THE DANDELION CLOCK

THE DANDELION CLOCK

Brenda McBryde

Severn House Large Print
London & New York

This first large print edition published in Great Britain 2006 by
SEVERN HOUSE LARGE PRINT BOOKS LTD of
9-15 High Street, Sutton, Surrey, SM1 1DF.
First world regular print edition published 2000 by
Severn House Publishers, London and New York.
This first large print edition published in the USA 2006 by
SEVERN HOUSE PUBLISHERS INC., of
595 Madison Avenue, New York, NY 10022.

British Library Cataloguing in Publication Data

McBryde, Brenda
    The Dandelion Clock. - Large print ed.
    1.   World War, 1939 – 1945 - Social aspects -
       Great Britain - Fiction
    2.   Large type books
    I.   Title
    823.9'14 [F]

    ISBN-10: 0-7278-7489-6

The author is grateful to the following for copyright permissions and acknowledgements:

Oxford University Press for kind permission to reproduce extracts of Robert Bridges' poem
I Will Not Let Thee Go from *Modern Verse*, 1940.

Stainer and Bell Ltd., London, for their kind permission for the extract from
The Immortal Hour by Rutland Boughton, with words by Fiona MacLeod.

Blue Moon. Music by Richard Rodgers. Words by Lorenz Hart.
© EMI Catalogue Partnership and EMI Robbins Catalog Inc., USA.
Worldwide print rights controlled by Warner Bros Publications Inc/IMP Ltd.
Lyrics reproduced by kind permission of IMP Ltd.

Begin the Beguine. Music by Cole Porter. © 1935 Harms Inc., USA.
Warner/Chappell Music Ltd., London W6 8BS.
Lyrics reproduced by kind permission of IMP Ltd.

Printed and bound in Great Britain by
MPG Books Ltd, Bodmin, Cornwall.

*To my children
Gay, John and Mark,
with my love.*

Acknowledgements

I am indebted to Joan Wilson, Territorial Army Nursing sister, for her memories of the Greek Campaign.

To Mary Johnston, Queen Alexandra's Imperial Military Nursing Service, for information relating to His Majesty's Hospital Carriers (ref. *The Ships of Youth* by Geraldine Edge, QAIMNS, and Mary Johnston, QAIMNS, published by Hodder & Stoughton, 1945).

To Marjorie Smith QAIMNS/R, who served on the Hospital Carrier *The Isle of Guernsey* at the evacuation of Dunkirk.

To Cyril Stephens of the Corvette Association.

To Inge Samson for her recollections of Nazi Germany.

Prologue

18 August 1995

'Fifty years ago tomorrow, eh, Andrew?' The brigadier tweaked his luxuriant moustache. 'Japan and Germany in the bag. Worth opening a bottle for that.'

'Not forgetting the reckoning.' Lean as a bean, his old friend of long standing spoke from the drinks table. 'What do you want in your Scotch? Soda? Ice?'

'Nowt.'

'I should have remembered.'

'Who's coming? Alec and Esme?'

'Flew in this morning. They're staying with Cathy. Evie can't come. She's organising the village party.'

'Eric and his missus?'

'Norah has just gone to the station to meet them. They will arrive in a state of collapse. Our dear girl is the worst driver in the world.'

Andrew carried the drinks to comfortable chairs by a window which gave a view of trees dressed in the full pride of May. 'Good to see you, old trout.'

'And you, dear boy. I've let too many years slip by.'

This friendship began before the outbreak of war in 1939 when Andrew Mount was a medical student and Simon Poole the star of the local rugby team in a town in the north-east of England. The outbreak of war in 1939 displaced youth's plans for a career and substituted in their place a hazardous enterprise from which some did not return.

Simon and Andrew belonged, in those carefree days before the war, to a group of young men and their girls, racketing about the countryside in their first cars, in love with life and love, George Gershwin, Big Bands and the Fox Trot. Survivors of that band of friends were meeting tonight, in Cathy's house.

The date was historic. This was the eve of the fiftieth anniversary of VJ day when the Second World War was finally won. Tomorrow these old friends would march in London before the Queen as war veterans, medals up, shoes shined, and umbrellas rolled. But tonight was for their own private celebration, to pay tribute to friendship, to share their good fortune in having survived against the odds, and to honour the memory of those who were not so lucky.

The Brig. contentedly nursed his single malt. 'Nice place you've got, Andy.'

'Norah found it for me when I retired. She has the ground floor flat. All very civilised.'

'Of course.' The brigadier's laugh emerged as a jolly rumble. 'Nothing remotely irregular in Norah's rule book. She surprised me, though, coming back from Australia. I thought she had settled there for good. You went out to see her, didn't you?'

'I was interested in the work she was doing. Running a clinic in the outback. Doing a marvellous job.'

'So – what brought her back to the UK?'

'She came back when Cathy became a widow. She could never share Cathy, you know.'

'I know.' Twiddling his glass, the Brig. shot an arch glance at his old friend. 'There was a time when I thought you and Norah...?'

Smiling, Andrew shook his head. 'A big brother is what Norah was looking for. Not a husband.'

'Is Hilde coming tonight?'

'Wild horses would not drag her away from her family of the dispossessed, not even for this momentous occasion. She sent her love to you all, though.'

'I was in Burma when she went to the Palace for her gong. She did a great job.'

'Still doing it. Another Müllerman Refuge has just been opened in Suffolk. She has no intention of retiring. Let me top you up.' Andrew stretched out a hand, a long thin hand, with the long thin fingers of a surgeon. 'We don't join the others until six thirty. You can fill me in with your latest conquests, my lusty friend.'

'For "lusty" read "rusty".' The Brig. drained his glass.

He leaned to look out of the window as the

9

sound of children's voices floated up from the park below. Preparations for the next day's celebrations were in hand ... Strings of coloured lights leapt from tree to tree and a Union Jack crept unsteadily up a flagpole. 'Which is Cathy's house?'

'Five minutes' walk. On the other side of the park.' The wistful look in the faded blue eyes of his friend was not lost on Andrew. 'When did you last see her, Simon?'

'At her father's funeral.'

That surprised Andrew. 'You went to that?'

'I had great respect for Mr Lewis.' The Brig. shook his head heavily like a dog with a sore ear. The memory of that melancholy day was with him still. Cathy, standing straight, like for 'God Save The Queen', with her shoes all muddy with yellow clay and her face awash with tears, as men lowered her beloved father into a hole in the ground. 'I will never forget that sad face under its little black hat.'

Andrew sighed. 'For both of us, life turned out so differently from the expectations we had.'

'Water under the bridge, old son.' Simon crunched on a handful of nuts. 'You surprised us all when you went to work for the Dame.'

'Best thing I ever did in an otherwise totally useless life.'

'Aren't you forgetting Dunkirk?'

'No one who was there could ever forget Dunkirk.'

'Then you will remember, my dear chap – and I am not likely to forget – that you saved

10

my life at Dunkirk.'

'My job.' Andrew said briefly, and consulted his watch. 'Time we were making tracks.'

Simon knocked back his whisky, stealing a glance in the mirror as he made to follow Andrew.

'Vanity, vanity, my friend,' mocked Andrew. 'All is vanity.'

'Not quite all, Doctor.' The Brig. patted his mop of silvery hair. 'Some of it is jealousy.' And he followed his sparsely thatched friend downstairs and out into the golden evening. They walked past the ladders and flags in the park until they came to Cathy's house

Through the open door leading to the kitchen Simon saw her, a chubbier Cathy than the one he remembered. Now she was like a grey-haired fairy godmother with a wooden spoon in place of a wand. He laughed out loud and barged in, wrapping her, pinny, spoon and all in one gigantic hug.

'You've got your plume of whiskers,' she greeted him, 'like you promised. Put me down, you great bear.'

His face was as red as the setting sun above his snowy whiskers. His voice was a warm caress, 'Cathy my dear, my very dear.'

'I knew he would turn into a D.O.M.' said Alec.

Simon spun round – for a moment at a loss to identify the speaker, a man with iron grey hair and a blobby nose grinning at him. 'Alec!' he grabbed the outstretched hand. 'Good to see you, you old colonial boy. Esme,

my dear,' giving the lady a discreet kiss.
'How's life in Canada? Always wanted to go
there.'

'What's stopping you?'

'A tribe of expensive grandchildren,' Simon,
reflecting upon the ease with which he lied,
roared with delight. Big and noisy, he seemed
to fill the room.

Here was Eric and his lovely Rosemary, and
Norah, too. He put his arms round her and
planted a kiss on the nape of her neck as she
stood defenceless at the Aga, with a saucepan
in one hand and a glass of wine in the other.
She smelt of nursery soap, and had grown
thin and spidery. The heavy golden hair he
remembered was as white as snow and as
insubstantial as cobwebs. Shocking posture.
His hands itched to take her by the shoulders.
Pull 'em back, girl! But Norah was not a girl
any more. She was a year younger than he.
Seventy-six. Same age as Cathy, but Cathy's
eyes, smiling at him across the room, were
still the eyes of the woman he had loved for
most of his life and her laugh, rippling, gusty
and explosive as ever, was singularly hers.
Cathy old, Cathy young. It made no difference.

She passed close to him, carrying plates to
the table, and he had to touch her bare
freckled arm. He remembered the freckles.

'Anyone caught interfering with the cook
will drop rank,' Andrew called out. 'Especially brigadiers.'

'How's Lorna?' Eric was the soul of

innocence.

'Lorna's very well.' Simon rounded on his tormentors. 'She declined the invitation to join you rough chaps. In her words, she was not a belligerent and feels she does not qualify for this occasion – though, mind you, she can come over pretty fierce at times!' He followed this with a huge guffaw.

'Tell him to sit down and behave himself, Cathy.'

'Open the champagne someone.'

'I expect you are good at this,' Norah handed a bottle to Simon. 'Brigadiers live on it.'

'Not retired brigadiers, my pet, but the knack has not deserted me. Pass me a napkin and I'll ease this out sweet as a nun's—'

'I know that one,' Andrew interrupted. 'Get on with the job.'

'I give you a toast.' Simon held his glass to the light, a surge of bubbles in a golden libation. 'We grateful veterans.'

'Or, put it this way,' said Alec, 'we doddering old has-beens.'

Yes, thought Simon, that is what we are. There's Eric, fat as a pussycat and lame in one leg, Esme with her arthritic hip, Norah with a hump, though she never got to be a dowager. And my sweet Cathy in her carpet slippers because her bunions are jumping. Andrew looks as though a puff of wind would blow him over, and Alec's homemade face ... and me, he reminded himself ruefully, praying that my bladder will hold out during the

13

march tomorrow. Public lavatories are thin on the ground near Buck House. Surreptitiously Simon popped a small pill into his mouth, but Cathy saw.

Hypertension, she guessed, with that high colour.

'Stay on your feet,' said Eric quietly. 'We'll drink to the friends who did not come back.' Eric, the timid bank clerk who would wear the Military Medal on his blazer tomorrow, had his own private memories. 'To Quentin, Colin and Jacky.'

'We're a small company now,' Cathy said quietly.

'Nevertheless,' boomed Simon, 'we'll put up a good show tomorrow because, my friends, this will most certainly be our last parade.'

Cathy took him by the hand and led him to a seat at the head of the table. 'Acting, unpaid,' she explained.

'If this is to be our last reunion,' Eric brought out more champagne, 'we will make it a memorable one.'

Cathy carried the joint of beef to the table and set it down before Andrew. 'Will the surgeon please carve.'

Andrew held out a hand. 'Forceps. Scalpel.'

One

Even as a little girl, Norah Moffat was beautiful. People looked at her and smiled because it was so pleasant to see a beautiful child: a peaches-and-cream complexion and huge dreamy grey eyes, with hair that hung like a curtain of pale silk. She had no idea that she was so pretty. Her modesty was charming.

Cathy Lewis accepted that her friend was beautiful while she herself was not and she did not mind at all, though she would have liked a straighter nose. She had her mother's tip-tilted nose. She would have liked blue eyes but hers were hazel, and her unmanageably thick shock of hair was a middling sort of brown. Their appearance, however, troubled neither of them. They were eight years old and best friends, and they lived near the sea at Eastport Bay in the north of England.

Seacliff School, which they attended, was for boys and girls. Some of the boys were nice and gave them pickabacks around the playground and even shared their sherbert sometimes. Some, like Albert Smith, were horrid. He was the most awful boy in the

15

school and was caned regularly, but he always stuffed an exercise book down his pants and took the beatings with a grin.

He pestered Norah and Cathy in particular because he was deeply in love with both of them and enraged them with love letters full of naughty words. His attentions were curtly dismissed.

'That boy makes me sick!'

'Him and his black-faced watch! Did you ever see anything quite so evil as a black-faced watch.'

When they were twelve Cathy and Norah joined the Girl Guides, passed their first aid badges and decided, there and then, to become nurses when they grew up. They won scholarships to the local high school and left Seacliff School for ever.

Albert Smith ran away to sea and his father said he'd scalp the little bugger if he ever set eyes on him again.

New uniforms were needed for the new school: gym tunics, reefer coats, velour hats and tussore blouses.

'Lucky your dad is working,' Chrissie Lewis reminded her daughter. 'There's many folk in Eastport who couldn't afford all this extra expense.'

Cathy's father had a reasonably secure job in local government, and Mr Moffat, Norah's dad, was mostly away at sea as a chief engineer on a tanker, so both men were sure of a steady wage. But many living in this northern port were less fortunate. Unemployment was the bogey that was reducing the families of skilled men to poverty. Repercussions of the 1929 Wall Street crash in America were making an impact all over Europe and Eastport, traditionally a shipbuilding town, had no work for its welders, platers, riveters and boilermakers.

Derricks stood idle by the great river which had provided a livelihood for thousands of workers for as long as anyone could remember, and now seagulls nested in the gantries. Winds blew through deserted shipyards and forlorn groups of men gathered at street corners, sharing a tab end, scratching around for rumours of work, of an order for the yards.

There was no work. No fresh orders. No one needed battleships and destroyers nor guns and shells from the armament factory up river.

'Things are a lot worse in Germany,' Cathy's father declared. 'Believe you me. They need a wheelbarrow full of money to buy a loaf of bread. Not that I have any sympathy for them,' he added. Cyril Lewis had fought against the Germans in the Great War. 'They brought it on themselves.'

After Seacliff, the high school was hugely imposing and offered many interesting diversions. Great sports – hockey, tennis and rounders – and new subjects like Latin, French, Science and Boys.

The boys' section of the school was a

playing field away and out of bounds to the girls but anyone with tuppence to spare for a fizzy drink could mingle with heroes after school in the tuckshop. There the long-limbed, gauche and spotty boys with croaky voices would foregather and show off to the girls. Rugger stars like Simon Poole and Jacky Whitmore, brainy blots like Quentin Ford and Colin Rankin with the gorgeous Scottish voice, who was captain of cricket – all would meet at the tuckshop after school. All were senior boys, terribly witty and self-assured.

'Who do you like best, Norah?'

'Don't know.'

'I think Alec Cruddas is dreamy,' Cathy's eyes glazed over with rapture, 'but he hasn't even noticed my existence.'

'Eric Dotchin is nice but he's so shy.'

'Eric's been nobbled by Eileen. I'm surprised she doesn't hang a notice round his neck, THIS BELONGS TO ME. He carries her school books and buys her coconut snow-balls.'

All the boys wanted to give Norah rides on the crossbars of their bicycles. She was the prettiest of all the girls in Cathy's group of friends but there was no need for any of the girls to fear competition. Norah always walked home with her best friend Cathy.

Life was yeasty, bouncy as a sorbo ball. There was tennis, swimming, the school play and the Annual Scouts Dance. Few of the pupils had ever heard of a man called Adolf Hitler but people in the world outside the school were beginning to talk about him.

The name of the Austrian ex-corporal cropped up one day in the tuckshop. As one would expect, Quentin Ford knew about him. Quentin's father was a well-known barrister and the source of most of his son's information on world affairs.

'He's started a new political party in Germany and promises to bring back prosperity and eradicate unemployment.' Quentin's audience was largely disinterested. He continued, nevertheless. 'My father says Herr Hitler has a huge following already.'

'And my dad says,' Cathy, remembering, put in, 'that Germany is in a worse mess than we are. They need a wheelbarrow full of marks to buy a loaf of bread!'

Simon Poole was the first of the crowd to learn to drive. Having proved to his father that he was a competent driver, he was occasionally allowed to borrow the family Morris Oxford to take his friends exploring the Northumbrian countryside. The back seat was a very cosy place for a cuddle. This was where he kissed Cathy Lewis and broke her duck.

'And not before time,' Cathy confided to Norah, 'I'm seventeen. Almost an old maid.'

Norah pulled her pretty face into a grimace. 'I don't like necking.'

'I do,' said Cathy.

Gradually the young men peeled off the end of the sixth form with their certificates of merit and headmaster's reports and predictions. Quentin, destined for the law like his famous father, enrolled at the nearby university with Colin, another lawyer in the making, but the university was not an option for those whose parents could not afford the fees. The others were lucky enough to find jobs when dole queues were growing longer every week.

Eric Dotchin, with his talent for mathematics, gravitated naturally to banking. Alec Cruddas convinced himself that he had taken the first step up the ladder to fame when he talked himself into the job of junior reporter on the *Eastport Gazette*.

In Simon's opinion, how he earned his living was of secondary importance. He was the star of the town's rugby team. Rugby was his *raison d'être*. He therefore accepted without question the job his father found for him in an insurance office. ('Steady. Dependable,' is what his employer said of him, and, 'not likely to rise to the top.') Well, the sports field was his métier, not the classroom. But he would be earning a wage and was assured of a game whenever the Eastport Valiants, who had signed him on as soon as he left school, were playing at home.

He was built for the game, broad shouldered and thighs like hams. The contours of his rugged face were regularly rearranged after wild collisions. Strong tawny hair, close cropped in order to deny a handful to the opposition, sprang from his head as fiercely assertive as a hard-pruned privet hedge.

20

'You'll have to pull your weight in the office,' his father warned. 'There are plenty of chaps lined up to take your place if you don't measure up.'

Simon came down to earth. He knew blokes who had left school the previous year and were still looking for jobs. He was lucky and it was up to him to make a success of insurance, although it sounded incredibly dull. His father, however, was usually right.

Jacky Whitmore was the other rugby player in the group, playing half-back for Valiant Firsts like Simon. A chunky fellow with sandy hair and freckles. His legs seemed absurdly short for his body but they served him well and carried him over the ground at a formidable pace. He had found a job in the office of a local estate agent but, like Simon, he lived for rugger.

Quentin's father bought him a sports car as a reward for academic achievement and there were now two cars available for jaunts into the countryside. Petrol was one shilling and tuppence a gallon. Life was good. They climbed the craggy hills of Cheviot, swam in trouty brown burns, fell in and out of love, knew all the songs of George Gershwin off by heart and dreamed great dreams about their futures.

The routes they took usually led north-west, following the course of the river Tyne, to its pastoral beginnings, to the foothills of the Cheviots. On this summer day, in the year 1935, they stopped for lunch at a favourite

21

spot, near the Tarset burn, a grassy hollow on the edge of a wood, sheltered from any wind and lit by sunshine. Simon was struggling with an obstinate fire while the others watched at their ease. They were discussing careers, as usual, but this time everyone was debating Norah and Cathy's decision to train as nurses.

Eileen McKay, ex-head girl, lumpish and bossy – she was only tolerated by the group because she was friendly with Eric – was scornful of nursing as a suitable choice for the girls 'What on earth persuaded you two nitwits to choose nursing for a career? They'll treat you like skivvies.'

'We want to look after sick people,' Cathy stated.

'We've always wanted to be nurses, for ever,' Norah echoed.

'In my opinion,' Simon said, 'there is no finer profession for a girl.' He was well aware that Eileen was planning to read economics at the university.

'What a lot of old-fashioned nonsense you talk. You need to wake up, Simon. Times are changing. Women have got the vote, you know. We do have a choice – if you've got the brains, that is.'

'You're showing your drawers,' he hit back, and she scrambled angrily to her feet.

'Where's Eric?'

'Gone to see a man about a dog.'

Jacky Whitmore raised his head from the cushion of his girl's lap to watch Eileen disappear into the beech wood. 'Stupid cow.'

Evie tenderly stroked his bristly sandy hair. 'Cows aren't stupid.'

'Coo-ee,' came a strident voice from the wood.

'Run for it Eric. Poor bugger.'

'You should be grateful to Eric,' Norah pointed out. 'If she didn't dote on him, it might be on one of you.'

'Perish the thought.' Quentin, the beautiful, delicately bred and academically brilliant young man, shuddered and moved a little closer to Norah, whom he greatly admired. 'I agree with Simon. Nursing is a wonderful profession.'

'She's found him,' Norah warned. 'Here they come.'

'Give him a beer, someone,' Eileen ordered. Evie's mother provided drinks at a discount from the pub where she worked.

'We're discussing careers, Eric. What's it like, working in a bank – all that lovely money?'

Tall and skinny, Eric flopped down on the grass. 'Oh. I'm not allowed anywhere near the real stuff.' Hastily he dispensed with any illusion of self-importance. 'I spend most of my day adding up columns of figures.'

'Crumbs! I'd die.'

'Eric got a distinction in maths,' Eileen reminded them. 'He's brilliant. That's one of the reasons why we get on so well.'

'Turumpty-tum,' mocked Jacky Whitmore with a grin. 'Couple of brainboxes, the pair of

23

you. Lesser mortals like me rise no higher than making the tea in a crummy estate agent's office.'

His girl, Evie, intervened. She was fond of Jacky, rough diamond though he was. 'You've only just started. Give yourself time to learn the ropes and I bet you'll be top salesman at Cook & Walters before long.'

'Thanks for that, sweetie.' He kissed the hand that lay by his stubbly cheek. 'The fact is, there's no money about,' he said flatly, blowing out a cloud of smoke. He had started early, smoking in back lanes and garden sheds, and now was coolly brazen and his fingers permanently stained. 'People are just not buying houses and the best salesman in the world cannot make them. Still, it's a job. I might be out on my backside tomorrow.'

'You could outstrip the lot of us,' Simon told him. 'As an insurance bloke I am not going to change the world.'

Jacky was still with his own affairs. 'What I really want to do,' he scowled into the canopy of leaves above his head, 'is engineering.'

'You could always make things work,' Simon agreed. 'My mum's vacuum cleaner for instance. You fixed that.'

Jacky continued, 'Only me dad can't afford what he calls "fancy training". University or tech, it all costs money. Not even an apprenticeship, though Morgan Wessel would have taken me on. No, I've got to get out there and earn money. Quick sharp. Not like you, Quentin.' Jacky's political views, while scarcely red, were decidedly pink and, as such, were at complete variance with Quentin's – a cause of frequent dissension.

Quentin flushed. 'I realise I am privileged.'

'Communism makes a lot of sense to folk who aren't privileged.' There was a mean edge to Jacky's voice.

Another voice came in at this point. 'There are pros and cons when you're talking about communism.' As a trainee reporter, Alec Cruddas spoke with the weight of the press behind him. A very handsome young man, he had been the heart throb of the Girls' Upper Fifth when he played Romeo in the school play and still displayed thespian characteristics. 'Full of bounce and bullshit' was the opinion of his father who failed to see that he, the father, was the role model for his son.

'Oh don't let's get on to politics,' Norah pleaded. 'It will only end by everyone getting cross.'

Evie removed the head from her lap. 'Ups-a-daisy, Jacky, I'm going to take over the cooking or those sausages will never be edible.'

She was a slight wisp of a girl with white gold hair and she wanted to become a teacher. She had won a place at the Dundee Teacher Training College and a bursary to help with expenses. Without this financial help, she would not have been able to accept the appointment. There was no money at home. Her father had been out of work for two years. Her mother worked as a barmaid in order to keep her daughter at school up to matriculation standard and now Evie had repaid her mother's faith in her by winning the bursary.

Sadie Dobson would have scrubbed floors and taken in washing, anything to make sure her bright little girl got a proper education, not like her own lazy-daisy ma with her tea-pot full of gin.

Amongst her friends, perhaps only Jacky would understand what the bursary meant to Evie.

Alec got up from the grass to take a drink to Nancy, who was sitting quietly under the trees some distance away, a sketch pad on her knee. 'Would our resident artist like a top up?'

Nancy Pringle held out her glass. 'I could demolish a sausage. What's happened to lunch? I've had to resort to chewing my pencil.'

Alec slid down beside her. 'Evie's taken over. Won't be long. I say,' he peeked at her sketch, 'that's good.'

'Thanks.'

With her head on one side looking critically at what she had just done, Nancy made Alec laugh. Her cap of tight black curls and rosy red cheeks reminded him of a cheeky little robin and he told her so.

Since she was not sure if this was compli-mentary or not, she stuck out her tongue and thumbed her pert little beak. He made a mental note to bag a seat beside her on the way home.

This band of companions, tried and true, would surely preserve such a friendship even if their paths were to part in the future. For the sheer joy of living, they sang as they drove home, holding hands with the one they loved. To be young and carefree was to know utter contentment. The world, it seemed, was at their feet and they took it lightly, as if this was their right...

Mr Lewis was at the window when Simon drove Cathy home.

'It's all right, Chrissie,' he called over his shoulder and put away his watch. 'She's with Simon Poole. She's back.'

Cyril Lewis had a high regard for Simon and a nodding acquaintance with his father, who was something big in the car export business. He went to the door and opened it and the lamp in the hall shot a broad beam down to the garden gate just as Simon was about to give Cathy a goodnight kiss.

'Hello there, Simon.'

'Good evening, Mr Lewis.'

'Bit on the late side, aren't you?' But he gave a jolly little chuckle to show he was not really cross.

'We've been up on the Ottercops. Fantastic sunset. Sorry we're a bit late.'

'I'm a big girl now Daddy-oh.' But like the little girl he still considered her to be, Cathy flung her arms about his neck and kissed his bristly cheek.

27

They stood, arm in arm on the doorstep while Simon swung the handle and finally got the Morris going. With a last wave of his gauntlet, he drove away.

Two

1936

Eastport in the rain. A wind turbid with the smell of seaweed cast up during the recent storms lashed the café windows. Jacky Whitmore and Quentin Ford looked down on streaming slate rooftops and glumly contemplated a wet Saturday in Eastport-by-the-sea. Below them a tumult of umbrellas concealed everything but the feet of indomitable shoppers, splashing through pools.

In place of the country jaunts of the previous year, the group had taken to meeting here, at the Haymarket Café, for coffee every Saturday morning. It was a very modest establishment and the coffee was not memorable, but it was conveniently placed in the centre of the town. As regular customers, their claim to a table by the window was never disputed. Quentin and Jacky were the first to arrive this morning.

'Game's off today, I suppose?' Quentin was handling Jacky with kid gloves. In a man-to-man, Jacky always won.

'Cancelled. Ground's waterlogged. No proper drainage. I'm brassed off, I can tell you. Nowt to bloody well do in this god-forsaken place when it rains – and that's most of the time.'

Quentin brightened visibly. 'Here's Alec.'

Alec, hurtling up the café stairs. 'Can't stay long. I'm on a job.' He signalled a waitress and tore off his dripping macintosh.

Quentin rather admired Alec's flamboyant personality. He knew himself to be something of a sobersides but that, after all, was as it should be for a respected legal presence. 'How's the world according to the *Eastport Gazette*?' he asked.

Alec ran a hand through his damp hair and took a seat by Jacky. 'In a bit of a flap, actually. Thanks, dearie.' He took his coffee from the waitress and gave her a winning smile.

'Oh, you boys in the Press are always forecasting doom, pestilence and disaster,' pronounced Quentin. 'What is it this time?'

'This chap Hitler. Got himself a bunch of thugs who are going around locking people up if they disagree with "the Führer".'

'Pure propaganda. Don't believe a word of it.'

The window was steaming up. A pleasant fug was being generated, of cigarette smoke and wet clothes drying, seasoned with the comforting aroma of hot coffee. Simon arrived with a friend, cutting the conversation short.

'Where are Cathy and Norah? I've brought Andrew Mount to meet them. He's a medical student at the hospital they are going to.'

'They haven't turned up,' said Jacky. 'Neither has Evie. She's helping her mother.'

'That's why you're looking like a stranded goldfish.'

'That and the weather.'

'Take a seat, Andrew. I'll order coffee,' Quentin said, moving his chair. 'Which year are you in?'

'About to go into the second year. I was hoping to meet your two budding nurses.'

'Are you another rugby player?'

'My game is cricket.'

'Then you must meet Colin. He's Captain of the first Eastport Eleven.'

'Where is Colin, anyhow?' Simon looked around him. 'Where is everybody? Frightened they might get wet?'

'Colin has taken his mother to Cornwall to see her sister,' Alec volunteered, 'and Nancy, that's our resident artist,' he explained to Andrew, 'is putting her portfolio together. She starts at the art college in the new term.'

Eric and Eileen arrived at that moment, bringing with them a smell of wet city streets. Eileen plumped down heavily. 'Anyone got a cig? Oh thanks.' Andrew was quick with his packet. 'Who are you?' She gave him a long straight stare before handing back his cigarettes. Nice eyes. Nice smile and dripping wet floppy fair hair. 'Your hair is leaking into your eyes.'

Alec drained his cup. 'I must be off, I was explaining to Quentin when you came in, there's a bit of a flap in the newspaper world.'

'Alec is a reporter on the *Gazette*,' Simon interrupted for Andrew's benefit. 'He keeps us up to date with the gossip.'

'Only this is not gossip.'

'It's propaganda,' stated Quentin.

'Well, spit it out,' smoke unfurled dramatically from Eileen's nostrils. Childhood pictures of dragons came unbidden to Andrew's mind.

'Something fishy is going on in Germany,' Alec's unaccustomed seriousness grabbed their attention.

'Like what?'

'This chap, Hitler. Throwing his weight around. Got himself a bodyguard of thugs. Anyone who gets up Herr Hitler's nose gets beaten up or worse – simply disappears.'

'And I say that is all propaganda,' declared Quentin. 'I don't believe a word of it.'

Alec darted a look of annoyance at him. 'There are some pretty scary accounts being told by people who have escaped to Britain. Especially Jews. He's got it in for Jews. Anyhow, I'll leave you to think about it. Got to go.' Alec reached for his macintosh. 'Been nice meeting you, Andrew. Come again.'

Eric glanced around the table. 'We're a small company today. I suppose it will be like this more often than not from now on. The nurses won't get much free time.'

'And Evie will be in Scotland most of the

31

time,' grumbled Jacky. 'The train fare is horrendous, so she won't be coming home much.'

There was a very good reason why Colin Rankin did not always join in his friends' activities. His circumstances were different from theirs – especially from Quentin's, who was a law student like himself. Colin depended on the benevolence of his elder brother, a farmer in Galloway, for everything; for tuition, for his comprehensive library of reference books and an allowance which provided him with his daily bread – even the clothes he wore. With commendable Scottish thrift, and in what he considered to be the best interests of his young brother, Alistair, senior by twelve years, did not encourage frivolous expenditure. The allowance was adequate, but ruled out indulgences.

This burden of indebtedness weighed heavily on Colin and dictated his lifestyle accordingly. He lived with his mother in a semi-detached house near the sea on Eastport Bay. They had moved from Edinburgh five years earlier when his father was offered a better position on the London–North Eastern Railway. Within a few months of taking up his appointment at Eastport Central Railway Office, Colin's father died of a heart attack, leaving a house and enough money to support his widow and very little else.

There had been another brother between

Alistair and Colin. Ian died of kidney disease while he was still at school, a tragedy which affected the elder son deeply. Seriously and conscientiously, Alistair had adopted a self-imposed guardianship over Colin. He meant to ensure that Colin's life, unlike that of the schoolboy Ian, would be a fulfilled one.

'One fine day,' Colin told his industrious little mother, always busy with dustpan and brush like Beatrice Potter's Mrs Tiggywinkle, 'when I'm a high court judge, I will buy you a fur coat and take you for a spin in my Rolls Royce.'

Maisie Rankin was a born stoic and did not yelp when he gave her bony little hand, rings and all, a hard squeeze. She was very comfortable with her younger son, more comfortable, she admitted privately, than with her firstborn, Alistair. Oh, Alistair was a good man, a very worthy man and, as soon as she caught herself thinking that, she wiped out the word 'worthy' with her mental eraser. That was no word for a mother to use with reference to one of her children. No, no. Alistair was a fine laddie, a successful farmer, president of she didn't know how many farming associations and chairman of seemingly every important committee dealing with Scottish agriculture. Pity he had never married. She had always known, though she had never mentioned this fact, that Alistair had had his eye on Isabel Gillies ever since his early twenties, but he would not court her until he had a home to offer and by that time he had missed his chance. Will Robson from the mill had snapped her up, though he had no more to offer Isabel than Alistair. The wee lass never knew that Alistair was breaking his heart over her. She might have waited for him had she known.

After that, Alistair never looked at another woman, though many would have had him, especially now when he farmed some of the best cattle country in Scotland. Anyway, here he was, taking over from her late husband, providing a training and the prospect of a good living for his little brother Colin.

She smiled to herself. 'Little Colin.' He was all of six foot. A fine, handsome lad with his father's strong features and, like his father, he never used two words where one would do.

He was sitting opposite now in a railway carriage bound for Cornwall, accompanying her on a visit to her sister who lived in Lost-withiel. 'Lost withal' was Maisie's little joke, for her sister Kate truly was lost among her hollyhocks and roses, refusing to stir further than her village shop. Maisie had to do the travelling on these twice-yearly visits and Colin always insisted on accompanying her.

He was reading the *Eastport Gazette*. 'Isn't that Alec's paper?' Maisie knew it was, but wanted to get Colin talking. He smiled at her over the top of the paper and a sudden familiarity made her heart contract. The deep, dark eyes under straight eyebrows, that was his father's legacy.

'That's right, Mother. He's got a piece in about the dangers pedestrians face on the new coast road.'

'He's doing well, seemingly.'

'He's a good reporter.'

She left him in peace for a while as she watched the stations whizz by. She travelled at a reduced rate on some of the trains, thanks to her husband Roy. Mind you, she'd rather pay the full price and have him still at her side.

Deviously she worked her way back to her favourite subject, 'Is Alec courting?'

Smiling at the old-fashioned phrase, Colin shook his head. 'Hard to tell. He was keen on Nancy but now that she has started at art college, we don't see much of her.'

Then it came, the question she always came round to in the end. 'And have ye no' found a nice wee lass to bring home, Colin? That's the day I'm waiting for.'

Colin regarded his mother with a whimsical lift of his eyebrows. They had been here so many, many times before. 'There are plenty of nice girls about,' he reassured her, though he was thinking of Norah Moffat in particular. 'They are a luxury I can't afford at the moment.' Nevertheless, the thought had crossed his mind that Norah was the kind of modest, good-natured girl to win his mother's wholehearted approval.

Maisie did not miss much. 'I do believe you have a young lady in mind, son, so don't dilly-

35

dally and miss the boat like Alistair did. I want to see some bairns running about in my English house to make it seem more like home.'

Three

'A friend of mine is a medical student at the hospital where you two are going to train,' Simon told Cathy and Norah. 'I'll fix a date so you can meet him. Good bloke. You'll like him.'

They did. 'When do you start your training?' He fell into step beside the pretty blonde one with the long shapely legs. They were on the way to the Empire Theatre to see Ivor Novello's new musical.

'Next month,' Norah groaned. 'I've got the jitters already.'

'Nurses are not allowed to get the jitters. That's my prerogative and I rely on you to protect me from angry ward sisters.'

He had a nice smile, she thought.

'Don't count on me,' Norah warned. 'I'm likely to pack my bags at the first encounter with an angry ward sister.'

In the darkness of the theatre, stirred by Ivor Novello's seductive melodies, Andrew sneaked a sideways glance at the girl sitting next to him. Blonde hair framing a high, smooth brow, a neat, straight nose, lips

36

slightly parted in an amused smile. He wondered about holding her hand, but Norah chose to turn her head towards him at that moment. By the flickering light from the stage, he caught the glint in her eyes. The message was very plain. Keep off. He turned his attention to the stage once more. OK. Softly, softly catchee monkey.

'Is she going round with anyone special?' he asked Simon. 'She's a jolly nice girl.'

'She's a smasher but if you are thinking of pressing your suit, you'll have to go on an assault course to breach that ivory tower.'

'I wondered.'

Simon stole a sly glance. 'Has Prince Charming been snubbed then?'

'Oh, shut up. But yes, in a way. I've made no headway.'

'That's how it is with Norah.'

'Cathy's different.'

Simon grinned. 'You noticed.'

Simon's doctor friend made quite a hit with the rest of the group. And even Nancy, the arty one, wondered if it was too late to apply for nursing.

'What shall we do on your last night of freedom?' Simon wanted to know.

'You make it sound like a prison sentence,' Cathy complained.

'I've got enough for two beers, one pork pie and two seats at the News Theatre.'

The *Pathé Gazette* news film showed floods

in Miami and earthquakes in Japan. Then came a film from Germany, which silenced all the toffee wraps. A troop of young boys aged between thirteen and sixteen years, striding along with picks and shovels over their shoulders, seemed the very picture of robust health. The banners they carried proclaimed 'STRENGTH THROUGH JOY'.

'They were off to till the land and grow food for the nation,' so went the caption – and a burst of spontaneous applause rippled through an audience grown used to the sight of disillusioned youths in the dole queues of Britain. The question which occupied many minds was, 'If Germany can work this miracle, why can't we?' This was the question Cathy put to her parents when she returned home.

Cyril Lewis's reaction did not match his daughter's enthusiasm. His experiences as a sergeant in the 14–18 war prevented him from ever again viewing Germany without prejudice. A stocky little man, he sat back in his chair and glared belligerently over folded arms at his wife and daughter. 'Ploughing the fields? Digging ditches? Don't make me laugh. Those lads are being taught discipline. They'll make good soldiers. Typical German thinking.'

'Really, Cyril,' Chrissie put her sewing aside. 'You've got soldiers on the brain. Why would they want soldiers?' Chrissie was short, like Cathy, with the same unruly hair which she kept under control with a nice tight perm. No longer lit by a fiery auburn gloss like Cathy's bob, the fat sausage curls showed streaks of rusty grey. 'Half the men in this town are unemployed and nobody is doing a thing about it.'

She believed in voicing her opinions. An inbred spirit of determination was responsible for the little creases at the corners of her mouth. The same characteristic was evident in the photograph of her late mother and would no doubt be inherited by Cathy at some time in the future. Not by Lydie, though. Cathy's sister Lydie was like Cyril's mother. Bone idle.

'There'll be no full employment here,' Cyril said with conviction, 'until we stop this crazy disarmament policy and start building ships and making guns again.'

'My,' his wife marvelled, 'you've changed your tune! You were all for disarmament not so long ago.'

Grumpily he picked up his tea cup. 'That was then and this is now. And I'll tell you something else before you start handing out the prizes to Germany. D'ye remember young Albert Smith? His dad works at the fish shop. He ran away to sea when he was no more than a kid.'

'He was at Seacliff School with Norah and me,' said Cathy. 'A perfect pest. Pulled our hair. Always fighting. What about him?'

'He's in the Merchant Navy and he wrote to his mother from Hamburg where his ship had gone for repairs. He said that the folk of

39

Hamburg are running scared of Hitler's followers. Brownshirts, they call themselves and they knock people up in the middle of the night and drive them away in trucks. No one knows where they go – and they don't come back.'

'Well,' said Chrissie, getting up to make the tea, 'I wouldn't believe a word that lad says. Proper no-hoper. Always was and always will be.'

On Cathy's first day at the hospital, the senior probationer marched her down to the sluice. 'You can carry eight at a time if you sling one on each finger but don't let them keep it in the bed.'

'Why ever not?' muttered Cathy as she handed a urinal to her very first patient. 'Nice and handy.'

'Because I'll no doubt spill it, dear.' Sadly the wizened old gentleman groped for his elusive member. 'I usually do.'

That was Cathy's introduction to a male surgical ward. She, who had never caught even a passing glimpse of male genitals, found herself in a close personal relationship with thirty-eight men of all ages, none of whom considered pyjama bottoms to be an essential article of clothing.

Norah's introduction was more refined. She was sent to a gynaecological ward, a place of pink nighties, talcum powder and tears.

The skills that the student nurse was re-quired to learn were almost overwhelming.

Discipline was hard and often unfair. There were more brickbats than plaudits. 'It *will* get easier,' Cathy and Norah comforted each other as they toughened their aching feet with methylated spirits at the end of each long, difficult day.

Simon suddenly became more important to Cathy. He was so normal, so sane compared to this strange, hostile world. Sitting next to him in the cinema one night, she suddenly leaned over and kissed him.

'What's that for?' He was pleasantly surprised.

'For being so awfully nice,' she murmured.

'I just can't help it,' he said modestly, and the people behind said 'shush'. 'You stink of anaesthetic,' he whispered.

'You should have smelt me before I bathed,' she hissed and the people said 'shush' again...

Andrew Mount, too, was proving to be a refuge when things were bad. One day he came upon Norah on the verge of tears after a dressing down by the ward sister.

'Don't let that old dragon get you down,' he took her hand reassuringly. 'When are you off duty?' Hastily he looked around for sight of the enemy. A nurse was not to be seen in conversation with a medical student unless it concerned a patient.

'Six o'clock,' she sniffed.

'Meet you outside the main gates.'

He took her to the King's Head. His cheerful company and two gin and limes worked wonders and, when Andrew returned her to

41

the hospital just before the ten o'clock curfew, Norah felt ready to brave the world and was even motherly towards Cathy who was preparing for bed in a fit of the miseries after a hard day on duty.

'I'll make you a cup of tea, pet.'

'You've had more than a cup of tea,' Cathy sniffed suspiciously. 'Where did Andrew take you?'

'The King's Head. The rugger team was celebrating. Did you pinch any milk from the ward?'

'Medicine bottle in my uniform pocket.' Cathy climbed into the high, hard bed with its regulation counterpane stamped with the name of the hospital. As if anyone would want to pinch it!

She set about putting her hair in curlers and her eyes travelled mournfully around the bilious green walls. Not a single picture allowed. She sighed a huge sigh.

Norah brought two steaming cups of tea. 'Here's the gossip. Evie has left for Dundee and Jacky is as heavy as dough.'

'Was Simon there?'

'Hero of the match for converting something. Nancy is in love with the drawing master. Colin's mum has knitted him a frightful orange scarf and Alec has a piece on page two about the state of the roads.'

All these old friends seemed so far away now. Cathy wished at that moment that she had picked any career other than this hard, joyless one. 'I couldn't do a damn thing right today. You know what I think? Women in authority are worse than men.'

After a while, however, the strangeness of hospital life began to wear off. Somewhat to their surprise, Cathy and Norah began to find the work intensely interesting. They no longer hid in the ward toilet for a good cry. They were growing a thick skin.

When they came off duty, they resisted the temptation to crawl into bed and sleep their off duty time away. They joined their friends at the Haymarket Café and, for a time, they forgot about hospital life.

Evie was finding Dundee and the training college very much to her liking. 'I've warned her off those men in skirts.' Jacky was in good spirits. He had moved a step up from tea boy in the estate agent's office.

'One day, Jacky, I'll wear my kilt for you.'

Jacky grinned. 'Sorry, Colin. I keep forgetting you're a barbarian from over the border. You've been growing more civilised since you came to England.'

'A veneer, my dear fellow. I can disembowel a foe as well as anyone.'

'I was on your ward yesterday,' Andrew was saying to Norah, 'and you walked straight past me. Cut me dead.'

She smiled. 'I'm under observation. I believe my ward sister thinks I'm a bad lot ever since she saw the houseman follow me into the secretion room.'

'Nurses must know their place.' Cathy energetically wiped the last of the egg from her plate with a piece of bread. 'I'm hungry,' she explained on meeting Quentin's reproving eye.

'Don't they feed you at that place?'

'Not enough,' said Cathy.

'Anyhow,' Andrew reminded Norah, 'we are waiting to hear what you were doing in the secretion room with the houseman.'

She smiled innocently, 'Testing urines.'

Four

One of Norah's patients was a sailor with a broken jaw who had been involved in a fight.

'George Bright's my name,' he told her, 'but my friends call me "Notso". We was bringing timber from Russia,' he explained when Norah asked him how he came by his injury, 'when we was caught in a storm an' the cargo starts to shift. Gives the ship a nasty list. The stokers, who were a bunch of scabs, got real nasty, threatened the captain and demanded he turn about. Me and my mate sorted them out.' He smiled ruefully, fingering his jaw. 'We laid the lot of 'em clean out on the deck. They were in a worse mess than I am.'

'What about your mate?'

'Two black eyes and a sore backside. Pardon, nurse.'

His mate arrived on visiting day, came

44

rolling into the ward in his bell-bottom trousers, with two black eyes and a cheeky grin.

Norah was cleaning out the medicine cupboard in the ward when Notso called her over. 'This is me mate, nurse. The one I told you about.'

After a moment of surprised silence, his mate broke into a guffaw. 'That's all right, Notso. No need for introductions. We're old friends, aren't we, Norah?'

With astonishment, Norah recognised the naughtiest boy in Seacliff School turned sailor. 'Albert Smith.'

He grinned, revealing a gap where his front teeth should have been. 'Do you still love me? My, you used to embarrass me with your love letters.'

An angry red flush swept over Norah's face. 'Behave yourself or I will report you.'

His injured pal intervened, 'If you're going to cause trouble, Smithy, you can take yourself off.'

Norah recounted this to an incredulous Cathy.

'What does he look like?'

'Pretty much the same. He's no beauty.'

'Never was,' said Cathy.

'His front teeth have been knocked out. What hair he has is bleached white and so close shaven you would think he was bald. Remember how he used to pull our hair?'

'And spy through the back of the girls' lavatories.'

'He got caned for that.'

'It didn't stop him.'

'But there's no denying that he and his mate were jolly brave to take on a mutineer crew.'

'He always did have guts, I'll say that for him.'

'And he turns up on my ward. When I said you were nursing here too, he said why don't we make up a foursome as soon as his mate can chew a steak!'

'Huh! Can't wait.'

'His mate is not a bad fellow. Very polite, which is more than I can say for our Albert,' Norah sighed. 'I just hope their ship sails soon.'

Able Seaman 'Notso' Bright did not stay long in the hospital. After treatment he was sent to a merchant navy convalescent home and Albert Smith was not seen in the ward again.

'I've lost me old mate,' Notso told Norah as she packed his belongings for him. 'Smithy, the one you went to school with. He's joined one of the passenger lines as a steward.'

In Britain there was a growing feeling of unease about events in Germany. Old soldiers like Cyril Lewis, Cathy's father, and Simon's father, Ken Poole, who had been a major in the last war, were full of misgivings but even they were taken by surprise when, in March 1936, Hitler sent troops to reclaim for Germany the Rhinelands which had been demilitarised in the treaty of 1919.

46

'What I want to know, Mr Poole, is how he managed to raise an army on the quiet. Strictly forbidden, wasn't it, after the last war?'

'I tell you, Lewis, Hitler's been rearming for months. When I go about my business over there, I see tanks, armoured cars and gun carriers rolling off the production lines in factories that are supposed to be producing cars. Conscription? Forbidden, you say? There are men drilling everywhere, not in uniform yet but that will come. When I try to warn out local MP, I am accused of warmongering.'

'Me, too.' Fiercely Cathy's father nodded agreement.

'Our blinkered lot at Whitehall would not believe that Hitler is rearming. Now they know. It's a bad business, Lewis.'

A little of the warnings did find a listening ear in the government, however, and the result was a modest move towards rearmament in Britain.

At last unemployed men in Eastport clutched at the hope of work in the ordnance factory up river and perhaps in the shipyards. It was rumoured in the King's Head that a naval order was also a possibility.

'What I heard,' Paul, the barman, was chief dispenser of news and rumours, 'was that the Grainger Yard is in the running for naval supply boats.'

Men inured to disappointment were too canny to throw their caps in the air at an unsubstantiated report. 'Supply boats? It'll take a bloody battleship to get Grainger's going again.'

An old riverman removed his pipe and spat 'middle for diddle' into the spittoon. 'An' it might get that an' all.'

Later that year when November fogs and chill draughts drew the regulars at the King's Head to sit by the cheerful fire, a very earnest conversation was taking place amongst Simon's friends. Andrew joined them when he was not 'on call' at the hospital. He had become a popular member of the group. Alec had moved up a grade to senior political reporter on the *Gazette* and had fresh, disturbing news to discuss.

'Where did he hold this event?' Quentin's legal mind needed facts before he could believe what Alec was telling them.

'In the huge amphitheatre at Nuremberg. It was filled with cheering crowds as columns of marching men, squadrons of tanks and gun carriers were paraded in front of them. The swastika hung from every pole.'

Simon looked stunned. 'This is going to make the rest of Europe sit up and wonder what has hit them.'

Jacky turned to Quentin. 'Do you still think Hitler is a good guy?'

'Well, we are rearming too,' but his reply came lamely.

'Hitler has fooled us all,' said Simon shortly, thinking, my old dad is not so far off the

48

mark after all.

That night the atmosphere in the King's Head was incandescent.

'Thinks he's scared the shits out of us with his bloody stormtroopers. Well, he'll learn we don't scare that easy.'

'We should have rearmed years ago.'

'That's your Ramsay MacDonald for you.'

'We're rearming now anyway.'

That was true. Cobbled ways leading down to the shipyards rang once more with the steel-tipped boots of riverside workers. Engineers gladly struggled into their boilersuits again and unwrapped prized tools. Eastport was working again. Britain was working again. Thanks to Hitler.

The new Prime Minister, Neville Chamberlain, started a recruitment drive for the Territorial Army. What was wanted, explained the posters, were young men who would be willing to train in their spare time as an auxiliary force capable of being used in a national emergency. Simon was the first of the group to join.

He met Cathy on her morning off. 'Passed my medical! I'm Gunner Poole now, so we'll have a little respect, please, from student nurses.'

She gave him a kiss and bought him a knickerbocker glory to celebrate.

Jacky and Eric followed Simon's lead. The commitment was two nights' drill every week and an annual camp in August. 'And we get paid for it, chaps! Money for old rope.'

'But what do you *do*?' demanded Eileen, somewhat piqued to be deprived of Eric's spare time.

'Strip guns,' Eric beamed. 'Mount them, take them apart, grease them and put them together again.'

'Thrilling,' she scoffed. 'What else?'

'Marching,' offered Simon.

'Digging latrines,' Jacky added.

'Map reading.'

'Instruction in the use of field telephones.'

'Playing at soldiers,' Quentin smiled indulgently. Such exercises were only marginally more mature than the things boy scouts got up to.

'As long as they don't make proper soldiers of them,' said Cathy's mother. 'They're such nice boys.'

Five

1938

Cathy and Norah were coming to the end of their second year at the hospital and moving into higher grades. They knew all the rules and how to break them without risk of discovery. They were happy in their profession and, moreover, they were good at it. Their salary had been increased to thirty-six shillings a month. They were rich and enjoying life and were not prepared for the sudden jolt to their everyday living that was to come.

At six o'clock on a summer evening Cathy was taking temperatures on the Men's Orthopaedic Ward. Young men injured in sport and old men who had fallen downstairs were brought here. Splints, pulleys and cradles poked from every bed. The late sun, angling through tall windows, bathed in its mellow light the junior probationer with her trolley of drinks. The senior probationer was removing vases of flowers which were not allowed to use up the patient's air during the night and Cathy, now a junior staff nurse, was about to record the temperatures and pulses of twenty-four men, all of whom, at this moment, were clamped to their earphones, listening to the six o'clock news on the wireless.

Cathy slipped her fingers under the sleeve of Mr Dawson's pyjama jacket, feeling for his pulse. Mr Dawson had funny toes, each going its own way. He had come into hospital to have them straightened.

'Ha!' he bellowed at her, still enclosed in his private auditorium. 'He's at it again!'

She popped the thermometer under his tongue but he continued to mouth his indignation.

'It's Hitler,' the young man in the next bed explained. He had crashed his motor cycle and his plastered leg was slung from an overhead pulley. 'He wants Czechoslovakia now.'

Relieved of the thermometer, Mr Dawson launched into a tirade on the satanic nature of the German Führer. 'It was Austria just a few months ago and he got away with that. Now he wants Czechoslovakia and we'll be soft enough to let him have it. You'll see!'

Cathy entered his temperature on the chart. 'Steady on, Mr Dawson. Sister won't let you go home at the weekend if you shoot a temperature.'

The temperature was rising in Whitehall, too. The government had turned a blind eye on Hitler's annexation of Austria six months earlier under the face-saving dictum that its population was mostly German anyhow. There was no justification whatsoever for the threatened annexation of Czechoslovakia. If Hitler were to take this step it would constitute the most serious challenge yet to France and Britain, who were pledged to come to the aid of any small European nation faced with aggression, which was exactly the situation at the moment.

The British people suddenly woke up. Did this mean war? Czechoslovakia was hundreds of miles away, surely nothing to do with Britain?

Norah came upon Andrew on his way to the main operating theatre. 'What do you think, Andrew?'

'I can't see how we can honourably do anything else but go to the aid of Czechoslovakia if Hitler persists. We have no choice. Neither has France.'

52

The day's operating began but the question, 'Will we intervene?' was debated by the surgeons as they scrubbed up, the instrument nurse as she laid out her trolley, the backshop nurse amidst her steaming sterilisers and the porter who collected the laundry. The Prime Minister flew to Berchtesgarten in Germany to persuade the Führer of the error of his ways.

'Chamberlain is a good man,' Cathy's Mr Dawson thought. 'He'll tell Hitler what's what.'

'T'other way round, more like,' said the sceptic in the next bed.

'I don't quite understand,' said Cathy, handing out laxatives to anyone with an '0' on his chart where he should have had a tick. 'What does Germany want it for?' Cathy was apolitical to the marrow.

'Oil and iron.'

'Why doesn't the League of Nations step in? Isn't that what it's for?'

'The League of Nations is *useless*!' someone bawled from the other side of the ward.

Standing at the ward entrance, the sister in charge clapped her hands. 'Hush! I will *NOT* have shouting in my ward.'

Cathy winked at the naughty men and proceeded with the medicine round.

Somewhat late in the day, Britain began to look to her defences. Cathy's father went with Ken Poole to Eastport Bay to verify rumours that gun positions were being constructed on the cliffs and found concrete mixers churning out grey sludge.

'My word! I believe we mean business at last.' Ex-Major Poole looked quite cheerful.

'Not before time, Mr Poole. This is Chamberlain's second trip to parley with that madman. It doesn't look good.'

The next move by the government, to put the Territorials on standby, underlined the growing feeling of alarm. Simon, Eric and Jacky were hastily recalled from camp on Salisbury Plain. The day was hot, their thick khaki uniforms unrelenting during the march from camp. Jacky, keyed up with excitement, was loudly aggressive towards anyone who got in his way when they boarded the train at Yeovil.

'Sit down, Jacky,' Simon said quietly, 'and button your collar.'

Because it was Simon, Jacky did as he was told and cut out the swagger. Had it been anyone else, he would have punched him in the nose.

Their local Territorial company assembled in Eastport drill hall to await orders. The atmosphere was taut with anticipation and some nervousness. War, they now realised, was only a step away. All the exercises they had undertaken so lightly could be for real: the map reading and projectile plotting; the endless cleaning of weapons; and the drill. Part-time soldiers no longer, they may be required to walk away from desks and offices where they earned a living, leaving letters unanswered for someone else to deal with. Few had seriously confronted this possibility when they'd joined the Territorials.

'What about our jobs?' Eric wondered.

'Anyone can have mine,' Jacky grinned. He was feeling extraordinarily buoyant. 'Bloody errand boy for a bunch of twerps.'

A warrant officer appeared. He waited, straight as a lamppost, until the shuffling ceased. His gimlet eye raked the assembled youths. 'You do not need me to tell you that our country is at crisis point. You have twenty-four hours to make arrangements for a possible call-up. After that period, you will remain at the ready and within reach of your company until the present situation is resolved, one way or another. That is all. Dis-miss!'

Those of Simon's friends not already committed hastened now to volunteer for the service reserves. Alec Cruddas enlisted at once in the RAF Reserve. His father had been a daring young pilot in the Royal Flying Corps twenty-two years earlier and was ready with a plethora of outdated advice for his son. Nancy, who was quite sweet on Alec, having fallen out of love with the drawing master, volunteered for the women's branch of the same service, the Women's Auxiliary Air Force.

Colin went along, albeit reluctantly, with the general impulse to do one's bit and joined the Royal Naval Reserve. Doubts invaded his mind even as he signed the necessary forms. How to tell his mother? What about his career? If he interrupted his studies to serve in the Forces would this not seem like ingratitude for his brother's generosity? At the naval recruiting office, he encountered a somewhat sheepish Quentin. 'Seems I was wrong about Hitler.'

Eileen volunteered for the ATS, the Auxiliary Territorial Service. Evie, as a teacher, was in a reserved occupation as were the two nurses. Cathy was furious to be left out of the excitement. She saw only the possibility of adventure in war, not knowing its underbelly of chaos, heartbreak and slaughter, and lacking the imagination to conjure up such images. Her father could have told her a thing or two about the Somme and Ypres but he did not.

'We're going to be stuck here with rotten lectures while the others will be away doing their bit,' she complained to Andrew.

'I happen to know,' he calmed her down, 'that in the event of war, ours will be a military hospital. You will be nursing wounded soldiers and, if that is not doing your bit, I don't know what is.'

'What about you, Andrew?'

'I'm here until I qualify. They don't want half-baked doctors in the Royal Army Medical Corps. By that time I expect the whole thing will be over.'

The hours, the days slid by in an atmosphere of suspense. The knowledge that Britain was teetering on the very edge of war was sobering yet because it offered a break from dull routine, a step into the unknown –

travel, perhaps, to faraway places – young men were eager to take up the challenge.

While the nation held its breath, the work of constructing air raid shelters continued un-interrupted. Concrete road blocks appeared at important crossroads, fortified pillboxes at strategic points. From the windows of the nurses' home Cathy and Norah watched gangs of workmen segmenting the common with trenches designed to prevent its use as a landing strip.

'Is this really happening, Norah?'

'My dad's ship has been recalled from the Med,' said Norah.

There was a delivery of a thousand gas masks to the town hall. As a senior council official, Cathy's father was required to assist in their distribution. 'It's not easy,' he told Chrissie, 'squeezing the cheeks of cross old ladies into these rubber things. "Stop it!" they scream, "you're pulling my hair out" or "you're ruining my perm". I tell them, "That's nothing compared with what a load of chlorine gas will do, madame!" '

Chrissie Lewis was remembering the earlier war. 'We never had to wear these nasty black snouts last time,' she complained.

'Aye,' her husband reminded her, 'and your brother got himself gassed and has never been right since. Just keep it in its box and keep it handy.'

'It doesn't seem possible,' she grieved, 'after losing all our young men in the last war and now, just time enough for boys to grow up, here we are talking about fighting again.'

Then, as suddenly as it had arisen, the crisis evaporated. At a point when everyone in Britain was preparing for war, when houses in vulnerable sites by the sea or near the river were already sprouting 'FOR SALE' notices and the value of country cottages trebled, when a certain acceptance of change in everyday life had come about, Mr Chamberlain returned from his third consultation with Hitler, this time in Munich, triumphantly waving a paper signed by the Führer.

'Peace in our time!' he proclaimed. 'Herr Hitler has agreed that our two nations will never again wage war against each other.'

There was to be no war. Rapturous applause. What a great man this Chamberlain was.

Nevertheless, there were some who did not applaud and they were not popular when they asked, 'What about Czechoslovakia?'

Simon put that same question to his father over a beer at the King's Head and got a terse answer.

'Czechoslovakia, my son, has been sold down the river in the name of appeasement and don't ever forget it. Our prime minister has nothing to be proud of. What right have we, who are supposed to be supporting the Czechs, to tell them that they must accept Hitler's demands? "War must be avoided at all costs," we told them. All right for us, but the cost to the Czechs is high. They have been sacrificed to take the edge off the tyrant's

58

appetite.'

Cyril Lewis joined them. 'May as well offer a currant bun to a hungry bear. There'll be no stopping him now. We've shown him our colours – yellow as mustard.'

Simon frowned, 'Are there no men of authority in Germany to restrain Hitler?'

'I believe there are,' his father said seriously, 'but they gave the horse its head in the beginning and now it has bolted with the bit between its teeth. They'll never hold Hitler now. Anyone who speaks out will end up in a labour camp.' He looked at his son, the apple of his eye. 'You'll be back in that uniform for real before long. The writing is on the wall. I am faced with it every time I go to Germany. Hitler means to rule the world.'

In the presence of these two old soldiers, Simon felt diminished and out of his depth. He perceived that this was no occasion for bugles, flags and big talk. If he were to be called, then he would do whatever was expected of him as honourably as possible. No big deal.

Cyril Lewis would have liked a son. What he got was three daughters. He had a great liking for Simon Poole, rugby fullback and a dependable team man. If he could not have a son, then a son-in-law was the next best thing and, in his opinion, Cathy could look far and not find a better prospect for a husband.

Six

The rape of Czechoslovakia took place unopposed. A certain blind self-interest persuaded the people of Britain that no dishonour was incurred. Into Germany's great maw went Czechoslovakia's huge deposits of coal and iron to feed the industries of a nation that was limbering up for war. Before the year was out German troops were marching down the streets of bewildered, defenceless Prague. Once again, Hitler had proved to his generals that the western allies were paper tigers.

Going back to his job at the estate office once the Munich crisis had subsided was something of an embarrassment to Jacky. The might-have-been Tommy Atkins now rather regretted the manner of his departure. Believing at the time that there was a better option open to him, he more or less told the boss where he could put his rotten job. His patriotism saved the day for him, however, since he was the only one on the staff to respond promptly to his country's call. A lifted eyebrow, the hint of a mocking smile on the face of the boss, this he could bear but 'See the Conquering Hero Come' sung by junior clerks resulted in a punch-up. Then Jacky settled down with a very bad grace to running messages once more. Fate had done the dirty on him.

Eric's reaction to the ending of the crisis was different. It was with a feeling of profound relief that he slid back on to his old familiar stool at his old familiar desk, modestly acknowledging the admiring glances of his colleagues. He had been ready to go and fight. That was true enough but now that Germany had signed the peace declaration with Britain, Eric could get on with his life. His mother was pleased. 'The cup hath been taken away from you, my son,' said she, in a loose quote.

Simon did what was expected of him, and resumed work in the insurance office – but with a deep sense of frustration. In that brief period of national emergency, he had discovered in himself a scarcely resistible urge to get out there and help Czechoslovakia. To return to his dull safe job threw him into a fit of depression. France and Britain had pledged themselves to come to the assistance of any small nation menaced by an aggressor. And yet both nations had looked the other way when Czechoslovakia was crying out for help. Simon was ashamed of his country.

He had glimpsed a different role for himself, something nobler than writing invoices and claims, and tracking fraudsters, something better than working in a poky little office above the Co-op with a view of waste

61

pipes and rubbish bins.

'You've been in a foul temper ever since Chamberlain made peace,' Cathy accused him and he bought her some licorice allsorts to shut her up. He didn't want to hear her say, 'I believe you really wanted to go to war.'

Evie, in her student lodgings in Dundee, decided that she could accept the offer of a year in the United States on an exchange of pupil teachers after all. When it seemed that war was inevitable, she was forced to turn down this chance of a lifetime, though it nearly broke her heart to do so. The offer was still open and she could now accept with a clear conscience.

Her mother told all the neighbours, of course, then wished she hadn't told the woman above the fruit shop who ran the Christmas club. The sour old spinster looked at Sadie Dobson in unfeigned amazement. 'Wherever does she get her brains from?' The bitch.

'You go to it, girl,' Sadie urged her daughter. 'Grab the chance. All expenses paid! It's a dream.'

Her father had not thought fit to congratulate Evie, although she had been selected from a wide net of applicants. 'No good squealing if you want to come home,' was his surly comment. He was sitting by the fire with his stockinged feet on the fender. The air was disgustingly thick with the smell of frying onions, cigarette smoke and sweaty feet. 'You'll have to stick it out.'

'I might even stay there,' she answered with some spirit. 'I certainly won't squeal to come home. Everything is more modern in America.' Dutifully, she made to kiss him farewell but he, anticipating trespass upon his person, retreated with alarm into his shoulders like a bad-tempered tortoise into its shell. 'Oh, you old curmudgeon!' Out of patience, she left him and went with her mother to the station to catch her train back to Dundee.

'Don't pay no heed to him.' Her mother slipped an arm through hers. 'Ignorant bugger. Now you get yourself a perm as soon as you can afford it. I'll make you some nice new clothes before you leave. Show them Yanks what a nice English girl looks like.'

On her return to Dundee, Evie wrote straight away to the principal of Miss Baxter's College for Girls, Marble Cove, Massachusetts, accepting the exchange offered. She would begin in the September term, 1939.

Privately, both Colin and Quentin welcomed the reprieve from service in the armed forces. They could now continue their law studies without losing face with their friends. They had done the decent thing. They had volunteered and their names remained on the Royal Naval Reserve list. Hopefully, they would never be needed. Nevertheless, the lighthearted insouciance of earlier years would never be recaptured.

Winter had taken up residence in the hospital. Icy winds coming off the North Sea sliced through Christmas decorations, whipping into paper chains and bunched balloons. Two well-stoked stoves in each ward made little impact on the volume of fresh cold air admitted.

'D'ye not t'ink we moight be havin' one o' them winders closed now, Sister, for it's freezin' cold oi am.' It took a bold Irishman, and an old one at that, to make such a suggestion to the sister of the ward.

'Fresh air kills germs, Mr Murgatroyd.'

She moved on and did not hear his bitter, 'It'll be after killin' me first.'

1938 was moving to a close. It had been a troublesome year but peace had prevailed, peace of a sort. At least Britain had nothing to fear from those ridiculous goose-stepping jackboots. Eastport shipyards were busy with naval orders. Life was good. There would be provision for a bottle of sherry and a bird for the table in every worker's home this Christmas.

The nurses went from ward to ward singing carols, Norah at the front carrying a hurricane lamp and an elderly home sister bringing up in the rear of the crocodile with a blanket in case of fire.

Happy Christmas everyone and a Guinness for every male patient.

Andrew was giving a party at his house, to see the old year out and welcome the new one in. Cathy and Norah were not among the lucky nurses who had evening passes, so it would be the fire escape for them. The leap from the last rung was always a challenge, more so when wearing evening dresses. But Andrew was there, crouched out of sight in the shrubbery, to lend a hand as Norah and Cathy and several other law-breakers parachuted the last eight foot, silver slippers in their hands.

Andrew's mother allowed herself a wish as her son led Norah to join the dancers in the drawing-room. With her shining blonde hair and dressed in primrose taffeta created by her mother, Norah was a golden girl tonight.

'We simply *adore* nurses,' Andrew's fifteen-year-old twin sisters chanted as they danced around the couple. 'So does Andy!'

Foxtrotting to Harry Roy's wild 'Hold That Tiger' playing on the gramophone, Simon held Cathy tight. 'I can't breathe,' she protested. 'My nose is squashed against your shirt front.'

Mr Mount, the large and beaming host, poured another whisky for himself and a gin for his wife. 'We can't be too much out of line,' he confided to her, 'or he wouldn't have brought his friends to meet us. Not too old hat, what!'

A wholesome bunch, he was thinking, as he looked around the room. Some he knew. Others he had not met until tonight. There was Quentin Ford, a dapper little fellow, very like his famous father; a serious young man who had engaged him in a rather obscure political discourse earlier in the evening. And another aspiring lawyer, the Scottish lad in

65

the kilt, who wished to be excused before midnight as he was his mother's first foot. Nice lad. That girl Andrew was dancing with, what a stunner! How in the world did that old sea dog Moffat sire such a beauty? Then there was Cyril Lewis's girl, another nurse, and Nancy Pringle with that extraordinary hair-style, one you'd expect from an art student. He remembered her mother when she was not much older than this flighty lass here. And Evie Dobson, home from Scotland for the Christmas holidays. What a transforma-tion there! A few years ago she was an undernourished waif. She had turned into this butterfly of a girl. They say, look at a girl's mother before you marry and you will see what your wife will become, but this slim, fair, wand of a lass could never turn into the blowsy barmaid who was her mother. Never in the world. By all accounts, she was a clever young woman, training to be a teacher. You would think that such a peach of a girl could do better than Jacky Whitmore for a partner. A rough diamond, that one, though Andrew said he had a heart of gold. Anyway, she was off to the States soon and would no doubt find herself a millionaire. Eric Dotchin had a pretty solid guardian angel in Eileen Whatser-name. Wouldn't like to get on the wrong side of that one. The big chap whizzing Lewis's girl round was Ken Poole's boy and the hand-some chap the twins had attached themselves to was a reporter on the local paper. What did the new year hold for them, these young

66

people on the brink of life? Pray God there would be no more alarms like that appalling Munich crisis.

'Five minutes to midnight, Andy,' Brian Mount bent to turn the knob on the Bakelite wireless set and lifted the needle arm from the gramophone record. 'Fetch the glasses, girls.' Corks popped. Champagne fizzed. Youth, he thought enviously at every pretty girl's smile, I remember.

'This is the BBC Home Service,' said the announcer and Big Ben began his sonorous declaration of the last minutes of an old and dishonoured year.

'I give you the toast,' said Mr Mount. 'Raise your glasses to this new year, 1939. May it be a year of prosperity for all of us and, above everything, a year of peace.'

Seven

1939

Norah was fishing instruments out of the ward steriliser when Andrew crept up on her and blew down her neck. 'What are you doing, Florence?'

'Andrew! You made me jump. Bladder wash out for bed ten.' And, quickly, before their conversation could be interrupted, Norah asked, 'Are you going to the King's Head tonight?'

'Unless I'm on call.'

'Cathy and I are bringing one of our new trainee nurses. She doesn't seem to have made any friends, so be nice to her.'

'What's she like?'

Norah's smile was conspiratorial, like his mother's. 'Very pretty.'

'Tell me more.'

'Big, black eyes. Black hair.'

'Of African origin, perhaps?'

'A Jewish refugee from Germany.'

Andrew sobered immediately. 'Poor girl.'

'She needs cheering up.'

'Bring her along. Simon, Eric and Jacky are going straight to the pub after drill practice. I'll be along later.'

Hilde Müllerman stood out from the rest of the new intake like an orchid amongst buttercups. Her somewhat heavy classical features conveyed a certain aloofness that set her apart from the giggling, whispering class of new students in the dining-room. With her large dark eyes 'like black olives', Cathy remarked, she looked impassively over a table set with bread and jam and Mrs Metcalf's rock cakes. Mrs Metcalf was the hospital baker and her rock cakes were serious. Seated amongst girls with the fair skin of northern people, the new student bloomed like some sultry eastern transplant.

Cathy and Norah, from the top of the table

where their seniority now placed them, regarded the newcomer with curiosity noting that, while the other new students chatted amongst themselves, this dark girl was left severely alone.

'She looks foreign.'

'She looks like a film star.'

No one was talking to her the next day nor the day after that. 'She seems unhappy.' Cathy found misery in another hard to bear. 'I wonder which ward she is on.'

'Women's Surgical,' said Norah. 'That awful staff nurse.'

Cathy snorted. 'She's enough to make any new probationer want to shoot herself.'

'Hope she doesn't do anything silly, run away or anything.'

'We'd better do something about her, d'ye think?'

'After duty tonight. Collect her for a cuppa. She's on my floor.'

They knocked on her bedroom door later that evening. 'Where do you think she comes from?' hissed Cathy. 'She doesn't look English.'

'I am Cherman,' the girl said, opening a chink. 'You vill not like me. I am also a Chew.'

'Pardon?'

The door was closed upon them. Cathy and Norah retired, rebuffed. 'Not a resounding success, that.'

They sat on Norah's bed, backs against the slippery painted wall and chomped on Norah's mother's shortbread biscuits. 'I borrowed a chair from MacDonald next door, specially.' They glared resentfully at the empty chair and proceeded to finish the shortbread.

For a while after that they left the new girl to her own devices, but when every glimpse showed her withdrawn and obviously miserable, they agreed to make another attempt at friendship.

'What's her name again?'

'Müllerman,' said Norah. 'Hilde Müllerman.'

'Perhaps she had to get out of Germany. Everybody knows Hitler hates Jews.'

This time when the door was opened a crack, Cathy and Norah stood their ground. They had seniority on their side and could pull rank.

'Come on, Müllerman,' they kept the tone lightweight but firm. 'Coffee in Moffat's room. No excuses.'

Since the two senior nurses refused to move from the door, Müllerman reluctantly and very slowly picked up her cardigan, locked her door and followed them.

They started off with ward talk, what a bitch the staff nurse was and did Hilde find the work difficult.

'For me is most difficult to understand the patients speaking,' she said. 'It is funny English.'

Cathy laughed. 'But yours is funny English, too!' a rejoinder that closed the German girl up at once like a clam.

'Just a joke, Hilde,' Norah said smoothly. 'You have to learn to take a joke. Life is not to be taken too seriously.'

Down came the girl's brows in a straight black line. She tossed her head in irritation. 'You know nothing, you English.' She did not attempt to disguise the scorn in her voice. 'Everything is a choke. But not for me. My father, my mother and my sister – we haf to leave our nice home in Berlin and come to this country vich I do not like.'

Norah broke the awkward silence. 'You are right. In England we cannot imagine such things.' Cathy and Norah were beginning to wish they had left the new student alone. They were only trying to help.

'Our nice garten,' the German girl's voice quavered and, as she looked away, Cathy and Norah saw her eyes brighten with unshed tears, 'mit statues and a fountain and a liddle shelterhouse for coffee in the sommertime. The Steinway piano and our paintings worth a lot of money and precious silver things and furniture – all that ve haf to leave behind for the Nazis.' She spat out the word so fiercely that flecks of spittle fell on her lips.

Cathy and Norah were silent.

'The night ve left vas terrible. Synagogues burning. The Nazis called it *Krystalnacht*. Pretty name, hein? Plenty krystallen on pavements from Chewish shop windows. Chewish peoples, some murdered, some taken away in trucks.'

'You escaped.'

'My father paid much money to get us to England, but almost too late. Ven we get away in a furniture van our house is burning. My uncles, aunts and cousins – they vould not come. They stayed and I think I shall not see them again.' There was no stopping her now that she had launched into her tale. 'Our ship vaits for us in Hamburg but my father must pay the monies for it all over again. Then the Nazis come and take our furniture from the van, all we haf left. Only our suitcases are ve allowed to take on the ship. They take everysing else.'

Any comment would seem futile and irrelevant. Finally Cathy said gently, 'At least you are safe here now.'

The German girl turned angrily upon her. 'Mit nothing. No money. Nothing. Ve are like the beggars.' She put down her cup and got to her feet. 'Thank you for the coffee.'

Norah detained her with a hand on her sleeve. 'Don't blame us because we have not been as unfortunate as you, Hilde.'

'We want to help,' said Cathy.

'You cannot help because you do not understand. Everything is all right for you English.'

'It is all right in England for you,' Norah pointed out. 'No Nazis here, remember that.'

There was pity as well as dislike in the girl's glance. 'Not yet and it vill soon be too late to stop them.'

After she had gone, Norah and Cathy looked ruefully at each other. 'Another bit of botched diplomacy. At least we tried.'

They were surprised when, a few nights later, there came a timid knock at Norah's door. Hilde Müllerman stood there in some embarrassment. 'I come to say I am sorry. You were kind and I vas rude. Please excuse.'

'Oh, forget it,' Cathy said lightly and was at that moment visited by a bright idea. 'Look. Are you off duty tomorrow night? We'll take you to an English pub.'

'I haf not been to an English pub. My father would not be pleased.'

'Your father won't know.'

She was unimpressed with her first pub. You could see from the hovering sniff on her perfectly chiselled nose as she followed Cathy and Norah into the saloon. Flyblown sporting prints crowded the nicotine-brown walls and a large stuffed salmon looked balefully down from its dusty glass case. There were cigarette ends on the unwashed linoleum floor. Someone with a daffodil in his buttonhole was bashing out 'I Don't Want to Set The World on Fire' on a tinny piano. A heated argument about football was going on at the bar.

'Over here, girls!' Eric, Simon and Jacky, in uniform after the Territorial drill practice, occupied a corner by the fire.

'This is Hilde, chaps.'

But in spite of their friendly welcome Hilde made little effort to communicate and sat glumly sipping lemonade.

'What's up?' Cathy demanded fiercely on

the side. The evening had got off to a bad start.

'You did not say ve vould meet mit soldiers,' Hilde said stiffly. 'I do not like soldiers.'

Cathy laughed. 'They're not proper soldiers! They're only Terriers.'

'Who's not proper soldiers?' Simon overheard the last remark. 'I'll have you know, Nurse Lewis, that I have just gained my first stripe.' Out of his pocket he produced a lance corporal's insignia. 'I'm looking for a nice nurse to stitch it on my sleeve.'

Explaining the Territorial Army to Hilde was not easy but eventually she warmed a little towards the three in uniform. And when Andrew and Quentin arrived followed by Eileen, she relaxed her straight back. They bought her potato crisps and another lemonade. 'It is kind of you to let me join you,' but her effort to be polite carried no warmth.

'Look upon us as your friends,' said Andrew.

'I do not haf friends,' she replied, 'because I am a Chew.'

In the fragile silence that followed, her listeners hesitated. To drop the subject or pursue it?

Jacky Whitmore, whose instincts were not as finely tuned as the others', came in very bluff with, 'Well. What odds? We're a mixed lot here. I'm a primitive Methodist and you can't get more primitive than that and he,' pointing at Quentin, 'is a Roman Catholic.'

'And I,' smiled Simon, 'am a "Don't

Know".'

Hilde sighed a huge sigh. 'You English. Alvays the choke.'

'Just ignore us.' Andrew leaned across and took her glass. 'Let me get you something more exciting than lemonade.'

'What's Hitler got against Jews anyway?' demanded Jacky.

Hilde's lip curled. 'Chews are more clever. Chews are the best doctors, the best musicians, the best artists. Chews hold the best positions and that is not permitted in Chermany. Chermans, says their Führer, are the Master Race. Chews must be their slaves.'

Andrew came back from the bar with a Pimm's for Hilde. 'Where are your parents now?'

'My father is a doctor. He has English doctor friend from many years. Now this friend gives my father and mother a small apartment near him in Liverpool and some work. He is very kind. My sister types his letters.'

'Why did you not apply to train as a nurse at a Liverpool hospital, near your family?'

She flashed an angry glance in Eileen's direction. 'You think I did not try? It is not easy to be refugee. This hospital said yes, so I come here.'

'She's prickly, isn't she?' Norah and Andrew were walking back to the hospital together. Cathy and Hilde were a little way ahead.

'Oh well,' said Andrew, 'it can't be easy for her.'

75

Despite friendly approaches Nurse Müller-man remained distant, preferring to spend her off-duty in her room, alone. There were no complaints about her work. She was quick, conscientious, and never forgot an instruction. The sister on Women's Surgical reported to the matron that Junior Probationer Müllerman was an excellent nurse but, she might have added, an occasional smile would not come amiss.

Nurse Müllerman shrugged off the good reports. 'I haf to be the best. I haf to get the best marks and get the best job at the end of training. I must study hard, for me work is not small thing. I must make money for my father who has lost all of his.'

The day came when Hilde had visitors. Cathy and Norah met her as she was leaving the nurses' common room accompanied by an older woman who was obviously her mother and a younger one who, by her strong resemblance to Hilde, must have been her sister. Making no attempt at an introduction, Hilde led them quickly past Cathy and Norah, who were left standing, somewhat nonplussed.

'You would expect her mother to be glad to know that Hilde has friends.'

'Maybe she dislikes anything English as much as Hilde does.'

Eight

The English summer of 1939 was memorable. The sun shone from blue skies as if there was nothing wrong with the world. Nevertheless, it was a frail peace which existed, balanced on a knife edge. The nasty fright of the previous year hung around like an undertaker at a wedding. Reports from Germany confirmed the emergence of Hitler's evil regime. How could the word of such a man be trusted? What was Chamberlain's piece of paper worth now? There was no surprise and not much opposition when construction of air raid shelters continued and suitable men in every town and village were elected as Air Raid Wardens.

As an ex-sergeant of the First World War, Cathy's father was a natural choice.

'Air raids!' gasped Chrissie.

'I'm too old to fight in this war,' Cyril told her. 'But I can still do my bit.'

'I thought there wasn't going to be another war,' she wailed. 'Chamberlain said so.'

'Best be on the safe side, dear.'

Cathy and Norah were not unduly concerned

with the political temperature in Europe. Their annual holiday was due and they still had to decide where to go. There was always the problem of poverty to spoil grandiose plans.

'If Evie were still in Dundee, she could have found us a cheap B&B in Scotland.'

'She'll be halfway across the Atlantic by now. Lucky beggar.' Cathy put aside the travel magazine. 'Are we going to stay in all night, moaning? What shall we do?'

'We've got exactly one shilling between us. There's not much we can do.'

'The Terriers are at camp, the lawyers are swotting and Alec has taken Nancy to the pictures, so do we stay in and listen to records?'

'Friday night. Fishcakes for supper and shop, shop, shop at the supper table. Let's go out. It's a lovely evening, too good to waste indoors.'

'We could go down to the river and see the trawlers go out.'

Cathy was peeling off her black stockings. 'We've got enough for one fish and chips and we can share it.'

On the quayside, work had finished for the day. An assembly of derricks, their empty buckets hanging black against an apricot sky, reared like a family of praying mantises over the ribs of half-built ships. The river, un-ruffled by any breeze, threaded the bridges like a silver ribbon. The noises of industry were silenced for the night. Only the fleet of

78

trawlers, straining at their hawsers at the foot of the river steps, bumping and nodding on the turning tide, and the rise and fall of voices from the nearby Mermaid Tavern disturbed the riverside peace.

Seagulls watched with greedy eyes as the girls spread the newspaper on a low stone wall and proceeded scrupulously to divide the fish and chips.

A string of men emerged from the Mermaid, cracking jokes, hitching their heavy-duty trousers, and wiping the froth from their lips on the back of their hands.

'Here come the crews,' said Cathy.

The men stopped to study the evening sky. A calm night by the looks of it. A good night for the nets. Neat-footed they tripped down the steps to their boats, throwing a wink at the girls perched on the wall as they passed by. The glittering river awaited them and the glittering sea beyond, full of glittering fish. Watched by the girls, they manned the boats and headed in an orderly fashion round the bend in the river, making for the open sea.

The sun had set up-river behind distant chimney stacks and a cool breeze sprang up, stroking the darkening water with wrinkles. Norah looked at her watch. 'It's nearly nine o'clock. We'd better be going.'

Even as she spoke, the sound of Big Ben chiming nine on the Mermaid's wireless reached them. The newsreader spoke no more than a few words before the hubbub of voices within the tavern ceased dramatically.

Norah, groping for a handkerchief to wipe her fishy fingers suddenly grabbed Cathy by the arm. 'Listen!'

The announcer's voice reached them clearly. 'Today Herr Hitler has made certain demands on Poland. They are as follows – that Germany be given the corridor to the Baltic and the port of Danzig. Failure to hand over these concessions would result in a German attack on Poland.'

For a charged minute no one in the Mermaid spoke. Norah and Cathy stood rooted to the spot while the newsreader continued. 'Britain and France have issued a stern warning to Germany against such action.'

There was an explosion of angry voices coming from the pub. Cathy and Norah regarded each other in dismay. 'Damn! Damn! Damn!' Cathy stamped with rage. 'Another crisis. Bang goes our holiday.'

When Poland refused his demands, Hitler was not surprised. When Britain and France warned him that they would support Poland, he was not surprised. Their promises were easy made and easy broken. What really did surprise him though was that this time the prime ministers of France and Britain meant what they said when they issued the ultimatum. 'Remove the threat from Poland or we declare war on Germany.'

Shame at taking no action over Czechoslovakia – unacknowledged at the time – now troubled the British conscience. People were determined that such a betrayal of a weaker nation must not be allowed to happen again. This time Hitler had gone too far. Outspoken men like Simon's father who had been labelled warmongers were suddenly speaking with the public voice.

'Hitler's got to be stopped ... The bully must be tackled. If we'd done it sooner...'

'You see!' said Hilde triumphantly. 'Now do you believe me?'

August passed, the tension slowly mounting.

Evie had already left for America and her mother was having sleepless nights on her account. 'She'll be there by now, won't she?' anxiously Sadie Dobson coughed her way through the first Gold Flake of the day.

'Should never have gone.' Evie's father was back in work at the shipyard, asserting himself once more. 'Wouldn't listen to me.'

Reservists of all the services, men and women, including Eileen and Nancy, were put on standby. Simon, Jacky and Eric were recalled from camp once again.

'Here we go again,' sighed Jacky. 'Is it on or off? There's a smashing bit of skirt in Yeovil. Twice I've had to scarper just as things were getting interesting.'

Simon was not taking the situation so lightly. 'If we give in this time it will be our turn next and Hitler will be that much stronger.'

'I agree,' Eric, the bank clerk, found himself speaking like a soldier. 'We've got to go for him. No two ways about it.' He was in the grip of an exhilarating confusion: a certain fear mixed with a new naïve belief in his own untried strength. With Simon and Jacky beside him all things were possible.

Colin was thrown back once more into the ill-considered role he had elected for himself. He, a warrior? An unlikely deviation from a planned future at the bar. Perhaps the political situation would be amicably settled before any irrevocable decision need be taken. Then he met Simon's father.

'I think we mean business this time, Colin.' He seemed quite jolly about it and so did Nancy, when he met her for coffee.

'It looks as though we really are going to be called up, Colin. Aren't you excited?'

'Actually quite the reverse.'

Nancy sobered immediately. 'Oh, of course. Stupid of me. This will seriously interfere with your career, won't it?'

Colin nodded.

'So why did you volunteer – if you didn't want to join up?'

'Good question. Got carried away, I suppose, when you were all rushing off being very patriotic.'

A fleeting look of censure crossed Nancy's face. 'And do you not feel patriotic, Colin?'

Colin refrained from exposing his financial situation. 'As patriotic as any of you, but there are complications.'

Nancy did not pursue the subject. The Scots were a cagey lot. 'Well, even if there is a war, my dad says it will be over in a few months.'

Andrew shared this opinion. By the time he qualified, the present situation would have been resolved, one way or another. He had never seriously considered life as an army doctor and had only the haziest of notions as to what was expected of his profession in time of war. Surgeons in the 14–18 war were known to have worked under horrific conditions but times had changed. Anyhow, this situation was unlikely to arise in his case.

The last days of August slid by without any sign of Hitler withdrawing his demands on Poland. He knew these wordy politicians of old and blithely disregarded their frothy fulminations.

Gravely and conscientiously the towns and cities of strategic importance in Britain, which included Eastport at the estuary of an important river, prepared themselves for war. The letters FAP were used to identify first aid posts. Inflated balloons like huge silver fishes soared giddily above the river on steel cables designed to ensnare enemy planes. Prefabricated hutments, to be used as gas decontamination wards, sprang up in hospital grounds.

The matron of Eastport General addressed the nursing staff. 'In the event of war,' she could not quite hide the tremor in her voice for she had never been called upon to deal with a like situation, 'this has been designated a military hospital and will take only military casualties. Purely as a precautionary measure, ambulances will begin transferring our present patients to hospitals in the countryside tomorrow. You have today in which to prepare them. For the moment, all staff holidays are cancelled.'

The patients did not want to go to some convalescent centre in the depths of the country. Nevertheless, on the following morning, they were bundled up in blankets and carried, willy-nilly, to waiting ambulances, clutching their handbags and their flowers, their baccy and their pipes, still protesting.

'You'll be safer away from here when Hitler starts dropping bombs.' The nurses were quite lighthearted. It was beyond their experience to imagine the chaos of a bombed hospital.

As soon as the patients had left, army trucks delivered 200 extra beds and several loads of sandbags to wall up the ground floor windows. When all daylight was shut out and blue bulbs replaced the standard electric lights, the wards were reduced to Stygian gloom. Cathy and a junior nurse, pushing a trolley piled with sheets and blankets, set about making up beds in readiness for the expected casualties. 'Anyone brought here will think they've taken a short cut to the mortuary.'

Nine

Matters moved swiftly now. Hitler removed any existing doubt as to his intentions by invading Poland on 1 September. Two days later, on 3 September, Britain and France declared war on Germany. In less than a year Chamberlain's ringing declaration, 'Peace in our Time', was recalled only with derision.

In the nurses' sitting-room there was a scramble for newspapers. 'WAR!', the head-lines in bold black type roared from every front page. 'Nothing,' said Norah, reaching for Cathy's hand, 'will ever be the same again.'

Instructions for nurses streamed from hospital offices. 'When you hear the air raid siren those nurses on duty will place the patients under their beds, protecting them from flying glass, and will make sure they have their gas masks at hand. Off-duty staff will proceed to the basement which, from now on, is the air raid shelter for the nursing staff.'

'That's the boiler-room,' hissed Norah. 'What if a bomb drops on it?'

'Boiled nurse.'

'Any nurse out of hospital on a pass,' said the matron, 'will return at once. Her identity card will allow her to commandeer any form of transport that is available.'

Such announcements created a feeling of imminent catastrophe. Ears strained to catch the first drone of an enemy aircraft. One very young student nurse cycled home in a panic wearing a tea-cosy on her head in lieu of a tin hat. Casualties could be expected at any hour. Hot water bottles in 250 empty beds were regularly refilled.

The nation's call to arms brought back old griefs to the aged but sent an uneasy thrill of excitement through the young. All talk of appeasement was over. An attitude of bravado prevailed in Britain which sprang from a totally unrealistic belief in her invincibility as an island fortress, the 'Land of Hope and Glory' syndrome.

'We'll teach the bounder a lesson,' mossy colonels assured the chaps in the clubhouse. 'The whole show will be over by Christmas.'

Nevertheless, the government decided that children should be evacuated from vulnerable towns to the safety of the countryside. This bold and complicated procedure was bravely embarked upon without delay.

Cathy's mother watched with tears in her eyes as a crocodile of children were led across Station Square holding hands. Each child carried his 'tatchy' case of precious things, his gas mask over his shoulder and a label bearing his name. Big sisters kept the noses clean.

Nobody cried except the mothers who were left behind while their children trotted away on little docile feet to live with strangers.

Simon, Eric and Jacky were given ten days' embarkation leave before sailing to France with the First British Expeditionary Force, 1st BEF.

'Why aren't we going to Poland?' Jacky wanted to know.

'Take a look at the map, laddie.' The sergeant major bristled. 'How would you get the British Army into Poland?'

Landlocked between greedy neighbours, Germany and Russia, Poland's situation was dire. Out of earshot, Jacky went on protesting, 'But what's the use of going to France? That cannot help Poland.'

'Got to defend the Western Front,' Mr Poole declared.

'Silly old fool,' Jacky muttered to Eric. 'He thinks he's back in the trenches of 1914.'

'I've always wanted to go to France,' Eric confessed but his daydream of France was his father's nightmare, coming back to haunt him now that history was repeating itself.

These three, Simon, Jacky and Eric, were in the army now for real. The rough khaki uniform they had worn as a bit of a lark twice a week on practice night would be their wardrobe from now on. And Eric's mother slipped a mothball into one of the pockets of his best suit before putting it away 'for the duration'. 'What I mustn't do,' she admonished herself, 'is make a fool of myself when it comes to

87

saying "goodbye".'

Quentin and Colin were now called up into the Royal Naval Reserve and would go their separate ways. Quentin was to undergo training on HMS *King Alfred* at Hove, Colin to HMS *Vernon*, the torpedo and mining school at Portsmouth.

Colin knew he was making a big mistake. He felt sick at heart with the realisation of what he had signed on for. He had not the slightest interest in either torpedoes or mines. There was a temptation to back out on compassionate grounds. None of his friends were leaving a widowed mother to cope with living alone in such uncertain conditions. He had tried to persuade her to close the house temporarily and move back to Scotland near her farmer son or to go to live with her sister in the safety of Cornwall.

'No,' she had said, quietly but firmly, 'I'll bide in my own place and you must do your duty.'

That was the rub. Where did his duty lie? But his pride would not let him make excuses when his friends were leaving their homes and jobs to fight for what was right. He let himself be carried along, deafened by the bugles of patriotism, but it was with a sinking feeling that he closed the law books and put them safely away.

Simon clamped his tennis racquet in its press and oiled his rugger boots.

'It's come to this, then,' his mother dabbed her eyes.

Her little boy who now topped her by head and shoulders put his arm about her, 'Can't let Hitler get away with it, can we, Mum?'

Ken Poole found his voice, both sad and proud at the same time, 'You're talking like a soldier, son.'

And Simon felt like a soldier. An infusion of energy and purpose seemed to course through his veins. He was bigger, stronger, taller than ever before. He grinned at his father, 'I'm not an insurance clerk any more.'

Andrew went looking for Norah. The atmosphere in the hospital was quite unreal. Everything was at a peak of readiness but nothing was happening: no operations were in progress in the theatres, though sterilisers hissed and steamed, and were continually refilled; no rows of frightened sick people waiting in the Out Patients department. Porters who would normally have been pushing their trolleys from ward to ward were taking the opportunity to clean and oil the wheels. A junior nurse staggered past carrying a flourishing aspidistra in a brass pot. 'Where on earth are you going with that?' Andrew asked her.

'I've been told to wash and polish every leaf of the wretched thing. Nothing else to do. I wish the war would start.'

He found Norah seated at a table between rows of empty beds, cutting gauze swabs. 'Tomorrow night, Norah, eight o'clock in the King's Head, a send-off for the boys. Simon, Jacky and Eric are off to France, Alec has been posted to an RAF training wing in the north of Scotland, Colin and Quentin are to go to Portsmouth. You've just got to get the night off, tell any lies you can think of. This is something we can't miss. Probably the last binge together for some time. Tell Cathy. I'll tell Hilde. OK?'

'We'll be there, Andy.'

'Lucky old you.' The hovering staff nurse watched Andrew go – tall, good-humoured Andrew with the flirty-flirty eyes. 'He's everybody's dreamboat and I'll swop nights off with you.'

Women, also, who had volunteered for the services during the Munich crisis of the previous year, were immediately called up. Eileen reported to the dean of her faculty and received his blessing, with a promise that she would be able to continue her studies as soon as His Majesty had no further need of her. Her initial interview with the Auxiliary Territorial Service (ATS) was with an imposing lady in khaki who wore red tabs on her lapels and laughed like a horse, as she promised Eileen honour and glory then sent her to issue underclothing to new recruits.

Nancy the art student, now aircraftwoman, was detailed as cook to the thirty-strong air crew at the balloon barrage station. She was appalled. Her friends were in hysterics. 'She can't even cook custard without burning it!'

Cathy and Norah, immensely jealous of their uniformed friends, joined the rest of the gang for one last night together before the winds of war scattered them like the seeds of a dandelion clock, the khaki, the navy and the air-force blue. The King's Head was crowded with such uniforms. Very ordinary chaps, who had been accustomed to play darts here in baggy flannels and a pullover, were wearing the King's uniform now, all at once cocky and smart.

Jacky had news of Evie. 'She's landed safely but it was a pretty scary trip across the Atlantic, by all accounts. German subs in evidence.'

'She'd better stay there till all this business is cleared up.'

'Why wouldn't Hilde come tonight?'

'She's in a bad mood,' Cathy told Andrew. 'Matron sent for her and told her that since we are now at war with Germany she must report to the police station once a week as an alien. "Like a criminal," she says. She's very cross.'

'That's fair enough,' said Simon. 'She could be a spy.'

'What a lot of crap you talk,' Andrew looked vexed. 'God! When you think of what that poor kid has been through...'

Norah and Cathy exchanged a faintly questioning glance.

'We didn't come here to talk about the ruddy Krauts,' Jacky broke in. 'Whose round is it?'

Quentin put some notes on the table. 'This is on my old man. Champers, he said, nothing less.'

'We'll make him an honorary member of the club for that.'

They were all high, tonight, a little bit over the top for no one could say for certain when they would meet again. The girls grew sentimental and clung to the young men who were now leaving them, the young men they had grown up with, had fun with and had loved from time to time. Cathy felt suddenly afraid for Simon. He felt her shiver and held her close.

'Will you write to me, Cathy?'

'Of course, Simon.'

Eileen was sharp with envy. 'It's all right for you, Eric. You will have all the excitement of going abroad. It's not fair. I will be stuck here in a quartermaster's store, making inventories.'

The nurses stayed long past the permitted hour. 'We'll have to go over the railings.'

'I'll come with you and give you a leg up.'

'Dear Andrew, we'll miss you when you go.'

'There'll be other medical students, my sweet.'

Jacky dreaded the emotional business of saying goodbye to his parents. Displays of affection did not feature in his family circle. He wished Evie was still around to smooth things over, but she was on the other side of the Atlantic and likely to be there for some time now that German U-boats were active. One ship making the crossing had already been sunk.

After that last night with his friends Jacky

went on his own private pub crawl, got blind, stinking drunk, and picked up a tart. Dawn was streaking the sky when he crept up the stairs to his bedroom, stone cold sober, carrying his boots in his hands. A few hours later he came downstairs, smartly turned out in army gear: boots shined, webbing blancoed, respirator and tin hat to hand and a mouth like the bottom of a parrot's cage.

The solemnity of the occasion pierced even *his* tough defences. Phrases from Sunday school kept running through his head – 'Off to fight the foe ... With the cross of Jesus, going on before'. He gave his red-eyed mother a hug. He had not done that for years and he noticed how much smaller she had grown, how much more frail. Nothing but a bag of bones. 'Don't you worry, Mum. I'll be all right.'

His dad was out with the cart, delivering coal, but had left a quid for his soldier son.

All the lovely young men, the lordly ones.

They were hearing the drums that had governed their fathers, seeing flags in a stained-glass window. What did they imagine they would be doing? Cathy and Norah would later reflect.

Shooting Germans? Did they consider in those adrenalin-packed days before they embarked for France that they could be looking into the terrified eyes of a German as they pulled the trigger or threw the grenade? Somebody's husband, or son, or daddy? Did

they ever think that it might be they themselves who received the bullet that pierced a
lung and produced a life-long disability? Or
felt the flames that burned off half a face so
that not even a mother would know her son?
Or caught the lump of mortar that made a
butcher's shambles of a man's intenstines, a
head wound that left a man as quiet as a
cabbage?

Did they consider that a shell bearing their
own name could send them straight into
oblivion in one astonished moment?

On that last night at the King's Head it was
not only the champagne that put the sparkle
in their eyes. They were in love with excitement, challenge and risk. They were off to
give Hitler a bloody nose.

Ten

1939–1940

On the other side of the world, the sun was
setting on Sydney Harbour as *The Lady of
Fortune* berthed. The contents of the cable he
had just received from Liverpool came as no
surprise to the master of the ship.

'Muster on the foredeck,' he instructed his
chief officer. 'I have an important announcement to make.' That was how assistant

steward Albert Smith heard the news that his country had just declared war on Germany. 'Life is going to change for all of us,' the captain continued. 'On the outbreak of war, all movement of merchant ships passes to the control of the Royal Navy. This entire ship's company will draw paint and brushes from the store and begin camouflage.'

When *The Lady of Fortune* turned about for the homeward journey her superstructure was no longer a sparkling white, but a dull battleship grey. A gun, which had been stowed aboard for such an eventuality when the ship left England, was mounted on the afterdeck, and there was a new set of rules for passengers and crew alike.

Before sunset, when 'Darken Ship' was announced over the ship's radio, portholes and doors were to be closed. Double layers of tarpaulin or army blankets were to be hung a yard apart at exit doors so that one fell into place before the other was lifted. Smoking on deck was forbidden, even the striking of a match.

There was a lot of water between Sydney and Liverpool. Enemy submarines were known to be hunting lone ships such as *The Lady*, easy prey to their torpedoes.

Albert Smith, on lookout during the dog watch and gasping for a Woodbine, cursed and prayed for the dawn. 'How the hell am I supposed to see a bloody periscope out there!'

The ship was a pimple, a solitary toy on a heaving mass of black water reaching unidentifiable horizons. Glimmering slivers of phosphorescence tricked the eye with phantom images. That long, dark cigar shape, the trough of a deep roller? Or a surfacing U-boat?

By the time they reached the Bay of Biscay, both passengers and crew were beginning to relax, comforted by the thought that the long voyage was nearly at an end. Their complacency was shattered when a merchant ship on the distant horizon suddenly exploded into flames.

From the bridge of *The Lady of Fortune* came the order for all engines to shut down. Total silence aboard ship. Submarines were in the vicinity and submarines move fast, might even then be under *The Lady*. Bereft of power, she rocked in a gentle waddle as the thick, black night seeped across her silent decks, dropping down into the still engine room where engineers stood motionless, by their turbines. Passengers, like listening effigies, felt the brush of eternity sweep close as minutes were agonisingly stretched. Albert Smith, for the first but not the last time, faced the possibility of a violent death and found himself unmoved. When the danger passed and the ship continued on her way, he notched up the incident as another of life's experiences and was prepared for the next.

When he signed off at Liverpool docks, a Royal Navy geezer told him he had two

weeks' leave followed by a course on torpedoes and electrics at Pompey. And when he
had that under his belt he was to pack his
gear and join a corvette that was being built
at Robbs' shipyard in Leith, Scotland. He
welcomed the change, though something
other than a corvette would have been prefer-
able. Too small. Too near the water and the
big bangs for his liking, but after months at
sea he was glad to be shot of a chief steward
with easy flies and the rest of the sea bandits
aboard *The Lady of Fortune*.

He was amazed at the change in Liverpool,
from the commercial peacetime port he
remembered to a city armed for battle.
Stumbling around in the total black-out – no
street lights, no lighted shop windows – he
was nearly knocked down by a car which
came upon him without warning.

'Put your bloody lights on!' he yelled before
he realised that the pinhole of illumination
scratched through black painted headlights
was all that was permitted. He was immensely relieved to find that behind the shuttered
windows and screened door of The Sailors'
Arms there was still good English beer and
good company to be found.

He put away a skinful in The Sailors' Arms
and then went in search of a lady friend who
usually accommodated seafaring gentlemen
at short notice. With his pay in his back
pocket and a rail ticket home, he meant to
enjoy his first night ashore after ten weeks at
sea.

★ ★ ★

Simon, Eric and Jacky went to France to fight, but the action was somewhere else. Poland, as the sergeant major pointed out, was geographically inaccessible to British and French troops and, despite the good intentions of her western allies, she was being carved up between Germany and Russia.

The 1st BEF took up positions in France which were very similar to those occupied by an earlier generation, and there they waited. The excitement and keen anticipation of those first weeks in France drained away. Corporal Poole wrote home from a field near Le Mans. 'The nights are cold. We are hoping to be out of tents before the real winter starts.'

Mrs Poole sent him some warm, hand-knitted vests, which he would never dare wear.

In his letter to Cathy, he wrote of interminable route marches through dreaming French villages. 'The people seem to like us. "Hello Tommy" they call out. Some of us are invited into their homes. I wish I had stuck at my French at school.' He finished with, 'I miss you, Cathy. I could do with a cuddle right now.'

In England, as skies remained free of enemy bombers, the alert state of readiness began to wilt. The hospital took back its civilian patients from the countryside since there was no sign of military casualties and surgeons were becoming alarmed over the lengthening list of operations pending.

There was one air raid. Cathy was on night duty with Hilde as her junior nurse. The piercing high-pitched moan of the air raid siren woke their patients just after midnight. It was a sound that would become very familiar in the years to come but, on this first occasion, it sounded like the wailing of banshees and chilled them to the marrow.

'You all right?' Cathy had thought for a moment that Hilde was about to faint. Her pallor was alarming.

'Of course.' Her answer was curt but the colour returned to her face.

'Come on, then. Bed one.'

According to instructions, they wrapped each patient in a blanket and laid him under his bed with all his paraphernalia of tubes, bottles, pads and splints, and his gas mask and then the All Clear sounded, sending the whole operation into reverse.

'This is ridiculous.' Angrily Cathy began tucking up her charges once more. 'We've just upset them and probably given ourselves a hernia at the same time. They'll never get off to sleep again and they will all want a bottle.'

They did.

Fortunately the authorities recognised the impracticability of this sytem and, in future, patients would stay in their beds with gas masks handy and hope for the best. Another relaxation of regulations came with the scraping away of some of the blue paint from the ward light bulbs, since night nurses could scarcely see in order to write their reports. The alert state of readiness leaked away.

There were spies and rumours of spies. Government posters urged awareness of the enemy in the midst of everyday life. A striking poster showing a British ship on fire, sinking bows down bore the caption: CARELESS TALK COSTS LIVES. Anyone with a foreign name was suspect. Was it true that the man at the Co-op with the funny name had been locked up? Anyone seen flashing a light near the coast was apprehended even if it were nothing more sinister than an old lady looking for her pussycat. And Hilde stumped off angrily to report at the police station every week.

January 1940 was the coldest January for forty years, the worst possible time to introduce food rationing. 'Two ounces of tea a *week*! It's a cup of tea that keeps Cyril and me going!' Chrissie Lewis, like all the other housewives, was wondering how she could possibly feed her family when sugar, fats, cheese, milk, eggs and bacon were all to be rationed from that day on.

Waiting in the queue for the issue of ration books, she and Eric's mother were full of complaints. 'Four ounces of bacon a week – my Cyril has that with a couple of eggs every day for his breakfast. He's not going to like this!'

A sharp-nosed man standing next to the two women snapped, 'Then your Cyril is going to have to lump it. Doesn't he know there's a war on?'

Huffed, Doris Dotchin and Chrissie conferred *sotto voce*, 'No need for that sort of talk.'

'Jumped-up nobody. That's what this war does to folk. Makes little Hitlers of them.'

Chrissie and her friends were soon in even greater straits when meat was rationed to one shilling's worth a week. 'Cyril has had his last steak. It's stew from now on.'

Without the ships and the sailors who crewed them to bring supplies across the Atlantic, rations would have been even smaller. The absence of any enemy activity on land was becoming known as 'the phony war' but there was nothing phony about the war at sea. German U-boats hunting in packs in the Atlantic sent tons of British shipping to the bottom of the sea every week. Despite the terrible loss of life convoys had to sail. Britain could not survive without raw materials and food from the United States.

The little cockleshell corvettes acted as scout, nursemaid, and rescuer to the convoys and Albert Smith was right up there with them. He was learning that life on a corvette was far from a bed of roses. A single-funnelled tub of a ship, she heeled so far over in bad weather that there were times when her long-suffering crew feared she would never right herself again.

'It's giving a bulldog's job to a terrier,' Able Seaman Smith wrote in one of his rare letters home. 'She's a bitch of a ship. The sea is swilling over the mess decks most of the time and the gear in your locker is permanent sodden.'

He came to recognise, like every other member of the crew, that sickening twist in the stomach when Action Stations sounded, when the convoy under escort was hidden in icy fog and somewhere, close at hand, a submarine lurked with torpedoes primed.

After his first blooding when six out of a convoy of forty ships went down, he was as tough as the next man. He sailed through the debris of many an unlucky tail-end Charlie and on nights that were pudding black he heard the cries of men drowning in oil. He pulled his weight with the rest of the crew and when he was required to help with the wounded, his big navvy's hands that Norah had noticed could be as gentle as hers. Courage was something he did not lack.

In March of that year, Andrew qualified and was acting as a houseman in Eastport General until his call-up papers for the Royal Army Medical Corps should arrive. A posting to France was imminent. Until then, he was to continue working in the hospital and was able to meet Cathy and Norah, and occasionally Hilde, to exchange news.

Cathy had received a letter. 'Simon writes to say they are all bored stiff with training exercises and route marches.'

Hilde pounced, 'But the danger is great!

How can they be bored? It is all "relax, relax,'" she mimicked scornfully. 'Nothing to excite about. Pah! You English vill vake up too late. Hitler vill not stop at Poland. He takes more and more *lebensraum* for his "master race". He vill come also here mit his *stoss-trupen* and you vill not stop him mit your bored soldiers.' Anger darkened her face, put fire in here black eyes.

Cathy exploded, 'Oh, for God's sake, Hilde! Turn it off.' Norah, the peacemaker, was absent that morning.

'We can do nothing in Poland,' Andrew said patiently, 'but we can prevent Hitler from invading France. Our troops are guarding the frontier and the French have built the Maginot defence line of concrete bunkers. Hitler will not get past that.'

'If Hitler comes to Britain,' Hilde went on morosely, as if Andrew had not spoken, 'there vill be no place left for my family to hide. Ve haf no money left to go to America.'

'We're all in this together, Hilde,' Andrew tried to reassure her.

'Hitler will get more than he bargains for if he attacks Britain,' Cathy added stoutly with nothing but patriotic fervour to back her declaration. Hilde's sniff was more eloquent than words. The British were well known for their stupidity.

Andrew turned the conversation to ask about Hilde's parents, who were now intern-ed with other aliens on the Isle of Man.

'My father is allowed to practice as a doctor

103

helping the other internees, so he is happy and my mother is content to see him happy. But we are poor.'

'But safe,' Cathy reminded her.

'Chews are never safe.'

Andrew reached across and took her hands in his. 'You must try to forget what happened in Germany, Hilde.'

He was so kind to her, so patient despite her ill humour. I have never yet seen her smile, was Cathy's unspoken thought. She's like a piece of sculpture, beautiful but as cold as an alabaster statue. And she needs her bottom smacked.

'This is England,' Andrew persisted. 'No one will harm you here.'

But she who was so much more aware of the dangers would not be pitied by fools. She closed her eyes and withdrew her hands. 'Only in America vill ve be safe. There is no safety here.'

Eleven

1940

Evie had a class of nine-year-olds in Miss Baxter's School for Young Ladies in New England, USA. She wrote to Norah and Cathy.

> It's paradise here. Everyone is so rich! Everything is different. Biscuits are 'crackers' and cakes are 'cookies' and scones are something else and I've got what American matrons call a 'beau'. His name is Ken and he has a car as long as a bus. No shortage of petrol here. No shortage of anything. No blackout. Have you any news of the boys? I haven't heard from Jacky for months. There is absolutely no news at all about the war over here. Did I dream it?

Evie met Ken Rauchenfeld at the tennis club, which she had been persuaded to join almost as soon as she arrived in Marble Bay. He asked her out once or twice to the soda

105

fountain, so that she could indulge her passion for ice cream. The choice was breathtaking. At home it was 'cornet' or 'sandwich' with a sprinkling of hundreds and thousands, if you were lucky. She was presently working through the alphabet and had got as far as 'H' for hazelnut crunch.

He was nice, Ken. She quite liked him. And it was fun to have money spent on her. Jacky had never been able to afford anything like this. Then one night, after they had been to the pictures, Ken said, 'My mom sure would like to meet you, Evie,' and now, here she was, in the home of Kenneth Z. Rauchenfeld the Third.

Her Ken was Rauchenfeld the Fourth. Funny little habit, that. You could say her father was George the Fifth. Her mother would die laughing. Anyhow here she was in the magnificent home of the tycoon himself, whose name was a byword for quality in every industry needing ring plugs and hose fittings, for things like washing machines, aeroplanes, motor cars. Like tanks.

Ken's mother was all the things that Evie admired in an older woman. Totally immaculate, from her lacquered cap of golden hair (shiny but not brassy like her own mum's) to her pearly pink fingernails which looked as though they had never been in a sink full of dishes. Probably hadn't. There was probably a kitchen out the back somewhere with machines for everything. And her suit of eau-de-nil linen was as crisp as a new pound note.

Evie, in her skimpy frock of flowered Tobralco, felt she must look as if she shopped at the church bazaar. Her mother had run it up for her when she left for America.

'Yes please, Mrs Rauchenfeld,' she held out her cup for a refill and Ken was on his feet at once.

'Well now,' his mother reproved her, 'that surely sounds awful formal. You must call me Sylvia. It is such a treat for us to entertain a little English girl in our modest home.'

Modest home! She should see ours back in England. They were taking tea in an elegant room with chintzy chairs and little polished tables to put your cup and saucer on. Gold velvet curtains, they called them 'drapes', reached from ceiling to floor at the French windows. Venetian blinds striped the sunlight before it could bleach the pretty Chinese carpet. Huge paintings on the walls. Huge vases of flowers. Enormous ash trays. In fact, everything was enormous. Ken was enormous, too, with great long legs in trousers which never seemed to crumple nor lose their crease.

'It's a simply beautiful house, Sylvia.'

'Speak some more, honey,' Ken smiled at her. 'Mom just loves your English accent.'

Ken drove Evie back to her apartment in his sleek convertible, with the hood down. Tucked inside Mrs Rauchenfeld's fur wrap, she felt proud as a queen. One thing would have made her pleasure complete. If only Jacky and the others could see her now. She

107

would have liked to show off a bit. Jacky would never be able to own a car like this. Not in a month of Sundays. Come to think of it, if he saw her now, he would only make some smart crack. Americans, Evie decided, were the most generous people on earth – and the richest. Everyone had a car, sometimes two.

As Ken drove back to town, the leafy suburbs, where mansions like Ken's stood back from the road, lawned and bedded, gave way to pretty little white, wooden houses, garages, diners and liquor stores.

'Have your parents lived here long?' Evie wondered.

He told her that Kenneth Rauchenfeld the First was actually named Conrad but folk could not get their tongues round it so he changed it to Kenneth. She wondered why he had not thought to change that awful surname while he was about it, but she kept that thought to herself.

'He was an immigrant toolmaker from Hamburg back in 1859. He built himself a split bark shack and raised a family not more than 500 metres from where my grandpop built our present house. That little ole German immigrant would sure be surprised to see what's happened to the piece of land that he bought with his first week's pay.'

'Rags to riches. Spectacular! I suppose it doesn't matter if you have a German name over here.'

Ken frowned. 'I don't get you, honey.'

'Rauchenfeld,' she explained. 'In Britain people with German names have to register as aliens.'

'Typical.'

She was not sure what he meant by that.

This was Cathy's twenty-first birthday. Just her bad luck to be on night duty, she reflected, for this especially important milestone. She got a box of Milk Tray chocolates from a first year medical student who was sweet on her, a nice boy but too young, and then, not to be denied at least a small celebration, she broke the rules for night nurses by 'nicking out' during the day to meet Norah, who was on day duty, for a Pimm's Number One and a lamb chop at The Eldon Grill – and that was about it.

'Some girls get champagne on their twenty-first birthday,' she told the very ordinary face reflected in her mirror. Sadly she regarded her springing auburn hair, the sort that did not take kindly to curlers and defiantly retained its individuality irrespective of fashion. 'Like a yard broom,' she cursed it and concluded, 'I'm not the type to be lavished.' Norah's face, by contrast, was one that everyone admired. The subject, Cathy felt, was not worth pursuing, 'Can't do anything about that.' She grabbed her dressing-gown and hurried to bag a bath before she went on duty.

The baths were massive constructions of cast iron, standing most empirically on great splayed paws. Those Victorian nurses were obviously big girls, she reflected, as she climbed in and blissfully sank up to her neck in hot water. Steam was rising from the next cubicle and pretty Ellen Cahill from Dublin, who was in love with a junior doctor, was singing 'Begin the Beguine' at full throttle. Cathy joined in with gusto.

'Let the spark that was once a fire...
Remain an em-ber...'

At once the singer in the next cubicle broke off. 'Who's that?'

'Lewis.'

'Then shut up, Lewis. This is my dirge. Get your own.'

'I don't need a dirge.'

'Neither do I. I need a wedding march.'

'It's my birthday,' sang out Cathy.

'Have a nice time. Which ward are you on?'

'Seven.'

'That gorgeous houseman!'

'He's been called up.' Fleetingly she hoped that Andrew would keep in touch once he was in the Army, especially with Norah. Norah liked him a lot.

'This is his last night,' she added.

'Then you do need a dirge.'

The day staff were coming off duty as Cathy tripped around the corner of the corridor into her ward with a swing of her skirt, her starched white veil flying, her head held high. She was twenty-one today, invincible, invulnerable. Tonight she could take on the world, dance till dawn, sing like a blackbird.

That was how she felt. In reality she would be in charge of thirty-two assorted men: old, young and in-between; nice, nasty, polite, rude and some quite barmy. Officially Andrew had left the hospital, but he had promised to put in an appearance on Cathy's ward to wish her a happy birthday after the Night Super's round at midnight.

Seen dimly in the lowered lights of the ward, white counterpaned beds stretched away into the shadows, their occupants tucked in, fed and watered – prepared for sleep. She passed by on her quiet rubber-soled shoes, nodding at the nice old men with prostates, the soldier who had fractured his femur by diving into an empty swimming pool, the cheeky footballer with the knee, who gave her a huge wink, and the road accidents. There were always road accidents, even though shortage of petrol limited the number of vehicles on the roads. With their blacked-out headlights, people drove into lampposts, garden walls and pedestrians. On dark nights, the old and the infirm learned to stay at home. There were no air raid casualties. No air raids.

The tramp from the Salvation Army Men's Palace lifted his bandaged head as she passed, 'Give us a kiss, norse!' he hollered.

At the central desk in a cone of light, the sister's starched purity was dazzling. The white cap, with its stiff little bow tied under the chin, was fixed to her shining bobbed head with white painted kirby grips. Lily hands rested lightly on the report book in front of her. She waited for Cathy, one eye on the ward clock.

Sister Milligan was one of the younger sisters, though not so young nor as attractive as Irish Nurse Cahill, who vied with her for the attentions of the junior doctor. Sister Milligan did not sing 'Begin the Beguine' in the bath tub, but her diary would have caused a sensation had it fallen into the wrong hands. Her report, delivered in low, modulated tones, covered every patient. Cathy scribbled away.

She walked with the sister to the end of the ward passage, as courtesy demanded, then she closed the swing doors and skipped all the way back to the ward. It was her ward now. She was in charge. The night was cold but coals were heaped high in the tiled stove in the centre of the ward. Cathy and her junior nurse would sit by that later on when all the treatments were finished and the Night Super had done her round.

She was in the kitchen carving up a birthday cake when Andrew put his head around the door. 'Happy Birthday, Cathy. Has she been?'

'All clear. Find another cup, McKinness.'

'There's only two,' said the junior nurse.

'Then Doctor Mount will have to use a specimen glass.'

'Unused, I trust.' Andrew helped himself to a piece of cake. 'How did you manage this?'

'Nancy sent it. RAF butter, sugar, currants.

112

We'll both go to prison.' She carried the tea tray to the comfortable chairs by the fire and handed him a glass of tea.

'Some day, Cathy, we'll do this properly – with bubbly.'

'When the gang has come home to roost,' said Cathy. 'After you have left, Andy, there'll only be Norah and me to hold the fort.'

'And Hilde,' he reminded her.

'And Hilde.' She handed the cake around again to cover her momentary confusion. 'All you smashing chaps are scattered. Alec in the highlands of Scotland, where Colin would like to be no doubt. Simon, Eric and Jacky in France, soon to be joined by you. Quentin at sea. Is Colin at sea or is he shore-based?'

'Still training in Portsmouth. Torpedoes and mining school. He hates it.'

Their voices were low so as not to disturb the sleeping patients. Out of habit, their ears were tuned in to the little noises of the night, the snores and mutters of dreamers, the splash of water as someone poured a drink. The new patient with the scalp laceration, who was still awake, regarded the little group by the fire with interest.

'Can't you sleep?' whispered Cathy.

'I'm not tired.' He smiled to himself thinking what he would tell his wife on visiting day. 'You should see what goes on in the night when the sister's not around!'

Andrew, no longer a hospital houseman, was already projecting his thoughts towards France. 'I hope to be posted somewhere near

Simon.'

'They are having a totally boring time, judging from his letters,' Cathy said. 'All Quiet on the Western Front.'

'There's probably all hell going on in Poland.' Andrew got to his feet. 'Must be off. It's almost tomorrow. Who knows where your next birthday will be celebrated.' He produced a flat package. 'A small gift, Cathy dear. I know you like the Inkspots. Remember me when you play it on your little gramophone.'

' "Ain't Misbehavin" ,' she read aloud the record label. 'I might not live up to that.'

'Don't even try.' He got to his feet and looked around the dark and silent ward. Not his patients any more. 'Is Hilde on night duty?'

'Day duty. Ward eleven, I think.'

'I must see her before I leave.' The firelight caught the sudden urgency in his eyes. 'I think she's keeping out of my way.'

He's in love with her! The revelation came to Cathy with sudden clarity. In retrospect it was obvious. Well, that sourpuss didn't deserve such a really nice fellow. And what about Norah?

He paid a final visit to the hospital to say goodbye to his chief and, if the truth were known, to show off a tiny bit in his uniform as a lieutenant in the Royal Army Medical Corps. He even walked like a soldier now, abandoning the sloppy gait of a medical

114

student. Already there was a military air about him, a hint of heroics enough to turn a nurse's head. Quite senior sisters gurgled and whimpered when he gallantly bade them goodbye.

Norah greeted him with delighted surprise. 'Andrew! How smart you look.'

'Came to say goodbye, Norah pet,' he dropped a light kiss on her forehead. 'Be good.'

'I will be thinking of you, Andrew, till we meet again.'

Well aware of the warm affection between them, he took her hand and turned it palm upwards, tracing her lifeline with his finger. 'Who knows what is in store for us?' Their eyes met. 'On my first leave,' he spoke lightly, 'we'll have a party at the King's Head, and damn the expense.' He let go her hand. 'Where can I find Hilde? I must see her.'

She was bending over the bed of a white-haired old lady, adjusting the pillows with infinite care. Andrew was looking at a different side to Hilde's character. Gone was the customary reserve that distanced her from any intimacy. In its place was a tender solicitude, creating a comforting bond with someone needing care. The radiance of her smile wiped away the other image making her, in Andrew's eyes, more beautiful than ever. It faded when she caught sight of him, waiting at the entrance to the ward. She hurried over to him.

'You are a soldier now?'

'I have come to say goodbye.'

115

Her head drooped in a gesture of sadness. 'Another goodbye.'

'It's not for ever.'

'I hoped that as a doctor you might be needed here.' When she lifted her head, he saw that her eyes were full of tears.

'I have to go, Hilde, dear.' He ached to comfort her.

A silence had fallen over the ward. Women patients interpreted the little tableau that was taking place as a special moment and stilled their chatter. The sister at her central desk saw, and took no action.

'Will you write to me occasionally, Hilde, please?'

Gravely she nodded, 'Farewell, Andrew,' and walked away.

Twelve

1940

'I've just said goodbye to our houseman,' Norah removed the thermometer from Lieutenant Webster's mouth. 'He's been called up. Into the Army.'

At that moment, her own emotional temperature was on a downward spiral. All the boys were gone now and for what purpose? Nothing seemed to be happening – and

Poland was lost.

Raymond Webster, twenty-seven, late of the Coldstream Guards, forced a small smile as if even that slight expenditure of energy made grievous inroads into his carefully husbanded strength. 'RAMC. Good. The Army needs keen fellows like him.' His voice was as light as the brush of a little bird's wing. 'Lucky chap.'

His own uniform hung in the wardrobe. There were grave doubts as to whether he would ever wear it again. He was a soldier who could not fight yet he had no wound to show. The staff on the ward were kind and sympathetic but there were days when his heart and mind rebelled against the fate that had brought him here, plucked him from the good company of the mess and the physically testing field days; the fate that had made an invalid of him.

He watched closely as Nurse Moffat read the thermometer but her expression gave nothing away. It never did. Each day dragged by without the slightest sign of improvement in his condition. All the tests that, at first, he had set so much store by, came back positive. Pulmonary tuberculosis confirmed. Would the day ever come when she would look across at him and smile and say, 'It's down.' No. She drew another mountain peak on his temperature chart just as she did every evening.

There were days when the hovering black cloud of depression enveloped him, when the will to fight it was beyond his reach. The inactivity, boredom and the feelings of rejection were intolerable. His own inexorable decay was sucking him dry of enthusiasms and interests and of life itself. A sigh escaped his lips, 'Up again, I suppose.'

Norah was desperately sorry for this handsome young man. The disease had shown up after four years in the regular army. Now his soldiering was over. He lay pale and insubstantial against supporting pillows, the only patient in a small side room off the main ward. One narrow hand outside the coverlet on his bed rested on his newspaper, the crossword unfinished. A broad gold signet ring seemed altogether too great an ornament to be worn on a finger where wastage revealed so sharply the phalanges of its skeleton.

'I'm going off duty soon,' Norah checked the black-out at the window. 'Is there anything you want before I go?'

She told Cathy about him over a bedtime cup of tea. 'He's a very good patient. Never complains. I feel so sorry for him. His family are all in the south of England so he has few visitors.'

'Why isn't he in a sanatorium?'

'Waiting for a bed. He's in the side ward on his own and gets very depressed at times. Come and cheer him up, would you, Cathy? When Sister's off duty.'

There was no reply to Cathy's knock. She waited a moment before opening the door a fraction then paused, arrested by the fragile

118

beauty of the young man who lay in the bed with his face turned away from her. Thick, light brown hair lay tousled on the pillow. His smooth, pale brow, unfurrowed as a child's, cut back sharply to the hollow of his eyes. As if in sleep, a fringe of dark lashes lay upon the high cheekbone. A portrait of Rupert Brooke sprang to mind. He was so like the tragic poet of the First World War, whom she and Norah had worshipped as schoolgirls. She stood for a moment, lost in the remembering.

Here am I, sweating, sick and hot,
And there the shadowed waters fresh,
Leap up to embrace the naked flesh.

Believing him to be asleep, she prepared to withdraw but he turned his head towards her. Dark brooding eyes met hers and held them. For a moment nothing was said. Taken aback to be caught seeming to pry, Cathy flushed scarlet. 'Excuse me. I did not mean to wake you.'

'Please don't go,' he spoke softly. It was hard for Cathy to hear him because of the clatter of enamel washbasins in the ward behind her. She shut the door.

'Please come in.' His smile encouraged her.

She took a chair some distance from the bed and explained, 'I'm Lewis. This is not my ward but Nurse Moffat and I are friends and she said you were bored. I can't stay long. The sister would kill me...'

'For saving me from boredom? I would not

119

allow it.' A light moustache was the only military detail about him. It curved with his smile. He was watching her through half closed eyes, as though the lids were weighted, yet plainly, he was anxious to talk.

'Nurse Moffat often talks about what you two get up to in your off-duty,' he said. 'Greatly addicted to ballet, I believe, the pair of you.'

She nodded enthusiastically, 'We saw the Ballet Joos when it came to Eastport and the Ballet Rambert. We can only afford the gods, but for sixpence we've seen Alicia Markova and Anton Dolin dance.'

'That sounds like good budgeting.' He spoke haltingly and with effort.

'Of necessity,' Cathy grinned, 'but, actually, we see the pattern of the dance better the higher we are. Are you interested in ballet?'

'Not really. I'm a philistine about tutus and men in tight trousers.'

There were bluish shadows under his eyes and the fine skin was stretched taut over his cheekbones. He is a sick man, Cathy reminded herself. I must not overtire him.

A little silence fell. Somewhat embarrassed by the slightly amused look with which he continued to regard her from beneath those droopy lashes, she cast her eyes about the room. 'Some flowers would cheer this place up.'

'I do not get many visitors. My family live in Surrey.'

She had noticed the photograph on his

120

locker. 'Is that your mother and father?' It was a family group: himself, debonair in uniform, a young girl in a tweedy skirt and an older couple.

He nodded. 'My father was a colonel in the regiment. He has retired now.'

This retired colonel looked out on the world from a position of authority. Every line of his face declared his indestructibility. His son had inherited the vulnerable looks of his mother, rather than the burly manliness of the father. There would be no high rank for the son. His lungs were as clogged as the bottom of a duck pond.

'Your mother is very beautiful.'

He nodded, pleased.

He loves his mother, Cathy thought. 'And is that your wife?' she asked, meaning the young woman in the tweed skirt – but she did not have the look of a wife. There was a sort of untried look about her.

'Just a friend,' he looked away as if tired of the subject.

'I think I must go now.'

'Come again, please. When you have nothing better to do.'

A smile was exchanged. A promise on Cathy's part. A contented nod from him.

In the solitude of her bedroom, Cathy opened McGillvray's *Practical Nursing*. Final examinations were in six weeks' time. Resolutely, she set herself to study cardiac disease and banished from her mind the patient in Norah's ward.

'Lieutenant Webster wants to know when you are going to visit him again,' Norah reported some days later. 'He says you make him laugh.'

'Indeed I thought I was doing some serious sick visiting.' All the same, Cathy went. She became a regular visitor when the sister of the ward was off duty. Such an association between nurse and patient would have been frowned upon. She would do little errands for him – buy his special shaving soap or a copy of *John o'London's Weekly*, his favourite magazine.

She asked him to test her on McGillvray's *Practical Nursing*.

'Refer your examiners to me.' He was feeling cheerfully expansive. 'I'll give you a first-class commendation.'

'And Norah, Nurse Moffat. We do things together, you see.'

She begged a big bunch of wallflowers from her father's allotment.

'What's this, then? Am I to supply flowers to the whole hospital now?' But Cyril Lewis did not really mind. Her mother asked whether the poor chap would like some calf's foot jelly but Cathy thought not.

'Come in, Cathy,' Webster greeted her when she appeared at the door of his room. 'Give me the gossip. I learn more from you than from the morning paper.'

There was no doubt that he had livened up of late. Norah said that there was no clinical improvement but she agreed with Cathy that he was in better spirits. She brought vases and scissors for Cathy to arrange the flowers.

'My father and his gang—' Cathy began.

'His "gang"?' Webster interrupted. Cathy brought him vivid images of the life outside the four walls of his hospital room. He wanted all the details.

' "Observers" he calls them.' Cathy explained. 'They keep a look-out at the coast for enemy landings. They found the body of a German airman washed up on the beach and my dad's in trouble with my mum.'

'Because he found a dead German?'

'No, silly. She's cross because we used to keep chickens and Dad made us get rid of them because he said they attracted rats and now meat is rationed Mum says we could do with a good fat boiler or two. By the way,' Cathy looked at him severely, 'you're not supposed to call me by my Christian name.'

'I don't mind if you call me Raymond.'

Cathy looked shocked. 'I'd be drummed out, defrocked and dishonoured. "No familiarity with patients, Nurse," ' she mimicked.

'To call you Cathy is no great excess of familiarity,' he sighed. He watched her as she carried the wallflowers to a place near the window where the evening sun lit them with sudden splendour. 'Thank you, Nurse Lewis.'

'My father grew them.'

'Then please tell your father how much pleasure his flowers and his daughter bring to me.' He saw her confusion – the colour which rushed to her face – and came to her rescue.

123

'Tell me how you and Nurse Moffat will amuse yourselves tonight.'

She pulled a face. 'Knitting circle at Norah's house. Socks and balaclavas for the troops.'

'No flicks tonight? No theatre?'

'No money. Not a bean and still a week to pay day. I dream of the day when I will be an army nurse – with wealth untold.'

He saw her glance at the temperature chart above his bed and grimaced. 'Unsettled. Like the western front.'

'It will settle,' she insisted. 'You have to give the treatment time.'

As if to give the lie to her assurance, he was seized by a violent bout of coughing. Cathy leapt to help him with an arm about his shoulders and a hand on his damp forehead to support his lolling head. Like a poor rag doll, she thought, with very little stuffing. She reached for his sputum mug when the paroxysm ended and gently laid him back upon his pillows. He was exhausted.

With a light hand, she felt for his pulse and was not prepared for the sudden wave of tenderness that engulfed her at the touch of his skin, of the satin-soft skin on the underside of his wrist. It was no more than a nurse taking the pulse of a patient. There was nothing to account for this extraordinary sensation which threatened to overwhelm her. She desperately wanted to comfort him, to wrap him in her arms as one would a child. When she consulted the pendant watch pinned to her apron bib, she found difficulty in counting the heart beats coherently.

He put away his handkerchief and turned away his head so that she should not see the misery in his eyes. 'Thank you.'

She left him then. Quietly she closed the door behind her and went in search of Norah to report that Lieutenant Webster's sputum was streaked with blood.

Some days later Norah told Cathy that a bed had been found for Raymond in Longhurst Sanitorium.

'Where's that?'

'Somewhere in Surrey. He'll be near his family.'

Suddenly, Cathy felt bleak as if the sun had gone in and clouds were closing in on her. 'When is he going?'

'Tomorrow.'

'I'll come and see him before he goes.'

But when Cathy came with her specially chosen get well card, the side ward was empty, the bed neat and flat, made up ready for the next occupant. A brisk wind blew in at the open window and there was a strong smell of disinfectant. Everything was cold and aseptic, including her heart.

Norah gave her shoulder a squeeze. 'Sorry, Cathy. I couldn't let you know. An army ambulance came early for him. He said to tell you how much your visits had cheered him up.'

Cathy nodded. 'That's good.' And added as casually as she could manage, 'Actually, I shall quite miss him.'

Norah looked sharp. 'Forget him, Catypus. His X-rays are awful. Sputum positive. Blood tests teeming with tubercle. No future, my pet.'

'I know, Norah. I know.'

'Come on. Let's go into town. We both need cheering up. Have you got any money?'

'Five bob in my stocking box.'

'Let the stockings wait. I can scratch up five bob so there's enough for a Pimm's each at the King's Head. And McGillvray's *Practical Nursing* can wait. We'll stay in and swot tomorrow night.'

'I suppose,' Cathy said, 'to be quite practical, one has to admit that Raymond Webster's chances of recovery are slight.'

'Nil,' said Norah.

A visitor to Britain at that time might have found it hard to believe that this was a country at war. To be sure, the King's Head was full of uniforms: Army, Navy and Air Force, land girls and the rest of the women's services, air raid wardens. And even indomitable Poles and Czechs. But the noise and carefree laughter were of people enjoying themselves and the subject under discussion was more likely to be the darts tournament than the state of the war.

The same could not be said of the war at sea. Quentin, an officer on one of His Majesty's destroyers, was necessarily circumspect in his letters. The truth was that he, in company with most of his shipmates, was taxed to the limit. The constant danger from U-boats, the ravages of the Atlantic Ocean itself, and the responsibility resting with the Navy to ensure the safe passage of convoys from America, allowed no relaxation for the men. Quentin had seen a sister ship, along with the men who sailed in her, go down in a blaze of flames, sending tons of urgently needed food and war materials to the bottom of the sea. His own ship could be the next to get in the way of a deadly torpedo but none of these disasters found their way into his letters. His friends knew that Quentin's job was tough but none knew just how tough. In one of his letters to Norah, he spoke longingly of leave that was due to him.

'He wants to take us both out for dinner at The Eldon,' she told Cathy.

'I bet he'd rather take you on your own.'

'That's not an option.' As ever, Norah was not interested in any male attention.

Thirteen

Andrew's orders were to proceed to a casualty clearing station near Le Mans as the replacement for a medical officer on the sick list. He landed at Dieppe on a chilly morning in March and shared the front seat with the driver of a utility truck on a slow journey over indifferent roads, frequently held up by troop movements. Darkness had fallen before they reached their destination, Le Château Dois, the site of the casualty clearing station (CCS).

The night was cold. Banks of crusty, dirty snow lined the roadside but Andrew was heartened by the thought of château billets. A roaring fire in a great hearth? Maybe a generous cognac before turning in? They drove into the courtyard of a building which, by the pale light of a timid moon, showed none of the characteristics which Andrew associated with castles. No turrets or battlements. No romantic moat or drawbridge. It was just a big house. If this was a château, Britain was full of them. Shadowy shapes came and went in the darkness; orderlies carrying jerry cans, blankets, buckets. He could dimly pick out ambulances parked in a tidy row.

'The CO's office is at the top of the stairs, sir.' The driver unloaded his passenger's valise at a side entrance of the building before he took himself off in search of a meal.

Any thought that Andrew might have had concerning château accommodation was quickly dispelled by the Lieutenant Colonel RAMC who commanded the unit. The owners were still in residence. Apart from the officers' mess, the hospital office and the operating theatre – previously the château kitchen – all other departments of the unit, including the wards, were in outbuildings. The dispensary was in a stable. Nursing and medical staff were under canvas in a nearby field. Andrew came down to earth with a bump.

An orderly led him to a camouflaged en-campment across ground that had been churned into a morass of mud by army boots in slushy snow. 'This is your tent, sir. Sharing with Lieutenant Bird. Your kit is here.'

'Hello,' his tentmate greeted him. 'Ian Bird. Radiologist. Did you bring any Nescafé with you?'

By the buttery light of a hurricane lamp Andrew saw a cheerful-looking character of about his own age seated on a camp bed. With some difficulty, he was negotiating his pyjama-clad legs into thigh-length woollen theatre stockings and, at the same time, trying to avoid contact with the muddy interior of the tent No floorboards. Not even a tarpaulin.

Andrew grasped the hand extended in welcome and introduced himself. 'I've got a tin in my kit somewhere.'

'Good man,' Lieutenant Bird proceeded to thrust his head inside a rugby jersey. 'It's like gold dust out here.'

'It's like gold dust at home but my mother knows a little man...'

Andrew's gear had been unpacked for him while he was served with a hot meal in the mess. His camp bed was erected, canvas wash bowl assembled on its tripod. A jerry can of cold water was at hand for the cleanly and the brave. He rummaged in his kit for the coffee. 'Boiling the water is going to be a problem, isn't it?'

Not a flicker of life showed at the mica window of a small oil stove standing self-consciously by the tent pole. The temperature in the tent was a degree above freezing. 'I could look for two sticks...'

Lieutenant Bird gave a great guffaw. 'Thank the lord you've got a sense of humour. The last chap was totally without. All will be well. Not to worry. We have a gem of a batman. Private Gilbertson. I can't understand a word he says. Comes from Stornaway. He's gone for paraffin. We've run out. When he gets back we'll get a good old fug going and brew up. What's your line of business, Mount?'

'General surgery. Bit of specialising with

ear, nose and throat.' Reluctantly Andrew divested himself of his greatcoat and hung it on a tent hook, at the same time taking careful note of his tentmate's preparation for bed. 'I wouldn't mind a pair of those stockings. Are they general issue?'

'Get on the right side of Matron. She's got a soft spot for poor young sawbones and I'm sure the Cheltenham Ladies' Knitting Circle would be happy for you to have a pair.' He crawled into his bedroll presenting a large behind as he did so, then proceeded to tie the overlap securely so that he ended up like a sizeable sausage. 'It'll be warmer when that heathen gets back with the paraffin. Ablutions? Hessian screens over by the hedge. Girls on the left. Boys on the right.'

'Are the nurses under canvas too?'

'Have been all winter. They're jolly hardy, actually. None have gone sick.'

'And the matron, is she in the field?'

'No, no. Matron's privilege. She's sleeping in the château with the colonel. That is to say, she's in the château and so is the colonel. No impropriety inferred. A very stalwart and godly lady is our matron. Where's that BLOODY BATMAN!'

Andrew decided to keep his boots on for the moment since his friend clearly expected him to make the coffee. 'Your colleague,' he ventured, 'the one I'm replacing, what's wrong with him?'

'Pneumonia,' came the voice from the depths of Lieutenant Bird's bedroll.

'One can understand a lack of humour in his case,' murmured Andrew, as he splashed icy water into his tooth mug.

When he was introduced to the wards the following day, Andrew found that most of the men were suffering from the cold and damp conditions: pleurisy, bronchitis and a couple of pneumonias. One of these patients was the medical officer he had replaced. The only surgical case was a ruptured gastric ulcer until Sergeant Poole, driving a scout car, delivered a gunner with a fractured wrist.

There was an astonished and joyful reunion. 'We're no more than ten miles away.' Simon laughed at the ease of it. 'On the Laval road. We're still together, Jacky, Eric and me. Come over and see us.'

Andrew flicked the three stripes on Simon's sleeve. 'Congratulations, Sergeant.'

Simon beamed. 'I'm getting to like the sound of Sergeant Poole. It's a very recent promotion.'

'If I looked into your kitbag, would I find a baton?' Simon would make a good sergeant, Andrew was certain of that. He carried his rank with confidence. The life out here, despite the total lack of comfort, seemed to suit him. He glowed with health. 'What are Eric and Jacky up to?'

'Ploughing,' Simon grinned.

'Ploughing?'

'The farmer whose land we are on is breaking his heart because now that the snow is melting at last he needs to get on with preparing the ground and all his men are away with the French Army, so our CO set us to work. None of your fancy tractors here. It's pushing a ploughshare behind a bloody great Percheron horse, but it's better than the everlasting route marches.'

Having seen the casualty into the care of a nursing sister, they walked together to Simon's transport.

'Did you see the girls before you left? How are Cathy and Norah?'

'About to sit their finals. Cathy had her twenty-first birthday the night before I left. Nancy was still at the balloon barrage but I believe she's been posted to a camouflage unit in Sussex. Her Wing CO decided she could paint better than she could cook. Alec, in Scotland, expects to get his wings any day now. Evie is in America, but you probably know that already. No news of Q or Colin. Cathy and Norah mean to join the QAs as soon as they qualify. You will probably see them out here before long.

'There are military hospitals all along the coast here – Boulogne, Dieppe, Le Treport – and CCSs like yours all over the place. It'll be great to see the girls again.' There was a wistful note in Simon's voice. 'I should get some leave soon but Eric and Jacky will go before me.'

'What's going on at the front? Have you had any contact with the enemy?'

'Not even a smell of them,' Simon spoke disgustedly. 'Troops on the Saar border have a bit of a flare up from time to time. Patrols, that sort of thing. They get relieved every so often, so I might get a chance.'

Andrew produced a pocket book and pencil. 'How do I find you? I'll come over as soon as I can'

But when Andrew made the trip a few weeks later, Simon's unit had moved and Eric and Jacky had left for England on ten days' leave.

Jacky's reception was, predictably, low-key. His dad was being called upon to fill the coal box and chop the sticks while Jacky was swanning around with French tarts. For Eric it was ten days of being indulged and made a fuss of – he was given first bath before the hot water ran out and a cup of tea in bed in the morning. He went with Jacky to meet Cathy and Norah and, to his surprise, Hilde turned up especially to see him. She wanted to know his opinion of the Maginot Line, and he suddenly realised, halfway through an explanation, that she should not be asking such questions. He shut up like a clam. After that, he wondered about Hilde, now and then.

Confirmation of Eileen's commission and posting arrived while he was there, so they were able to have a last night out together. When he took her home after a dance at The Riverside Ballroom, he caught the whiff of a plot. Mr and Mrs McKay rose as one from the cut moquette, grabbed their spectacles, newspaper and *Ladies' Journal* and took themselves off to bed with coy admonitions directed at Eric, which completely sabotaged his plans. Mrs McKay, he realised, with something like alarm, was behaving like a prospective mother-in-law. Eileen was more bossy than ever now that she carried one bright pip on her shoulder. Eric was an unambitious private and did not stay any longer than necessary with Eileen that night, although he enjoyed the generous nip of whisky left out for him by Mr McKay.

On their return to France, Eric and Jacky were detained by the rail transport officer at Cherbourg. 'Your unit has moved,' they were told and were issued with a pass to take them to the town of Albert near Amiens. A glance at the map showed that this was a considerable leap forward, which raised their spirits since they would be nearer the action – what action there was.

'My dad was there in the last war,' Jacky said. 'He never tells anybody about it, but he's got a photo of it in his workshop. A heap of ruins with a church still standing. He wrote Albert 1917 on the bottom.'

On the long drive from Cherbourg, they watched from the back of a 15 cwt truck as the French countryside unfolded. Some of the fields were still waterlogged after the late thaw.

'Too wet for ploughing,' Eric was surprised to find himself thinking like a farmer. 'I'll miss that old horse,' he confessed, 'I know every contour of its backside like the map of England.'

'I'll miss more than the horse.' Jacky was back on form. 'I was getting on rather well with Veronique. You've got to admit her contours leave that old horse for dead.'

'Which one was Veronique?'

'The youngest.'

'Just as well we're leaving – before her father puts a round of lead into you.'

They rattled over cobbled streets, through small villages. 'DU-BON-NET,' Jacky spelt out the letters of the ubiquitous advertisement. 'Piss weak, that stuff. So's the beer. The cognac's all right, though. They can stick the rest.'

'I hope the NAAFI finds us. I want some cigs.'

'I want some writing paper. Got to write to Evie to tell her I saw her father and mother.'

'How's she liking America?'

'Fine. There's some Yank with a big car taking her around.'

'That's tough, Jacky.'

Jacky shrugged. 'Plenty more fish in the sea.'

Eric's thoughts wandered. 'I'm sorry we missed Andrew.' He'd always admired Andrew, envying his self-confidence, and his good looks so casually borne. 'Insignificant' is how Eric described himself. A silly little mouth like a girl's over a cleft chin. Nothing very manly. And that sickening expression he wore and seemed unable to change, an 'anxious to oblige' look. His mother had brought him up that way, not to be pushy and to heed

136

his betters. Sometimes he wondered what Eileen could possibly see in him. He failed to acknowledge something else that his shaving mirror showed – alert observation in the deep-set eyes and steadiness revealing the habit of self-control. The baby mouth he so despised was none the less resolute, and, if he stopped to think of it, he could beat any of them, Eileen included, in a mathematical contest.

Jacky, too, looked up to Andrew, a few years older and a proper doctor now. 'If his unit moves north we might meet up with him again.' He felt in his breast pocket for a packet of Woodbines. 'Cig?' His roughened hands with their splayed-out thumbs cradled the match for Eric. They were the hands of a fixer, an artisan. He could strip an engine, car or boat. He could mend things. 'Do you think he and Norah will get hitched?'

'I always thought so till Hilde came on the scene. I think Andy fancies her.'

Jacky scoffed at the idea. 'Norah's worth ten of her. What can he see in Hilde but a bad-tempered, bigoted Jew?'

'Come off it, Jack. She's a damn good looker.'

'So's Norah. Unfortunately she resists my charms. Hard to believe but there it is. What about you and Eileen. I wondered if you might get spliced on your leave?'

Eric gave a little self-conscious laugh. 'You know us. Darby and Joan.' He and Eileen had been going around together ever since he used to give her rides on the backstep of his bicycle after school. 'There's too much going on at the moment without any added complications.'

Nevertheless, he had thought about his relationship with Eileen quite a lot during his recent leave. Eileen was not bad looking and she was *so* passionate! She had surprised him with her ardour when they got into a clinch. But he wasn't sure if the passion and declarations of love would last. What could he offer her that would keep such fires burning? Eileen was clever and since going to university she had acquired an air of sophistication that he could not match. In any case, he could not afford to get married at the moment and so, since the time had not seemed right to speak of an engagement, he had not done so. Mr and Mrs McKay were no doubt disappointed in him. Most people were.

All seemed peaceful and normal in the towns and villages Jacky and Eric were passing through. People waved a cheerful greeting, 'Allo Tommy!' Few young men were to be seen. Men of an older generation and women carried out essential work on the farms. Tram drivers in the towns were grey-haired. All the young men, like their British counterparts, were drilling and marching and digging while Hitler and Russia proceeded to ingest Poland without interruption. And Hitler finalised the plans for his next move.

The truck pulled into the transit camp in

Rouen to pick up stores. 'That's it for to-night,' their driver told them. 'We'll get crack-ing 0600 hours tomorrow.'

It was bully beef and beans for supper and a mug of tea, then a bed in a Nissen hut full of Welshmen in the Pioneer Corps.

'I hope the buggers are not going to sing "David On A White Rock" all night long,' Jacky squinted, red-eyed through drifts of cigarette smoke. 'Hey, boyos! Anybody know why we're moving up? Is something on?'

Fourteen

The row was coming from Cathy's room, gales of laughter. Careless of authority, the newly qualified nurses were tipsy with suc-cess – and sherry. Hilde knocked on the door, timidly at first, then boldly.

'Come in,' yelled Cathy, and Hilde peeped in. A blast of the Inkspots singing 'Ain't Misbehavin' hit her. Through the haze of cigarette smoke, she could see nurses flopped on Cathy's bed and on the floor, caps and aprons abandoned, singing lustily, 'I'm saving my love for you-oo—' to the record on Cathy's portable gramophone.

Norah waved a bottle of Sandeman's sherry at her. 'Go and get your tooth mug, Hilde!'

139

'She can have mine,' Cathy held out her arms. 'Come! Dance with me, Hildegarde and be my love.' She had drunk more than a mug full of sherry.

Embarrassed and confused, Hilde thrust a bunch of tulips into Cathy's arms, 'For both of you. Congratulations.'

Melting with slightly drunken emotion, Cathy planted a kiss on Hilde's cheek and Hilde, seeing the tears start to Cathy's eyes, held her close in a warm and surprising embrace.

The home sister was on her way to the second floor in the nurses' home with a message for Nurses Moffat and Lewis. A visitor awaited them in the common room. She would have sent a junior pro on the errand but, aware that she was carrying a little more weight than was good for her, she resolutely climbed the stairs, two flights. Now, however, on hearing the music and the yells of laughter, she changed her mind and sought a junior to deliver the message after all.

She was remembering how she felt, years ago, when she earned the right to add S.R.N. to her name. She had added a few more letters since those long past days, but that first explosion of disbelief into joy was a sensation never to be forgotten – nor repeated. With the hint of a smile crinkling one corner of her mouth – both corners would have been excessive – she creaked her way downstairs again leaving the newly qualified nurses to their noisy celebrations. She wasn't the killjoy they all made her out to be.

The junior pro arriving at Cathy's open door had to shout to make herself heard since no one heeded her polite knock. 'Visitor in the common room for Staff Nurse Moffat and Staff Nurse Lewis. A man.'

'Ooh-ooh! Bring him up!'

'You go, Norah. You are more respectable.'

The well-dressed gentleman holding a labrador on a short lead had tugged several times at the bell pull of the nurses' home, to no effect. He pushed open the door and went inside.

A home sister passing by was brought to a sudden halt. 'Dogs,' she enunciated crisply, 'are not allowed in the nurses' home.'

The charm of the man was irresistible, however. The trilby was doffed to show a fine head of expensively barbered iron grey hair. 'Do forgive me, Matron.' His motto was always to start high. One can drop seniority but rarely make an upward correction without causing offence. 'My mission is of considerable importance. You would be doing me a great service if you would permit me to speak – for a moment only – to one of your young ladies. The matter concerns my son who is a naval officer on board one of His Majesty's destroyers. He was to have come home on leave and had made arrangements to meet his friends, Nurses Moffat and Lewis. Sadly, his leave has been postponed.' A sad shrug of the shoulders begged her compliance. 'Exigencies of the Service, Matron.'

'Home Sister,' she corrected.

'Home Sister,' he amended with a slight bow. 'By the by, my dog is house trained and, rather than tie her up outside where she will make such a hullabaloo that all your patients will be disturbed, perhaps I may be allowed to stand on this doormat with her? I promise I shall not move from this spot if either of the two nurses may be permitted a few moments with me?'

She was pursing up ready to protest when he spied the hospital benevolent box and made certain that the contribution he pushed through the slot was clearly seen to be the fine white tissue of a five pound note.

When Norah arrived, somewhat breathless and flushed, he engaged her with a nice combination of fatherly smile and roguish twinkle which plainly said, 'I was a bit of a dog myself when young and I still admire a pretty woman.' When he left, he thought Quentin should press home his advantage there. Jolly nice girl. Snap her up before she gets into the Army with all those roistering brown jobs.

The following Sunday was their morning off. Norah, lolling on Cathy's bed, idly watched her friend sort through a heap of possessions, very few of which would accompany her to the Army.

Cathy held up a pottery rabbit. 'Who shall I give this to?'

'Spitfire Fund Jumble Sale. The whole lot,' Norah said without hesitation. Her thoughts were elsewhere. 'Quentin's parents must have been so disappointed when his leave was cancelled.'

'After such a long spell on Atlantic convoys,' Cathy agreed.

'His father,' Norah blew out cigarette smoke, reflectively, 'thinks something big is brewing. That's why leave was cancelled.'

Cathy looked up, 'Like what?'

'Didn't say.'

'What's his father like. Very posh?'

'But nice. Lovely dog.' Her long, black stockinged legs found a patch of sunshine on Cathy's bed. It was late March and a watery sun could not disguise a nip in the air. 'Handsome. Like Quentin.'

'You know what?' Cathy stuffed all her old theatre programmes and lecture notes into the waste-paper basket. 'I have to keep reassuring myself, Norah. We are state registered nurses. Yippee!' She aimed a kick at the pottery rabbit.

'Stage one accomplished,' Norah nodded. 'Queen Alexandra's Imperial Military Nursing Service Reserve, here we come!'

They had qualified in medical, surgical, gynaecological and orthopaedic nursing. They could treat diseases of the eyes, nose, throat and skin. They were word-perfect in diets, sewage disposal and ventilation, skilled in the use of poultices, blisters and enemas. They had no conception whatsoever of how the remains of a young man's body might appear if he steps on a mine, how a pilot looks

143

when his nose, lips and ears have been burnt off.

'I hope we can stay together, Cat.' For a brief and unpleasant moment, Norah imagined life without Cathy. Their partnership was indivisible. Cathy led with headlong – and sometimes experimental – initiative. Norah followed with common sense. This had been the pattern since early schooldays.

'That old biddy in the red cape and bosoms promised we would,' Cathy reminded her.

'You'd better learn to be a bit more respectful. She was a Principal Matron of the QAIMNS. Regular!'

'Every inch of her,' Cathy agreed.

'What are you going to do with the gramophone and records? You can't take those into the Army.'

'I've decided to give my gramophone to Hilde.'

'Goodness!' Norah was understandably surprised, considering what pleasure they had both derived from the little wind-up portable throughout their training. 'What do you want to do that for?'

'Well, I can't take it with me into the Army,' Cathy agreed. 'My dad has a much better one at home, so he won't want it and Hilde is going to feel pretty very lonely when we go. She really hasn't made any other friends.'

'Whose fault is that? But the boys will look her up when they come home on leave. Andrew will, I know.' She paused. 'I think he is in love with Hilde.'

Cathy looked up quickly. 'Does that bother you?'

Norah shrugged. 'I've always been fond of Andrew, but only as a good friend. I wonder how Hilde feels about him.'

'Hilde,' Cathy said firmly, 'will break his heart. Hers is made of stone, except...' she recollected, 'she did give me a cuddle at our party.'

Norah stubbed out her cigarette. 'What about your heart? Simon is devoted to you, you know.'

'He's a nice bloke.'

'Is that all?'

'That's all.' Cathy went to the dressing table to brush her hair. 'Come on. We'd better go down to lunch.'

Norah reached for her shoes. 'I wonder how Raymond Webster is getting on.'

'Poor chap.'

'Do you ever think of him?' Norah asked softly.

'Practically all the time,' Cathy said quietly and then, catching sight of her own reflection in the mirror, she briskly turned away. 'What are you going to do with your cuckoo clock?'

'Hilde can have that, too.'

Cathy giggled, 'It will drive her mad. She calls it "der dumm vogel"!'

Norah picked a record from the pile. 'You're not parting with this?'

Cathy peered at the record in Norah's hand. 'Ah. Not that one. "The Faery Song". It will always remind me of the boys, of picnics, and banging about the countryside in Mr Poole's Morris, and of those interminable arguments, as we put the world to rights.'

'And seeing the boys go off to war.'

Cathy slipped the record back into its paper cover. 'When we are very old, we can sit by the fire in our cottage in Scotland.'

'Or Cornwall,' said Norah.

'And play that record on a posh new gramophone, and remember how things were in 1940 when we were twenty-one.' Cathy began to sing.

'How beautiful they are, the Lordly Ones
Who dwell in the hills, in the hollow hills.'

She paused and Norah joined in.

'They have faces like flowers,
And their breath is a wind,
That blows over summer meadows
Filled with dewy clover.
Their limbs are more white than shafts of moonshine.
They are more fleet than the March wind.
They laugh – and are glad – and are terrible.
When their lances shake and glitter
Every green reed quivers.'

'Oh, Cat,' Norah's eyes were filled with foreboding, 'I do hope all our Lordly Ones come back safely.'

Fifteen

The BEF was doing its job well enough in France, sharing with French troops the task of guarding their frontier. Belgium and Holland were neutral, consequently no armed defensive troops could be deployed there. Apart from a few patrolling incidents, all was quiet on the western front. Inevitably the enthusiasm of the troops was blunted by months of inactivity. The daily round of a soldier's life had taken on the dull predictability of a civilian job. Mr Ford's suspicion, however, that something big was brewing was very soon to be confirmed and it was the British Navy which bore the brunt of Hitler's next move.

From the day war began, British ships crossing the Atlantic were the target for German U-boats. Quentin's leave was well earned and overdue. He was desperately tired and looked forward to catching up on sleep in his own comfortable bedroom. He had even made a date to take Cathy and Norah out to dinner. The anger he felt when leave was cancelled was understandable, but unproductive. He knew as well as any serviceman that in an emergency personal circumstances were secondary to the functioning of the unit. In Quentin's case this emergency involved his ship in an attempt to intercept and prevent a landing by German troops in Norway.

In April, his ship left the port of Rosythe as part of a naval force heading for the Norwegian ports of Oslo and Narvik. The following days brought only bad news, which rapidly grew worse. The mission to pre-empt the German landings failed. German troops captured all the main ports of Norway and overran Denmark within a few hours of landing.

A new word found its way into the English dictionary – 'Blitzkrieg', lightning war. Hitler caught the allies by surprise, demonstrating that no declaration of neutrality by any country would be honoured by him if it stood in his way.

Fierce battles raged at sea. Many ships on both sides were sunk. One of these was the destroyer on which Quentin served.

The information took a little time to reach his parents. Then, despite his personal devastation, Mr Ford remembered Quentin's friends. 'Missing, believed drowned,' he wrote to Norah. 'I wanted you to know. You share our loss.'

Until this moment Norah and Cathy had avoided a face to face confrontation with the risks undertaken by their friends. Other men would be wounded or killed, but not their lighthearted companions. They were too young, too full of life to die. The shock of

Quentin's death brought them face to face with reality. More than his leave was cancelled. His life was cancelled. Within their circle of friends, there was a space once occupied by Quentin.

'Quentin,' Cathy grieved, 'the confident, the indestructible Quentin, the boy with the brilliant future.'

'The beautiful, spoilt boy,' said Norah, 'blown away like a fleck of foam.'

Thoughts wavered uncertainly over the rest of their friends. They, too, were suddenly glaringly vulnerable.

Mr and Mrs Ford had no more sons to give, no more children at all. The war, for them, might just as well be over. Lost or won. No matter.

Norah's mother was accustomed to do the church flowers with Mrs Ford. 'I'll go and see her, poor soul.'

Other parents in Eastport, with sons like Quentin, felt a shiver of apprehension, which up till now had been concealed by pride in their brave offspring. The photographs of smiling young men in uniform, gracing piano tops and mantlepieces, desks and private places where a candle burned, took on an altogether ephemeral quality as if the little boys they had raised did not belong to them any more. The nation had borrowed them and might not give them back.

More than ever were Cathy and Norah impatient for their call-up papers. 'We can help. We can at least look after the wounded.'

The War Office obliged within the next few days. Sisters Moffat and Lewis were to report to a military hospital in Scotland at the termination of their contract with the training hospital.

'When do you leave?' Chrissie passed the cake to her youngest daughter. In any crisis her instinctive reaction was to offer food.

'Beginning of June,' Cathy drained her cup of tea. The cake was as dry as dust.

Chrissie was much put out. 'It's not easy, you know. Dried elderberries for currants. Liquid paraffin instead of butter and scarcely any sugar.'

They were sitting in the pleasant room at the front of the Lewis home. Solidly built at the turn of the century, its generous sash windows looked straight into the setting sun on this evening in early May. Soon the black-out curtains must be drawn over the frilled muslin and the twilight banished, but in this last golden hour before the sun disappeared over the rooftops it enlivened the cabbage roses of the wallpaper, touched the dark mahogany of the piano with a roseate glow and alighted, pink and irreverent, on Cyril's bald tonsure.

'Well,' he said, over the top of the *Gazette*, 'there's one thing for sure. You won't be going to Norway now.'

'They wouldn't send you to France, surely?' There was a quiver in Chrissie's voice. She had thought, having no sons, that she would be in the clear, but now here was her youngest child walking into danger.

'I hope so, Mum. That is what we trained for.'

Cyril, a man who knew what was what in times of war, stamped on the soft edges of relationships. Though Cathy was just a bairn to him, he would suffer no sentimental outpourings. If she had to go, she had to go. 'You might meet up with the lads. Have you heard from Simon, by the way?' He still had hopes of a liaison there, though Cathy did not appear all that interested. Still, plenty of time for that when life was more settled.

'He's got sergeant's stripes.'

'So I heard. And isn't his father proud of him. Quite right, too.'

'Poor Mr Ford,' said Chrissie. 'He was proud of his boy as well.'

Uneasiness tugged at Cathy's conscience. 'We didn't seem to understand, when Quentin went, that he would be in such danger. On his last night it was all champagne and fun.'

'Better that way,' said her father. 'You sent him off in good spirits.'

'None of us said goodbye. Not properly. Not seriously.'

Her father broke the fraught silence. 'Not even his parents would do that. In wartime, tearful partings are counter-productive. Now then,' he took out his pocket watch and studied it, 'nearly time for the news.'

Chrissie picked up the tray and carried it to the kitchen. 'Look at that,' her father directed Cathy over the top of his glasses. 'Typical.

She always disappears just when the news is about to begin.'

Britain had got herself a new prime minister. After the disastrous defeat in Norway and Hitler's annexation of Denmark, the country demanded a new leader. Neville Chamberlain, man of peace, resigned and Winston Churchill, man of war, took his place.

'Leave the dishes, woman!' Cathy's father called out. 'Winston Churchill is going to speak to the nation.' He twiddled the knob on the Bakelite oracle and the chimes of Big Ben emerged loud and clear.

Chrissie appeared and stood silently by the door, a tea towel in her hand, to hear Mr Churchill tell the nation that Hitler had struck yet again. On that morning, 10 May, he had invaded Holland. England was finally shocked out of its complacency. Holland was just across the water.

'We could be next,' said Chrissie.

'Britain and the Commonwealth,' Churchill declared in a voice of stern authority, 'will wage war by land, sea and in the air until Hitler is beaten. On the beaches ... in the streets ... we will *never* give in!' The splendid rolling phrases inflamed his listeners with fierce national pride. The spirit that had lately languished in Britain flared up once again. Blood, toil and tears, Churchill promised. No soft options. So be it. The phony war was over. This was the real thing and this was a real leader, an orator to stiffen resolve.

Cyril Lewis punched his clenched fist

against his palm. 'Now we've got the right man on the job.' He was full of fight and fervour. He had been an admirer of Winston Churchill for years. 'Now you'll see the sparks fly!' Already he looked ten years younger. Sergeant Lewis once again.

He grabbed his stick and his cap and went to see Simon's father to see if there was a useful job in the town for two old soldiers. He was asked into the sitting-room where Ken Poole and his wife sat by a modest fire and Simon's young brother struggled with homework. Mrs Poole got up to give Cyril a cup of tea before retiring to another room, taking the boy with her. 'Dad and Mr Lewis want to chat.'

Ken Poole was pleased to see his friend, anxious to talk over the latest news. 'So, it's Holland now.'

'And he'll not stop there.'

'We've had a letter from Simon. He's on the move again.'

Lewis looked knowing. 'On the way to Belgium, I'll be bound.' Instinctively he fingered his temple for that is where the memories sometimes throbbed. 'Same old battlefields. Same old cemeteries,' he muttered. Then, feeling he may have gone a mite too far, he hurried on. 'My Cathy has just received her call-up papers. She and Moffat's lass are to report at a military hospital in Scotland when they're finished here, but my guess is they'll be over the water before long.'

Ken Poole's face was set and grave. 'It's a

153

bad show, Lewis. We should never have let Hitler rearm.'

'He hoodwinked the lot of us.'

'Let's hope it wasn't too late when we did eventually start to rearm.'

'Now, I was thinking, there must be some way we old soldiers can help? Count on me, Mr Poole, if you've got any ideas.'

'We may be too old for the forces, Cyril, but we can defend our homes. You can depend on that.'

Holland fell in four days.

Lieutenant Webster, late of the Coldstream Guards, listened to the news on his earphones and wondered if his regiment was involved in this new development in Europe. His friends, who once figured so large in his life – large and noisy – were diminished to little more than distant acquaintances. They were gone quietly about their duty without him. He had no place now in their world. His place was a bed in a sanitorium.

He missed not a single news broadcast and felt more dejected after each one. Hitler was sweeping the board. German armoured divisions were now attacking Belgium. This guardsman should be out there now with the BEF, instead, he lay there, useless, a maundering failure. It had taken three years to make an efficient soldier of him. All had been wasted. Expensive, hard training, wasted. His remoteness from all that was manly made him curl evermore within himself.

154

A nurse came rushing in, all agog, 'Did you hear that?' she dumped a vase of flowers on his locker. 'Hitler's invaded Belgium now! Holland has caved in! Have you had your bowels moved?'

He cringed at her insensitivity. How different she was from the two nurses he had left behind in the north. This was not at all their style. Moffat so serene. Lewis so ... electric, might be a way to describe her. They would have discussed Churchill's speech together, talked things over. And another thing, they would not have spilt water from the flowers all over his writing pad nor left his sputum pot out of reach.

During his stay in the Eastport Hospital his days had been enlivened by the company of those two nurses. He could find nothing in his present surroundings to lift him from despondency, although the sanitorium was cheerfully modern. The grounds, manicured lawns and tidy rose beds, were immaculate. From his verandah he had an unspoilt view of the Surrey countryside, but these things gave him no joy. His parents were close enough to visit him but to look upon their anxious faces only reminded him of his own mortality. Each day was for him nothing more than a period of stagnant hours to be endured, each night a treadmill of black thoughts and fruitless regrets.

At this time every evening, when rooks circled the primrose sky in a noisy routine manoeuvre, depression drove out any faint wisps of hope. He hated the rooks. The message they wrote with their raggy black wings as they made for the black-green wood told him that another interminable night stretched ahead of him.

He pulled the blankets close to his chin. It was growing cold out here. He was the last patient to remain on the balcony and would be wheeled inside at any moment. But fresh air was good for him, they said. Fresh air! Where had he got this damned infection from if it was not from too much fresh air? That and a chap coughing at his side, night after night, in a bivvy where there was plenty of fresh air. Plenty of damp, chill, fresh air.

He closed his eyes under hot, gritty eyelids, making an effort to recall happy incidents that might banish self-pity and bring him rest. And, as always, it was Nurse Lewis who came to mind: Cathy bouncing in through the doors of the side ward with a bunch of bluebells or a tin of her mother's biscuits, once a priceless banana; Cathy making him laugh with her improbable stories, exaggerated, he suspected, for his entertainment.

Understanding, sympathetic Cathy. Funny Cathy. Out of bounds Cathy.

Sixteen

Events in Europe were moving so fast that yesterday's news sheet issued to the troops was out of date almost before it reached the company offices.

Belgium, her neutrality abused, now welcomed British and French troops to her aid, as she faced the might of the German army. The allied front moved into Belgium.

The sergeants' mess at Albert was in a building that had not seen a lick of paint since the previous war when it had served roughly the same purpose. A large map of France and the low countries hung on one wall and Sergeant Poole was not the only member of the mess to feel the need to study it in some detail.

Staff Sergeant Cowan was all chest and shoulder. No fat anywhere on his big frame. He topped Simon by a good five inches, though Simon was not far short of six foot. A lower lip permanently thrust forward reinforced the bulldog image. 'The Maginot line,' he spoke with authority, 'is all right as far as it goes but it doesn't bloody well go far enough.' With his forefinger, he stubbed the map where the French fortifications ended, in the upper reaches of the River Meuse where, it was believed, the mountainous terrain would be impassable for motor transport. 'Natural defences, they say. Well, we'll see. And what about the rest of the line?' He ran his finger north-west from the town of Sedan, through Dinant, Namur and Louvain to Antwerp. 'We've been building pillboxes and anti-tank ditches all winter long in the British sector, but there's nowt much anywhere else.'

'Plenty of troops,' Simon reminded him.

'French.'

'First-class soldiers, Staff. Isn't that right?'

Simon's instructions from his commanding officer the following day came as no surprise. 'We're moving up, Sergeant, into Belgium to back up the 12th Royal Lancers. Get your men ready to move at 0600 hours tomorrow.'

Simon saluted.

'In good spirits, are they?'

'They will be when they hear this, sir. They're itching to have a crack at Jerry.'

'There will be some hard fighting, Poole. Make no mistake about the strength and efficiency of the enemy, but our troops are fit and well trained. We will have the Belgian army on our left and the first French army on our right. An excellent fighting command and we will give a good account of ourselves. Go to it. No time to lose.'

'Send important letters home tonight,' Simon advised his platoon. 'There may not be a lot of spare time once we are in Belgium.'

A current of excitement ran through the company and also some unacknowledged trepidation, but smutty wit and crude buffoonery served to neutralise apprehension. Private Eric Dotchin, looking at his sergeant, cool and assured, could scarcely believe that this was the boy he had once gone to school with, the one time insurance clerk. He had grown so in authority that Simon the Civilian was by now totally eclipsed by Simon the Soldier.

Jacky dug him in the ribs. 'The real thing this time, old lad.' And went off to pack his kit singing what Hilde called that 'dumm gesang'.

'We're going to hang out the washing
On the Siegfried line...'

Simon took his own advice and wrote a short note to his parents and one to Cathy, warning that there might be a gap in his letters for a while. He carried two photographs about him always: one of his parents with his young brother, smiling for the camera; the other of Cathy, taken unawares, standing up in Quentin's car with the hood down, her face held smiling into the wind. She had not asked for a photograph of him but that, he told himself, was Cathy all over.

Andrew was also on the move. The CCS at

Le Mans put its affairs in order, evacuated its patients to a base hospital on the coast, packed its equipment and took to the road. Its destination was Béthune, a little town south-west of Lille, some thirty miles from the Belgian border. Here the unit established itself in a sports pavilion. Two large tents to serve as wards and several smaller tents for the unit's sleeping quarters were erected on the football field. The refreshment room, equipped as it was with running water, was hosed down and adapted for use as an operating theatre. All these preparations were carried out without any sense that a chaos of unimaginable proportion was about to envelop the unit.

The first indication of trouble came with the appearance of long lines of refugees fleeing their homes in Belgium. From a trickle, the exodus turned to a flood: old men and women – carrying children and babies – all their worldly goods piled into carts, vans, taxis, babies' prams, even wheelbarrows. Frail invalids in wheelchairs were pushed by equally frail relatives, all of them bewildered, hardly knowing where they were going except to get away from the pursuing Germans. They clogged the roads and seriously hindered the movement of troops to the front. When the dive-bombing Stukas came on the scene there was no shelter but the ditch for these desperate people. Kid's play for the machine-gunners.

The newly established CCS was thrust into

160

action, dealing with civilian casualties. That was something Andrew had never envisaged. He was witnessing at first hand the appalling obscenity of war when an old woman with a bullet wound in her leg stumbled into the reception tent of the CCS. Her hand-knitted stockings were torn. One foot slithered inside a shoe filled with blood but it was not on her own account that she sought help. In her arms, she carried an unconscious child whose paper pale brow was mapped by coagulating trickles of dark red blood.

Andrew took the child from her. His heart was wrung by the look of despair in the old woman's eyes. He had been prepared for wounded soldiers, not for little children and grandmothers.

With touching politeness, the old woman explained that she had left her daughter, the child's mother, in the ditch where the three had been sheltering when the Stuka dived. 'Ma fille est morte.' She did not cry and, though she was plainly exhausted by the ordeals of the last few days and the shock of the Stuka attack, her sense of responsibility for her granddaughter overrode any concern for herself.

After this first influx, military casualties were not long in coming. They arrived in a sudden rush of ambulances, bumping along the rutted roads leading out of Belgium. Civilian casualties at the CCS were transferred to the municipal hospital in Lille in order to make room for them. The old

161

woman was loath to go. The English doctor was kind.

As the days passed, the picture became progressively more confused. Ambulances were arriving from a variety of directions. A nugget of concern was forming in Andrew's brain. Where were Simon, Jacky and Eric in all this? He asked several of the wounded about the whereabouts of the Tyne Borderers, but all he could glean was that they had been seen in Belgium.

He was crossing the football field with the radiologist, Lieutenant Bird, one morning when the sound of gunfire coming from a new locality stopped them in their tracks. 'Where the hell is the fighting?'

The answer was provided in a report shortly to be confirmed of bitter fighting to the east and south of Béthune, as well as on the Belgian front. 'How did the Germans get behind us?' was the question on everyone's lips. Weary soldiers told alarming stories of allied positions being attacked from the rear. 'Bloody Huns are everywhere.' The sudden increase in the number of casualties arriving at the CCS bore this out.

The unit was now working at peak strength. Stretchers occupied every set of trestles in the reception area and every yard of floor space. Two nursing sisters went among the wounded, cutting away stained uniforms, applying dressings, giving injections and preparing casualties for operation. The sweet, nauseating stench of blood and sweat was all around.

162

There were two operating tables in use, two teams working continuously, breaking off only when the makeshift theatre needed to be cleaned. The senior surgeon led one team, Andrew the other. They dealt with every conceivable injury, gunshot wounds of stomach, penetrating chest wounds, amputations, fractures, tank burns.

Little in his previous surgical experience prepared Andrew for this. Compared with the almost churchlike calm of civilian operating theatres, this seemed like chaos. Nevertheless, casualties were anaesthetised and operated upon, and sent to the wards for post-operative care at a speed he would not have thought possible in such circumstances.

The noise of the guns drew ever nearer as the rows of men waiting on stretchers increased. Andrew kept his head down, concentrating on the injured man on the table before him. He held out his gloved hand to the sister at the instrument table. 'Retractor.' Like the rest of the team, the sister was now wearing a tin hat all the time. Their eyes met over their masks. Was she thinking the same as he? If the CCS had to make a run for it, as well they might, what chance of surviving had this nineteen-year-old youth with the stitched-up abdomen? A few hours earlier, while eating a breakfast of porridge and tinned bacon, he had possessed a perfectly whole body.

From time to time, the senior surgeon cast a quick glance at Andrew's table. 'OK,

Mount?'

'OK, sir.'

An extra loud explosion sent down flakes of plaster from the ceiling.

'Christ! What's going on?' Ian Bird was setting up blood transfusions in what had once been the changing room for 'le football' and was now the resuscitation department. He was a radiologist but in this time of crisis everyone assisted in whichever way he or she could.

'I'll tell you what is going on, Bird.' The CO was there, assisting, directing. 'The Powers that Be said that no one could drive a tank through the Ardennes. Hitler has done exactly that. He is at our backs. We're packing up tonight. Move off 0500 hours tomorrow. If we stick around here, we'll be caught with our trousers down.'

'So much for the Maginot Line,' grunted Bird.

'The Germans,' said the CO, 'have simply driven round the end of it.'

One of the casualties raised his head and looked about him at the room full of wounded, helpless men. 'What happens to us, sir?'

The CO's voice carried across the department. 'Don't worry, men. We'll get you on to an ambulance train tomorrow. From there you will be taken by ship to England.' The confidence he expressed was far from what he truly felt but it served to put fresh heart into men who could no longer defend themselves,

164

who were confused and disorientated by the unexpected trap they had fallen into. It was enough for them that they were going back to Blighty in the morning.

At first light, the unit was packed and ready to move off. Andrew was ordered to accompany the convoy of ambulances to Lille station and see the wounded safely transferred to the hospital train waiting there. 'Then head south.' The CO handed him a map reference. 'We're setting up shop in a factory on the outskirts of Amiens. Get on your way, Mount. Lille station is getting some stick. The train won't leave without you but it can't hang about. Two hospital ships are embarking wounded at Dieppe and the train can't afford to miss the boat.'

Lieutenant Bird came to see Andrew off. 'Good luck, Andy,' he shook his hand. 'See you in Amiens.'

But Andrew never reached Amiens. The Germans got there first.

Lille railway station was already under heavy bombardment when Andrew's driver pulled up close to the siding where the train, well marked with huge red crosses, awaited them. The train driver already had a head of steam up, prepared to move as soon as the transfer of wounded was completed. Orderlies ran across the lines carrying stretchers. When all were embarked, Andrew turned to his driver. 'Next stop Amiens, Charlie. Make it snappy.'

It was soon obvious to both Andrew and his

driver that there was no possibility of moving with any speed. The roads were congested with refugees all heading south for Dieppe, hoping for a boat to England. Many were on foot, some in trucks, taxis and on bicycles. The road was repeatedly blocked by some vehicle which had run out of petrol or had stuck fast in a shell hole. When this happened the following vehicles took a detour across the fields, which were rapidly turning into a quagmire.

By the late afternoon Andrew and his driver were still some distance from Amiens when the road ahead was barred by a British military policeman.

'Sorry, sir. Road closed. Turn about, please.'

Andrew stuck his head out of the window. 'What's going on, Corporal? I have to get to Amiens to join my CCS.'

'All roads south are cut off, sir. The enemy has reached Abbeville on the coast.' He pointed to flickering flashes in the end-of-day sky. 'That's Amiens they're bombing now. And likely to take it soon.'

Andrew's mind was on the ambulance train filled with wounded men. 'They left Lille early this morning,' he told the MP, 'making for Dieppe to board a ship. Have you any information on it?'

The MP shook his head. 'All I know is, two hospital ships have been sunk in Dieppe harbour. Your train might have been diverted to Boulogne. Hospital carriers are loading there. Better get on your way,' when Andrew seemed undecided, 'with respects, Jerry's not far away.'

The news that the Germans had reached the coast was devastating. It was exactly ten days since Hitler launched his attack on the low countries. By breaking through at Sedan he had been able to throw an armoured phalanx across the north of France behind the allies' frontline, reaching the sea at Abbeville and trapping within its boundaries almost the whole of the 1st BEF, as well as many French regiments. Under his breath Andrew said a prayer for Simon and the others, wherever they were...

Night was falling. Gun flashes lit up the sky. Andrew turned to his driver. 'Make for Boulogne, Charlie, though we have about as much chance of finding the unit as a bat in hell.'

Fleeing refugees, like mindless sheep, turned about and made for Boulogne. There was still a chance to escape by sea before that port, too, was lost. A hostile moon illuminated targets – long lines of slow-moving vehicles, terrified cowering civilians – for the Stukas. Trucks burned, crashed into each other and were wrecked in unseen craters. Charlie Dunsford gritted his teeth.

His peacetime occupation was delivering groceries to remote farmhouses in Yorkshire and on this nightmare drive he wished with all his heart that he was back in Skipton driving his little van. His neck and shoulders were locked alert as he crouched over the steering-wheel of the cumbersome army ambulance, ready to take evasive action if one of those dive-bombing bastards came at him. His unblinking eyes were red-rimmed with the dust of explosions, as he peered ahead into the trail of humanity. The wailing of women and children behind him in the body of the ambulance played havoc with his concentration. The doc had insisted on picking them up.

He had never imagined a situation so truly horrible as this when he had volunteered as a driver. Better than the poor bloody infantry, he had thought. Now he wasn't so sure and he whined quietly to himself, 'I'm not cut out for heroics. I'm only a grocer's delivery man.'

'You OK, Charlie?'

The driver glanced sideways at Andrew. One look at that calm face, cool as a cucumber, restored his courage. Steady as you go, he told himself 'OK, sir.' I'll get this lot to Boulogne if it's the last thing I do, and once or twice during that nightmare drive it seemed as though it would, in fact, be the last thing he would do.

Seventeen

The time was almost nine p.m. Ken Poole and Cyril Lewis were at the bar of the King's Head. 'Things are just about as bad as they can be, Lewis.'

Cyril Lewis looked at the clock on the wall. 'I'm getting to dread the nine o'clock news.'

There had been disastrous news every night this week. Almost the entire Expeditionary Force was caught in a trap in northern France and the enemy seemed to be tightening the screws with every hour that passed. At the first stroke of Big Ben, all conversation ceased. The barman stayed his hand on the beer pull. The landlord froze at the open drawer of the till.

Tonight's message stunned the entire company and drove home with ever-increasing finality the hopeless position of the BEF. The King of the Belgians, after his army had fought most valiantly against terrible odds, was seeking an armistice with the Germans.

A sudden intake of breath by everyone present followed this announcement. Almost everyone in the pub had a member of his family or a close friend involved in what now looked like a major catastrophe.

'The Belgian Army has laid down its arms.' Even the newsreader's voice sounded forlorn and hopeless.

Cyril Lewis's apple-cheeked face was owlish in its bewilderment. 'Our boys have been betrayed!'

'I reckon the Belgians fought until they had nothing left to fight with.' Ken Poole pushed away his empty tankard in a gesture of despair. 'Belgium was neutral and unprepared.' He looked suddenly old and tired. 'They'll leave a gap in the line.'

'What gap?' demanded the landlord. 'The Jerries are pouring in from all sides. They don't leave many gaps. Our chaps are in the bag for sure.'

Ken Poole bridled. 'That's no way to talk, Sam. The BEF isn't done yet.'

'Listen!' There was a further announcement.

'The Royal Navy is preparing to evacuate our troops from northern France. Boulogne is lost. Calais is now under threat. That leaves only Dunkirk as a possible exit port.'

'Take off a whole army!' The suggestion was beyond belief.

'Under the nose of the *Luftwaffe* and Hitler's troops? They'll never do it.'

'They've got to do it,' said Cathy's dad, 'or we're done for. Somehow our men have got to get to the sea.'

'And quick—'

'Or we'll never see wor lads again.'

The dire situation revealed itself to families throughout Britain. Mr and Mrs Dotchin were in their sitting-room, she knitting socks, he, with pipe clenched between his teeth, glowering at the wireless set as if that mischievous box were responsible for the bad news. Andrew's father and mother, playing rummy with their daughters, put down their cards and exchanged a look of barely concealed alarm. One of the girls said, 'Will Andy be coming home now, Daddy?'

Jacky's mother, Mrs Millie Whitmore, put on her hat and coat and went off to see Mrs Lewis. 'She might have heard something,' she told her husband, who needed a long spell of concentrated thinking before any action at all was undertaken. Evie Dobson's mother was there already, sitting with a cup of tea in her hand, straight up as if she didn't want to dirty her pale blue costume on Chrissie Lewis's kitchen chairs.

'Sit you down now,' Chrissie took pity on Millie, tousled and flushed. In a state. 'Kitchen company,' she said kindly, 'but there's tea in the pot.'

'Any news of your boy, dear?' Sadie Dobson, too, felt sorry for the poor thing. What a hat!

'Not a word.' Millie hoped she was not going to break down, not in front of Sadie Dobson with her fancy manners and her little finger sticking out. If the wind changed it might stay like that. Serve her right. 'Two weeks since we heard from Jacky and the wireless says our men are on the run.' Her trembling lip could no longer be concealed. 'I wondered if your Cyril—' haltingly to Chrissie, 'had any news? Or Mr Poole?'

Chrissie shook her head. 'We're all waiting for news. But we've got to keep our spirits up. That's what the boys would want.' Suddenly she, too, was trembling and on the verge of tears.

'I'm glad my Evie is out of it all,' Sadie chirruped. 'She's having a great time. The Americans make such a fuss of her, being English. All the boys want to "date" her.'

Her tin words clattered into the small, quiet space that would have been put to better use by a gesture of sympathy. The tears which Chrissie and Millie might have shed were instantly replaced by anger. Millie's face purpled. 'My Jacky's not "dating" many girls right now.'

The staff of the New England school were being excessively kind to Evie. Americans generally were shocked to hear of the collapse of the allies in northern France and were eager to help in any way short of actual military involvement. Hundreds of Jews fleeing from Germany had found sanctuary in the States and there were not many citizens who, like Ken Rauchenfeld, admired the Führer.

Complete strangers approached Evie knowing that she was from England. What could they send? What did ordinary people in Britain lack? Parcels began to find their way

172

across the Atlantic: knitted singlets, tins of pears and sock-eye salmon, turkey slices in cranberry sauce, maple syrup, raisins and packets of waffles.

The art master, one of the three male teachers at the school, joined Evie at the morning break, bringing his coffee to her table. She was on her own today, no longer the gay little English girl bubbling over with high spirits but withdrawn and miserable.

'May I?' he asked, pulling up a chair.

She could only nod, not trusting herself to speak.

'I'm sorry to hear the news from Europe. It's tough on you to be so far away from your own folk when they're in trouble.'

Only a few years older than Evie, he was a quietly spoken young man who usually chose to sit alone during the morning break. She had often seen him with a book propped up against the ketchup bottle, a significant hint that he did not wish to be disturbed. Today the book stayed in his jacket pocket.

Evie stirred her coffee vigorously. 'I don't know what to believe,' she faltered. 'Each newspaper tells a different story, all of them dreadful.' Her eyes filled up. 'It seems our soldiers are trapped in France and will either be killed or taken prisoner. A lot of my friends are there, boys I grew up with.'

He sought to reassure her. 'They will fight their way out of this, you'll see. They'll send Hitler back the way he came.' This was just to cheer the poor girl up for he could not

173

honestly believe his own words.

She hunted for a handkerchief in the pocket of her skirt. 'You are very kind. I don't even know your name.'

'Hugh Greenway. Senior art department.'

'Everyone here is so kind.' A hefty nose blow strengthened her voice. 'I wouldn't worry so much if I knew what was going on at home. I haven't had a letter from my mum and dad for ages.'

Ken Rauchenfeld expressed his feelings differently. He was walking Evie home after a night at the cinema where scenes of destruction and chaos in northern France silenced the rustling audience. Evie had watched in horror as women and children crouched in ditches, seeking protection from dive-bombing enemy planes. She had peered at the tired faces of British troops trudging along muddy lanes between burning tanks and wrecked gun carriages. Was Jacky amongst them? And Eric, Simon, Andrew? Already one of the old gang was lost. Norah had written to tell her about Quentin. And what of Alec and Colin? She was starved of news.

'You sure are lucky to be over here, babe,' Ken took her arm in his customary proprietary manner, 'away from all that.'

'I'd rather be with my mum and dad,' she said miserably.

'Put them out of your mind, kid. You chose to come here. That was real lucky for you. England should never have gotten herself into this quarrel.'

Evie looked up at him, frowning. She found his complacency intensely irritating. 'We couldn't stand by,' she protested. 'We were pledged to help Poland when she was attacked. Britain and France were *pledged*.'

'Well, honey, you didn't, did you?'

'Didn't what?'

'Help Poland.'

She hated him for that the more so because what he said was true. 'Poland,' she said lamely, 'was inaccessible.' She wished she could find something clever to say, to cut him down. Nothing sprang to mind. 'But we are determined to fight Hitler,' she said fiercely, 'and everything he stands for, no matter how long it takes.'

He smiled and patted her shoulder, which made her more cross than ever. She nearly mentioned Jacky, fighting in France, but thought better of it. She heard her mother's voice – 'Don't burn your boats, dear' – and controlled her anger.

'That's where your country is making a great mistake,' he went on. 'It is backing the wrong horse. Britain should have backed Hitler from the beginning.'

'What!' Evie almost screamed.

'Hitler's no fool,' he seemed oblivious to the effect he was having on Evie. 'Given the chance, he would have made reasonable terms. I'm afraid, Evie honey...' He darted a quick smile at her and the thought struck him that she wasn't half so pretty when she frowned. Downright bad-tempered. 'You British

175

are on the wrong side. You don't recognise a genius when you see one.'

'Genius!'

'Yeah, genius. Hitler is the leader Germany has been waiting for to pull them out of the gutter.'

'He's evil.' She could not keep her voice down and people on the sidewalk turned to stare.

He frowned in annoyance at the scene she was making. 'You've been taken in, kid, by British propaganda.'

'What about the Jews? And the terrible things he has done to them. That's not propaganda. That's truth. I know. I have a Jewish girlfriend back home,' suddenly she found herself championing Hilde whom she had never liked anyhow, 'and the Nazis burned down her home, stole everything in it and left her family penniless. They escaped to England in the nick of time.'

'Think again, little girl, and please don't shout at me. How d'you think the Jews came by their gold and silver and precious works of art in the first place? They took them from good, hard-working Germans. The Jews are parasites in any country.'

'This girl's father is a medical specialist!' Evie said hotly. 'Some of the most important people in Berlin went to him for medical treatment.'

'Exactly!' Triumphantly Ken guided her up the steps to the school entrance. 'My point exactly. That position should have gone to a

German doctor, an Aryan.'

'Perhaps he was better at his job than they were.' Now that she had started, she would have her say. Damn Ken Rauchenfeld and his big car. And his money.

He was about to make a rejoinder, then changed his mind. 'Quite the little stirrer.' He turned his most winning smile upon her. 'Forget it, honey. You are safe here in America.'

Everything he said tonight seemed to nettle her. That condescending air, for one thing, and she had never liked men with pale eyelashes. She was beginning to wonder what she ever saw in him that was attractive. She groped in her pocket for her door key. 'I didn't come here to be safe. In fact I wish I were back home.' She stomped up the steps. 'Thanks for taking me to the pictures.'

'Movies,' he corrected automatically. 'Hey! Wait a minute I could come in for coffee if your roommate isn't in.'

But she had gone, through the doors and through the scented cedarwood corridors of Miss Baxter's College for Young Ladies without a backward glance. 'When I think of my poor Jacky with his daft jokes and silly grin,' she told the mirror, dabbing at her eyes, 'mebbes wounded, mebbes killed, I could murder that Big Mouth.' She had a good howl before her roommate came in and felt better.

Eighteen

Simon's company had its baptism of fire up front near Menin on the border between Belgium and France. No sooner had they moved up from Albert when a heavy armoured attack by the Germans forced them to fall back and regroup. Casualties were heavy. It was first blood for most of the company – and last for some.

There was no certainty that they would hold this new position. Pressure from the German frontline was unremitting. Another move 'to consolidate' was beginning to look extremely likely to the hard-pressed men of Simon's unit. Sleep was in short snatches. Ablutions were a quick sluice with a bucket of water, but the morale was high until the rumour spread that the enemy they faced was now also at their backs. Confirmation was not slow in coming. German armour had broken through French defences and was now carrying out a sickle movement behind the advanced British and French forces. 'Sichel-schnitt' – that was another German word which found its way into a British soldier's vocabulary.

Staff Sergeant Cowan, when he heard this report, seemed to blow up huge like a killer spider. With his great boxer's shoulders and murdering hands, he looked capable of taking on the whole German race and grinding it to dust. 'How did the buggers get behind us? That's what I want to know.'

The men were taking advantage of a lull in the firing to brew up. 'If he reaches the coast in our rear,' said Simon, 'we're in the bag. That right, Staff?'

'Right. And the rest of the BEF with us.'

At that moment a shell landed uncomfortably close. Dirt and gravel rained down on them. Staff Sergeant Cowan downed his tea and got up from his perch on a provisions box. 'Relieve the platoon that collected that one, Poole. Call the stretcher-bearers and send an answer straight back to Jerry with our compliments. What we are,' he told his NCOs, 'is a perimeter force which means, my lads, holding back the Jerries long enough to let the rest of our troops get back to England.'

The BEF was getting out. That was hard to take and every man there was thinking, what about us? But none so craven as to voice his fear.

'We can't hold this position now that the Belgians are out of the ring,' Cowan continued. 'There's a bloody big hole in the line where they used to be.' He shoved his tin hat forward to get a good scratch at his sweating head. 'We withdraw slowly. OK? Tighten the line as we go and blow up every bridge we

179

cross. The navy is standing offshore at Dunkirk. Evacuation has already begun.' He spoke in what Simon recognised as his cheer-up voice. 'With a bit of luck we'll all get away.'

Privately, Simon thought their chances were wretchedly small. They fell back and crossed another bridge, another river. Simon's platoon dug itself into whatever cover was available. From this vantage point they watched the sappers lay explosives beneath the bridge and scurry away, bent like a confabulation of beetles.

And then time seemed to slide out of the hourglass, to hover unmeasured over a drama in the making on the bridge. A young woman was in the act of crossing it from the far side. She carried a baby in her arms and held by the hand a small child running alongside. Men gasped and held their breath but not the Staff Sergeant. Without a moment's hesitation he leapt on to that primed, doomed bridge. With a speed incredible in a man of his size, he gathered up the woman, children and all and ran with them across the remaining few yards. It was almost a miraculous save. It was certainly a deed of great bravery, but by a margin of seconds the timing was against him.

Stunned after the explosion, Simon could only stare at the unidentifiable mess slipping into the river amongst the broken spars and dust of shattered masonry. The Staff Sergeant, the young woman and her children, with scarce a cry of protest, were blown to

180

kingdom come.

When his mind cleared, Simon wanted to yell out loud, to protest against this terrible end, this awful, rotten waste of a first-class soldier and the slaughter of an innocent woman and her babies. He wanted to vomit, shit himself. His gorge rose up. His insides turned to water. He wanted to weep.

He caught sight of Eric, with his face buried in his hands, sobbing hysterically. The sight put steel back into Simon. He grabbed the boy who had shared his inkwell at school. 'Come on, kidder. Grieve later. Right now it's the Jerries or us. Give the bastards all you've got. Make them pay! Give them bloody hell! Do it for Staff Sergeant Cowan.'

A small delay in the enemy's advance was achieved by the blowing of the bridge. The respite was temporary and the British line fell back once more and regrouped. With each re-grouping came a tightening of the perimeter cordon of defending troops.

Simon's commanding officer moved up alongside him, 'Right, Poole,' his voice was grim. 'You are acting Staff Sergeant from now on.'

Simon did not see the detail of destruction he caused with his Bren gun nor the faces of men he killed and wounded. He knew nothing of their homes or their families. They were the enemy. Them or us, that was the only equation. No time to mourn a friend. Ungovernable savagery gripped him. A head-ache, or something like it, hammered in his head. His once eager, boyish face had grown hard with resolution, dirty and haggard through lack of sleep, intent only on delaying the enemy by every means possible. That was Staff Sergeant Cowan's last command.

Day merged seamless into night. Food came or it didn't. Inexorably the perimeter was shrinking. The defending force was also shrinking. Amid the confusion and the shellfire Simon lost sight of Eric and Jacky. Fighting alongside him now were the non-belligerent elements of the BEF: army cooks and clerks, signals and service corps, a padre even. Dummies filled with sandbags filled gaps. With a tin hat balanced on top of the sandbag and a stick laid on the shoulder, they were sufficiently lifelike to fool the enemy into thinking that the defending force was greater than it actually was. Even this small delay allowed more men to escape to England to fight another day. The retreat went on.

At the back of Simon's mind, as he marked the telltale flashes of enemy guns and pounded their positions, was the knowledge that his charmed escape from shells and bullets could not last – and it didn't. Suddenly he felt a violent blow to his shoulder, a sudden taste of salt in his mouth, blackness all around. His legs gave way and he sank to the ground. He was no longer in charge, neither of himself nor anyone else.

The Navy was doing a great job under constant bombardment. Back and forth from

Dunkirk to Dover and Newhaven went the destroyers, sloops, corvettes, packet boats and minesweepers, loaded to the limit with exhausted troops. Enemy bombers harassed the operation continuously. Ships were sunk, lives were lost, though casualties would have been greater had it not been for the calm sea. The elements at least were on the side of the retreating army.

The men were bewildered, worn out. Personal bravery and stamina had not been found wanting yet here they were, a well-trained, disciplined army on the run. Amidst the relief of returning home was a feeling of shame and a need to know how this had happened.

The nightmare began to recede when they stepped ashore at Dover. Children bearing bunches of flowers were there to greet them and kindly women with urns of tea, English voices sturdy English policemen. Another world. One where sanity prevailed, at least for the present.

There were those whose wounds had not been dressed for days, who had walked with the help of a friend. Blinded men stumbled into darkness with a hand on the shoulder of the man in front. There was the occasional stalwart carrying a mate on his back. Many had been fighting for days without respite. Without sleep, often without food after British supplies had been captured. Once in England, they fell asleep where they stood, on the roadside or under a tree. It was enough for the moment to know that it was an English road, an English tree.

Throughout the length and breadth of Britain, hospitals had been alerted to this huge influx of wounded men. Operating theatres were ready. Nurses were there to ease stinking feet out of soggy boots – feet which had marched for days – and help them into the indescribable comfort of a hot bath. Some, after rest and food, were able to move on to their homes with a leave pass and a travel warrant. At the railway stations, they would find women, as agitated as a crowd of starlings, seeking a particular face, a husband, son, brother, and if they found the one they sought they would be shocked by his sudden ageing. After Dunkirk young men grew up. Older men grew down, bludgeoned by the experience.

As soon as Chrissie Lewis heard the news via the milkman, who called at the Dotchin household before her own, she put on her hat and coat and caught the bus to the hospital. Straight up to Cathy's ward she went. Cathy and Norah were staff nurses now awaiting mobilisation orders and Chrissie no longer concerned herself with the rules for visitors. She surprised Cathy in the linen room. 'Good news, Cathy pet! Eric and Jacky are home. Both all right.'

'What about Simon? And Andrew?'

She did not know anything about them. 'But they are coming over in boatloads, so we will probably get news of them soon.'

184

There was joy and relief in the Dotchin household. Eric was home, safe and ... Doris Dotchin paused before she let herself think 'sound'. He was not himself. That was clear but, as his dad said, the poor lad was dead beat. She went to put the kettle on and left the men to themselves for a spell.

'Thank you, God. Thank you, thank you,' she addressed the sea-blown clouds scudding past her kitchen window. Somewhere up there was a kindly old man with a white beard who looked after people who said their prayers. 'Thank you for bringing our son back to us.' Weeping quietly into her hankie, she could not see how much tea she put in the pot and, when it was poured, it was so strong you could stand up a spoon in it.

They did not rush him with questions. He went up to his bedroom with a mug of tea and left his dirty boots on the dining-room carpet. 'Give him time,' her husband said. He reached for his hat and his stick. 'I'll just slip over the road to the Poole's. Tell them Eric and Jacky are back. See if Simon's home.'

'Mr and Mrs Mount will be anxious, too.'

It was late May in England and wild roses bloomed in the hedgerows around the football pitch at the back of the Dotchin's house. Eric wakened to thrushes, blackbirds and tinkling springtime poplars. No planes. No guns. He turned on his side and groaned. No shaming, shaking terror.

'No. Mum. I never saw Andrew. Simon did, early on at Le Mans but not since then. Last

I heard, Andrew was with a medical unit near Lille.'

'What about Simon?'

'Simon.' Simon at the Bren. Simon full of courage. Simon when the bridge was blown. Staff Sergeant Cowan and the little children. The images were burnt into his brain. He controlled his voice with difficulty. 'I was with Simon and Jacky for most of the time. We were perimeter force.'

Mr Dotchin winced. He was old to be the father of a young man of Eric's age. Eric was the much loved offspring of a second marriage. They had watched over the little boy, Doris and he, and kept him from harm – till he grew up and his country needed him more than his parents. Now he tells them he was part of a perimeter force in a monumental manoeuvre to save the bulk of the British Army. Up front, that is. Under the very noses of the enemy guns. George Dotchin had been in the infantry himself in the 14–18 war and never thought to see young Eric in the same position.

Cathy and Norah went to see Eric on their next free afternoon. The haunted look in his eyes was new. They let him do the talking while they listened with deep concern.

'It was one bloody muddle,' he told them. 'Most of our platoon bought it. Somehow, I never imagined it would be quite as awful as this. Jacky and I made it to the beach and swam out to a motor launch but we lost sight of Simon long before we got anywhere near

Dunkirk. God knows what happened to him.'

Norah gave his hand a squeeze. There was nothing much anyone could say. Eric and Jacky were lucky. They had come home. Jacky, when they met him, had sloughed off the bad dreams and said he would go back tomorrow if they would let him.

'You're smoking too much,' Norah told him. 'It's not good for that chest of yours.'

He blew out a defiant cloud. 'Neither is standing up to my armpits in the sea for three hours, pet.'

Colin, isolated from the rest of his old friends at HMS *Vernon* in Portsmouth, wrote anxiously to Norah.

> What news have you of the chaps in France? Everyone here is desperate to hear about friends and relatives. I know that boatloads have been rescued but what about our blokes? Please let me know as soon as you have news.
>
> Yours, Colin
>
> PS Alec's got his wings and expects to be posted soon. We might be able to meet. It's damn lonely down here.

There was the good news concerning Eric and Jacky, but no news yet of Simon or Andrew.

'We keep hoping, every day, to hear they're safe.' As Norah sealed her letter to Colin, she thought how glad his mother must be to know that he had not been involved in the hazardous evacuation from Dunkirk.

As the precious days slipped by during which this manoeuvre was still possible the number of wrecks in Dunkirk harbour made it hard for the big ships to come inshore. Hundreds of men still waited on the beaches under constant enemy fire. Desperate measures were necessary. The call went out across Britain for small craft to act as ferries between the shore and the big ships. An impossibility, some thought, but it was a chance that must be taken. There was a place in history awaiting the owners of small boats who were capable of navigating the Channel. Their orders were to assemble immediately with their vessels at Westminster Pier, London, for briefing.

In the northern port where Cathy and Norah lived many men made their living from the sea; men who had handled small boats at their grandad's knee. They, like hundreds of other small-time sailors throughout the country, responded to the call for help without questioning. The bar at The Lobster Pot in Eastport was the place to hear the latest news of who was taking up the challenge.

'The Shields' trawlers are going. Jimmy Donkin. Mac Stronach. Bert Smith from the fish shop is crewing for Mac.'

'Bert's a bit long in the tooth for that lark, isn't he?'

They recalled that Bert's lad, Albert, was on Atlantic convoys, on a corvette. 'He wants to do his bit, like his boy.'

'No good little bastard, that lad was.'

'If he's on Atlantic convoys he's a bloody hero. Make no mistake!'

'So's his dad if he sails to Dunkirk with Mac Stronach.'

They drained their pint pots and wished that they, too, might be heroes, but miners were in a reserved occupation and made rotten sailors anyhow.

'Micky Lisle wants to take *The Seagull*.'

'Why, man, he can hardly get from Watt's Bank to the lighthouse in *The Seagull*, let alone sail to France!'

But Micky was there at Westminster Pier when the young sub-lieutenant briefed the weirdly assorted armada of little boats. 'Take full water tanks with you, gentlemen.' He used a megaphone to make himself heard over the bumping and scraping, clinking of spanners, tapping of hammers and testing of reluctant motors. 'There'll be a lot of thirsty men out there. Pick 'em up. Take them to the nearest naval vessel or bring them home yourselves. You have a vital job to do. Go and do it. Good luck to you all.'

Away they went to France – paddle steamers, motor boats, fishing vessels, some of which had never been outside the Thames estuary before, and luxury yachts more accustomed to the Mediterranean than the variable English Channel.

Albert Smith's father was there feeling thirty years younger and Micky Lisle, with his *Seagull*, confidently pulling a string of dinghies behind him.

Nineteen

Dunkirk blazed. The oil storage tanks were on fire. The foreshores were alight with burning trucks and tanks, a bonfire of army equipment jettisoned and rendered inoperable by the retreating BEF. The land was being grilled under high explosive shells. They exploded on beaches and on piers. If they landed on the beaches their effect was lessened by the sand, but there was no shelter from machine-gun bullets for the men crowding there. Medical officers, struggling to save lives and limbs under impossible conditions, saw injured men wounded again and again.

Andrew had lost all sense of time. With his driver, he had escaped from Boulogne a few hours before it fell to the Germans and he had joined the troops making for Dunkirk. He had long since given up any hope of finding his own unit. Instead, with Charlie Dunsford acting as a nursing orderly, he had set up an aid post in the shelter of a bombed warehouse on Dunkirk harbour, where he treated the wounded. Some of the injuries, neglected for days, were crawling with maggots. Some men were past help. Only the ease brought by morphia remained for them. He worked at speed, transfusing, carrying out urgent surgery, amputations, stitching open wounds.

Time was running out. The date was 9 June and the game was almost up. His Majesty's Hospital Carrier *The Isle of Guernsey* was embarking casualties. She had been shelled, repaired and shelled again, but here she was on her fifth, and without doubt, final trip. For Andrew she represented the last chance to send his wounded men back to England.

The ship's officers and crew, fully aware of this, were assisting the RAMC orderlies, picking up casualties from the beach and running with the stretchers along the rapidly disintegrating Mole. All three piers in the harbour were now out of action. Only the Mole remained and even that was beginning to burn.

With 600 men on board packed into every foot of space, the captain of the *Guernsey* prepared to leave. He must now run the gauntlet of fire from the German batteries ashore. There was little reason to think that the enemy would respect the ship's non-belligerent status. The Hospital Carrier *Paris* had been sunk here despite her prominent red cross and definitive markings.

Andrew straightened his aching back. His rubber apron ran with blood. The turned-back cuffs of his battle jacket were sodden. Private Dunsford, on Andrew's orders, had accompanied the last stretcher to be evacuated.

'What about you, sir?'

'I'm staying, Charlie. Good luck and – thank you.' Andrew was one of a number of medical officers who had volunteered to stay with the wounded. He would not be going home. 'Go on!' he shouted angrily as Private Dunsford stood irresolute. 'Get the hell out of here. That's an order. And hurry or you'll miss the boat.'

When his very loyal driver-turned-medical-orderly left him, Andrew closed his eyes for a moment, aware of overwhelming fatigue which seemed temporarily to blot out the crescendo of explosions that surrounded him. He was alone in hell.

When he opened his eyes a few seconds later he saw Simon, slumped in the sidecar of a French dispatch rider's motorcycle drawn up on the quay.

"*Au secours! Médecin! Sergent anglais pour le bateau!*" the rider shouted.

Andrew was already there. Simon's eyes were closed. His face was chalk pale, his lips bloodless. 'My God, Simon! Where are you hurt?' Feverishly, Andrew tore open the battle jacket and found a sticky pool under his back. As they moved him, Simon groaned and opened his eyes. Unfocused at first, they cleared in recognition.

'Andy...'

'Deep flesh wound left shoulder,' Andrew muttered. 'Hang on, old chap. We'll fix you.'

When they laid him face down on the stretcher a diagonal wound was revealed exposing torn muscles and blood vessels amongst shredded khaki cloth and dirt from the ditch where he had lain. Andrew breathed a sigh of relief. The blood was already beginning to coagulate. No main arteries involved. He was busy with syringe and morphia, conscious all the time of the ship's immediate preparation to sail. 'I've got to get you on that ship, Simon. No time for stitching. I'm filling the wound with sulphonamide, stop infection and,' he prepared another injection, 'anti-gas gangrene. That will hold till you get on board. Hang on, old lad, this is going to be a bumpy ride.'

Without hesitation, the French driver picked up the other end of the stretcher and the two men ran with it along the burning Mole. Already the ship had a head of steam and the gangway was up.

'WAIT!' yelled Andrew.

Willing hands reached down and grabbed the stretcher. Simon was hoisted aboard the crowded deck. 'Take him below!' Andrew shouted instructions to the army nursing sister at the rail. 'He needs urgent surgery. He's lost a lot of blood.'

As though there were not 200 other exhausted men crowded on the deck, Andrew saw only Simon, peaked in shock, drained of blood. They would transfuse him on board, stitch and repair the back wound. Tidy him up. He was in good hands. Calm settled upon Andrew. Panic was replaced by an acceptance of the appalling pattern of Fate. Simon was his dear friend and he might not survive. He himself would be taken prisoner by the Germans. He might never see Simon again. 'Goodbye, Simon,' he called. 'Good luck, my old friend.'

The distance between the ship's side and the Mole was already increasing.

Surfacing to consciousness for a moment before he was carried away, Simon stared in stricken comprehension. 'Andy...' He tried to shout but it came out small. 'Come on. Jump.'

'I'm staying with the casualties.' Andrew cupped his hands to make himself heard. 'Give my love to Mum and Dad and the girls.'

Simon remembered nothing after that.

The French soldier turned to Andrew in enquiry, would he not leave also on the ship?

Andrew shook his head.

'Ni moi non plus.' The Frenchman looked even more exhausted than Andrew. *'Je reste ici. La France a besoin de chacun de ses soldats.'*

Together they walked unhurriedly along the burning Mole to the smoke and destruction of Dunkirk. The die was cast.

Micky Lisle mislaid his dinghies on the way back from Dunkirk but he brought *The Seagull* home with a full complement aboard.

There was a sticky moment on the homeward trip when her engine developed an alarming attack of hiccoughs while bullets smacked into the sea around her, but Micky knew every trick of that old engine and brought his weary passengers safely into Dover, still carrying their small arms.

Back in the north a respectful audience awaited him at The Lobster Pot. He was halfway through his free pint and his mates were waiting to hear about his trip but Micky, for once, was tongue-tied. Gabby Micky was lost for words.

'What was it like then, Micky lad?' They thought he looked half shot. Done in.

'Them boys out there on the beach,' he managed at last. 'They got guts. Waiting their turn like it was the Saturday night queue for the Dogs only they're up to their necks in water and Stukas and Heinkels spraying them with bullets. One bloke had a mouth organ. "Danny Boy", he's playing and the rest sing along. Christ A'mighty! Oh boy.' Micky's eyes filled with tears. His friends were hushed. 'I'll not forget this trip in a hurry.'

The British Army had been saved to fight another day and, despite the fact that all the guns and ammunition, trucks and tanks had been left behind, Britain rejoiced. To have retrieved 200,000 troops from Dunkirk seemed like an amazing victory.

It was left to Prime Minister Churchill to remind the nation that wars were not won by evacuations.

Twenty

The nation's feeling of relief over the Dunkirk 'miracle' was fleeting. The greater part of the 1st British Expeditionary Force had been rescued from northern France but their tanks, armoured cars and guns had all been left behind and what good was a fighting force without its armaments. The loss would have to be replaced before the 2nd British Expeditionary Force could be sent to help French units, who were struggling to hold back the Germans from Paris. There was no time to be lost. Armament factories in Britain went into overdrive. Gaps in military ranks were filled.

Cathy and Norah, as newly enrolled army sisters (QAs) at a military hospital in Scotland, anxiously awaited news of their friends. 'Do you think they will send Jacky and Eric back with the next force?' Cathy wondered. 'Eric was shattered after Dunkirk.'

'What did Eileen have to say about that, do you think?'

' "Pull yourself together, Eric," that's what Eileen would say.'

Cathy's father wrote as soon as he had the news.

Mr Poole came round to our house to tell me the bad news that Simon has been wounded, it's pretty serious. A shell got him in the back. He's in hospital somewhere in Surrey and his ma and dad are going to see him. They've promised to let me know how they find him. The message they got from the hospital was that he was 'poorly'. You will know better than me what that means. No word of Andrew. Mr and Mrs Mount are in despair. Look after yourself, pet.

Simon was seriously wounded. Cathy felt her heart flip. A wound in the back could mean one of many things and, yes, she did know what was meant by 'poorly'. She passed the letter to Norah.

From his wheelchair, Raymond Webster could see the nurses preparing beds on the adjoining verandah. Previously used as a store for medical equipment, it was now equipped with four army beds. He had learned, via the grapevine, that Dunkirk casualties were expected at the sanitorium. Unable to relax, he waited for their arrival with trepidation and a certain amount of humility. He should have been with them in France, sharing the risks and the consequences.
He watched as they were lifted into bed, still in their stained uniforms, and he was able to

check that none was from his own regiment. To judge from the urgent attention of the nursing staff, their condition was serious. The men lay still and quiet, each linked to an intravenous drip, one to an oxygen cylinder.

The soldier in the bed nearest to Raymond Webster lay on his stomach, the weight of the blankets supported by a bed cradle over his back. His face was turned away but from the thick tousle of hair and the strong neck above the bandages, Webster judged him to be a young man.

He looked down at his own thin, pale hands. How long since they had handled a weapon? They could not strangle a sleeping sentry now. They could not strangle a sleeping cat. He was useless. Eminently expendable. Not for the first time, he contemplated opting out. It would not be too difficult. A slash on the wrists. Over and out.

Later, when only a dimmed light on the night nurse's desk relieved the hateful dark of endless night, he said a prayer. 'For a change, God, I'm not asking for anything for myself. Please help these innocent soldiers. Relieve their pain. And if, because of my inability to help my country, I take my own way out, I know You will understand.'

The black mood lifted with the coming of the day. He took the first opportunity, after the routine consultations on the ward, to propel his wheelchair to the verandah rail and check on the new arrivals. The welfare of these unknown soldiers concerned him as if they were his own men. During the night there had been a traffic of porters taking the men to and from the theatre and drifts of residual anaesthetic swamped the sweet scent of the honeysuckle on his verandah rail.

Frightened relatives came in the afternoon, moving chairs to bedsides with scrupulous care to make no noise in these oppressive surroundings. They spoke in whispers and when their vigil was over they went quietly away, looking back from the doorway with hopeful, brave little smiles.

'You should not concern yourself so, Lieutenant Webster.' The ward sister felt that such a morbid interest in the wounded men was not good for a TB patient for whom a hovering depression was a constant companion. 'Why not push your wheelchair to the other side of the verandah? The library ladies will be around this afternoon. A good book will take your mind off these poor boys.'

In the following days, one of the four men was transferred to a hospital nearer his home. One died. But Raymond Webster persuaded himself that the man next to him was getting better. His optimism was justified when the nurses removed the drip intubation and turned the patient round to face the world. Webster lowered his paper with interest. The young man Raymond had watched over, since his arrival from Dunkirk, was propped up on pillows, taking a look at his surroundings.

'Good morning,' Raymond greeted him like

an old friend. 'How does it feel to be right side up?'

He would be no older than twenty-three or -four. To a layman like Raymond his pallor was alarming. There were violet smudges beneath his eyes. His nose was nipped and white, his face drawn – but his answer was perky enough.

'Bloody awful,' said Sergeant Poole, 'but I expect it will get better.' His head fell back slackly on the pillows and his heavy eyelids drooped.

Raymond Webster went back to his crossword and automatically resumed his role as minder, greatly reassured by the improvement in his charge.

As days went by and Simon's condition continued to improve, Raymond Webster had to remind himself that, at some point, the companion who had enlivened his lonely days would be transferred. 'Don't overdo it,' he ventured his advice as Simon applied himself with fanatical determination to the exercises prescribed by the physiotherapist.

'Got to join my mob again,' Simon answered. Grim determination hardened his jaw. 'When they go back to France, I'm going with them. I've got some old scores to settle with the Hun.'

'There's something I've been waiting to ask you.' Raymond edged his chair closer to the common rail. 'I was afraid at one time that you were going to peg out before I had a chance to talk to you. Did you come across

200

any of my chaps at Dunkirk? 2nd Battalion, the Coldstream Guards?'

Of course, thought Simon, looking at Webster, guards officer. He had the bearing, even in sickness. He shook his head. 'Can't say I did. We had to run for it when the King of the Belgians capitulated. Units were separated. Lines broken. Men from any regiment fought alongside each other. Bloody shambles. I don't remember the Coldstreams but the Guards were there, for sure.'

Simon's eyes narrowed in nightmare recall, lifting his thoughts over the trembling cherry blossom and cool green lawns to a raging inferno on the other side of the Channel where men's bodies were tossed about in the spuming earth to fall in fragments like a curse upon orchards and pastures, streams and rivers. What evil fruits would grow from soil enriched with this grim compost of war? He saw again Staff Sergeant Cowan's boot, with the foot still in it, being washed down the river. That *excellent* man.

Raymond Webster noted the clenched fists. 'Where did you collect your packet?' he asked gently, anxious not to probe but hoping that to talk of his ordeal might be helpful to a man wounded both psychologically and physically.

'I think it was about fifteen miles inland from Dunkirk. A French dispatch rider picked me up.'

'Entente cordiale indeed.'

'And delivered me to an RAMC doctor at Dunkirk who patched me up and got me on

201

board the last hospital ship for Britain. He stayed behind himself to go into captivity with the remaining wounded.'

'He was a brave man.'

'He was my best friend. We grew up together. He saved my life and threw away his own.' Simon's voice grew thick. He turned his head away and Lieutenant Webster welcomed the distraction of a nurse offering tea.

'Pity you two old gossips can't sit together. Save my poor legs.'

Simon looked curiously at Raymond. 'Why are you in splendid isolation?'

'TB lungs.'

'You look all right to me.' Simon could not be expected to tell the difference between the rosy cheek of health and the dark, febrile flush of tuberculosis.

'I wish I was. What's your regiment?'

'1st Tyne Borderers.'

'I know your part of the world. The artillery range near Otterburn especially. It was sleeping in damp heather up there that did for me.'

'Can they fix your lungs?'

'Probably not.'

Simon fell silent at his neighbour's calm acceptance.

Raymond shrugged. 'I get bloody-minded at times but what's the use?' He smiled to show it didn't matter. Nothing mattered.

To Simon his own wound seemed of little consequence compared with the unclean infection which had brought this soldier, this regular army officer of one of the most prestigious of regiments, to this – a bed in a TB sanitorium with seemingly only one exit.

Through the window of her office the ward sister regarded the two patients in conversation at the verandah rail. 'Lieutenant Webster is going to miss his company,' she remarked to the medical officer who was at that moment completing the authority to transfer Sergeant Poole. 'He has been so much more cheerful of late.'

The doctor nodded briefly. 'Sergeant Poole has been good for him. Taken his mind off himself.'

'I think it is a little more than that,' the sister persisted. 'I see a real improvement in Lieutenant Webster.'

'Wishful thinking, Sister. He's a nice chap. We'd like to think he had a chance but—'

'His last blood tests were no worse.'

'They were no better.'

On the day of the transfer, Raymond was at the rail, watching Simon struggle into battledress. 'Some kind person has drawn a new jacket from QM Stores. But look at my trousers,' he stuffed a fist down the waistband, 'miles too big for me now. I'll have to put on some weight soon or my mother will sue the War Office.'

'So – sergeants have mothers?'

Simon grinned, 'Mine's a smasher. She'll insist that I have a diet of porridge and cream and treacle pudding in the hospital I'm bound for.'

'Which hospital will that be?'

'Eastport General.'

Raymond's eyebrows lifted. 'I was a patient there for a short time before coming here.'

'Really? My girl is one of the nurses there. She may have left by now. She was waiting to join the QAs.'

It was instinct that made Raymond say, 'Cathy Lewis.'

'That's the one,' said Simon in surprise.

Nurse Müllerman, now in her second year, was still a very solitary person, repelling any attempts at intimacy on the part of either nurses or medical students. The young men found her extremely attractive, but cold as a block of ice. They laid bets as to who would get to take her out. She froze them off, every one of them. She sought no one's company, although, privately, she confessed to missing the times spent with Norah and Cathy and the rest of that lighthearted group. Such thoughts were quickly overridden. Her vocation, for such was her dedication to nursing, provided all the company she needed. In some obscure way she felt that, by caring for the casualties of war, she was getting back at Hitler for the misery and chaos he had caused.

The patients adored her. They were amused to see how coolly she treated the ogling medical students and how downright unfriendly she was towards her fellow nurses, yet to her patients she was an angel, a beautiful dark angel with gentle hands and ever ready sympathy, and they loved her.

She still had difficulty in writing English but Cathy and Norah must be told without delay that Simon was a patient in her ward.

He has deep shoulder wound, muscles all messed up and still draining but now begins to heal. He asks for you both and hopes you will write soon. Sad you have gone away. Also sad news of Andrew. He puts Simon on board the last hospital ship to leave Dunkirk but himself stays mit the wounded on the beach so Simon says for sure he is now prisoner of war. When Simon tells me this he is very upset and I cry, too, for Andrew is a brave, good doctor. Please write a letter to Simon. He cannot write easily to you.

I am sorry I do not answer all your letters but it is hard for me (you can see!) to write in English. I am senior probationer now. I hope you are both well and happy.

Your amiable friend,

Hilde

Twenty-One

Their hospital was on the draft to accompany the 2nd British Expeditionary Force to France. Cathy and Norah had no reservations about this. Satisfaction was uppermost in that now they would be able to put their long training to practical use and, since they were sublimely ignorant of what might lie ahead, they were filled with excitement at the prospect. They went home to Eastport on ten days' embarkation leave and visited Simon straight away.

To return to their old hospital in their new rôle as army nursing sisters was a novel experience for them. Free of its disciplines, they stepped out smartly along old familiar corridors, boldly demanding a smile of recognition from senior members of the staff.

The sister in charge bent the rules to allow them into the ward where Simon was a patient, although this visit was outside regular hours. 'Sergeant Poole is making good progress,' she told them. 'Looking forward to seeing you.' Her eye ran over their appearance with undisguised envy. 'You both look very smart, I must say.'

At the ward entrance Norah halted diplomatically. 'You go ahead, Cathy. I caught sight of Hilde in the treatment room. I'll be with you in a moment,' which left Cathy to walk down the ward on her own as she had done so many times before, on both day and night duty. Old Mr Parsons had been in that bed and cheeky Jimmie Wilkinson in the next. Little Georgie, whose head had been crushed between two coal tubs, died in bed seven. Seated in a chair by bed fifteen, supported by pillows, was Simon, his face alight with anticipation at her approach.

'Cathy.'

She bent close and kissed him on the cheek. 'Can I hug you or will you crack?'

'Hug me to death and I'll love it.'

He smelt of tobacco, hospital issue White Windsor soap and methylated spirits. With her arms about him, she could feel his shrunken frame. How desperately ill he must have been to lose so much of his substance in so short a time. Where were the rugby shoulders now? Aware that the whole ward was enjoying the spectacle, she gently disengaged herself and pulled up a chair close to his. 'We've been so worried about you, Simon dear.'

'I was worried about myself.' A beam of sunlight streaking through a nearby window set a sparkle in his eyes. He was all smiles. His white teeth seemed quite startling in his unfamiliar thin face. 'Wondered if I would ever tote a Bren gun again, but now I know I can. Give me a few more weeks and I'll be back in the line.' He leant towards her and took her hands in his, his eyes searching her face. 'I thought about you, Cathy, whenever there was time to think, and I wondered if you ever thought of me?'

'Of course I did,' she spoke lightly, although she knew that he was seeking a more thoughtful response. 'Norah and I pestered your father and mother for news of you. It's such a relief to find you looking almost the same as the old Simon despite all you have been through.'

He released her awkward hands reluctantly. 'I am the old Simon. I'm the Simon who has been crazy about you since you were a scatty kid – and look at you now! If I were in uniform, I would have to salute you, Lieutenant Lewis.'

'So,' she smiled at him affectionately, 'we'll have a little respect then.' She poked into her mother's string bag. 'I've brought presents. My sweet ration of chocolate. That's the measure of my regard for you! Strawberries from my uncle's allotment and some of my mum's ginger biscuits. They'll blow your head off. Everyone sends you their love and hope that you'll soon be fit and well again.'

His mind switched to a more serious matter. 'Cathy,' there was an unaccustomed sternness in his voice, 'You musn't go to France.'

Her eyes widened. 'Simon, you ought to know. We have to go where we are sent.'

'It's madness to send women out there now.'

'Where there are British soldiers there have to be British nurses and doctors to look after them.' She laid her offerings on his bed. Then, meeting his darkening eyes, 'Was it terrible, my poor darling?' she asked quietly. The lines and grim creases in his face were new drawn by his experiences.

'No more terrible for me than for the other chaps but, yes, it was terrible. I cannot bear to think of you going into that abattoir.'

'I think we are supposed to be making for the south, some distance from the fighting.'

He snorted. 'No one, least of all the generals, can keep track of the fighting. Here today. A hundred miles retreat tomorrow. "Consolidating the line," it's called. "Running scared" is another name for it. We couldn't stop the Jerries when we had all our guns. How the blazes can we hold a position now with scarcely any armaments?'

To deflect his concern, she asked, 'Have you any news of Andrew?'

'The War Office has just confirmed that he is a prisoner of war.'

'At least we know he is alive.'

'In a POW camp. That's no life.'

'Is there an address we can write to?'

'It will follow.'

'He had just qualified and he's such a good doctor.'

'That won't be wasted. He'll have plenty of patients in the clink.'

'He got you on the last ship out of Dunkirk, didn't he?'

'Mine was one of the many blokes he saved but he didn't try to save himself. He stayed behind voluntarily to look after the wounded. Our Andy deserves a medal.'

'Norah and I are proud of you all.' She lifted his hand, grown soft and pale, and pressed it to her lips.

Simon caressed her cheek. 'There's something I must tell you, Cathy.' He looked into her eyes and held her gaze with great seriousness. 'I'm not an insurance clerk any more and never will be again even if I survive this war. I'm a soldier. I will go on fighting Hitler and everything he stands for as long as I have breath in my body. That man is evil itself. He wants the whole of Europe for his "Master Race". And when we've settled the score with him, after the war, I mean to join the regular army. We must never again make ourselves defenceless through disarmament. It is important that you should know that, Cathy pet.' She was beginning to look restless, looking over her shoulder to see if Norah was in sight, 'Because I want to know if you will marry me if I am a regular peacetime solder? Not right now,' he said hastily, seeing the panic leap to her face. 'One day, some day, would the idea be too preposterous? After all, we've known each other for long enough. Please don't take fright. I've been rehearsing this speech for days, ever since I knew you were coming.'

Cathy, taken by surprise, could find no words.

'You know my feelings,' he pressed her, 'but what about yours? You've never said if you love me a little, ever.'

Her laugh was shaky and inappropriate. It quickly became a little moan of misery, 'Simon, I am so very fond of you.'

'OK,' his voice flattened. 'I'll have to be content with that for the moment. I hope I haven't frightened you off. You won't run away and marry someone else? Wars loosen tongues, my sweet. Even my wooden clapper has managed a proposal at last, of a sort. You will think about it?'

Cathy could only nod.

Simon continued quietly, 'I'll never change. Just remember that. Never. When I come back from foreign parts with crowns and crossed swords on my shoulders, I'll still go down on my knees and beg you to marry me.'

Grateful for the laugh, Cathy said, 'To a mere lieutenant? Bit of a come down. I think the anaesthetic hasn't worn off yet.' She greeted the arrival of Norah with relief.

When it was time to go, Cathy and Norah turned at the door of the ward. Simon sat, still as a rock, unsmiling, one hand raised in farewell.

Cathy gave him her smartest salute before they turned away.

'I wonder when, if ever, we will meet again,' Norah said.

'He's just asked me to marry him.'

'*What!*'

'Not right now. Some time in the future.'

'What did you tell him?'

'Not very much.'

Norah had stopped in her tracks. She shook Cathy's arm. 'Don't be so utterly infuriating. Are you going to marry him?'

'Oh come on. Don't stand here in the middle of Out Patients arguing about my future. I don't know if I want to marry him. I don't even know if I love him. Never really thought about him like that.' They walked on down the hill to the market. 'I don't feel any bursting, yelping, agony of emotion. I don't think of him every minute of the day. I like him, of course, very much. Is that a good enough reason to marry him? I'll have to wait and see. Life is much too busy for all of us right now for such earth-moving decisions.'

They had reached the Haymarket Café. 'Come on, Norah, let's have a cup of tea for old times' sake.'

The linoleum on the stairs was worn on the treads. The curtains were dingy and dirty. 'Funny we never realised it was so scruffy.'

'Too busy talking. Remember how Quentin and Jacky used to argue, and Alec making speeches...' They sat by the window at their old accustomed table, deserted now. The waitress brought them tea.

'I've been thinking about you and Simon, Catypus,' Norah regarded Cathy solemnly, 'maybe we're just not the marrying kind.'

'Oh,' Cathy said readily, 'I think we are,

212

with the right person.'

'Then I haven't met the right person. Neither have you.'

Cathy picked up the teapot and began to pour. 'I think I did once but he wasn't interested. We'll need some hot water. This pot is too small for two of us.'

Norah's brow knitted. 'I don't remember that drama. Was he a medical student? A doctor?'

'A patient. One of yours.'

Norah looked blank.

'In the side ward.'

Enlightenment dawned on Norah's face. 'Raymond Webster. Pulmonary tuberculosis.'

Cathy nodded. 'I was in love with him all right. I would have married him on the spot if he'd asked me – but he didn't.'

'You must be mad. He was a very sick man!'

'So? Forget it. It didn't happen. Here's your tea. Move your bag. Simon is in a blue funk about us going to France.'

'Hilde says he is lucky to be alive.'

'He's lost a lot of weight. What he needs is a long convalescence but he's determined to get back into the fight at the first opportunity. What's Hilde's news?'

'She had a letter from Nancy. Alec is getting his wings and expects to "join the circus", as he puts it, any day.'

'And our poor Andrew has just left it.'

Twenty-Two

'We've got to get back to France without delay. The longer we wait, the harder it will be.'

On their nightly black-out check, the air raid wardens in the area usually stopped by the King's Head to hear the 9 o'clock news. Ken Poole's opinions were always listened to with respect because of his experience as an officer in the 14-18 war.

Everyone knew about his boy lying in Eastport Hospital with a serious wound, but the major always put on a brave face. 'He's doing well but I doubt if he'll ever be fit for soldiering again. Desk job probably and he won't like that. You should see his back!' He sucked in his breath. 'Bloody great gash. A miracle his spine wasn't smashed. He's got young Mount to thank for being alive today.'

Cyril wagged his head. 'Tragedy that. Just qualified and now he's in the bag.'

As Big Ben opened his sonorous overture an immediate silence fell, except for the landlord's fractious baby in a distant part of the building. Then came the worst news of all.

'France,' the announcer said slowly and

clearly, 'has asked Germany for an armistice.'

The date was 17 June, the day France laid down her arms. From now on she was out of the war. The landlord's baby, with a triumphant grunt, settled to its bottle.

For a moment, no one spoke. The leaden tick of the bar clock sounded like the countdown to doom. A falling cinder in the hearth called men back to the reality of the awful present.

The barman was the first to speak. 'That leaves only us in the ring.'

Someone said, 'What price the 2nd BEF now?'

Cyril Lewis cleared his throat. 'There isn't going to be a 2nd BEF. What we had was the first and the last British Expeditionary Force to France.'

'And the frontline,' Ken Poole added grimly, 'is right here.'

There was a further BBC announcement. 'The Secretary of State, Mr Anthony Eden, urges men of any age who are not members of the Armed Forces, who are prepared to defend their homes against invasion, to join a force that will be known as the Local Defence Volunteers.'

'It's come to this, chaps,' Ken Poole was the first to grasp the situation. 'Every man jack of us will have to pull his weight.'

He and Cyril Lewis were at the head of the queue the following day to sign up for service in the LDV. They were two of thousands of like minded men throughout Britain.

Invasion was no longer inconceivable, no longer improbable. It was possible and probable. Hitler was virtually master of the greater part of Europe. His last enemy was Britain. When would he jump the Channel?

On 22 June France signed the armistice terms in the same railway carriage in the forest of Compeigne which had witnessed Germany's humiliation in 1918. Hitler had a long memory. Mussolini, the Italian *duce*, judging the time to be propitious in view of Hitler's successes, threw in his lot with the Führer and declared war on Britain.

Without doubt, Hitler expected Britain to follow France's example and seek an armistice. What other action was open to her? She stood alone against the might of Germany's war machine. With her arsenal depleted, with U-boats preying on her lifeline of food and raw materials from Canada and America, she could not survive. She had no alternative but to admit defeat. Such was Hitler's assessment of the situation. Even Britain's friends abroad could see no other option open to her.

They were instantly disillusioned by the prime minister. When Hitler boasted that Britain's neck would be wrung like a chicken, Churchill's response was a snarled, 'Some chicken! Some neck!' and the construction of tank traps and other anti-invasion devices was speeded up. Infantry divisions took up position on the vulnerable south-east coastal regions. Coils of barbed wire snaked along beaches that were now closed to the public and the sun shone as if all the world was at peace. On the other side of the Channel this same sun beamed down on the rape of Europe.

The reaction of the British people was totally irrational. Far from being downcast by the impossible odds against them, they were lifted up. The spirit of the people had never been as high as it was at this moment of extreme danger.

'Right, lads. We're in the Final and we're playing at home.' That was the mood. Other nations looking on were nonplussed.

'What do we do now, Mr Lewis?' Herbie Graham had just left school and worked in Cyril's department of the Council Offices until he was old enough to join up. Until then he was an enthusiastic member of Cyril's ARP group.'

'We watch, Herbie. We keep watch on every yard of our shores, day and night. We are a coastal unit with a big responsibility and we won't be caught napping.'

'There's no blueprint to go by,' said Ken Poole. 'It's a mighty long time since we were invaded.'

'All we gotta do is shoot 'em, Mr Poole,' Herbie assured him. 'Just let them set foot in our country and we'll blow their brains out.'

Military patrols armed with rifles and grenades were posted at every railway nexus and road junction of importance. The Local Defence Volunteers, now known by the more stirring title of 'Home Guard', made do with

217

shotguns and loaded clubs and anything else that would serve as a weapon. Aristocratic families went feudal and raised their own militia from tenants and employees, arming them with halberds and pikes taken from displays on ancestral walls. Simon and other casualties from that first disastrous expedition to France chafed at their helplessness at this time when every soldier was needed.

Hilde astonished Simon one evening with a hysterical outburst quite unlike her. In some distress she flopped down on Simon's bed in a totally unprofessional and uncharacteristic fashion.

'What's up with you?' He stared in some puzzlement. 'You look as though you don't know whether to laugh or cry.'

Hilde shook her head fiercely then nodded. 'That is true, Simon. I am feeling so sorry for you that I cry for you, but you are English and mad like all the English, so you do not even see why,' she began to giggle uncontrollably, 'you don't even see why I am sorry for you!'

Simon was at a loss to know what she was on about nor why she found it funny.

'You are all so mad it is hard to believe. You think you can beat Hitler?' Her voice rose shrilly then gave way to tears. She seemed oblivious of the stir she was causing in the ward. 'And since I live here and you let me make a home here, then I must pretend to believe it too. It is so stupid that I do not laugh, I cry.'

Simon stretched out a hand, 'Look here, old girl—'

Hilde's shoulders shook helplessly, 'Simon. I am twenty two years old. I am a young woman.'

'Just a manner of speaking, old thing ... Hilde. But honest, there's nothing for you to get worked up about. OK, we took a beating at Dunkirk but we're back in business now and ready for Hitler if he dares set foot in England.'

'A roll of barbed wire on the beach,' she scoffed. 'A pillbox made to look like a bathing hut! If German parachutists land you are going to ring church bells. What good will these things do?'

'There's a lot more than that to our defences,' Simon was somewhat nettled. 'We're digging in concrete tank traps all round the coastline. The government is doing everything possible.'

'I hear soldiers say their guns are rusty old things left from the other war.'

'Pay no attention to that kind of talk, Hilde, and don't repeat it.'

She shrugged. 'But if it is true?'

'It may have been true right after Dunkirk but we are rearming fast,' he grew angry with her for making him face unpleasant facts. 'Factories are turning out tanks and planes at a record rate. There's no room for dismal johnnies. We're going to give Jerry the fright of his life if he attempts to invade Britain. Listen hard, Hilde, and you'll learn something. This is Britain. It is not Norway or Denmark, Holland or Belgium or France. It is Britain and we will give Hitler a bloody nose if he tries his blitzkrieg tactics here.'

'Simon,' Hilde said softly, 'I am sorry for Britain because she is brave but she is also foolish. Peoples running about with buckets of sand to put out bombs. Peoples looking everywhere to chase off parachutists with a big stick. Peoples taking away the spark plugs from their cars every night so Germans cannot use them. You think a little no-good car will stop a row of Tiger tanks, hein?'

'I'm not hearing you. You talk like a fifth columnist.'

She was quick to deny this. 'Ach, nein! Simon, not me. Britain is a friend to Jews like me.'

'Then stop talking rot.'

'I tell you something funny, stop you looking so cross. Matron now wears a big hat-pin in her cap. She says no German will take her without a fight.' She collapsed in giggles again. 'You tink German soldier might fall in love mit Matron?'

Wheedled back into good humour once more, Simon smiled. 'Come on, Nurse Müllerman, help me back to bed. My bottom is sore.'

Twenty-Three

Cyril Lewis was one of six men who made up Sergeant Ken Poole's Home Guard platoon. Their duty was to patrol a section of the cliff top overlooking Eastport Bay. At the first sign of a seaborne invasion young Herbie Graham would run with the news to the Home Guard captain who sat in the little back room at the King's Head drawing plans on the back of old bills. Herbie was a good runner. His mother's sideboard was adorned with the cups he had won in school athletics.

The Home Guard captain would then inform the bell ringer who was ready at any time of day or night to climb the bell tower of St Oswald's church and sound the alarm. There had been a false alarm the previous week when the rector, seeing in the moonlight a swan coming in to land on the rectory pond, mistook it for a parachutist and set the bells ringing.

On a starless night Ken Poole stood with Cathy's father on the cliff top scanning the sluggish sea as it moved, thick and black as oil, breaking silver with will-o'-the-wisp phosphorescence as it washed over the

221

Corkscrew Rocks.

'Black as your hat tonight. A good night for an invasion.'

The lighthouse beam was doused long since but a pin point of light on the dark sea tonight would be spotted at once. Listening ears would hear the first splash of an oar, the hum of a motor. The men were well aware that utmost vigilance was demanded of them. Straight across from where they stood was Holland, a country already crushed beneath the weight of the swastika. Aerial photographs had revealed invasion barges being built on the River Scheldt in Belgium. Any night, this night, might be the night when Hitler decided to launch his attack on England.

There was one pair of binoculars in the platoon and Will Jackson, the coal merchant, had a telescope. In peacetime he was something of an amateur astronomer. Another man had a pair of exquisite ivory-mounted opera glasses. The rest relied on a seaman's sharp sight. This was a four-hour duty. They synchronised their watches. They would be relieved at 0200 hours. The light airs settled salty on their lips.

Each man had provided himself with a thermos of tea and a packet of sandwiches. Ken Poole poured steaming coffee into the cup of his thermos and sharpened it up with a drop of something different from his hip flask. 'Instead of sugar,' he winked at Cyril.

'Swop you sugar for Scotch any day,' but

Cyril's ploy did not work. He unwrapped his corned beef and pickle sandwich, the bread cut thick and the beef cut thin, and turned his attention to the sea once more. Time passed slowly.

'Any news of Simon's friend, the young doc who is a POW?'

'The War Office has come up with an address for him. Simon thinks it's in Poland.'

'Waste of a good doctor.'

'Herbie! What the hell are you doing?'

'Pumping up my leg muscles, Mr Poole. Ready for a sprint.'

'This is an undercover exercise,' hissed Sergeant Poole. 'D'ye want all the spies in Eastport to know what's going on?'

They conversed in low tones. 'You heard they've locked up the green keeper at the bowls club?'

'Flashing messages, they say.'

'I don't doubt there's more like him about. I'd tar and feather the lot of them.'

As the two men made to turn about at the end of their beat a dark form sprang out from a scrub of gorse bushes and they found themselves looking down the barrel of a rifle.

'Halt! Identify yourselves.'

'Sergeant Poole and Private Lewis. Home Guard patrol.' Ken Poole was unruffled. Cyril Lewis's heart had missed a beat.

'Password,' demanded the soldier.

'Green bananas,' and the man put down his weapon. 'Carry on.'

'Wait a minute. What was yesterday's password?' Ken demanded, much to Cyril's admiration. He himself had not thought of checking the soldier.

'If that had been a German we would be dead meat now,' said Ken as they resumed their patrol.

'Scared the pants off me till I saw his uniform,' Cyril was ready to admit.

'You can't always go by the uniform, Lewis. Simon says the Jerries were wearing the uniforms of dead British officers in France, giving false orders, creating chaos.'

Which put Cyril in mind of that poor Dotchin lad who was in a terrible state when he got back from Dunkirk. 'I hear the Dotchin lad and Jacky Whitmore have sailed for the Middle East,' he said.

'With the rest of the Tyne Borderers.'

'Seems a queer time to be sending troops away from home.'

'Suez Canal,' Ken wagged his head sagely. 'With Italy against us now, there's a real threat to Egypt. Got to hang on to the Suez Canal or we lose the Med and all routes beyond.'

'They'll mebbes send my Cathy out there. She's never tired of reminding me that where there are soldiers there must be nurses.'

Despite all the brave show, apprehension was mounting. Waiting for Hitler was what they were doing and the rector was not the only one whose nerves were on edge. Signs and portents of Hitler's intentions were there for all to see. The number of enemy planes over Britain increased daily. Reconnaissance planes at the moment. Bombs had yet to fall but construction of air raid shelters went ahead with all speed.

A stranger walked down the road that led to the sea in Eastport Bay, to the little redbrick school, with its dusty flowerbeds of monkshood and golden rod. He was a stocky, deep-chested fellow and, though he wore no uniform, his gait was enough to identify him as a sailor. Few would have guessed that this was the ne'er-do-well son of Bert Smith from the fish shop – him that ran away to sea, years back, and was never anything but a trial to his poor old ma.

Albert Smith's ship, the corvette *Trumpeter*, was in dock for a refit. Not before time. The wretched cockleshell of a boat had survived explosion and storm in the Atlantic for more voyages than was good for her. She was lying at Pompey now and Smithy had ten days' leave. What had suddenly prompted him to take a look at his old school he didn't rightly know but here he was, peering through the railings at a bunch of little kids who were being addressed by their teacher.

'Now you all know where the air raid shelter is, don't you?' All heads turned to look at the concrete bunker.

What the 'eck have they done with the lavs, thought Smithy.

'And when you hear the siren you don't all rush straight across the playground, do you.

Why not, Billy Purvis?'

'Because a Nazi pilot will see us and kill us.' He was a little fair-haired boy wearing his big brother's pants, by the look of him.

Poor little sod, thought Smithy.

'What do we do, Mary Jenkin?'

'Walk in line by the railing where he can't see us.'

Smithy watched them go through the motions but knew sure as eggs is eggs that as soon as the siren sounded they'd run for their lives, taking the quickest route to the shelter, Nazi pilot or no. It was all a waste of time anyhow. If their luck was out, they'd cop it.

He marvelled at the smallness of the playground. He remembered a big yard where sticky black bubbles of tar appeared in summer and stuck to his knees when he skinned them. He couldn't hide the grin on his face when he remembered how he used to chase the girls, pulling their hair and making them scream. He watched just such another little bastard making a nuisance of himself, another bloody little fool, throwing away the chance to improve himself, to use his brains to get what he wanted out of the big wide world.

An education, as he bitterly realised now, can win an argument better than a pair of fists. His own fists, clenched around the school yard railings, a bunch of knuckles that could break a man's jaw, had got him out of many a tight corner but he recalled the headmaster's words: 'There are plenty of fools in

226

the world who have no brains, Smith. You have a brain. Use it.'

Time and time again, the head had told him that, but he was too bloody daft to listen. If he had taken that man's advice he would be an officer today with a spirit ration and snotties to call him 'sir'.

A man on a ladder holding a pot of paint was covering up the name of the school.

'Hi! You with the paint pot. What d'ye think yer doin', apart from making a bloody mess?'

'Shut yer gob and eff off.'

'That's the name of my old school you're painting out. It's still called Eastport Primary, you know.'

'I know what I'm doin'. I'm confusing the Germans.'

'They won't want to go to school, you silly bugger.' But as he walked back through the town Smithy noticed that the man with the paint pot had been busy at the post office and the Co-op, and had blotted out the signpost to the station. 'Hope I can find me way back to Portsmouth,' he said and sent his poor old dad into a wheezy guffaw.

Bert Smith had never been the same since the Dunkirk trip. In hospital for six weeks with pleurisy after getting wet through in Mac Stronach's old boat, he had never really picked up again and spent most days sitting at the back of the fish shop with a shawl about his shoulders gutting fish.

These preparations against invasion were getting on Albert Smith's nerves, sitting

227

waiting to be clobbered was not his style. After a few days, he wanted out and wished himself back at sea with his mates. There was nothing here in Eastport for him. He took his ma out for a fish and chip supper and a bottle of stout and stood his dad a round or two at The Lobster Pot. And that was it. Nothing else to do unless he volunteered for digging tank traps and that was not the Navy's job.

All the young folk were away in the Forces. Everything pitch dark at night. Shop windows blacked out. Nothing in them, anyway. And at any corner you were liable to get a pitchfork through your guts from an over-excited member of the Home Guard. He stood on the top of a cliff watching a tanker go out of the estuary and wished – and wished – he was on it.

'You don't know what we've had to put up with, son,' his mother said. 'You've been out of it all, away at sea.'

He grinned ruefully but didn't say anything. Out of it all? Torpedoed twice. The second time he had been picked out of the water stiff as a lump of frozen cod. A lot of his mates had gone under. But it was better that his ma didn't know too much about that.

Cathy Lewis's father stood him a beer in the King's Head one night. 'Thought I recognised you, Albert. On leave, are you?'

'My ship is in dock for repairs.'

'Corvette, isn't it?'

Albert Smith nodded, ill at ease with such friendliness from the father of one of the little girls he used to torment. More than once in the old days Cathy's father had threatened him with a good hiding.

Cyril laughed encouragingly, 'No Queen Mary!'

Smithy grinned. 'It's a treat to be in dry clothes.' He wiped the froth from his lips, 'an' it's a treat to be back in a British pub again with a pint of the real stuff. Your health, Mr Lewis.'

'Good luck,' said Cyril and he meant it. The Merchant Navy had done wonders for this lad, he was thinking. Taught him some manners. Not a bad lad at all. A rough diamond, mind you. Wouldn't like to get on the wrong side of him. Neck like a bull. Sharp little eyes, on the lookout for trouble. 'You'll see a difference in your dad,' he suggested. 'He was very poorly for a time.'

'He should have had more sense than to go to Dunkirk at his age,' Smithy said, and added more kindly, 'but I'm pretty proud of the old bugger just the same.'

'We're all proud of him.' Cyril shook his head sadly. 'Dunkirk. Doesn't bear thinking about.'

Smithy pulled out a tin of cigarettes and offered them. Cyril held up a hand, 'I won't smoke yours. They've gone up again. A shilling for ten now.'

'We get a free issue in the Navy,' Albert insisted and flashed his jazzy lighter. 'I don't seem to know anyone in the town now. To tell the truth, I can't wait to get back to sea.'

'Have the other pint and cheer up.'

'My round.' Smithy put his hand in his pocket. 'What's Cathy up to these days? Is she still at Eastport Hospital?'

Cyril Lewis exhaled luxuriously. These were full-size proper cigarettes. 'She's an army nurse. She and her pal, Norah Moffat, are working at a military hospital in Scotland. They were down to go to France with the next lot of troops but that is all off now. A lot of her friends have sailed for Egypt to protect the Suez Canal from Mussolini. Her hospital might be sent out there. Anything could happen.'

Smithy frowned, crinkling up his little eyes. 'What d'ye reckon Mr Lewis? Have we got a fiddler's chance in hell of standing up to Hitler?'

The cheerfulness faded from Cyril Lewis's face. 'We're in a desperate situation, Albert. Make no mistake about it. Churchill says we will fight to the last man and that's about the size of it, but it will be women and children, too, if Hitler invades.'

'And what's to stop him? Nowt much.'

'They say German troop commanders have been issued with maps of Britain.' Cathy's father paused. 'No need to worry the women-folk with that bit of information, Albert.'

On the other side of the Atlantic, the art master at Miss Baxter's College for Young Ladies came seeking Evie. She was always glad to see him. 'Will you not come in for a
230

coffee? Actually, I'm better at tea.'

Politely, he declined. 'I want you to know, Evie, how much I admire your country for standing up to Hitler. The whole civilised world is threatened and, since the US will not commit itself and because I want to help, I am leaving now to enlist in the Canadian Air Force.' He handed her a note. 'This will find me, if you want to write.' It was said off-handedly, almost a dismissal, but he turned his warm smile towards her and that seemed to make her a party to his decision. 'Wish me luck, little English girl ... and *au revoir*.'

Twenty-Four

Before they left England for the Middle East, Cathy and Norah paid a last visit to the hospital to bid goodbye to Hilde. Simon had been transferred to an important plastic surgery unit near Basingstoke for skin grafting. 'He is strong now and wants to fight again, silly man,' said Hilde. Alec and Colin had visited him before he left. Alec, very proud of his wings, was at a base in England, flying Spitfires. 'And now,' Hilde said sadly, 'you, too, will leave me and I will have no friends left.'

Norah and Cathy promised to write, and gave Hilde Andrew's address.

They had embarked on the troopship with their hospital from Liverpool at the end of July, before Hitler launched his attack on the RAF. Having witnessed that force in action, Hitler had postponed any plan to invade Britain until this critical weapon of defence was wiped from the skies. Since then England had been under daily attack from the *Luftwaffe*.

Throughout August and September deadly battles took place over the hayfields of southern England. Blazing planes, both British and German, spiralled down into summery pastures where cattle grazed, plunged into the Channel where vicious flames were finally extinguished along with many an airman's life.

When the troopship finally sidled into the calm waters of Port Suez, the men and women on board were desperate for news of home. Cathy and Norah were two of the army nursing sisters crowding the rails after a voyage of almost two months. Via the Cape. The shorter route using the Mediterranean was out of the question ever since Mussolini had entered the war. Italy's navy was considerable.

On the ship, apart from troops, were armoured vehicles, armaments and a field hospital – all destined as reinforcements for the small British force safeguarding the Suez Canal against a possible Italian attack.

Under the pale gleam of a melon slice moon the ship came to rest at her berth. Shadowy figures on the quay wrapped in flowing burnous made her fast. The night air, soft and spongy, sought to seduce the Englishness of these visitors with smells of cumin, ginger, cinnamon and bad drains. Cathy and Norah looked across the black glittering waters of the Bitter Lakes to a foreign land made more mysterious by night's dark shadows.

'Eric and Jacky are out there somewhere.'

'I wonder if we'll ever meet them.'

The first tanks came swinging out from the holds. The shout went up, 'The mail's on board!'

From the purser's office came a trail of servicemen and women, with envelopes impatiently torn open, seeking a quiet place where they might immerse themselves in news from home.

With sinking heart, Cathy and Norah read of bombs falling in the streets of Eastport, streets they used to cycle along on their way to school.

'The air raid shelter at Riverside, a direct hit. Many people killed.'

'Mrs Daly at the post office, only six weeks off retiring with a pension.'

'Poor, poor Mrs Daly.'

'The paddling pool—'

'And the Trinity Wesleyan church. Cathy, I shouldn't be here. I should be helping my mother. With Dad away at sea she has to manage on her own. Listen to this,' Norah read from her mother's letter.

We go down to the shelter every night, the three of us. The siren goes without fail at eleven o'clock. We play Halma until the children fall asleep or the All Clear sounds. When we come up out of the shelter we never know whether our house will still be standing.

'What's up, Cathy? Is Simon OK?'

'It's Alec.'

'What? What's happened? Cathy, what's happened?'

'Shot down over Kent. A Messerschmitt got his fuel tank.'

'Is he – dead?'

'Severe burns, Simon says. Mainly face and hands. He's in the same hospital as Simon. Park Prewitt. Burns Unit.'

'Sir Harold Gillies. Best plastic surgeon in the country – if that's any comfort.'

'It was only his third mission since he had his wings. Simon says he got the Messerschmitt. His second kill.' Cathy looked up. 'Alec? A killer?'

'Them or us, Cat.'

'Handsome Alec,' Cathy grieved. 'Heart throb of the Upper Sixth.'

'At least he's alive and he's in a first-class Burns Unit.'

'I just can't imagine what hell it must be, to be in a burning plane. All that petrol. Poor, darling Alec.'

'What about Simon?'

'He's OK. The grafts on his shoulder have

taken. He's having physiotherapy every day.' Cathy folded the letter. 'Terribly cut up about Alec. He'd been to see Simon only the week before. Now he's a patient in the same hospital.'

'Nancy is billeted not far away,' Norah suggested, 'near Basingstoke. She'll be able to go and visit them both.'

By the time this news reached Cathy and Norah, Nancy had already paid a visit to the Burns Unit. She was directed to the Day Room where most of the up and walking patients spent their time. Almost without exception, they were air crew, some in uniform, some in pyjamas and dressing-gown. The treadmill of their days was worked out here, from operating theatre to recovery ward, to Day Room and back to the operating theatre. So the dreary days went by as skilful surgeons patched and sewed, excised scar tissue, transplanted whole skin from other parts of the body, repaired torn muscles and, in so doing, released the claw grip of roasted hands. They restored, as far as they were able, an acceptable image so that men could face the world again.

At the door of the Day Room Nancy hesitated, aghast. She had strayed into a world peopled by Hieronymus Bosch characters: men with slugs of fatty yellow flesh, eyelids in the making, above lashless eyes, men with pendant tubes instead of noses, men with no chins sprouting steel aerials, men with no ears.

They looked up from dog-eared magazines, domino and card games, and smiled at the pretty girl in WAAF uniform, but all Nancy saw was a room full of leering freaks. The blood rushed to her face and it was with the greatest effort that she stopped herself from turning back and running away from this nightmarish place.

Alec saw that his girl did not recognise him and held up a hand to guide her. Haltingly, she crossed the floor to where he sat in a wheelchair, an open book on his lap. Certain areas of his face had already received skin grafts and showed livid against untreated burned flesh. No lips. The slit of a mouth suggested cruelty which was not in Alec's nature. The eyes without lashes gave him a clownlike appearance. His hair was straw-coloured stubble and it seemed to Nancy that he still had a burned smell about him.

She tasted bile in her mouth. She could find no resemblance whatsoever to the young man she had loved, and could not bring herself to touch the red claw he extended towards her. Rejected, it dropped to his lap. Shakily, Nancy took a seat beside his wheelchair, unable to think of a single relevant thing to say. A silence had fallen among the other occupants of the room. Card games were suspended for a poignant moment before conversation and activity were vigorously renewed.

Alec's eyes swivelled her way. 'Thank you for coming, Nancy.' Even his voice was different. There was nothing here of the Alec she knew. They had been lovers and planned to marry. She cringed now at the memory and lacked finesse in hiding her feelings. She wanted to leave. She wished she had not come. Romantic, fun-loving Alec was not here in this ... zoo.

Turning his head was difficult. He had to move from the shoulder to look at her. 'I understand,' he said quietly.

She heard the pain in his voice, knew that she should try to comfort him, but could not.

He nodded, accepting this. 'It will get better. Takes time.'

She prepared to leave and this time he did not attempt to touch her. She laid the bunch of black market grapes on the table beside his chair. 'I must go now, Alec. I'll try to come again if I can get transport.' Even as she spoke she knew she would not come again.

Only the red-rimmed watery eyes moved in his expressionless, patchwork face. She walked away with quickening steps. The wise, world-weary eyes of disfigured young men watched her go in a silence that was louder than catcalls.

Oh God, forgive me, she cried within herself, I cannot help it. That is not the Alec I knew. Relief at her escape fought with shame, as she tried to stem the tears of self-reproach. She did not hear the light footsteps behind her until the woman spoke.

'Aren't they a crowd of jokers in there? Did you know that they hold a beauty competition every week? My hubby won it this week with the funniest nose. Good job they can laugh about it, poor sods. Oh my dear!' Hastily, the woman was all concern for Nancy who was crying into her handkerchief. 'You're upset and here's me prattling on. Is this your first visit?'

Nancy could not trust herself to speak. Dumbly, she nodded.

The woman took her arm in a motherly way. 'They look dreadful at first but it gets better after a while. But of course, they'll never again be as you remember them.'

Nancy nodded miserably. 'He was my boyfriend. Now he's a stranger.'

'What you have to keep telling yourself is, it's not the face you fell in love with in the first place. It's the person inside and that person is still inside. My husband was a handsome six-foot warrant officer. See him on the dance floor! All the girls envied me. Now he's got a monkey face and an artificial leg.' She turned suddenly vicious. 'Bloody war. We'd only been married six months. But we women have got to stick with them. If they lose us, what have they got left? And remember too, how they got mashed up. Fighting the bloody Germans! Who for? For us and our families. Never forget that, dear.' They had stopped at the entrance to the hospital. 'Here's my bus. Cheerio, then, and chin up! We'll probably meet again.'

Nancy doubted that very much.

Twenty-Five

Personnel of the newly arrived hospital spent their first night in Egypt as temporary guests of number thirteen General Hospital near Port Suez, later to become known as the 'bed and breakfast' hospital because of its turnover of incoming and outgoing casualties. On the following morning, these temporary guests were taken by truck across the desert to join a hospital already established not far from Cairo.

The sisters here were now used to the desert conditions, having been in their present site ever since Italy declared war on Britain. They had nothing but scorn for the complaints of the newcomers who had yet to adjust to the difficulties of nursing patients in tented wards where the heat was excessive, water was in short supply, and patients, as well as the staff, were plagued with mosquitoes, sandflies, bugs and rats.

Cathy, returning one night to her tent after a visit to the latrines, carrying the advisory stick and torch, complained bitterly. 'I whack them with my stick and I blind them with my torch but still they come. How can I concentrate with these brutes watching me! I'll probably go off sick with chronic constipation. Some heroic war record, that.'

'For God's sake stop whingeing,' said the old hands. 'What d'ye expect. The Savoy?'

After a while, however, the desert showed its own peculiar charms, breathtakingly beautiful dawns of mother-of-pearl skies, blazing sunsets and deep dark velvet night skies scattered with brilliant stars. On these occasions, it was easy to forget sand in the tea, scorpions in boots, the sapping heat and plaguey rats.

There were no battle casualties. The men lying in the wards suffered from dysentery, malaria, sandfly fever and other tropical diseases, but this situation was not expected to remain much longer. A large Italian army was known to be advancing across Libya, heading for Egypt and the Suez Canal.

'Why don't we stop them?' Norah was helping one of the junior surgeons to set up a saline drip for a dehydrated young soldier.

'Luckily for us, they've had to halt to refuel. Lines of communication overstretched. Saved our bacon. We had neither enough men nor tanks to mount an offensive until now.'

'We came out here with a shipload of troops and tanks.' Norah said.

'They're moving up now. We can expect battle casualties at any time. Make the most of your off-duty now, Sister. You may not get any once we go into action.' He slid an appreciative glance at the girl standing there.

In her white uniform and starched head veil she looked cool and beautiful despite the oppressive heat. 'Come with me to Cairo this afternoon and I'll stand you a cream tea at Groppis.' Lieutenant Barsdale had the rubbery face of a comic which was unfortunate for him since he took himself extremely seriously.

More tents were erected within the hospital compound in preparation for expected casualties. The recently arrived hospital was surprised to hear it was being sent to Greece.

'Greece! We thought we were needed here.'

'There are several hospitals here now,' the commanding officer explained, 'an adequate provision for casualties without us. The Italians have invaded Greece from Albania. A small nation under attack from an aggressor. We are duty-bound to go to her aid.'

'Like we did with Czechoslovakia,' whispered Cathy to Norah.

The CO's hearing was acute. 'It is precisely because of that earlier omission, Sister, that we are sending a token force to help Greece and a hospital to serve those troops.'

'It's all academic anyhow,' said Lieutenant Barsdale as the company broke up. 'The Greeks are more than a match for the Italians. We'll probably be back here in time for our show.'

'We always seem to be running away when things get lively,' Norah complained. 'Our parents, as civilians, are facing more danger back home than we are here.'

In the event, Cathy and Norah were soon to have their baptism of fire. The convoy in which their ship sailed had barely left the shelter of Alexandria and the protection of shore batteries when enemy planes attacked. As instructed, the nursing staff remained in their cabins, wearing life belts and tin hats as the ship rocked to a series of explosions. Huge waterspouts battered the portholes at each near miss. The noise was intense as the convoy's anti-aircraft guns flayed the dive-bombing planes. Doors rattled. Crockery crashed. The very bones of the vessel seemed to be shaking apart.

Norah reached out and gripped Cathy's hand.

'I don't like being stuck in a cabin while all this is going on,' Cathy yelled against the noise.

'It'll be worse on deck.'

The attack was short-lived. The damage to their ship was superficial, but another in the convoy suffered heavy casualties and had to turn back to port, listing badly.

'I was just thinking,' said Cathy, 'this is what Quentin had to go through, day after day.'

'We never even got to have that last date with him,' Norah sighed.

Once out of range of enemy planes, the convoy continued on its way undisturbed. This so-called token force was made up of chirpy British Tommies, leathery Australians and rangy New Zealanders. The welfare of these troops would be the sole responsibility of the British hospital until Australian and New Zealand medical units arrived.

As the voyage continued without incident, the atmosphere on board ship lifted and took on a holiday air. There was an out of tune piano in the saloon and a talented pub artist was persuaded to 'tickle the ivories'. Then it was 'Roll out the Barrel', 'Waltzing Matilda' and 'Now is the Hour' until they docked at Piraeus. The last song, before the pianist shut the lid on the beer-spattered, cigarette-burned old upright, was 'We'll Meet Again', sung with sweet mindlessness by all the troops.

Norah composed a letter to Andrew, adding 'By Jove' at the end. 'He may guess where we are from that.'

On disembarking the soldiers marched away to their stations, cheered by a welcoming crowd, and the hospital party climbed aboard the trucks that would take them to their destination, the small town of Kifisia, some twelve miles north of Athens. Three hotels there had been requisitioned for their use with provision for wards and offices. Staff billets were in private houses.

Cats with triangular faces slipped silently into crevices to watch the antics of the new arrivals as smiling black-shawled Greek women showed the nurses to their simple whitewashed apartments, which they themselves had vacated for the comfort of their guests.

Once the equipment was installed, the hospital was functional. Casualties were few and restricted to accidents or infections, and Norah, remembering the battle that was imminent when they left Egypt, reflected that there must surely be a greater need for nurses in Egypt than in Greece at that moment.

The allied troops were to protect the long, meandering Bulgarian front, though no threat was anticipated in that part of the country. The Greeks themselves were well able to deal with the Italian invasion at the Albanian border. Masters of guerrilla warfare in their inhospitable mountains, they proved themselves superior fighters despite the enemy's much greater force, but their sufferings from the intense cold were horrific.

Inadequately clad and with little shelter in extreme weather conditions, they suffered greatly from frostbite. Gangrenous limbs were amputated on the spot with crude surgery and by the time the sufferer was brought down from the mountains, a six-day journey, the wound was in a seriously infected state. They were stoical and brave beyond belief.

The Greek hospitals had scant facilities while the British hospital had a fully equipped operating theatre and X-ray department, a dispensary, several small wards and many empty beds. It seemed reasonable to offer to care for the Greek casualties. The gratitude of the Greek families was overwhelming. At the same time, it was an opportunity for the British nurses to repay the many kindnesses shown to them by the Greek women.

They were not prepared for the alarming physical appearance of their new patients. Black-browed, with piercing eyes and strong, rugged features. Cathy wrote to Simon.

They looked like a band of brigands, especially those from the Cretan division with their luxuriant black moustaches trained to a wild upward sweep. In addition, they were crawling with lice. But after our orderlies bathed them, shaved and disinfected them, they were scarcely recognisable and so delighted with their nice clean beds and Red Cross pyjamas that they roared with laughter. Norah and I have never nursed such truly joyful patients though most of them have lost a leg or an arm – or both – with frostbite. They laugh and sing all the time and you've no idea how happy that makes us, even though we cannot understand a word they say nor can they understand us. But we get the messages across somehow and it doesn't seem to matter if we don't. They trust us.

In many cases, the original surgery for frostbite had been by crude guillotine, leaving no flap of skin to cover the open wound. To tell these men, who had already suffered so much, that a further amputation was necessary before healing could take place was a hateful necessity.

Norah looked over the top of her mask at

the owner of the botched limb she was dressing. He was nodding cheerfully at her, delighted with her attentions. As she wrapped the strong hairy stump of his badly mauled leg in cotton wool and laid it gently on a small pillow, he grabbed her hand and kissed it. 'I felt a complete toad,' she told Cathy. 'My brave Cretan will never trust me again, when he discovers he has to go through that operation all over again.'

The village women, grateful for the care given to their men, brought flowers and sticky sweetmeats in screws of paper for the nurses while tucked in their apron pockets were bottles of retsina, a local wine made stringent with the resin of pine trees – guaranteed to restore their men's virility and, incidentally, strictly forbidden in the hospital by the sober British.

A month passed, a month during which the British hospital did much to help the guerrillas back to health. In their off-duty, Cathy and Norah wandered on the hills behind the little town where wild flowers bloomed even in December and the only sound to interrupt the serenity was the tinkling of goat bells. War seemed far away.

They were delighted to receive, at long last, a card from Andrew in his POW camp, bearing its mouth-gagging definition, KRIEGSE-GEFANGENEN POST. They pored over the small personal insertion permitted between the printed text. 'Dear Norah, I am well. Take good care of yourself. Love Andrew.'

'He's safe, then. I hope he's getting our letters. He doesn't say.'

'He doesn't say much!'

'His dad thinks he's somewhere in Poland.'

From North Africa came good news at last. The allied forces had won a great victory. The Italian army had been driven back along the way they had so recently advanced. Hundreds of prisoners had been taken. Christmas was approaching. Here was something to celebrate at last.

As they decorated the wards with evergreens, the nurses were thinking of their homes in Britain where the merciless bombing of towns and cities continued unabated.

Norah and Cathy kept up a regular correspondence with the friends they had left behind. Some of his old wit was there in Alec's scrawled notes. Their letters, he wrote, saved him from total boredom. Simon was now at an army convalescent depot in Aldershot. 'Retraining,' he wrote.

Evie, they learned from Hilde, was coming home, 'to be mit her father and mother in the air raids. I am hoping she vill come to see me. Maybe bring me a little tin of butter. America is so rich.'

Cathy wrote to her parents for news of Jacky and Eric and in his reply her father told her about Colin.

Colin was still a probationary sub-lieutenant RNVR at the torpedo and mining school at

Portsmouth when he was called to deal with a random parachute mine in the East End of London. The mine, containing 1,000 pounds of explosive, had crashed through the roof of a house and was dangling from the chimney by its parachute canopy.

He picked his way over rubble and came face to face with the landmine, hanging there, quietly waiting for him. He understood what he must do. He had been through the procedure many times with dummy bombs. His hands were steady, though his heart pounded and sweat poured from his brow, stinging his eyes. No hurry, he told himself. Take it easy.

There was a difficulty. He could not shift the fuse. Suddenly without warning the chimney above him crumbled, crashed, dislodged the mine. He heard the whirring mechanism start up. He stumbled, scrambled back over the mounds of rubble. He had twelve seconds to get away. Not enough. That was Colin's first live bomb and his last.

Colin's brother, Alistair, at the scrubbed deal table in his farmhouse kitchen, buried his head in his hands and wept. His young brother, whom he had loved and watched over since he was in short pants, had gone from him for ever. Alistair's conscience belaboured him, beat him about the head with heartless persistence reminding him of the harsh things he wrote on hearing of Colin's decision to join the Navy in what was now his last letter to a most beloved young man.

Twenty-Six

Evie Dobson was glad to be back in England where everything was happening. It was a different world from the one she had just left. Tobruk could be on the moon as far as America was concerned, while people in England danced in the street at the amazing victory in North Africa.

Happy as she was to come home, Evie was loyal to her American hosts. 'They are the most generous people in the world.' She was at pains to spread the word. 'Even society ladies raise hundreds of dollars for Britain, organising garden parties, balls, clothes sales, fêtes. Everybody shells out for the Spitfire Fund, and food parcels for Britain.'

Such glowing praise cut no ice with her father, who couldn't get comfortable in the Anderson shelter at night and was grumpy from lack of sleep. 'Never mind the parcels,' he grunted, 'why don't they get themselves over here and give us a hand! Guns, not butter, is what's wanted. Hitler was right about that.'

'Some of them *are* coming over, Dad. An American friend of mine, a teacher at the school where I worked, has thrown in his job to join the Canadian Air Force. He's based in England now. And he's not the only one.'

'Is he the boyfriend with the big car?' asked her mother.

There had been a dramatic change in mood of the average Briton during Evie's absence. There was energy in place of the apathy she remembered. Everyone, old or young, was intent on helping the war effort in any way possible, be it selling national savings stamps, surrendering pots and pans or digging up their garden railings to make Spitfires, even giving a bed to a bombed-out neighbour whom they had never liked anyhow. 'Dig for Victory' the posters urged and everyone had gone mad on allotments. Evie's own dad, who had never lifted a spade in his life till now, produced enough pallid rhubarb for a pie.

'Don't you know there's a war on?' was the rebuke for anyone who dared to complain on any account, such as lack of offal – 'A lamb's only got two kidneys, madame' – or the late arrival of trains due to enemy action. When the main air raid shelter in Eastport received a direct hit, Evie saw how a common tragedy pulled the people together. Lady Strachar, a well-known local personality, working for the Red Cross, was scarcely recognisable, dirty and dishevelled by the dust of the explosion, sitting on the church steps comforting a distressed old woman who had not taken a bath since the first air raid.

Evie, herself, helped at the Aid Post,

handing out cups of tea, taking messages from wives whose husbands, on their return from work, would not think of looking for them in hospital. Some relatives would have to look in the mortuary.

A man emerging from the ruins of the shelter saw her smudging the tears that ran down her cheeks and laid a comforting arm about her shoulders. Through brimming eyes she saw Cathy Lewis's father, his tin hat and overcoat, even his face, overlaid with a film of grey mortar.

'It's something we all have to get used to, Evie. You're doing a good job.' She watched him grab a stretcher with another man and clamber down over the rubble into the moaning dark and wondered if she could have been a nurse like Cathy and Norah. That, more than teaching youngsters, was such an important profession in wartime. But when Mr Lewis emerged with an injured child on the stretcher, she knew that she had better stick to teaching.

'Come and have a chat with Chrissie,' Cathy's father had said. 'She'll give you the latest news of Cathy and Norah.' So she did.

'It takes that long for letters to reach us that we never get up to date but we do know that they are in Greece.' Chrissie gave her a great welcome. 'They get on well with the Greeks, but Cathy says it's very cold at night. I thought it was always warm in Greece but it seems their winters are cold and there's no heating in their little flat. I've sent Cathy

251

some knitted vests but it'll no doubt be summer before she gets them.' She poured the tea. 'You're looking that bonny, Evie. America seems to have suited you.'

'But I'm glad to be home, Mrs Lewis. I wouldn't have missed the visit to America for anything, but I belong here. They've got so much of everything over there and we have so little, it doesn't seem fair.' She helped herself to a piece of Chrissie's eggless, fatless sponge cake.

Chrissie laughed. 'We save every blessed thing. Paper shortage, so we take our own paper bags for shopping and use them again and again. We save string and jam jars and tins and safety pins. We make one clothes peg do for two on the washing line. When Cyril's shirt collar starts to fray, first I turn it then, when that starts to fray, I make a fresh collar from the tail of his shirt!' She gave a peal of laughter. 'He doesn't like it, mind. He says when the wind is in the east there's a terrible draught up his trousers! Now, just take a look at this,' she opened a pocket-sized women's magazine, 'I'm going to make this for my little granddaughter.' She turned the page to the instructions for making a child's coat from two chamois leathers generally used for cleaning windows. 'If I line it with a piece of blanket it will be nice and warm for her.'

The good-tempered acceptance of these numerous restrictions amazed Evie. Every smear on the wrapping paper of butter or margarine was used. Fuel was precious and must be conserved. Even the King, it was said, had a black line painted around his bathtub marking the regulation five inches of permitted hot water. Everyone bought raffle tickets for the Spitfire Fund and the first prize was a lemon.

She liked this new Britain where neighbour helped neighbour, stranger helped stranger. It was as if the thought 'we are all in this together' was in everyone's mind and it broke down barriers of any sort. Even her mother, who was not given to social work, had volunteered to help at beetle drives organised for the entertainment of the troops stationed in the area.

When the new term began, Evie would be required to report to her old school, now evacuated to the countryside, but until then she joined her mother at the tea urn in the Riverside Ballroom. A blonde twenty-two-year-old with a shapely figure and a ready smile, she was a popular addition to a committee of solid matrons.

The ballroom was full of chaps like Jacky, all a long way from home, in khaki, navy and air-force blue and you couldn't see across the room for cigarette smoke. A private in the pioneer corps bashed out popular tunes on an ancient piano, a natural pianist, every bit as good as Charlie Kunz. Couldn't read a note of music.

With the first bars of 'Smoke Gets In Your Eyes' Evie was back to the dances held there before the war. As she went from table to table handing out score-cards and pencils, she was remembering how she used to swish across this same floor in her diamante slippers to Don Dawson's band, for the military two-step, the tango, the foxtrot and the rhumba. Jacky was great at the foxtrot, sending other couples for cover when he whirled her round the corners. Simon would stomp around like a policeman holding Cathy tight. Andrew and Norah, the handsomest couple on the floor, graceful, elegant ... and now Andrew was a prisoner of war. She had been shocked by the terrible casualties of war. In her own group of friends, first Quentin and now Colin. Gone. Both gone. Never to sing and laugh and dance together again. Evie came back to earth when a too friendly hand slid round her waist.

'Hands off, sailor. I'll tell mother. That's her with the hatpin.' Not that she sat at home moping for Jacky all the time. When boys asked her out, she told them about Jacky, but that didn't stop her having a bit of fun. Well, why not? Jacky couldn't care all that about her or he would write more often.

She arranged to meet Hilde at the Haymarket Café as of old. 'Good to see you again, Hilde. Gee, you look smashing.' Evie's compliment was perfectly sincere. Hilde was now in her third year, one more year to finals. The hang-dog, resentful look had gone. There was an air of confident authority about her which even penetrated the bored inattentiveness of the waitress.

'Please do not keep us waiting,' Hilde instructed and she didn't.

In a small voice, she whispered, 'Such sad things happen, Evie. You know that Colin, the nice Scotch one, is blown up by a mine?'

Evie nodded. 'He was very brave. My mother does the washing for Mrs Rankin. She looks very old now that she has lost her Colin. They were close. She wanted so much for him to be a lawyer.'

'So did Colin.'

'Simon is properly mended now. He was in my ward, you know, with bad wounds, but he is a soldier again and came to say goodbye to me before he went out to North Africa. He is going to look for Cathy.'

'Her mother says Cathy is in Greece.'

'Then he will not find her. Maybe he will meet with Eric and Jacky. I do not get letters from them.'

Evie shrugged. 'Neither do I. Not often. But Jacky wrote to me after the capture of Tobruk. He and Eric were there, at the sharp end. We should be very proud of them. Is Alec still in hospital?'

'He comes home between operations. He has many operations to make a new face.'

'That bad?'

'Simon says that bad.'

'Nancy is stationed not far from Park Prewitt Hospital. I expect she visits him.'

The statement prompted an answer but Hilde merely shrugged. There was an implied significance in Hilde's manner which Evie decided not to pursue. 'An American friend of mine joined the Royal Canadian Air Force. He is over here now and is stationed near Nancy's wing. I gave him her address. He knows no one over here. I hope she will look after him.'

'I think she will.'

Thoughtfully sipping her coffee, Evie made a mental note of the decided unfriendliness of Hilde's tone.

'Eileen is fat officer now,' Hilde continued, 'and knits all the time. Knit, knit, knit, even when drinking tea, making khaki socks for Eric. I think he must be centipede.' Their spontaneous laughter restored the good humour of the meeting.

'I don't know what we will do when you leave the hospital, Hilde. You keep us in touch with each other.' Evie almost added 'those who are left'.

'I do not leave the hospital, so that is all right. Matron asks me to stay as a sister when I pass my finals. I will be here. All the time.' She gave a little laugh. 'Funny, hein? Always I am the outside but now I am the inside. You are all my family instead of cousins I left behind in Chermany.'

Evie warmed to this new approachable Hilde. 'No news of them?'

'In Hitler's Europe there are terrible places where Jews are murdered. I will not see any of my aunts and uncles or cousins or friends ever again.'

Her matter-of-fact tone sent a shiver

through Evie. Risking a rebuff, she leant across and took Hilde's hand in hers.

'It's all right, Evie,' she did not withdraw her hand, 'I have grown harder and stronger. Now, what will you do since you are come home?'

'Back to school. The new term starts next week.'

'I think your school is now headquarters for Home Guard.' Hilde picked up the teapot and refilled the cups.

'The school has been evacuated to Slabridge in the country. I will try to see you whenever I come home.'

Hilde looked genuinely pleased. She had a lovely face, Evie told herself, but it was so much prettier when she smiled. 'And another thing,' Evie added on a sudden impulse, 'on my first weekend off, I will go to Park Prewitt to see Alec.'

'And I,' Hilde said simply, 'will come with you.' They smiled at this amicable agreement. Hilde handed Evie her refilled cup of tea. 'You see I am now very English. I drink tea all day long.'

Evie laughed. 'I never imagined I'd hear you say that.'

Hilde smiled, enjoying her little confession. 'Tell me how you liked America? I envied you so much to go there. Always I wanted to go to America.'

'America astonished me, so big, so rich, and 150 different flavours of ice cream. Lovely clothes in the shops. Nothing old or mended

257

there. Coming home to England, everything looks so shabby.'

'They are not at war, in America.' It was almost a chiding and Evie loved her for it. Was Hilde at last coming round on Britain's side?

Twenty-Seven

1941

Simon was right back on form. One shoulder perhaps not quite 100 per cent yet, but he was working on it. He was glad to be on active service again after his long spell in hospital, and the western desert, where he was now, was a place of intense activity, the scene of recent allied victories. Promoted to Staff Sergeant after his part in the perimeter force at Dunkirk, which also won him a Mention in Dispatches, he was now with a reserve gunnery unit in a relatively quiet location. Allied troops had romped along this road, scooping up Italian prisoners by the hundred, capturing Tobruk and now Benghazi. He was a long way from the frontline but recognised ruefully that he was not quite fit enough for the sharp end.

He had been bitterly disappointed to find that Cathy's hospital was now in Greece. He had hoped to surprise her with a visit. Instead he found that his bird had flown. Returning to his company, dusty and depressed, he was met by his superior officer.

'We're moving on, Staff.' The unit was re-fuelling, mounting equipment on trucks, packing tents. 'Corporal Burt is packing your gear.' One look was enough to tell Lieutenant Charlie Pollard that Simon's trip had been unrewarding. 'No luck?'

'Their hospital moved to Greece two months ago. Thanks for transport, sir.' Putting the disappointment behind him, Simon joined the men in loading the trucks. Their high spirits were infectious. Like them, Simon itched for action. For too long he had worn hospital blues.

The Greek winter was drawing to a close and spring was in the air. Girls in Kifisia put on bright shawls, came out from the dark houses into the white light of the streets, laughing and tossing their black heads whenever the British medical orderlies walked by. Friendships blossomed between a nation which still called its sons after the ancient gods and the Berts and Bills of a newer, less romantic civilisation. Between the army nurses and the village women, in spite of language difficulties, there was a warm relationship.

Guerrilla casualties who occupied most of the hospital beds were noisy, unruly, amazingly cheerful and always gallant. Demetrius, a young peasant boy, had been brought to

Cathy's ward more dead than alive with severe wounds, a lacerated liver, a fractured arm and a botched amputation of his right leg. The nurses shamelessly spoiled him and when, against all odds, he recovered, they were overjoyed. Twelve years old, with a cheeky, bright-eyed face and a mop of black hair, he was totally without self-pity, choosing to look upon his injuries as honourable scars suffered for his native land. There was a happy atmosphere in the wards despite the many disabled men.

Cathy and Norah shared a cell-like room in the village where the high, square window showed sky and distant olive groves. It was spartan accommodation. The primitive wash place was attended by one of the young girls in the village. The only furniture was their tin trunks and camp beds. A hairy rug in glorious reds and blues, their inspired purchase at the local market, blazed defiance at the austere white plastered walls and gave an illusion of warmth. No more than that. There was no heating and the nights were cold. No place for the glamorous black silk nightie Cathy had bought in Port Said. They slept in jerseys over winceyette pyjamas and woollen operation stockings up to the thigh. Since their couches were truly virginal, their nightwear was an unconsidered trifle.

On this fine evening in late February they had just come off duty and were preparing to go down to the village in search of supper and entertainment. Cathy was changing into more comfortable shoes. 'When you think about it,' she said, 'nursing is really a selfish profession. Look at the kick we get when someone as messed up as Demetrius gets better. My little ego is nourished by playing God when, in fact, it was his own fantastic courage which did the trick. He's shouting now for moussaka the way his mother makes it.'

Norah, at the little mirror on the wall, peered through her hair, 'Your modesty is impressive, Cat, but you have to take some credit. You have a certain touch with patients, you know. I don't think you are aware of it. It's something I lack. Oh no,' she forestalled Cathy's protest. 'I don't mean the actual nursing. I'm as good as the next one at that but there's a sort of loving understanding about you that seems to comfort men when they are really up against it. I've seen it. They lean on you. You give them strength, as if you were their sister.' She scrumpled her face to excuse the sententiousness.

Cathy spluttered in astonishment. 'What a load of rubbish you do talk, my dear old thing.'

'Do I? Remember a TB patient called Raymond Webster?'

'I do.'

'You would do well to forget him but my point is, I could do nothing for his depression. You came along and his spirits soared.'

'Much good it did him ... or me. Are you going to sit and gas all night? I'm hungry.

Grab your cape. The wind is chilly.'

The way to the market square was down a flight of wide shallow steps, of easy rise for old folk carrying water from the well and convenient seating for idle cats, old men and hens. On either side, modest houses, square as children's building blocks, all newly whitewashed for the spring, descended in neighbourly disorder, their pink tiled roofs reflecting the fire of the setting sun.

Look inside each dark little entrance and you would see, alongside the cheap print of a holy icon, a framed photograph of Herakles or Kostar or Mattias, complete with bandolier and rifle. There would not be many families here who did not have a man away in the mountains, fighting the Italians.

Little domestic sounds came on the evening air: a woman singing, a child being scolded, the sizzle of frying fish and an invitation from a balalaika somewhere close at hand. Cathy cocked an ear. 'Pericles is in good form.'

Women buying oil and soap and olives and sewing thread in the square called a greeting to the nurses, their bright, cheerful faces giving the lie to their dowdy black garments. Norah had a special smile for the fat old woman who came to the ward every day to collect the patients' washing and left a bundle of figs or an orange for Norah, whom she clearly regarded as a saint. 'What right have the Italians or anyone else to invade this peaceful country?'

'Rights don't come into it. They're all wrongs.'

'Let's come back here, Cat, after the war, and live on figs and honey and music, happy ever after.' Visions of Arcadia filled Norah's dreamy eyes.

'What about our cottage in Scotland or Cornwall?' Cathy was teasing but perhaps Norah was still faithful to the childhood dream? As far as Cathy was concerned, those teenage plans had been left behind with Dornford Yates and Angela Brazil. 'If there is an "after the war",' she said. 'Sometimes I think the War Office has forgotten about us and we'll never go home again. We'll turn into two old ladies dressed in black getting sozzled on retsina every Saturday night.'

'I don't like retsina.'

'Ouzo, then.'

There were two tavernas in the village but the one with the balalaika player was favourite with the hospital staff. Here they could relax at the end of the day, sip ouzo with *metzes* and listen to music until their fish was brought to the table, grilled over charcoal, the crispy crunchy skin scored and basted with lemon juice, the whole redolent of thyme and coriander. Maria would bring it to them with pride. Maria was wife, mother, cook and cleaner, clothed in smiles and dignity.

Men of the village who were not away fighting sat around the walls drinking coffee and raw, red brandy. They would not consider bringing their womenfolk here, but accepted the presence of the QAs with a good enough grace. They had reason to be grateful to the British hospital.

Sometimes they would dance. Sometimes they would not. The hospital staff had learned not to request this treat or it would most certainly be denied them. It was always by a seemingly spontaneous decision that the men would stub out their cigarettes and get to their feet without any reference to the assembled company. Not in any way to be hurried, they would draw themselves up, chest out, chin high with a sniff so charged with intention as to lift their moustaches. Then, in their own time, they would begin their stately performance to the music of the balalaika, just as generations of Greek men had done before.

It was not women's business. A stir was caused, therefore, when, on one occasion, and never again, a sister from the English hospital was invited to join the dance.

Cathy, who loved dancing, had not been able to conceal her longing to join the men on the floor. She could not keep her feet from tapping the beat as she watched from the side, and she accepted with pleasure when Apostolos, the sponge diver, led her into the middle of the room.

Although still a young man he was bent like a hairpin from deep-sea diving with inadequate equipment. 'The bends' was a common enough condition here, yet, awkward and

264

ungainly as he was in his walk, he danced with infinite grace, transformed into a pin-toed elf by the music; attitudes of feet and hands meticulously placed in the manner of tradition.

Aware of the singular honour offered to her, Cathy conscientiously tried to follow his every movement. Critical black eyes watching her so impassively might have awarded her performance a grudging acceptance had she not spoiled her act by an excess of enthusiasm. The mounting pace of stirring eastern rhythms got the better of her common sense. She began to improvise, wheeling, whirling in a western style, laughing with sheer pleasure, and was brought back to earth by Apostolos breaking off the dance. Politely but firmly she was handed back to her seat with a sad little bow.

'Well, you properly ruined that, didn't you.' Lieutenant Barsdale considered that QAs should not make an exhibition of themselves.

'Ach, well,' Cathy answered testily, knowing she had indeed made a proper fool of herself. 'I bet they can't dance a Highland Fling.'

As well as Greek patients there were now some allied soldiers in the Kifisia hospital, suffering from the effects of the cold weather. It had been a hard winter and there were few comforts for troops under canvas. Among the men in Norah's ward was a young Australian suffering from bronchitis. She was present when his officer came to visit him.

'Excuse me, Ma'am.'

She looked up from the injection she was preparing. The visitor was a tanned Australian soldier wearing the definitive shako and the rank of captain.

'I want to tell you, Ma'am, how sorry all of us Aussies feel about the air raids on London,' he spoke with diffidence.

She was surprised and touched by his concern. 'That is kind of you, Captain.' He looked about thirty years of age, standing tall in a loose-limbed, easy way. His eyes, chinks of brilliant blue in a sunburnt face, were set about with tiny wrinkles suggesting that here was a man used to long years of peering into the sun.

'Eight Wren churches destroyed by fire,' he shook his head in disbelief. 'Whole streets of historic places gutted. History will come down hard on the Germans for this.'

'You know London?'

'I was there in '36,' his grin was a white flash against the tan, 'with a guitar and a backpack. The usual growing pains. London bowled me clean out. After my homespun town in the Australian outback, London was something, I can tell you, and now I kinda feel a bit of it belongs to me. I hope your folk are not in London, Sister?'

'No, my home town is in the north of England but since it is a busy port it's getting its share of air raids.' A look of anxiety crept into her eyes. 'Letters from home take so long to reach us.'

266

He seemed in no hurry to go. She picked up the tray of injections. 'Excuse me. I must attend to a patient.' He stepped back, politely touching his hat. As she walked across the room, she was uncomfortably conscious of his eyes upon her back.

He came once more a few days later to tell his batman, the Australian patient in Norah's ward, that the company was moving to a new location and to leave directions for it. Cathy was working in a nearby ward and found him wandering about in one of the passages. 'A tall blonde sister,' he pleaded, 'where can I find her?'

'Who was that gorgeous Australian?' Cathy demanded later of Norah.

'One of his men is in my ward.'

'He wasn't looking for his man when I saw him. He was looking for you. He's taken a shine to you.'

'Don't talk drivel. He just came to say goodbye. Their unit is moving.'

Twenty-Eight

In the spring of 1941 fresh detachments of British and Dominion troops were beginning to arrive in Greece from North Africa. Truck-loads of them rattled through Kifisia heading north, giving rise to much speculation amongst the villagers. When, in March, the trucks were followed by tanks of the 1st Armoured Brigade, a ripple of unease spread through the town.

Apostolos, appointed spokesman, loped after the hospital staff as they left the taverna one evening. 'One moment, please, I ask you something. You think we win this war very soon?'

'Sure thing,' the giant pathologist towered above the little twisted diver. 'Just a matter of time.'

Apostolos's prematurely aged face wrinkled in perplexity. 'Then why more troops come?'

'Just a precaution, old chap. Defence of the border.'

Which border and why? Apostolos would have liked the big doctor to explain further but he had no wish to embarrass by his persistence, so he smiled his 'efharistos' and shuffled away. His young brother, however, was sent without delay to saddle up the mule and take a present to his auntie who lived in Salonika in the north of the country.

'Take care.' Apostolos wrapped the bottle of first press olive oil in straw and packed it in the saddle bag. 'Give greetings to our relative and look about you. Use your eyes and your ears. Where are all these troops going and why. Do not alarm your auntie but tell her if many soldiers gather in Salonika, she must come to stay in our house in Kifisia.'

A month had passed since Captain Keith Russell of the Australian 6th Division, while on a visit to the British hospital at Kifisia, had chanced upon an English nurse with the looks and the demeanour of a madonna. He had not been able to get her out of his mind since then and inwardly cursed his timidity in that encounter. For the first time in his adult life, he had muffed a chance. He was thirty-one years old, a rugged sort of bloke and, if past records were anything to go by, girls did not find him unattractive. Back home he was spoiled for choice. So, why had he not 'followed through', to put it in golfing terms, and made a date? He couldn't rightly say. 'Cat got your tongue?' his mother would have said. She had been trying to marry him off since he left school and would certainly have approved of this one. A cut above the good-time girls he used to take to the picnic races at Gunnedah, that's for sure. Well, too bloody bad. The chances of ever again meeting that

English nurse were nil and he didn't even know her name.

Events soon put all such romantic notions out of his head. His unit was now stationed in Macedonia on the Bulgarian border alongside a Greek division, 350 miles north of Kifisia. For some time he had questioned the thinking behind defending this border when the Italians were attacking through Albania. The explanation was soon made clear when it became known that German troops were massing in large numbers in Bulgaria. Their purpose could only be hostile. When he looked at the map his heart sank. If Hitler meant to invade Greece from Bulgaria – and for what other reason was he concentrating troops there – the task of defending that long, convoluted border with the existing defence force would be well nigh impossible. The hairs pricked on the back of his neck as the awful danger in which Greece now stood revealed itself. Two enemies were at her borders, the Italians in Albania, the Germans in Bulgaria. 'And it's our job to keep them out.'

He studied the map again. There was no possibility of defending the entire length of the Bulgarian frontier in any depth. The allied forces would have to fall back and regroup in a more strategically placed position. The logical move would be to consolidate with Yugoslavian forces at their border which was equally threatened by a German invasion, but *Jesus!* Germany *must* be stopped. If Hitler

270

took possession of Greece, Crete and the Mediterranean would be vulnerable – and the British fleet based there. His mind leapt further, to Egypt and the Canal. Without the watchdog of the Royal Navy what future was there for Egypt and the Canal and for the whole of the Middle East?

What had begun as a minor campaign to support the Greeks against the Italians was turning into a dilemma of unimaginable proportions. With a decisive gesture, he closed the map. If the Germans come, let them come. They would meet face to face, gun to gun, with a well-trained army of Brits, Kiwis, Aussies and Yugoslavs. The Greek division, willing as they were, could not be relied upon. They had been fighting for five months and were tired men.

'We can do it,' he told his company. 'We've got the right men for the job and the guns to do it with.'

The fears of all, including Apostolos and his friends, were realised on 6 April when German troops invaded Greece from Bulgaria. As Captain Russell had anticipated the frontline of the allies was ordered to fall back and reform further west to be in line with the Yugoslavian frontier. What he had not foreseen was that Hitler would invade Yugoslavia and Greece simultaneously. German troops lost no time in exploiting the weak points facing them. Yugoslavia, the hoped-for ally, was overwhelmed.

★　★　★

In what was once the entrance lobby of the Hotel Cecil, a place of brown varnish and bored pot plants, a small crowd had gathered. Daily Orders, pinned to the noticeboard there, generally related to the management of the occupying hospital and dealt with such items as sanitary disposal, missing sheets and other domestic details. Today's orders were causing a stir.

'What's up?' called Cathy from the back of the crowd.

'Our Greek patients have to be transferred to their own hospital.'

'What for?'

Sergeant Major/Wardmaster Rogan, passing by at that moment, obliged with the reason. 'To make room for our own lads, Sister. British casualties expected. Some nasty arguments with the Jerries on the Bulgarian border.'

A sudden distant reverberating explosion startled them all, shook plaster from the ceiling on their heads. The sergeant major disappeared at once to investigate.

Twenty miles away, the *Luftwaffe* was engaged in making the harbour at Piraeus inoperable. They sank thirteen ships there, one of which was the *Clan Fraser*, which was unloading her cargo of ammunition when a German pilot scored a bull's eye. Windows were shattered in Athens. Mothers ran in the streets seeking their children. Men working in the olive groves stopped working to stare in disbelief at the towering column of smoke staining the sky over the port. If Hitler's design was to prevent a Dunkirk-type escape of allied troops from Greece he succeeded brilliantly.

Alarm was clearly written on the faces of the village women who came to bundle up their men's belongings for their transfer to the Greek hospital. Tales of German tanks sweeping over the border had already reached them by the grapevine. Relatives in the north of the country were fleeing their homes and seeking refuge in the mountains. More blood-shed. More widows.

Their menfolk were philosophical about the move to their own hospital but demanded the immediate return of their weapons without which they would not budge. They would fight one-legged or one-armed if need be, but they would fight. Only the shepherd boy, Demetrius, objected to the move. Convinced that he was being transferred because of some misdemeanour he protested loud and long. 'I not want to go,' he screamed. 'I like it here.'

Eventually he was persuaded to join his fellows but, as he was hurried away, lurching on his crutches, he turned to plead with Cathy, 'Mees Sister, I not bad boy. Why you send me away?'

'Please explain to him, Georgio,' Cathy urged one who had a knowledge of English. 'We would keep him if we could.' And, after she had helped the boy into the ambulance, she promised, 'I will come and see you, when all is quiet again.'

With the Greek patients went the often lightsome atmosphere of the wards. Their hearty guffaws and rollicking singing had generated an atmosphere of optimism and hope despite their injuries. All this leaked away with the last transfer. Stale tobacco smoke and a breath of retsina hung over empty, disarranged beds, somebody's pipe, a last-minute urinal and Demetrius's comic under his pillow.

There was no time to waste. The ward must be quickly prepared for British and Commonwealth casualties.

'There's a New Zealand hospital now north of us at Larissa,' Cathy reassured her orderly as, together, they began stripping sheets from the beds. David Jenkins, small, dark and busy, was a park attendant in Swansea in peacetime; butter-fingered not green-fingered when it came to making up beds, as Sister Lewis was never tired of telling him. 'They'll get the first convoys of wounded. We'll be the back-up.'

A quick wipe of the bed frames with disinfectant, a turn of the mattresses then the beds were made again with fresh linen ready for casualties. When the first ambulance drew up at the doors of the Hotel Cecil the wards were ready.

More ambulances were to come trundling over the brow of the hill in the next few days. The casualties told of confusion at the front, of heavy fighting, of the enemy's supremacy in tanks and planes, of losing ground, giving way. The trickle of ambulances turned into an uninterrupted convoy.

'What on earth is going on?' gasped Cathy as she eased the boots from a new arrival.

'The Yugoslavs have packed it in,' the weary soldier told her. 'German troops are pouring in from all sides.'

When all the beds, and spaces for beds at the hotel were occupied, tents were erected in the grounds to serve as extra wards. Cathy was in charge of one of these tented wards with an orderly to help her, Norah in another. Conditions were far from ideal there. There was no running water. Washbowls, bed pans and urinals, and drinking water all had to be carried to and from the hotel. This made hard work of bathing injured men who came with the grime of several days upon their bodies.

Casualties continued to increase in numbers. Ambulance drivers arriving at the hospital stayed only long enough to put the stretchers down in the nearest empty space before returning to the frontlines to pick up more casualties. Sweating stretcher-bearers, panting with fatigue, carried them into the rapidly filling wards. There they were laid on the tarpaulin floor of the tents until beds were freed by evacuation or death of the occupant.

Cathy's orderly brought a mug of tea to the makeshift desk where she was entering name, rank and number of the latest admissions, 'I thought there was a hospital up front of us now, Sister? At Larissa?'

'It must be full.'

The entire staff of the Kifisia hospital was now called upon to help the nurses. The QA home sister, with the aid of Greek kitchen maids, made huge jugs of soup and carried it to the men under the sheltering trees who were waiting their turn to be admitted. Many had not eaten a square meal for days. The matron rolled up her sleeves and helped to lay out the dead before undertaking that most harrowing duty, the letter to families.

As each formation of enemy planes flew unchallenged over the hospital, the same thought was in the minds of all. Would the pilots respect the bold red crosses painted on the roofs and slung over the tents.

'They're bombing the ports,' David Jenkins informed Cathy. 'How are we going to get the wounded away?'

'Why aren't there any of our planes up there?' Cathy demanded of a young airman who had broken both legs on baling out of a stricken plane.

'First thing Jerry did was to shoot up any kites on the ground,' he explained wearily. 'We only had seven squadrons to begin with and we've lost most of those now. He's got the whole show going his way, on the ground as well as in the air.' Like most of the new arrivals he was totally dispirited. He was spread out like a spatchcocked chicken with both legs in traction. 'Could you ease the left splint, Sister? It's digging into my groin.'

As she adjusted the splint, Cathy was

remembering the young airmen who, until recently, were based at a nearby airfield. The nurses had been invited to their Christmas party in an old Nissen hut. This lad with broken legs might have been one of the dancers. 'What about the rest of your crew?' she asked. 'Did they get out?'

He said, no, they had not. (Memories of Alec.)

So, thought Cathy, if we have no planes and the ports are being bombed how *do* we get these boys to safety?

The sound of the guns, distant until now, grew louder. Still wearing his theatre gown, one of the surgeons, a clever young fellow from a family of surgeons, came seeking Cathy. 'We are to evacuate casualties twenty-four hours after operation,' he told her.

Cathy's brows came down. 'Twenty-four hours! They won't be fit enough.'

'Those are the orders, whether we like them or not.'

'Where are they going?'

'By sea to Alex.'

'The Germans are bombing the ports.'

He ignored this. 'I'll write up each man for morphia before he goes. Twenty-four hours,' he emphasised, 'OK? Except abdominals, of course. Got to give them a little longer...' his voice trailed away, 'If we can.' The outlook for men with abdominal wounds was unpredictable.

'What's happening at Larissa?' Cathy asked.' I thought a New Zealand hospital was operating there, but we seem to be getting all the casualties direct from the firing line.' She poured a mug of tea for the tired young man.

He nodded. 'The Kiwis had to scramble, fast. They were able to operate for only two weeks. At the moment we are the only military hospital functioning in Greece.'

That was a chilling thought 'Isn't there an Australian hospital somewhere?' Cathy asked.

'With no gear. That was sunk – or maybe never left Egypt. Anyhow, it never arrived. There is supposed to be another Aussie hospital on the way.' He drained his cup. 'It had better be quick.'

At last Cathy saw how nakedly dreadful the situation had become.

'All right, Cathy?' he suddenly smiled at her worried face. 'Just do your best. That is all that any of us can do.'

Twenty-Nine

The allies regrouped again, further south, at Thermopylae. 'Miracles,' said Cathy's orderly, 'seldom happen twice in the same place.' David Jenkins was a bookish young man.

The entire staff of the hospital was stretched to the limit, medical, clerical, catering and

278

sanitation. Sergeant Major Rogan was much in evidence, handling stretchers, giving out urinals, preparing men for evacuation. They were to be taken by truck on a far from comfortable journey along the winding coastal road, hopefully to rendezvous with a rescue ship. By his casual air of bonhomie, as he helped injured men, the sergeant major kept the lid on any tendency to panic yet it was obvious to everyone that the situation was desperate.

Only the necessary cleaning periods interrupted operations in the two theatres. No sheets now on the beds. No time. No laundry. The men were made as comfortable as possible between grey army blankets. New arrivals, seriously wounded as they were and in great discomfort, were amazed to find British nurses still working there. 'You girls should get the hell out of here. Jerry's not far away. You're not safe.' But, as yet, there was no plan to evacuate the nurses and the work went on.

The staff grabbed snatches of sleep and faced each new day with as much resolution as they could muster. Transfusions, operations, injections, dressing of wounds. And young men dying. The noxious humours of war's degradation lay thick on the air about them as they worked. They did not dwell on what lay ahead for the helpless men under their care. The present was all that they could cope with. 'Do your best,' the young doctor had said to Cathy. There was no more that anyone could do. The medical officers were now wearing revolvers.

'Do you know how many patients we have at the moment?' Cathy demanded of her totally unfazed orderly. '1,300 at the last count.' She could have added, 'And the numbers are growing with every day that passes.'

There was a measure of relief for the British hospital when the long-awaited Australian hospital arrived and opened up near the town of Daphne. Australian wounded brought to Kifisia could now be passed on, delaying only for a hot meal and a change of dressings. After treatment at Daphne, they would join the long, long trail of trucks winding down to the ports.

'Where are they taking me, Sister?' Cathy was preparing a young soldier of nineteen for evacuation. He had the torso of a gymnast from the pelvis up and nothing but two stumps below. Did he, this young son or some mother somewhere in Britain, look at her and begrudge her her legs? The unfairness of war bore painfully into her consciousness with the drive of a screw. What had he done to deserve this butchery? That is all that it was, butchery. Slicing off a young man's legs. What kind of civilisation was this?

'Crete or Alex,' she answered and bent her head as tears blurred her vision. Pity was the last thing this soldier wanted. 'You will be able to rest there and get your strength back before you go home.'

He took her word for it, being beyond all

decision-making himself. All such things as commands, patrols, storming an enemy position, helping a mate, cleaning his boots – especially cleaning his boots – all that was finished with. He had shed all that with his legs. Cathy gave him a quarter-grain of morphia and he was at peace.

Norah was now in charge of wounded German prisoners in a tent set aside from the rest of the hospital, at the top of a hill. She had one orderly to assist her and a guard on duty outside the tent. Every day brought more German casualties.

'They are in high spirits,' she told Cathy, 'even the very badly wounded amongst them. They know their comrades are not far away and that they will soon be released.'

'What sort of men are they?'

'The ordinary soldier is all right, grateful for any treatment. The SS officers are rude and arrogant, but I don't stand for any nonsense from them.'

Cathy smiled. She could imagine.

'They need me to dress their wounds, relieve their pain, feed them, so they do what I say.' She allowed herself the hint of a smile, 'I enjoy cutting them down to size, especially those jackbooted officers. I really almost hate them but' – she pulled a face – 'some of them are seriously wounded, you know, so...' A shrug.

'It has been reported,' said the matron, 'that German parachutists are being dropped behind our lines wearing British uniforms. In case we should be challenged by our own men, we are requested to learn a different password each day and to pin a different emblem on our uniforms.'

Cathy exploded quietly. 'That I must see! A Gauleiter dressed up as a QA. Queen Mary won't like it.'

'It's not funny, Lewis.'

The next announcement came from the Greek government. Grateful as it was for the initial support of British and Dominion troops it now requested them to leave in order to save the land from further destruction. Towns and villages, tidy homesteads, olive groves and orchards, tobacco and cotton plantations, mules in the marketplace and goats in the hills were being blasted by bombs. The livelihood of the people was being destroyed and the countryside despoiled before their eyes. The Greek government decided that the time had come to call a halt to the fighting, to surrender before nothing was left of Greece but scorched earth and starving peasants.

To retreat, to pull back all the British, New Zealand and Australian troops and their wounded, to evacuate them to Crete before they could become prisoners was a daunting and dangerous task, likely to be costly in lives. Even a blindfolded Stuka pilot could scarcely miss the target of long lines of trucks making for the ports and the rescue ships waiting offshore were as vulnerable as sitting ducks. Nevertheless, the chance of escape must be grasped and was grimly undertaken.

All except men too ill to be moved were sent on their way, along with one half of the medical officers and orderlies and twelve of the older nursing sisters. Cathy's staunch Methodist orderly was one of those detailed to go with the patients. 'I'm staying, Sister,' he announced firmly, 'as long as you are.'

'You've got to go, Jenkins.'

'Not without you.' But he had to go in the end, reluctantly.

They were to head south for Megara Bay where, it was said, a naval destroyer awaited them.

Cathy shook him by the hand. 'You have been a wonderful support to me, Jenkins. Even if we never meet again I will never forget your kindness to the wounded. Goodbye and good luck.'

'You'll never manage.'

'Probably not.' Oh, very probably not, she thought, as she waved goodbye to those who were leaving. More wounded, fewer helpers. She had only one pair of hands.

The matron, who was staying, made sure that all who remained were fully aware of the gravity of the situation. 'We have to face the fact that the rest of us may not get away.' She was older than any of them. She could have left but she chose not to do so.

Casualties continued to arrive, to be operated upon, fed, washed and sent on their way by any means available. One such truck, loaded with post-operative patients, was bombed

283

soon after it left the hospital. Most of those on board were killed. Some were brought back to the hospital for further operations.

'Is Sister Lewis here?' said one.

Cathy had dressed his abdominal wound not half an hour earlier. Now both eyes were covered by a field dressing. She helped him back into bed.

'Sorry to be such a bloody nuisance.'

Every day was like this, full of tragedy. Every night, Cathy and Norah fell into bed, weary beyond words. The present situation seemed so devoid of hope that Cathy took to saying her prayers again, a habit long discarded. Too embarrassed to go down on her knees in Norah's presence, she sought privacy under the sheets. She prayed for everyone, for the family at home, the boys in the services, for Andrew in his Oflag, for all the lost boys and girls who grew up into a world at war. She finished with, 'and if Thee can' – that didn't scan very well – 'please look after Norah and me.' Had she looked across at Norah's camp bed she would have seen her head also, emerging from the sheets.

When the increasing sound of gunfire could no longer be ignored the commanding officer of the hospital made a tour of the wards. 'I want you all to keep calm,' he urged, but the nurses did not even lift their heads, too busy for any pep talk.

They wondered sometimes if they would ever see their families again. Thoughts went back to those carefree peacetime days which might never come again. When Cathy allowed herself this sad indulgence, the memory of a Guards officer with the looks of Rupert Brooke and the lungs of a dying man flickered through her mind. Long, long ago, it seemed, in another world, away from guns and slaughter, she had loved a man as she would never love another. She could recall the warmth of pleasure which would flood her whole being when she was with him, the pain when he left. She could never forget him.

On Norah's conscience was the image of her mother coping with air raids, rationing and two school children, knowing that her husband in the engine room of an oil tanker faced a terrible death every day that he was at sea. Bitterly Norah blamed herself for volunteering to nurse abroad when she was needed at home, though heaven knows, she wa. needed here in Kifisia right now.

Another hundred German wounded arrived.

Sergeant Major Rogan put up the necessary extension tent himself in a furious temper because he and the rest of the warrant officers had received their movement orders. They were to leave within the hour with most of the remaining senior officers. That he should be leaving while there were as yet no plans to evacuate the nurses drove the sergeant major to barely controlled anger.

Norah and Cathy were breakfasting on

tinned bacon, bread and marmalade when the fresh intake was announced. Norah was in despair. 'There are not enough blankets, or washbowls or cutlery. They have to eat their food with their fingers.'

'Too bad!' Cathy grunted. 'My heart bleeds.'

'And I have had to show some of those who are not too badly injured how to dress the wounds of their comrades. I cannot get around them all. They know that most of the hospital staff have already left and they've promised me all kinds of things: silk stockings, perfume, even a holiday in Vienna after the war if only I will stay and look after them.'

' "After the war",' Cathy repeated. 'And what will that be like? Beyond any imagining. I wonder what will become of us, Norah.'

'Funny if we end up as POWs like poor old Andrew.'

Cathy flashed furiously. 'Shut up, Moffat! We're not going to be taken prisoner by any damned German even if we have to swim to Crete.'

'Oh, keep your wool on, Cathy.' Wearily, Norah pushed back her chair. 'Come on. I've got to go and keep order up there. Actually there is one officer who really tries to be helpful. Not SS, of course.'

As she climbed the hill she saw at once that something was missing. The guard was no longer on duty outside the tent. Then her orderly was dispatched and she was alone with over a hundred German prisoners who knew that very soon the present captor/captive role would be reversed.

She sought advice from the matron. 'Some of the POWs are in great pain, Matron, and no medical officer has been up the hill for some time. I have had to give morphia at my own discretion.'

The matron understood very well the strain that all the nurses were working under. 'The few medical officers who remain are working in the theatres with scarcely a break, Sister. Use your own judgement. Give morphia where it is necessary. I chose you for this difficult duty as I knew you would deal with it better than any of us. You will do whatever has to be done and I will see that a medical officer comes to you in the event of a serious emergency.'

The gunfire, which had become an accustomed background, suddenly ceased. The ensuing silence fell with the authority of a clap of thunder, the finality of doom. Its message registered at once on the face of each helpless casualty. The defenders had left and taken their guns with them.

At this dramatic moment, when it seemed that the nurses were to be left to fend for themselves, a relief team appeared. Sisters of Mercy from the convent in Kifisia, accompanied by Greek nurses, presented themselves to take over the care of the British wounded and allow the QAs to escape.

'You looked after our men when they needed help. Now it is our turn to look after yours.' They took charge at once, embraced the English nurses with tears in their eyes and wished them Godspeed.

'It's all right,' a soldier called out on seeing doubts on the faces of the British nurses. 'You've got to go. And quick. While you've got the chance.'

But Cathy cringed before the despair in their eyes. At the last moment she hesitated. Every instinct called out to her that she should stay with them but the matron was calling her. 'Come quickly, Sister Lewis. These are our orders. Only one small suitcase allowed. Pick up some rations from the mess. Transport is waiting.'

She let go the hand of a man who would not survive, but turned once more at the exit to take a last look at the tent in which she had witnessed so much pain, bravery but also light-hearted companionship. Here stood the beds, jammed close together, stretchers touching on the ground, the drip stands and bottles of blood and saline, the oxygen cylinders and the helpless, hopeless men, the fractured spines, the burns, the men with stomach wounds on continuous gastric lavage – what would happen to them? Someone raised a hand, 'Good luck, Sister, and thanks.'

Fighting back the tears, she hurried to the mess, stumbling clumsily over the guy ropes in her distress. She went to bid farewell to the few medical officers who would be staying with the patients. It was a sad parting. The medical team had worked well together but

288

this was the end of the road. Their surrender-ed revolvers lay on the table in front of them. There was nothing to say but goodbye.

Then she went looking for Norah. 'She's gone back up the hill to her POWs,' someone offered.

'Surely to God she doesn't want to bid them a fond farewell,' groused the anaesthetist who had insisted upon staying behind, though his extra years would do him no good in a POW camp. As Cathy set off to find Norah, a shadow slipped like a wraith, a curiously crooked shape, along the walls of the tent. No one but she saw him snatch one of the revolvers from the table and disappear whence he had come.

'Apostolos,' she found him outside, 'be careful. If they find that on you when they come...'

'No worry, Seester. I not afraid to die but I take one German with me.'

Captain Keith Russell could scarcely be-lieve his eyes when he saw the British Military Hospital still functioning at Kifisia. A week ago he had driven past the burnt-out remains of the Larissa hospital. Caught in the Ger-man advance, there had been no time for that unit to pack equipment. All was destroyed. He had assumed that the Kifisia hospital would have packed up and left long since and he was astonished to find it still operating. He and his men were making for the ports, like all the other vehicles on the road, but, on catching a glimpse of an army nursing sister in one of the tents at Kifisia, he called a halt and leapt from the truck.

'Find the cookhouse,' he yelled to his men, 'and get yourselves some tucker. You've got ten minutes.'

He ran to the tent where he had first met the English nurse and found only Greek nuns there. Perhaps they had got away? 'English Sisters?' he bawled. He was a frightening sight. A bloodied field dressing was soaking through the torn sleeve of his shirt. His eyes, red-rimmed with lack of sleep, burned with fierce urgency. The nuns pointed him towards the mess where he found the padre on his knees. Rudely, he interrupted, 'The blonde sister, Padre?'

The padre's sad and gentle smile was ice to the Australian's fire. 'With the POWs in the tent on the hill. Please bring her down. The Sisters' transport is about to leave.'

Cathy had raced up the hill, arriving out of breath at the POW tent to find Norah giving a last injection of morphia to those who desperately needed it.

'Quickly, Norah We've got to go.'

The men lying there in the hated uniform of the enemy turned sharp eyes to Cathy, alert to the signs even if they could not understand the words. A German officer rose from his knees at the side of a sick man, and, with the feeding cup still in his hand, he came to a heel-clicking salute in front of Norah. There was respect and gratitude in his eyes. 'Mille

290

danke, Schwester. Wiedersehn.'

The Australian soldier burst into the tent. 'Never mind the bloody Krauts!' He grabbed Norah and Cathy by the wrist. 'Get out of this place. Quick!' he yelled and pulled them down the hill at such a rate that they could scarcely keep their feet. Not for a moment did they connect this wild and bloodstained soldier with the spruce Australian captain of some weeks previously.

Their transport was waiting, engine running. 'The bastards are only ten miles away,' he shouted at the nurses already seated in the truck. 'You women should have left weeks ago.'

Hands stretched down to help the latecomers over the tailboard. Cathy turned to help Norah and stopped in amazement. The Australian held Norah in a fierce embrace.

'Tell me your name. Quick.'

'Norah Moffat.' She seemed too stunned to protest.

'Norah Moffat. If I get out of this alive I will find you and take you to my home.'

'Sister Moffat!' From the back of the truck came the matron's indignant screech. 'This is neither the time nor the place.' Her position was weighing heavily upon her. She was responsible for twenty-five young women, who might at any moment be surrounded by lusting Germans.

Norah broke away from the Australian and climbed on board. 'Sorry, Matron.'

Curious, half-amused glances came her way

291

from the rest of the nurses. 'Cutting it fine, you two. Where did you find your ardent Romeo, Moffat?'

And Cathy smiled. Here was one who had raided the citadel. Trust an Aussie.

The truck was at once on the move. The driver had an appointment with a ship and wanted no more hanging about while nurses kissed Krauts and Aussies goodbye.

The Australian in question stood in the middle of the road with a small group of Greek men and women, Apostolos and Maria from the taverna and the old woman who did the laundry, and Pericles who played the balalaika. Would he play for the Germans? And Demetrius, Demetrius in tears. All waving farewell.

'Goodbye Demetrius,' Cathy shouted. 'Goodbye.'

The Australian stood watching until the truck was lost to view, as it turned round a bend in the road.

'Your friend had better get moving, Moffat, or he'll end up in the bag.'

Amongst the nurses sitting on jerry cans and overcoats in the bumping, rattling truck, conversation wilted and died. Thoughts of the men they had left behind lay leaden in their minds. 'We deserted them, didn't we?'

'If we had been ordered to stay,' said the matron, to quieten her own conscience as well as the guilty feelings of her nurses, 'we would have done so. But we were ordered to leave.'

Thirty

Tucked away in the village of Slabridge in rural Northumberland was Evie Dobson's school, housed in temporary wooden huts. The pupils, evacuated from Eastport at the beginning of the war, were now able to tell a bull from a cow, a thrush from a blackbird, but remained unreconciled to the countryside because of the dearth of fish and chip shops. Evie read them improving literature, and taught then how to spell.

She shared Sunday duty with young Mr Brown, the geography teacher. There was another Mr Brown on the staff, very much older and no joy in him because of his sciatica. He taught mathematics and, because of his aches and pains, was excused from Sunday duty. So, on alternate Sundays, Evie, with considerable ill will, was required to organise some sort of recreation for her evacuees. Young Mr Brown put her to shame. He was so enthusiastic about bringing the joys of the countryside to his 'rural heathens', as he called children from city slums. He was nice, young Mr Brown, and he wasn't married.

Once a month she used her free Sunday to go home to Eastport and each time she saw fresh destruction caused by air raids and heard of new casualties. The station goods yard suffered a direct hit and burned for days. The firefighters, all of them volunteers, had not been able to control the huge blaze and three of them perished. Only the walls remained of her auntie's house in Beach Parade. You could see her lavatory still stuck against an upstairs wall, festooned with streamers of wallpaper. Evie turned her eyes away from such exposure. Her auntie was a nice, refined little lady and it seemed a gross liberty to stare at her lav. Fortunately she had been away at the time of the bomb, staying with her brother who was a pitman. She had gone to look after him when his wife was poorly.

'You see,' said Evie's mother, who rarely did anyone a good turn, 'goodness gets its own reward.'

Then Evie went to call on Jackie's mother for news but there had been none for weeks. Mrs Whitmore's tea was as weak as water for she used the tea leaves twice over because of rationing.

'I thought *you* would have news, Evie.' Mrs Whitmore didn't like Evie. 'He'd write to you sooner than write to his mother.' She could make tears as easy as winking. 'Lads never think of their mothers back home, worrying themselves to death about them.'

'He's not much good at letter writing,' Evie

admitted, 'but, mind you, they are having a hard time in the desert by all accounts. I don't suppose there's much spare time for any of them.'

Mr and Mrs Dotchin were very pleased to see her. They had just received a few lines from Eric written in haste – 'because they were on the move again'.

'And we all know which way they are going,' Mr Dotchin added grimly. 'This German general Rommel is giving them stick. Different cup of tea altogether from the Eyeties.'

'At any rate, we were glad to know that he and Jacky are still together but he doesn't seem to know where Simon is, except that he's been made an officer.'

'Good for him!' Evie was delighted.

Mr Dotchin nodded. He had always thought Simon a cut above the other lads. Chaps like Jacky Whitmore, for instance, would never make an officer. Never in a month of Sundays. The Scottish lad was different. All the makings of a good officer, blown to kingdom come. 'Simon is a lieutenant now. According to his dad, he took charge when his superior officer was wounded. Got the platoon and its guns out of a nasty scrape.'

'And there's us thinking he'd be a crock for the rest of his life after that awful wound.'

'Not Simon,' Mr Dotchin asserted stoutly. 'Simon's got guts and his dad has a good right to be proud of him.'

'I don't suppose,' Mrs Dotchin suggested a little uncertainly, 'you have any news of Cathy and Norah?' She was one of nature's second-in-command ladies. Dad didn't admire pushy ones.

'Not for some time. Hilde might have heard from them.'

'Cyril Lewis is worried out of his mind,' Mr Dotchin said gravely. 'He believes the girls are still in Greece and no one seems to know what's going on there since the Germans went in.'

'Like North Africa,' said Evie. 'Same story since the Germans joined in.'

'But they'll surely look after the nurses,' Mrs Dotchin said comfortably.

'Surely,' said Evie, but she wasn't sure. 'Hilde may have news of Andrew, too. He writes to her.'

'Such a nice young man,' Mrs Dotchin sighed. 'But at least he's safe there.'

'He'll not get fat on the rations, Doris, as you well know.' Mr Dotchin had been a POW himself for a short time at the end of the 14–18 war and remembered cabbage soup and black bread.

It was visiting day at the hospital. Little groups of friends and relations pattered along the corridors carrying bunches of flowers, clean pyjamas wrapped in brown paper and the sacrificial precious egg, a week's ration for one person, carefully inscribed with the patient's name with an indelible pencil. All patients' eggs went into the pan together to be boiled for the regulation four minutes, and relatives who had been to some trouble to obtain a farm egg of high pedigree for their loved one were loath to have it confused with a common grocer's egg.

The visitors spoke in undertones and shushed the children. Hospitals were terrible places and you musn't make a noise. The overpowering smell of disinfectant increased the apprehensive atmosphere. Evie stopped a nurse hurrying by. 'Can you tell me which ward Nurse Müllerman is on?' and she was relieved to find, after steeling herself to face diseased old people with suspect tubes and bottles, that it was the children's ward. Children would be all right.

Hilde was surprised and, what was more, *pleased* to see her. A senior nurse now in her last year of training, she was in charge of the ward that afternoon. 'Look, Evie, can you vait a little while? I come off duty in half an hour, then I take you to my room. Come talk to Billy while I work.'

Billy was eight years old. He had been helping out at the chip shop when his arm was caught in the potato-slicing machine. Plastered and splinted in a position at right angles to his chest, his arm smelt appallingly of pus.

'It's called an aeroplane splint,' he explained to Evie and described a zooming action, missing the top of his locker by inches.

'*Oh*! Do be careful!'

It was a trick which never failed to scare people, especially girls.

'How long have you been in hospital, Billy?'

'Two months.'

Evie was horrified. 'What about schooling? Do you have any lessons?'

'Nah! I work. I help the nurses. I can change a nappy with one hand, if the sister's not on duty. She wouldn't half go her ends if she knew.' He enjoyed a private giggle, then a sudden look of suspicion crossed his little old face. 'You won't let on, will you?'

Evie pledged secrecy. She took Billy's one good hand in hers. It was a small, working hand with nails bitten to the quick. His pinched face was pale as parchment, his eyes huge and wise with the knowledge of what the world can do if you don't look to yourself. 'I'll be your visitor for today.'

'We're not allowed visitors.'

'Why ever not?'

'Cos all the kids would start bawling, the sister says, when their ma goes back home.'

'I'll scoot before the sister comes.' As she watched Hilde go from cot to cot, changing wet sheets, doling out spoonfuls of Syrup of Figs, checking dressings, Evie's feelings that she could never be a nurse were confirmed.

There were babies here with little arms splinted, so they could not scratch infected sores. And burned little girls who had stood too near the fire in their flannelette nighties. And wasted little bodies with tubercular lesions which would never heal. And the pale silent toddlers grieving for mothers who had so inexplicably deserted them. She was glad when six o'clock came and Hilde signalled her to wait outside.

Hilde's bedroom in the nurses' home was as comfortable as she was allowed to make it. A small basket chair with cushions, a bedside table, a lamp and the portable gramophone donated by Cathy. Among the regulation seventeen objects permitted on the dressing-table were photographs of her family, a dignified father and mother and a pretty smiling sister.

This was Hilde's substitute for a home. Other nurses regarded their bedrooms as temporary refuges. They all had homes to go to but this plain, pea-green room was all Hilde had. She was permitted to visit her parents and sister in the Isle of Man when she could save up the fare. Her own freedom from internment was due to her employment. Nurses were in short supply. She poured tea from a small teapot of blue Spode into matching cups. No tooth mugs for her.

'Have you any news of Cathy and Norah, Hilde?'

Hilde shook her head. 'No letters. No news. Not of Eric, nor Jacky but good news of Simon in the desert. You know about him? And Andrew writes little cards with not many words. Eileen is a lady captain and Nancy does not like me, so she does not write. No letters from Alec.'

'Do you still want to come with me to visit

Alec?'

Hilde nodded. 'Of course. As soon as the line is repaired.'

'And before the *Luftwaffe* has time to bomb it again. But right now we're worried about Norah and Cathy. Mr Lewis thinks they're still in Greece.'

Hilde nodded vigorously. 'I think so too.'

'And there is a lot of fighting going on there.'

'I think the nurses will be safe. Faraway from fighting. Maybe soon we get some letters. Hein?' Hilde the comforter. This was a new role. 'Now tell me of your school. You like Slabridge, Evie?'

At that moment Evie had the splendid idea of inviting Hilde to stay with her in Slabridge and wondered why she had not thought of this before. 'Would you like to, Hilde? On your next day off? It's an hour on the train from Eastport. I get board and lodgings in the village and I'm sure Mrs Martin would be able to put you up as well.'

Hilde was totally charmed by the village of Slabridge and the surrounding countryside. Wild flowers on the roadside, trout in the river and deer nibbling at the fringe of woods. 'I did not know that England could be so *schön*.' Her enjoyment was so plain to see that the people in the village took a liking to the German girl who was staying with the teacher. After all, the Germans could not all be bad.

300

Evie pointed out the village hall, a wooden building with a corrugated iron roof and a gun from the Crimean War mounted outside. 'There's a hop in there tonight. Would you like to go?'

'Hop?'

'Dance. Not much choice of partners. Most of the men are away in the forces except the farmers and men with flat feet or piles.'

'Piles?'

'Haemorrhoids.'

It was good to hear her laugh outright and see her black eyes light up with amusement, 'Haemorrhoids! I tink no man want to dance mit haemorrhoids!'

And then a totally unexpected dancing partner turned up at Mrs Martin's private guest house. He carried with him the letter Evie had written months earlier.

'How did you find me!' Surprised and delighted, Evie greeted Hugh Greenway, the ex-art master from Miss Baxter's School for Girls in New England.

'The young lady in the store pointed me in this direction.'

'Bring him into the sitting-room.' Mrs Martin dropped the lace curtain and plumped up the cushions. She never could resist an airman's uniform. 'I'll put the kettle on.'

Evie sat him down on a squeaky Lloyd Loom chair amongst the pot plants, paper flowers and pre-war souvenirs from Whitby. 'This is Hilde. I mentioned her in my letter to you. She's a nurse.'

Even in a tweed skirt and cardigan Hilde would never be mistaken for an English country girl. Despite time spent out of doors in this fine spring weather her olive skin showed no rough usage by either wind or sun. Her dark hair lay in a neat, thick coil about her head. Hugh held her hand a little longer than was necessary.

'You are Canadian?' She had noticed the maple leaf emblem.

'American. I got tired of waiting for America to put the gloves on so I joined up in Canada.'

Mrs Martin came in with the tea tray. 'I'll leave you to have a chat amongst yourselves,' but she lingered at the door with one more make-yourself-at-home smile for this nice young man, who looked just right for her pretty schoolteacher.

'Alvays I vant to go to America,' Hilde addressed Hugh seriously, 'because it is a long way from Chermany and Hitler. And I did *not* vant to come to England. England, I tink, is an ostrich mit head in the sea. No fire in her belly, you say? But I vas wrong. She has fire, a great fire in her belly. Such a fire that no one, not even Hitler, can put out. So, I am happy to be here. That is not what I mean. I mean I am *proud* to be here.'

Evie clapped her on the back. 'Thank you, Hilde. What a speech! I'm not sure that we deserve all that praise, but I'm glad you are happy here.'

'And I, too, am proud to be here.' Hugh's

smile sealed the new relationship. 'Sink or swim, I want to be part of it.'

'What are you doing up here in the north, Hugh?'

'I've gotten some embarkation leave and nowhere to spend it, no one nice to spend it with, and I thought of your letter. Guess I should say sorry I never got around to answering it, Evie,' he hung his head and smiled disarmingly. Her little schoolteacher nod could have implied forgiveness or censure. 'And I wondered if you would be offended if I came to visit, unannounced, like this? Say the word if I am making a nuisance of myself.'

She hastened to reassure him, 'And here's something you didn't know. You're taking the two of us to the village hop tonight, so polish up your dancing pumps.'

He was cagey when she mentioned Nancy. It was Evie who had given him the introduction to Nancy. They were at the same RAF base but all he said was, 'Haven't seen her lately.'

He was given a room at the local pub, a dainty pink and white room intended for honeymooners. It smelt of new mown hay, oil of citronella for the midges and an occasional waft of poultry manure from the yard below. 'Glad to oblige,' the rosy landlady told him. 'Not many guests in wartime, you know. We have our permanents, of course. Old Mr Brown from the school. He's in the room next to you, but you won't hear him snoring.

I tested that myself. Then there's the man from the Forestry. He comes and goes. I'll give you the key if you want a bath and it's two and sixpence extra. High tea at six o'clock and I'll need your ration card.'

'Better beware of beetle-crusher boots,' he warned the girls later when he went to escort them. 'The Home Guard has been drilling and they mean to come dancing when they've sunk a few pints at The Black Horse. No licence at the village hall, they tell me. Hope we don't have an air raid tonight!'

'No air raids in Slabridge. That's why the school was moved here. Our only bit of excitement was when Rudolph Hess dropped out of a plane just over the border.'

Certainly, Hugh thought, as they walked up the quiet main street to the village hall, this is far removed from bombing missions and pranged crates. Birds in the chestnut trees were settling themselves for the night filling the sweetly scented air with their twittering. Hopeful girls with shampooed hair – 'Friday night is Amami Night' – and dabs of Soir de Paris behind their ears came fluttering out of cottage doors, all eyes upon his uniform. Hugh liked Evie's pad, was glad he had come. A quiet spell in a little English village before North Africa. Just the job.

Thirty-One

The three members of the band – the accordion player, the fiddler and the pianist – were excluded from active service because of flat feet, chronic asthma or some other debilitating affliction. The music was wild and noisy. The night was warm and the faces of the Home Guard red as the setting sun, as they pranced around in boots and gaiters. Willy Parker, bashing out the beat with his club foot, kept the assembled company in a state of perpetual motion. 'Take your partners for the Circassian Circle ... Dashing White Sergeant ... Military Two Step ... Eightsome Reel.'

Evie, sipping lemonade at one of the small tables with Hugh, watched Hilde get up for every dance. The bravely smiling wallflowers looked on enviously as every male who was not actually crippled or cuckoo whisked her off. 'I'm glad Hilde is enjoying herself. Her family had a bad time escaping from Germany.'

'Jewish? I guessed.' His eyes followed Hilde's swirling dirndl skirt around the little dance floor. 'She's one of the lucky ones.'

He looked very handsome in his air force

uniform. Interested glances came their way. 'Look who teacher's found. One in the eye for Mr Natty Brown!'

'How long can you stay?' she asked him.

'Till Monday morning.'

'Then what?'

'Middle East.'

She sighed. 'So many of my friends are there.'

'Your boyfriend, Jacky?'

'Yes, but he never writes.'

'I'm not surprised. Our troops are up and down the desert like a yo-yo. Rommel's got us on the run. We've lost Benghazi. Tobruk is under siege. Not much time for letter writing. It's a pretty grim situation.'

'And what's happening in Greece? Two of my best friends are army nurses there and we've had no news for ages.'

'Greece is a disaster. The king has abdicated, and our troops have been asked to leave. Greece seeks an armistice.' Evie's look of alarm prompted him to retrack, 'I expect all nurses will have been evacuated to Crete by this time.'

'Oh dear, Hugh. I feel such a fraud, here in this peaceful countryside, teaching running writing to eight-year-olds while my friends are risking their lives. Already two of our close friends have been killed and another is a POW.'

'And one has had his face burned off.'

She looked up in surprise. 'Alec.'

He nodded.

'You visited him? I suppose Nancy took you?'

'Nancy did *not* take me. Nancy has been once to see Alec and not again.' The line of his mouth hardened.

Evie was thunderstruck.

He continued, 'I contacted Nancy, as you suggested, when I joined the unit. Didn't know a soul. I took her out, several times. I think I was in love with her a bit. She's a pretty girl. Didn't know she had a boyfriend. She never mentioned him.'

'Nancy and Alec have been going around together for years. They were on the point of getting engaged when he was shot down.'

'My squadron leader put me wise. He didn't believe me when I said I knew nothing about a boyfriend. "Don't give me that crap." Thought I was shooting a line. "Go and see the poor chap for yourself. Burns Unit. Park Prewitt Hospital. You'll learn a thing or two." I did, and I never saw Nancy again.'

Evie was silent, remembering Alec the charmer. She had intended to visit him before now but it was a long journey, and expensive, and you never knew when air raids would hold up the trains. 'Is he very disfigured?'

Hugh blew out a cloud of smoke, arranging his thoughts in acceptable words. 'I never knew Alec before his crash, but you did. You would not recognise him now. He's got guts. He's not crying over his lost looks. What knifes him is the fact that his girl has forsaken him. I know that sounds corny but I don't know another way of saying his girl has dropped him in the shit. I get angry about it, Evie. I'm sorry. Anyhow, whether Nancy is to be blamed or not I'm not going to be the guy to take Alec's place. No sir,' he stubbed out his cigarette and looked about him. 'Where's our fraulein?'

'Gone to the refreshment room with a large fat farmer.'

'Come on then.' He grabbed her by the hand. 'Let's get high on lemonade and then you can show me how to dance this Dashing White Sergeant, and, by the way, you can stop thinking you are not pulling your weight in the war. Educating the next generation is as important as and much more civilised than shooting Germans.'

Beneath a skyful of stars Evie and young Mr Brown were walking hand in hand along the fell path above the blacked-out village of Slabridge. Her visitors had gone. A rather unlikely friendship had developed between Evie and Hilde, and she found that she was missing their company now that they had gone, Hugh to somewhere in the Middle East and Hilde back to the Eastport General Hospital.

She was glad when young Mr Brown suggested a walk on the fells, though darkness had fallen. Only the stars were out tonight and the fellside path, made by sheep for sheep, was winding and narrow. She matched her stride to his so as not to bump him into the rough. She had no thought of Jacky. No ties or obligations there. He was good fun but if she meant anything to him he would surely write. On the other hand, she had become quite fond of this clever young geography teacher. Ask him any mortal thing and he'd be sure to know the answer.

She had reason to believe that her feelings for him were reciprocated although the holding of hands had been a very recent development. He seemed not to be a very passionate sort of chap. Still, if you've got as many brains as he had perhaps the physical side of a relationship doesn't seem too important. The physical bit was what Jacky was good at but then, to support her theory, he didn't exactly shine when it came to headwork.

Tonight, young Mr Brown was preoccupied with the category of a reserved occupation as it applied to him. 'I know I'm not *obliged* to go,' said he.

'Certainly not,' Evie said firmly, her opinions, having been recently reinforced by Hugh. 'Like me. We're needed here.'

'That's perfectly true.'

He always spoke as if at a public debate. Evie was proud of his distinguished delivery, as though he was reading from notes.

'The question I must face ... and I welcome your views, Evie,' he turned to her and marked with some surprise that her face had taken on a strange, pale green colour in this weird starlight.

She nodded in agreement. Her views were certainly worth hearing.

'The question is, am I of more use here, teaching young children, equipping them for a better world or,' he screwed up his mouth and threw back his head seeking enlightenment from on high, 'or getting myself rigged up in some sort of uniform and going off to make what I fear would be a very inferior soldier.'

'No doubt about it,' Evie said stoutly. He had no sort of figure to carry a uniform, sort of bendy. Not in any way heroic. Jacky scored over him there. 'Our job is here with the children. These poor kids, evacuated from their homes, separated from family, deserve the best education possible and you, Gladstone' – she did not often make use of his rather embarrassing Christian name but the moment seemed appropriate – 'you are one of the most talented teachers I have ever met.' She had not met many, but that point did not arise.

With becoming reluctance he agreed that she was probably right. Evie pursued her argument. 'My American friend, Hugh, the one I told you about, says that many of his pals back home are following his example and enrolling in the Canadian armed forces. There'll be plenty of volunteers without taking our schoolteachers.'

He was nodding solemnly. That was the only thing, Evie told herself. He was a bit short on humour. You'd never catch him having a real belly laugh. Not him!

'Is he a Very Special Friend, Evie? I would like to know where I stand.'

A blinding flash of intuition told her that this was a question of importance, one which he had rehearsed. 'Glory no! Not a special friend. Just a nice guy.'

He looked just the tiniest bit critical. 'One can tell that you have spent some time in America. "Nice guy",' he explained.

'Well, so he is. When I was new at the college and a bit homesick, he befriended me. Nothing more than that. He's somewhere in the Middle East now. Bombing Rommel, I suppose.'

He gripped her hand at that and put it in his pocket which, she thought, was a rather surprising thing to do. She could feel his keys, and some coins and ... his leg!

Thirty-Two

The driver's instructions were to get the nurses over the Corinth bridge without delay and proceed to a port near Argos where a ship was waiting to take them and himself to Crete.

'But it's not going to hang around waiting for us,' he told himself, 'not when enemy planes are bombing every port. No chance of a Dunkirk this time.' He had just witnessed a Heinkel sinking a ship as wounded men were boarding, some of them on stretchers. Comrades on the beach, watching, waiting their turn to be picked up, saw their hopes of escape go down in flames.

The driver kept his attention firmly fixed on the road ahead. He needed to keep his eyes peeled. Other drivers like himself were grimly trying to force the pace before all escape routes were cut off, but shellholes and occasionally a burning vehicle which had to be shifted off the road made progress desperately slow.

The nurses whose safety he was charged with dozed fitfully in the back of the truck, rocking and bumping with each rut in the road, snatching at sleep which had been denied them over the past weeks. Myfanwy Jones's face was green. Cathy felt an ache of sympathy. What a time to get your period. She always did have a bad time, but this must be the worst ever situation. Someone said, 'Does anyone know where we're going?'

'Argos, wherever that is.'

The matron had once spent a holiday in Greece. 'In Peloponnisos. The other side of the Corinth canal. Still a fair way to go but, once there, our troubles will be over. The Royal Navy is waiting for us.'

Cathy glanced at the older woman. Did she believe all that? Or was it just a front to keep up morale. It was obvious to everyone that her expression of cheerful determination was

312

stitched on top of a less confident mode.

They drove through Athens at a racketing pace. At Daphne they joined the tail end of a long line of trucks carrying the wounded and a party of Australian army nursing sisters who, like their British counterparts, had stayed at their hospital until relieved by Greek nurses.

After Daphne the road ran close to the shore, a stretch where the *Luftwaffe* was especially active, as now. A stick of bombs straddling the road ahead jerked the exhausted nurses into wakefulness and brought the convoy to a sudden halt. A vehicle ahead of them burst into flames. There was a shout – 'take cover!' and passengers spilled out from the trucks into the fields of barley bordering the road. A second explosion shook the ground. Shrapnel spattered the fields. Cathy, face down on the red, suffering earth, groped for Norah's hand. 'Please God,' she whispered, 'please, God.'

The whole scene was grotesque and unreal, but these were real lethal bullets pinging into the ground and that was a lifesize Stuka diving low. It was that other world, teatime in her mother's sitting-room at Eastport, that was unreal. Would they ever see their families and friends in England again? A nurse cried out in pain.

'Somebody's hit!'

'Keep your head down, Moffat!'

'Is someone hurt?'

'Kennedy's got a piece of shrapnel in her

leg, Matron. We're dealing with it.'

The planes wheeled away leaving a foul black cloud in their wake. Heads were cautiously raised. The transport officer in charge of the convoy appeared. 'Keep under cover until I give you the word. Everybody OK? The sister who was injured?'

'I'm OK.'

'Five minutes to brew up then get back in the trucks. We'll drive through the night.'

Grubby figures emerged from the scarred field and from the nearby cemetery where Australian army sisters had sought shelter behind tombstones. There were others like Yvonne Kennedy with minor shrapnel wounds which their friends had bound with field dressings.

While the men in the convoy busied themselves with tommy cookers the nurses sought some discreet cover. 'The first thing I do when I get back to England,' came a plaintive voice from the bushes, 'is to book myself in for a hysterectomy.'

A light breeze sprang up, dispersing the fumes from burning trucks. Shadows lengthened. A cow bellowed to be milked and a bent old woman, prodding a pig before her, went by without a glance at the convoy. Her face was a map of life's vicissitudes. A long line of walking wounded went by, looking straight ahead, hanging on, feet dragging. The nurses watched in silence unable to offer help. This was how defeat looked.

'We're leaving ruined houses where the

people lived and shellholes in the fields where their crops grew. Perhaps we should never have come if we couldn't do the job properly.'

'They'll hang that hideous red and black swastika over the Acropolis.'

'Jackboots in the market square.'

'What will become of our Greek friends?' said Cathy, thinking of a young boy called Demetrius.

The sun set in splendour over a modern Greek tragedy where might had so demonstrably conquered right.

'All aboard, Ma'am. Got to get over the canal bridge before our lot blows it.' The driver was already starting up the engine.

Darkness now fell swiftly. Progress was slow. The road to Corinth was badly broken up and the only illumination allowed was a pin point scratched through blackened headlights. The night grew cold and the women were glad of their greatcoats. Hours went by. Conversation had dried up long since. They all realised that their journey was perilous, that they might not, in the end, escape ... Burnt-out vehicles littered the roadsides. Their own truck might suffer the same fate.

Sappers were laying mines beneath the bridge at Corinth even as the trucks rumbled across it. Gunners were mounting anti-tank guns on the Peloponnese side, directed towards the mainland.

'Last ditch,' said Norah, 'to let us get away.'

They drove through Mikini, Mycenae and Argos. Names to dream about in other times, but not tonight. With relief their driver arrived at the port of Nauplion and pulled up on the end of a long line of abandoned trucks. 'This is as far as we go.'

The nurses, stiff from their cramped positions, slid down on to a sandy path. There was a taste of salt in the air and the smell of wet wood and boats and the stink of discarded fish. A timid moon glittered on water. They were at the edge of the sea, the edge of Greece.

A transport officer silently appeared out of the darkness. He was young and justifiably tense. His task was to organise the evacuation by sea of men, many of them wounded, and two truckloads of women. His voice was low and stern. 'The lives of all of us depend on complete silence. No noise. No talking. No smoking. No torches. No lights, not even the strike of a match. You are to march from here to the jetty, about a mile. There you will wait your turn to board a caique which will ferry you to a freighter lying offshore. Understood?'

He had a home, like all the other young men. He had a life outside of soldiering. He wanted, hoped, to get back to it but despaired at the moment of ever seeing his family again.

Cathy and Norah collected their suitcases from the truck and set off into the darkness, walking by the water's edge. The air was pleasantly cool and a blessed silence prevailed. No sound but the lap-lap of a creeping tide and its rattling retreat. The light crunch of shoes on gravel. The thick garment of night cloaked this undercover operation, giving no hint that here were many desperate men and women taut with apprehension and praying for deliverance before the telltale dawn broke.

To the weary nurses, burdened as they were with greatcoats, tin hats, respirators and suitcases, the mile seemed to stretch forever. Walking hand in hand with a friend, short-sighted Janet McGregor, bat-blind without her spectacles which she had lost in the barley field, threw away the rug she had brought from home. 'It'll nae doubt come in verra handy,' her mother had said. Well, her mother had never envisaged a scene like this. Into the ditch went the cherished product of a Scottish woollen mill. She hoped some Greek peasant would find it and not a rotten storm-trooper. One by one, items of luggage were jettisoned.

There was an altercation at the jetty, the outcome of which was that soldiers must have preference over the nurses. The women were to wait in a nearby ditch until given the signal to board the caique. The ditch, which was dry and would afford some shelter, was found to be already occupied. There was a muffled exclamation as a rat abandoned its home.

From their shelter, such as it was, the women heard the splash of the caique as it disappeared from sight with its load of soldiers, many of whom were wounded, their bandages a startling white in the pitch darkness of the bay. The turn of the nurses would come. It would have been a comfort to talk, but that they dared not do.

Over the little noises of the night the rhythmic thud of marching feet on hard-packed sand came faintly at first, then clearly. By the shifting grey light of an inconstant moon, a body of men became palely visible, their featureless faces looking steadfastly ahead. Not a word was spoken as the column passed by. Behind a curtain of silence the phantom army was swallowed up into the night.

A whispered order reached the nurses in the ditch. They were now to board the caique. This they accomplished in good order, but the transfer from the bobbing boat to the waiting freighter was fraught with difficulties. For Janet McGregor, without her glasses, it was terrifying. From a standing position in the launch, she was required to grab a slippery rope ladder which she could not see and, by this means, climb up the side of a ship knowing that one false move would send her into the swirling dark waters of the Aegean. She was not surprised when she lost her footing and fell between the ship's hull and the launch. Weighed down by greatcoat and tin hat, she must have drowned, but for the quick action of a sailor on the freighter who leapt into the water, grabbed her by the thick collar of her coat and held her while the crew of the caique pushed away from the freighter to avoid Janet being crushed. Even in such dramatic circumstances, Janet remembered the order of silence and did not make a sound.

A cabin was found for her on board the freighter. Ministering sisters pounced, stripped her, rubbed her down and bundled her into some sailor's bunk wearing an outsize pair of pyjamas donated by the chief engineer, but it took the arrival of the matron with a bottle labelled 'For Medicinal Use Only' to still her chattering teeth.

AB Albert Smith was also chattering with cold as he dried himself with a towel rough enough to curry horses. Petty Officer Siddons handed him a measure of rum. 'Get that down you, Smith. Think you're a bloody hero, do you?'

Smith grinned, a flash of white in a pomegranate face. 'Yessir. Thank you, sir.'

'Well, the young lady requests your presence in her cabin when it is convenient. She wishes to thank you personally.'

'Bollocks.'

'I didn't catch that.'

'Right, sir. Thank you, sir. I could murder the other half of that rum.'

'Get yourself up on deck. These chaps'll have to shift their gear from the companionways. See to it ... and Smith!'

'Sir?'

'Don't fall overboard again.'

The ship was crammed to capacity. The matron came seeking Norah to help in the ship's sick bay. 'You and Sister Anderson are to report there at once.'

319

Cathy looked for a space on the crowded deck. There were three thousand wounded men on this medium-sized freighter. She squeezed down beside a trooper of the Northumberland Hussars.

'Welcome aboard, Sister. We've met before. Trooper McDonald.'

Cathy peered at the face beside her. The white of a bandage showed beneath his tin hat and one arm was in a sling. 'I can't recall ... So many men passing through.'

'You sisters were being run off your feet at Kifisia. You dressed my arm, gave me a cup of tea and wished me luck.'

'It didn't work, then. Where did you pick up the head injury?'

'After we left the hospital our truck was bombed. Most of us were wounded again. Some of the lads were killed so, in a way, your luck stayed with me. I got a bloody head but it's still attached. We all wondered how you nurses would get away.' Like all the walking wounded, he was dirty, unshaven and weary. 'I'm glad you made it out of Kifisia.'

'Greek nurses relieved us to look after those casualties who were too ill to move. It's awful, having to leave like this.'

'My mates in the Northumberland Hussars are holding the bridge at Corinth. They'll blow it before the Jerries get there.'

'We crossed about an hour ago.'

'You'd be about the last.'

'Can I get you anything? A drink?'

He shook his head and patted the water

320

bottle at his side. She saw that he was fighting off sleep and made no further attempt at conversation.

The ship's engines started into life. The anchor chain rattled home to the fo'c'sle. Crew members appeared, stepping over figures already asleep on the deck. A distant bell sounded deep in the belly of the vessel and she began to move.

'Goodbye, Greece.' Cathy was thinking of the medical officers and orderlies left behind who would be taken prisoner with the remaining patients. Vivian Barsdale, junior surgical. Michael Stewart, medical. Capt. Radlett, anaesthetist, the padre and some dedicated orderlies. I would have been happy to stay had I been needed, she told herself and then, on cross examination, found this to be untrue. No, she admitted, I would have been scared out of my wits.

Dark shapes of other ships had silently taken up position alongside. It was a comfort to know that they were travelling in convoy. Her neighbour slept. She wondered how Norah was getting on. The sick bay was usually in the very bowels of the ship, an awful place to be in if the weather turned nasty, as it could, even here in the Aegean. She recalled Jason and the Argonauts, Children's Hour on the wireless. B.H. (Before Hitler), like so many memories.

Under cover of darkness the convoy made unhindered progress towards Crete, but daylight brought an enemy spotter plane and

321

bombers quickly followed. Sleepers awakened to the sound of shells falling port and starboard. Waterspouts encircled the convoy.

The trooper next to Cathy woke with a start and, with his one good arm, grabbed his rifle. There were several near misses by the bombers when their ship seemed to lift right out of the water, hover eerily, then smack down with gut-churning impact. The noise was deafening as the ack-ack guns of the convoy went into action. People on deck scrambled for cover as shrapnel and bullets slapped about them. Trooper McDonald banged away with his rifle, one armed, at the diving planes. Able Seaman Albert Smith, running to his station, fell headlong over a prone body, sending his tin hat flying over the side. The man he had tripped over was lying in a pool of blood. Smith knelt to turn him over. Cathy, field dressing in hand scrambled over the deck to help, but the man was past help. The contents of his skull spilled out on the deck. 'Too late, sailor.'

At her voice, Smith looked up. 'Well I never! Cathy Lewis!'

Equally astonished at this encounter, Cathy collected her wits, 'Don't stand there gawping for the love of mike.' She picked up the dead soldier's tin hat. 'Here, put this on, Smithy. He doesn't need it any more, poor chap.'

There was a huge explosion, a blinding light and the air was filled with cries. A nearby ship had been hit.

'Stay under cover, Cathy Lewis. I've got to go and look for survivors. We'll be lowering a boat.' And Albert Smith was gone leaving her feeling strangely disorientated. Making her way back to Trooper McDonald she was sorely grieved to see that his luck had run out at this third encounter with death.

For the rest of the voyage the nurses were occupied with tending the wounded. Two more ships in the convoy were sunk and some of their survivors were brought on board, picked up by rescue parties, perhaps by Albert Smith's boat. When land appeared on the horizon, the attackers gave up and wheeled away to their bases with empty bomb racks.

As she made her way to the sick bay to tell Norah that Suda Bay was in sight, Cathy looked for Albert Smith but he was not amongst the crew who were clearing up the shambles on the deck and there was no time to make enquiries. Recalling his cool courage during the bombing attack, she was revising her earlier opinion of the Bad Lad of Seacliff School.

The 7th British General Hospital, the only military hospital based in Crete, did its best to cope with this sudden intake of exhausted and wounded troops and nurses. Sandwiches and tea awaited them as they stepped ashore. The nurses made for the tent which had been set aside for them. With only a quick scour around a jaded mouth and a wipe with a wet face cloth by way of ablutions, they crawled into prepared beds and were asleep almost at once, each within her own web of peace that not even the continuous movement of trucks and troops could penetrate.

When it seemed they had just closed their eyes, the bellow of a sergeant was cruel. 'Sorry, ladies. We need this tent. Another 200 casualties just come in. You'll have to sleep out in the open. The men will carry your beds for you.'

Bedraggled and weary, with a blanket thrown about their shoulders they trailed out of the tent, and, to the astonishment of passing troops, lay down to sleep under the Cretan sky amongst the wild snapdragons and sweet-smelling thyme. Cathy caught the ghost of a grin on the face of the orderly carrying her bed. With unaccustomed venom she hissed, 'Take that grin off your face, Corporal, or I'll put you on a charge. Go away and don't come back for a long, long time.'

Some hours later the Australian Captain Keith Russell brought an overloaded fishing boat to the safety of Suda Bay. When all possibility of escape for his men and himself appeared to have gone, a fishing boat left untended at a quiet bay in the Peloponnisos offered a last chance. They took that chance leaving behind a 'Promise to pay' note for the Greek owner. The weather had been kind, the sea calm and now they were stepping ashore in Suda Bay. 'We've made it this far,' he told his men, 'but don't kid yourselves. Jerry's not going to leave us in peace. He'll do his damnedest to winkle us out of here. We've been assigned to guard Rethymno airfield. Once we get there we'll wash up and work out duties. Right now Sergeant Hoddle and I will try to rustle up some transport.'

At the top of the cliff path he came upon a spread of sleeping women. 'What the devil?'

A passing RAMC orderly explained, 'Some of the British nurses, sir. Just got out of Greece in time.'

'For chrissake couldn't they have a tent?' His eyes scanned all the heads – black, brown, ginger … and blonde. The blonde hair was stringy with salt. There were blue shadows under her closed eyelids. She was utterly out for the count, her breathing deep and regular, impervious to everything going on around her, heartbreakingly vulnerable. He had to control the desire to take her in his arms and comfort her. Instead, he tore a page from the notebook he carried in his breast pocket, scribbled a line and laid it lightly by the grubby fingers at her cheek. 'Friend of mine,' he explained gruffly to his straight-faced sergeant.

The matron, at least, had a little privacy in a small tent of her own, but her sleep, too, was disturbed in the early hours of the new day. 'Message from the CO, Ma'am.' An orderly stood outside her tent. 'All nursing officers to report to docks immediately for embarkation to Alexandria. Sailing 0500 hours.' The time was then half-past four.

Wearily the matron dragged herself alert.

'Thank you. Please let the sisters know.'

'You're joking,' Cathy pleaded, her eyelids remaining steadfastly glued together. 'Tell me you are joking.'

'You've got half an hour, Sister. You might not get another chance.'

She leant over and shook Norah by the shoulder. 'Ups-a-daisy. We're off again. This time to Alex and,' she noticed Keith Russell's note, 'the postman's been.'

Thirty-Three

Twenty-five bedraggled members of Queen Alexandra's Imperial Military Nursing Service climbed down from the truck which had brought them the eight miles from Alexandria to this military hospital in Egypt where they would be able to rest and recover from their recent experiences.

The building, previously a boys' school, looked reassuringly solid and safe. Down the steps to greet them came Miss Wilson, the resident matron, immaculate in tropical whites, accompanied by some of her staff.

'My dear girls! How glad we are to see you. We feared you had drowned.'

Her opposite number, newly arrived from Crete, felt inexplicably weak at the knees now

326

that her long ordeal was over and her nurses were safe. 'I must apologise for our state, incredibly dirty,' she faltered.

The *Caterini* was one of many boats packed with troops attempting to escape from Crete. Once spotted by the *Luftwaffe* they were mercilessly bombed as they made for the comparative safety of Alexandria. The *Caterini* played her part in picking up survivors from vessels sunk. Badly burned men, naked and slippery with oil, were hauled on board to be cared for by the nurses, as far as the meagre medical facilities would allow.

The nurses' uniforms, hands and faces were streaked with oil. Their hair was lank and filthy. Water on the *Caterini* was rationed to one pint per person per day, so there was none to spare for washing. A cat lick with the corner of a damp handkerchief was the limit of the nurses' toilet.

Resident nurses came forward to help the weary travellers up the steps. 'Have you no kit? None at all?'

'None at all. All lost.'

Miss Wilson accompanied her guests to the dining-room. 'Tea and hot baths straight away. I'll ask one of our doctors to check you over later. And incidentally,' she smiled reassuringly at her subdued and weary guests, 'there's no need to wear your tin hats here. Just keep them at the ready.'

They sat on wooden forms polished over many years by the trouser seats of little boys. Local girls employed in the mess brought hot sweet tea. On the *Caterini* tea was made in kerosene containers. They drank it out of cigarette tins.

Cathy looked around the table and thought, we've made it. The agony of Greece, that would stay with her for ever, the last four horrific days at sea, all that was behind them now. We have survived. Norah looked washed out. But then, she never was as tough as me.

Kennedy's leg was inflamed and painful. She looked as though she was running a temperature. The matron had put her down as a priority. Robinson had the runs. She had just left the table in search of a loo – again. 'We all look fagged out,' Cathy admitted. 'And poor old McGregor, bumbling about half blind.' She glanced across at wiry little Michelson from the Shetlands, gritting her teeth, keeping her troubles to herself – a survivor if ever there was one.

But what of the hundreds of casualties left behind in Greece? This was on the conscience of all the nurses from Kifisia. Wounded German troops had been impartially treated there. Would the same treatment apply to wounded British prisoners of war?

A distribution of letters with news of home, weeks in arrears, lifted the nurses' spirits as nothing else could do, then Norah passed a grubby little note to Cathy. 'I didn't show you this. I had a visitor while we were asleep in the open in Crete. My Australian friend.'

'God bless. Perhaps you'll be awake next time.' Cathy read. 'Signed Digger K. Russell.

So he managed to get out of Greece.'

'I'm glad. He was very concerned about our safety before we left Kifisia.'

'He has a knack of turning up in unexpected places, your Digger.'

Sleep came at once after the luxury of a bath. The five-foot-small home sister, busy as a bantam, bore away their dirty clothing for the incinerator. 'We'll find uniforms to fit you tomorrow. Don't worry about anything else tonight.' She was in her element. Looking after people was what she was good at. She had been doing it for most of her life.

Before she succumbed to the sweet seduction of sleep, however, Cathy wrote a note to Number Three, The Crescent, Eastport, England. 'Just to let you know Norah and I are all right. Will write a proper letter later. Don't know where the Eastport boys are.'

She was the last to turn off the light. The darkness was safe and friendly here. Kennedy was snoring after medication. She was for operation in the morning.

The world was a different place in the morning. Everything about them was orderly, clean and correct according to King's Regulations. The home sister produced a selection of uniform. 'You are all to have ten days' leave in Ismailia.' Sister Flowers (Bloomers) was as delighted as if she were going herself. 'Staying at the YWCA there. Very comfy. Except the poor dears in sick bay. They will go later.'

Robinson, who was found to be suffering from dysentery, had joined Kennedy in the sick bay. 'It was the foul water in that ship that did it. Just as well it was in short supply.'

'What's happening in the desert war, Sister? We're out of touch with what has been going on here.'

Bloomers obliged with spirit. 'We're about to knock Rommel for six.' Gleefully she smacked her fists together. She was a very political little lady, a born optimist reared on porridge, Mr Churchill and the British Empire. And was at pains to assure the new-comers that darling General Wavell knew exactly what he was about. Admittedly, most of the gains of the previous year had been retaken by Rommel. 'But put your trust in Wavell. He'll scotch this Desert Fox. We still hold Tobruk, a thorn in the enemy's back-side.' She would not put it quite like that to the troops of course.

She cut a comic figure in the hospital with her waggling behind and her dyspeptic nose, but the men respected her too much to laugh at her.

'While in Ismailia,' the resident matron addressed them, 'you must take the first opportunity to replace all your lost kit and uniform. Sister Flowers will give you the address of the military tailor and you must insist on priority. You will be needed here before long. Later you must put in a claim to the paymaster for your lost uniform. You will be reimbursed.'

'I wouldn't count on it,' came Bloomers, *sotto voce*. She had been shipwrecked twice in the 14–18 war and was still waiting for the cheque. After serving in the Territorial Army Nursing Service in that war, Kathleen Flowers forgot to resign in 1918 and, as a result, was called up promptly in 1939 and ordered to take a casualty clearing station to France with the 1st BEF. When France fell she escaped with her staff of thirteen nursing sisters via Cherbourg after a headlong flight in a Salvation Army mobile canteen. And here she was in Egypt with chronic indigestion and a determination to stay the course, albeit in a more relaxed position as home sister.

She saw the girls off in their transport with a coy, 'Don't do anything I wouldn't do!' and ten blissful days began for them. In borrowed uniform, they sat sprucely in the truck so as not to lean against the grubby canvas sides and prepared themselves for any indulgence on offer.

The YWCA building was a handsome private house before the war. Vines clambered over white-painted porticoes and colonnades, bougainvillea over its balconies. The interior with its high ceilings and gently revolving fans offered a refuge from the tireless sun. Patterned rugs on white-tiled floors.

There were a number of servicewomen here sitting around in comfortable, easy chairs and wicker sofas, sipping tea, nibbling cakes, ATS, FANY, WRNS, WAAF and members of the British Red Cross Society. The murmur of their conversation dropped for a questioning moment as the new arrivals came under scrutiny for possible recognition and then took up again.

Norah tugged at her skirt. 'I feel a freak in this tight uniform.'

Cathy looked about her wonderingly, remembering Greece. 'Is there a war on somewhere?' Here were starched white cloths on the tables and jugs of bright flowers everywhere, cannas and lilies, oleander and hibiscus. And dishes piled high with fresh dates and green figs. Waiters slipped silently between the tables serving cool drinks and, coming to meet them, striding across the tiles, unembarrassed by the noise of his boots or the admiring glances directed his way, was Lieutenant Simon Poole.

'Thank God you're safe.' His smile stretched from ear to ear. 'My two lovely girls.'

Cathy fell into his arms in delighted surprise. 'Simon! Dear, darling old Simon. Dad wrote that you were out here somewhere but I never expected we could meet.'

'My spies told me you were coming and here you are at last, looking a bit the worse for wear but nothing that a glass of bubbly won't put right.'

They went, the three of them, arm in arm to a table on the verandah where three tall-stemmed glasses awaited them and a silver-capped bottle poking out of an ice bucket.

'You're an officer,' Norah said accusingly. 'What have you been up to?'

'When we last saw you,' the tremor in

Cathy's voice revealed her excitement, 'in Hilde's ward, you were a bit of a wreck and look at you now.' She laid a light hand on his back. 'Is it OK?'

'Never mind about me,' he was applying himself to the champagne cork, 'I'm fighting fit. But you two ... God, I've worried over you. At first the rumour went round that the QAs had been left behind in Greece, then that your ship was sunk on the way to Crete. It's been so hard to get any reliable news. Get ready with a glass. This is going to pop. Your matron at Victoria is a good stick. Told me to get myself down here if I wanted to see you. I'm on four days' leave. Two left. I've bitten my nails to the bone and chewed my moustache to a whisker in case you didn't arrive in time. But here you are.' He handed round the glasses of golden bubbles. 'We are going to drink a toast to Poseidon, the god of the sea, who brought you safely here.'

Privately, Cathy thought it was her God who worked it, but no matter.

They ate chicken with roasted almonds and fresh limes, dishes of rice flavoured with cardamon, sweet figs and honey and yoghurt and champagne, a banquet after the hard tack of recent weeks.

Cathy did a genteel burp. 'Pardon. It's so marvellous to feel full.'

'And clean,' said Norah.

The coppery light of a setting sun flooded the girls' faces with colour and touched their newly washed hair with glints of gold. Cathy looked across at Norah. 'Tell me I'm not dreaming.'

Simon had no news of Eric or Jacky. 'It's damn difficult to keep track of anyone in the desert, but I believe they are attached to the Durham Light Infantry at the moment. No one stays in the same place for long. There's been a lot of falling back and not much going forward since Rommel came on the scene. We've got a tough fight on our hands.' His own battery, Simon said, was at a place with a name like Hellfire, 'Which it assuredly is.'

He scarcely left their sides during the two remaining days of his leave, toting them around the markets, accompanying them to the military depot for uniform replacement, treating them to coffee and cream cakes at the officers' club. On Simon's last evening, however, Norah stayed behind to sew name tapes on the new uniform while he took Cathy in a borrowed scout car to a smart French restaurant on the shores of the Bitter Lakes.

This, Cathy told herself as she applied Max Factor pancake to her freckles, is a significant evening. Usually she discovered significant moments in retrospect when it was too late to take appropriate action, but she knew in her bones that tonight was indeed to be taken seriously. There was no knowing when ... if ... she and Simon would meet again. And Simon was a very dear friend.

Chez Nous was small, discreet and very French. A frangipani tree framed the entrance, enveloping every newcomer in its exotic perfume. Dimmed lamps shed a rosy glow on small marble tables, one of which, set in a discreet little alcove, was reserved for Lieutenant Poole and guest. They danced to the music of an accordion in a small space crowded with uniformed couples. Simon held Cathy close. She had forgotten how comfortingly big and strong he was and she laid her cheek contentedly against his chest. He was happy too. Humming off-key, dancing off-beat, he steered her through the close-packed bodies, 'With all the determination of a man with a wheelbarrow full of manure,' she later regaled Norah with an account.

'That moustache is new,' she observed. 'There's not much of it.'

'I'm only a second lieutenant. Wait till I'm a brigadier. I'll grow a great plume of whiskers and you will be very proud of me.'

'How did you get to be a second lieutenant so quickly from a sergeant?'

'My CO was killed. His number two seriously wounded. I was the next one down. My turn to take over.'

He refilled her glass with rich red wine from Gascony. 'That's enough of war. Forget it for tonight. Here comes the food.' But he had noted the glow of admiration in her eyes and felt proud.

Melons and ginger, ham and artichokes and sherbet doused in Benedictine liqueur. Cathy and Simon were easy as easy with each other. With two friends of such long standing it could not be otherwise, but such a scenario as the present could never have been imagined in those far off days of hockey on Eastport's sands on a Saturday morning, fizzy drinks and coconut snowballs in the school tuck shop, kissing in the dark.

'Will life ever go back to normal again? Like it was before?'

'No, my darling Cathy. Never the same again. We've moved on. And if we live to see the end of this war we will be different people. All we've been through, good and bad, and I've done some bad things,' he looked down and stirred his coffee, 'all these things cannot be absorbed like a meal, digested and passed into the pot. We're going to be stuck with them, good, bad and indifferent, to the end of our lives, one way or another.'

'I expect all soldiers think that way, Simon.' This was a different Simon talking. This serious self-analysis was out of character.

'Some of us will never be the same again,' he repeated. 'If I survive I intend to join the regular army. If we had been prepared in 1939 with a standing army and squadrons of tanks, Hitler would never have got away with plunging the whole world into misery. Colin and Quentin would be halfway to a law degree. Alec would still have the looks of a film star.'

'Married to Nancy.'

'And married to Nancy,' he repeated in a tone of disgust. 'That's one mistake he's been saved from.'

Cathy felt a sudden chill at the stark review. 'Simon, my dear,' her hand slid across the cool marble table to his. 'Please, please don't take risks. Don't be the first to stick your head above the parapet or gun turret or whatever. You've already suffered a serious wound. Don't tempt fate. Go easy – to please me.'

His young man's hand, strong, smooth-knuckled and tanned by the desert sun, covered hers. 'I have no choice, my sweet. Neither more nor less than any other soldier. I keep my fingers crossed and my ammo dry.' He turned her hand over. It lay quiescent in his big palm. 'Like a little baby chicken,' he said. 'How do you manage to do miracles of healing with such small hands.'

He held it firmly there. 'On this particular finger,' he continued, 'will you let me one day place a ring of promise and on this one a plain gold band?'

'Simon,' Cathy protested, 'you're leaping ahead again. How can we think of such things at a time like this? If I were to make such a promise now, and I might because of that great pale moon ogling us and the reflection on the lake and the magic of Egypt, and the fact that neither of us knows what tomorrow may bring ... if, because of all that and the fact that I'm a teeny bit squiffy, if I should say "yes" now because I want to make you happy and then later change my mind, how cruel and stupid that would be.'

'I know, I know and I want no promises like

that but if...' He paused and, in the rosy halo cast by the table lamp, Cathy glimpsed Simon the schoolboy once more – the winning smile, the pleading charm that could always be counted upon to get him out of scrapes, 'if you will just say that you will think about it, I will try to content myself with that for the time being.'

She leant towards him and took his broad, firm face in her two hands and on his unready lips beneath their golden moustache, she planted a kiss. 'I do love you, you know, in a nice cool sort of way. Whether it will warm up to a marrying heat I can't rightly say. If you don't want to wait then you must go seeking in other pastures green.'

'Don't talk rot. You are my girl. Always have been.'

He poured the last of the wine into their glasses. 'Since it is "tell the truth" time, I have to come clean and reveal my dastardly intentions now foiled by your brazen chastity. I hired a room here tonight, a seductive little nest, lit by candlelight and reeking of every known aphrodisiac and I planned to lead you there, after filling you with wine, to a bed of silken sheets strewn with rose petals.' He cocked a quizzical eye in her direction. 'I don't think you would come?'

'That's right,' she nodded equably. 'I wouldn't be any good, anyhow. I've never done it before.'

Outside the perimeter of their candlelit table, ancient Egypt wove its mysterious backdrop. Bumbling night bugs buzzed against wire screens at the open window. Mosquitoes whined spitefully to be let in. The ferryman's song drifted over the water.

Foreign soldiers and their love affairs were of no concern to Egypt.

Thirty-Four

June 1941

Andrew crossed off the date on his calendar and reflected that two years had passed since he marched from Dunkirk into captivity. Another dreary day to be endured lay ahead. How many more?

Oberleutnant Golze was about to tell him. He was in excellent humour as he strode into the hospital hut. Visits to the camp hospital by the German army doctor were infrequent. He left the running of that to Andrew, interfering only when Andrew's demands for more drugs, more dressings reached a totally unacceptable level. All demands were unacceptable to the next in seniority in the German medical hierarchy and if Kampmeister Oberleutnant Doktor Golze was seen to be favouring the POWs he would be made to pay for his alien generosity in any one of a number of ways – all of them unpleasant.

Nevertheless, he had to confess to a certain liking for the English doctor. Clever man. Good surgeon within the limited scope of his equipment. Civilised fellow. Could do with a few more like him in the Third Reich. Andrew was sometimes pleasantly surprised by the results of his petitioning, but not always. Doktor Golze could rage on occasion.

'Sulphaguanadine!' he would roar. 'For prisoners! We have not enough for our own frontline troops.'

'It will clear up the dysentery,' Andrew told him mildly. 'If you could persuade your pharmacists to produce more, you would reduce sickness in your troops.'

Dysentery. That was the dread sickness of the camps, that carried off lives already wasted by poor living conditions. Andrew was privileged, however, to receive a major share of the Red Cross parcels for his patients, nourishing extras like condensed milk, Bengers food, malted milk and wheatgerm.

On the arrival of the German doctor this morning, Andrew looked up from the leg ulcer he was dressing, noted the beam in Golze's face and waited for the bad news. Whatever pleased the German was unlikely to have the same effect upon himself. 'Good morning, Oberleutnant.'

'I haf good news for you, Doktor Mount. The war, I tink, will soon be over.'

In the expectant pause, Andrew continued to roll a bandage with exaggerated care while, inside his head, he was snapping, 'Out

340

with it, man.'

'The Third Reich now controls Greece and Crete!'

The smirk on the German doctor's face was almost insupportable but Andrew's expression was inscrutable except for the faint suggestion of superiority, which always maddened the Oberleutnant.

'Also, we will soon haf the whole of Nort Africa and Egypt and the Suez Canal! Your Meester Churchill will haf notting left to fight for. That is good. We make treaty.'

'We are not fighting for land, Oberleutnant,' Andrew spoke mildly, as if to a rather dimwitted child. 'We are fighting for freedom. Not only for ourselves but for people of all the countries you have annexed. May I have some more aspirin, please?'

The good humour vanished. Golze swivelled the monocle into his starting eye and glared at Andrew. Detecting there the fleeting image of a smile, he whacked his boot sharply with his cane and turned on his heel, shouting as he went, 'Nein! You shall not haf aspirin, *dumkopf*!'

All Andrew's patients were smiling now. Nevertheless, the news, if true, was alarming. 'D'ye think it's a leg pull, sir?'

'I expect it's propaganda as usual. Forget it.'

'Greece gone? And Crete? Blimey.'

Andrew could almost hear their thoughts in the uneasy silence that followed, broken by a Welshman with a gangrenous foot.

'Are we downhearted!' he yelled.

A Cockney answered, 'Yes! I'm bloody downhearted. I've lost me effing teeth. Some bloody Hun's nicked 'em. Begging your pardon, sir, but how'm I going to chew me steak an' chips?'

At the end of the day, having briefed the night orderly with instructions for care of the seriously ill, such as was possible, Andrew retired to the hut he shared with five other officers. Had they heard the latest news, he wondered. It was always bad news. This was worse than most.

'Johnnie' Johnson and Ron Jewitt were playing draughts. Barnfather was cooking something in a tin hat over the primus stove and the other two clever beggars, Winstanley and Stevens, were working on the task that would take them to the end of the war – how to accumulate immense riches and defraud the tax man at the same time.

'My German colleague tells me Greece and Crete have fallen. I wonder if it's true.'

The draughts' players looked up from their game. 'It was a foregone conclusion about Greece. But Crete? I would have thought we could hang on to that.'

'If they've got Crete, that's a poor outlook for the fleet in the Med.'

'The corporal will get it on the BBC if it's true.' The tax dodgers resumed their calculations.

'I know two QAs out there,' Andrew said slowly. 'At least, I think that's where they are, with a British hospital.' He went to his bunk and extracted Simon's letter from a bundle in his haversack. A letter from Simon was something of a miracle. He was no letter writer. This one contained two pieces of interesting information. He read, 'I got there to find that Cathy and Norah had just moved on. Of all the rotten luck...' Then he followed with the usual stuff about all the celebrations they would have at the King's Head when the war was over. That was Simon. Ever the optimist. Still he had survived his serious wound at Dunkirk and no one but an optimist could have forecast that.

According to Simon, then, the girls had moved on from the Middle East. That earlier posting had been deduced from a letter his father had sent. In Norah's letter there was a further clue to their whereabouts when she wrote in what was an unlikely phrase for her, 'By Jove, we're busy.' That seemed to point to Mount Olympus and Greece. He had one remaining lettercard of the current ration. He would write to Hilde for news of Norah.

The other bit of interesting information in Simon's letter was to be found on the back of the envelope. Name of Sender: 2nd Lt S. Poole. Andrew was pleased but not surprised. From the start, Simon was cut out for promotion. Andrew tucked the letters away, as Captain Tony Barnfather called them all to the table, a packing case stood on end.

He was an enterprising, if not always successful cook, concocting his own menus from the contents of Red Cross parcels. 'Barnfather Special tonight for my mother's birth-day. Fried meat roll in a piquant sauce of tomatoes, finely chopped preserved ginger and fresh nettles.'

'The cat in hut fifty-four piddles on the nettles.'

'Not these nettles. These are homegrown in my tooth mug and, for afters, you lucky lads – prunes and condensed milk and a drop of poteen to toast me lovely mother. Come on now, boys. Draw close to the festive board.' He began dishing up the contents of his tin hat into six mess tins.

The draughts' players got up from their game. The fashioning of board and pieces had taken hours of patient filing of bits of a broken packing case. The games that followed filled in days and weeks of superfluous, use-less hours of leisure for Lieutenants Johnson and Jewitt. As they rose now from their seats, each instinctively checked the position of his opponent's pieces. There had been unholy rows over suspected cheating in the past.

All six men showed loss of weight, slackness at the waist of their trousers and bony shoulders. Barney's once chubby cheeks had grown a mite saggy. Two years on prisoners' diet had done little to maintain their phys-ique. Regular Red Cross parcels saved them from actual malnutrition.

'Happy birthday, Mrs Barnfather.' They toasted her in a gulp of mouth-screwing, gut-bending, homemade poteen.

'God, that's terrible stuff, Barney!'

344

'It is indeed. But she'll be glad we thought of her, just the same.' Barney loved his mum, so they all puckered up and drank to her health.

There was a knock at the door of the hut. 'Corporal Lemington, sir.'

The man who was a wizard with radio communications only came in person when there was very good or very bad news to report. He always carried some part of an officer's equipment, such as his boots, to explain visits to their hut. Andrew took up position by the door to check that the coast was clear, as the corporal came inside.

'Let's have it, Corporal.'

'Crete's gone.'

'Herr Doktor Gobbleguts was telling the truth for once then.'

'There's more,' said the corporal.

'I'm not sure I can stand it.' Flight Officer Winstanley, still the dandy despite patched shirt and drooping trousers, collapsed theatrically on his bunk.

'Rommel has pushed us back across the desert and retaken Halfaya.' Corporal Lemington was not to be distracted. He was a man who did one job at a time and did it well.

'What about Tobruk?'

'Still holding out.' He refused a drop of the poteen and left, carrying a different pair of boots. If his wireless set were to be discovered, he was for the chop.

After his departure an atmosphere of gloom descended on the hut, not to be relieved in any way by Barney's poteen. Greece. Crete and most of North Africa, all gone. The future, which could usually be embroidered a little to tide the POWs over the bad times, stayed resolutely bleak.

In the early hours of the morning, Andrew was awakened by the night orderly. 'Thompson, sir. The ruptured ulcer. He's bad.'

There was nothing to be done. Peritonitis had set in. Kevin Thompson slipped into unconsciousness and never recovered. By the light of a hurricane lamp, Andrew filled in the soldier's medical notes. Age twenty-three. Next of kin. Wife.

As he walked back to the hut, his khaki greatcoat slung loosely over pyjamas for the night was warm, Andrew's spirit, usually kept under strict control, coiled shamefully, wormlike, in forbidden despair. The hopelessness of his situation bowed him down. Here he was trying to treat very sick men with nothing but the bare minimum of supplies at his disposal and scant equipment for any but the simplest of surgical procedures. He was wasting his life, somewhere in Poland, while his friends were fighting for their country. Even the girls were in it, making their contribution. And what if Golze was right? Was Britain really at the end of the road?

As he made his way back to the hut he was caught in the swivelling searchlight from the guard tower. He raised two fingers. 'Get that, you bastards.' The medical officer was allowed to make nocturnal visits to the hospital

346

hut. He was OK. Couldn't care less, anyway.

Andrew's father, Mr Mount, had a large scale map of Europe in his study. The bits which were now in German hands were coloured green. Britain owned the pink bits. So which pink bits were left? A dot at Gibraltar, another in the Mediterranean – that was Malta. Cyprus, Palestine and Egypt, still pink but for how long? The rest was green. Even Libya, which had seen so many British victories over the Italian forces, was now held by Rommel, except for Tobruk and that was a pink dot in an expanse of green.

His eye travelled up through Greece, Yugoslavia, Hungary, Czechoslovakia ... to Poland. Somewhere in the midst of a continent ruled by a cruel and obsessive tyrant was their son. He took his walking stick from the hideous green umbrella stand and his hat from the peg. 'Just taking the dog out, dear,' he called. He needed to get out of the house. Clear his head.

'All right, dear.' She was sewing new school uniforms for the girls. No point in burdening her with his worries.

He saw Cyril Lewis from afar and Cyril Lewis saw him. Too late to take evasive action. Not in the mood to chat. Can't be helped. So he was extra hearty to make up for his reluctance.

'Ha! Lewis. How's your girl?'

Lewis was jumping for joy. 'A letter today. They're all right. She and Norah Moffat.

347

Couldn't say much, of course, because of the old blue pencil, but it's clear they got out of Greece just in time. Been a close shave, it seems. Lot of our lads didn't get away, once the King gave up...' Then, recollecting himself, 'And what about you, Mr Mount. Any news of Andrew?'

'Just the same.' he said. 'Just the same.'

'You heard Simon Poole's got a commission? He's in the thick of it in North Africa. Eric Dotchin and Jacky Whitmore as well. We've got our backs to the wall, Mr Mount, and no mistake.'

'As I see it,' said Mr Mount, 'the only spark of good news right now is that Hitler has declared war on Russia. That makes Russia our ally.'

'Bloody queer ally, I must say.'

'Better than none. Well, must get on. This chap,' he tugged the lead on the docile golden labrador, 'is getting restive. My regards to your good lady.'

Thirty-Five

Bloomers had a crick in her neck, standing there, talking to this tall Australian. Her chin was on a level with his umbilicus. It would be so much easier if he would sit down but, of course, he was too polite to do that. He had arrived with the previous intake of men rescued by submarine from Crete, all of them in a poor state, having fought to the finish to save the island from German occupation.

The Cretans, at the risk of their own lives, hid allied soldiers in the mountains until a ferry service by submarines to and from the south coast of Crete offered escape. With the invaluable co-operation of the Abbot of Preveli the daring scheme continued to operate under the very noses of the enemy. At the end of July Captain Keith Russell, boarding the submarine HMS *Thrasher* with other grateful servicemen, was beginning to wonder how many lives he had left.

From Alexandria the servicemen from Crete were taken to the military hospital at Victoria for a medical check-up and any necessary treatment. After some surgery on a neglected bullet wound he approached the little home sister on the question of the British army nurses he had seen on Crete. 'They left in a leaky old tub and I'm anxious to know if they arrived safely. Can you help, Ma'am?'

'Certainly, Captain. They were brought here, thoroughly exhausted after a terrible trip. Running the gauntlet. German planes bombing right, left and centre. Lots of ships sunk. The girls did splendidly, helping with the wounded. I put the poor lambs straight to bed. Nothing seriously wrong except one had dysentery rather badly. She is still here, working on our staff. Light duties. She can tell you where the others are stationed now.'

He found Sue Robinson at a desk, filling in diet sheets. 'Excuse me, Sister. I'm trying to track down Sister Norah Moffat. Can you help?'

Her eyes widened in recognition. 'I remember you! When we were leaving Kifisia, seems like a million years ago, you came to see us off and gave Norah a whacking big kiss. We were all green with envy.'

His grin followed a proven formula of cheek nicely modified with respect. 'I hadn't time to kiss you all.'

She liked his flirty eyes. Norah was jolly lucky. Smashing guy. 'I'm sorry we had to split up after all we went through together, but I got a bug and had to be warded. Here you are,' she handed a slip of paper, 'this is their unit. Give them my love and,' she smiled encouragement, 'good luck.'

Then it was simply a case of drawing fresh kit and a twenty-four hour pass before reporting to the Australian Divisional HQ in Cairo. He had no difficulty in borrowing a scout car and while that was being arranged he learned from the transport officer that General Wavell had been replaced by a long, dry Scotsman called Auchinlech, which surprised him. He had always had a pretty high regard for Wavell, but it now appeared that a recent British offensive had been unsuccessful. Wavell out. Auchinleck in.

So what was going on now? There were a lot of troops about and they were not moving forward. Redeployment, it was called. He knew all about that. He must find his girl without delay and then rejoin his unit or lose it in this regimental mêlée.

He found her present hospital, a large tented area not far from Cairo. Wasting no time with smaller fry, he sought out the regimental sergeant major who held the position of wardmaster. Sister Moffat? Ward B was the answer.

She was in the ward annexe, padding a splint. She spun round in surprise at his, 'Hello, again, Norah Moffat.'

'Goodness! Where did you spring from?'

'It's a long story. If you'll have dinner tonight with me at the New Zealand Club in Cairo we can swap yarns. Let me look at you.' He put one finger under her chin. 'You've had your face washed since I found you asleep on the grass at Suda Bay.'

Instinctively she drew back from that possessive finger. 'I'm glad you didn't waken me. We were all deadbeat.' She was noting the changes in his appearance, the gaunt face. That was new. 'I remember you had a bullet wound,' her eyes darted to his shirt sleeve.

'Nothing much. I had it cleaned up at your old hospital. Sister Robinson told me how to find you.'

Her eyes lit up. 'Robbie! How is she? She was pretty ill with dysentery.'

'Your pint-sized home sister is keeping a watchful eye on her. Light duties. She sends her love to you.'

351

At that point the steriliser boiled over. Hastily Norah adjusted the lid.

'You're busy.' He prepared to go. 'I'll pick you up outside the hospital. What time? Six thirty? Ah yes, my dear Norah, you simply must get off tonight. It is important.'

Cathy was quite enchanted by this romantic situation and pleasantly surprised that Norah had not seen this determined soldier off the premises at once.

'Well, I must admit that my first reaction was to decline,' Norah hesitated, 'but he has obviously had a tough time, holed up in Crete.'

'You don't have to make excuses, Norah dear. He's a smashing bloke. Grab him.'

'And it was thanks to him that we got out of Kifisia before the last truck left.'

'Exactly.'

'He seems a well-mannered sort of chap.'

'If a little impetuous,' Cathy smiled

'Ah well. Now that I am on my guard I can handle that.'

So she went. After duty.

She changed from the trousers which were now general issue on the wards as protection from mosquitoes and dressed in white uniform, white stockings and shoes. Civilian dress was not allowed. She brushed the sand from her regulation white felt hat with its grey and scarlet band, a touch of lipstick, a dab of Coty powder on her tanned face and she was ready.

'At least I'll get a good dinner,' she told

Cathy, thus damping down the feelings of pleasurable excitement which hovered.

Cathy, reclining on her camp bed, looked up from her book. 'Yes, of course. That's the only reason why you are going, I'm sure.'

Norah found him in the sisters' mess, chatting up the assistant matron, who was all arch twinkles. 'Have a happy evening, Sister. I'm sure that Captain – er – will look after you.'

When he took her arm, he knew she was nervous. He handed her into the waiting gharry and released her hand as soon as she was seated, aware that if he rushed his fences, he would lose her. Yet time was so short. No time for gentle wooing. That was not his style, anyhow. But when he glanced sideways at her he felt an urge to take her, felt hat, starched frock and all in one great embrace. And he knew darned well that if he did she'd be mad with him and would run away for ever.

Instead he told her a funny story about the Australian who thought he'd got the hang of all those weird English names when he called a certain lady, Mrs Fanshaw. 'My name,' she said coldly, 'is Featherstonehaugh and that is the way I pronounce it.'

That amused her. Her laugh was light and wonderful to his ears. He was beginning to feel extraordinarily elated. The girl he had dreamed about ever since that first glimpse in Kifisia was sitting at his side. A star of a girl. A dinkum Sheila, his mates back home would say. Then, steady on, he told himself. She's not your happy-go-lucky Aussie female and

353

she'll cut you down to size if you step out of line.

He had booked a table at the right distance from the three-piece band for them to enjoy the music without having conversation overwhelmed. Champagne stood in the ice bucket, ready and waiting.

'Let's start,' he said and poured it, golden, sparkling. 'I reckon we have something to celebrate. We're both alive.'

Norah raised her glass to his, boldly meeting his lingering look. 'There were times when I thought I wouldn't make it.'

'And how did you react? Scared?'

She thought a while. 'A bit. But mostly disappointed that all the things Cathy and I meant to do with our lives would never happen if I were to be killed with the next shell. All the dreams we had as kids.'

'You're good mates. You and Cathy.'

'For ever. Best friends.'

The New Zealand Club prided itself on its catering. Norah chose roasted peppers and spicy lamb kebabs and peaches stuffed with almond paste. The music was sweetly caressing, made for lovers. Many of the servicemen here were enjoying a break from recent hard fighting and would soon be returning to face more of the same. Champagne flowed like water. There was an air of recklessness – anything goes – perfectly understood by their partners, especially by the nurses there. None understood better than they the thin line between handsome

354

youth and an unidentifiable weight on a stretcher.

Somewhat to her own surprise, Norah felt completely at ease with this unpredictable Australian. She smiled at him over the rim of her glass. 'Here's to happier times.'

Coloured spotlights flickered over her in washes of indigo, ruby, violet and green. 'You look like a beautiful genie,' he said, watching the transformation of her golden hair. 'Please don't ever go back into your bottle.' Their eyes kindled on meeting.

'There's magic around tonight,' she said. The champagne made her feel loving towards the whole world. 'A special magic for soldiers.'

As he led her on to the tiny dance floor he caught a whiff of her perfume. Her cheek was in easy kissing distance, but he resisted. He danced well, gliding her skilfully among the couples.

'I didn't know Australians could dance,' she teased. 'I imagined that riding bucking broncos would be more in your line.'

'I can do that too.'

'Most of the time he talked about his family,' she related to Cathy over breakfast. 'They run a cattle station somewhere in the middle of Australia. His sister and her husband help the father run the place.'

'Hasn't he got a mother?'

'Oh yes, he's got a mother. She's his template for womanhood. She's everything a mum should be; runs a school for the aboriginal children on the station, first aid expert, gardener, dressmaker and goodness knows what else.'

'What is he telling you all this for?' Cathy demanded.

'Well, it's nonsense really, but he wants me to go and visit his family some day, when all the fighting is over; to go either with him,' she paused, 'or, if he is killed, to go on my own.'

Cathy checked to see if Norah was serious. 'What a strange request, unless he is thinking of making you his wife.'

Norah's face clouded. 'Maybe that is in his mind.'

'Good heavens! He's a quick worker. He's seen you only three times – and you slept through one of those.'

'Well,' Norah said dismissively, 'there's unlikely to be a fourth time. He has rejoined his unit, wherever that may be.'

Cathy was interested; to give any admirer a second thought was a new departure for Norah. She was expert at the cold freeze. 'Do you like him?' Eggshell business, this, with Norah. There were limits, even to a best friend.

There was just the slightest hesitation. 'Yes, I do, but I'm not looking for a husband.'

They left the mess to walk to the wards. The sun's glare was already dazzling, though the day had just begun. Heat shimmered over the metal tracks laid over the sand for vehicles. 'The Auk's batman is on my ward. I might

356

meet The Big Fellow if he comes to visit.'

'What's the matter with his batman?'

'Diphtheria.'

'Then I don't think you'll be meeting the Auk.'

An ambulance nosed over the skyline. And another.

'Convoy.' They quickened their steps.

Thirty-Six

1941–42

The nights grew colder, though daytime heat was still oppressive in the desert hospital where most of the nurses rescued from Greece now worked. It was November. 'This time last year we were on our way to Greece,' they reminded themselves sadly. 'I shall always remember our first day there.'

'I shall never forget our last,' said Cathy.

She and Norah were off duty on the evening when a major transfer of patients was announced, sounding a warning that another battle was looming. Their present hospital, which had previously occupied a base position, was considerably nearer the frontline after Rommel's latest advance. It was essential that men, suffering from dysentery and other tropical illnesses, occupying beds at the moment should be transferred in order to accommodate battle casualties in the event of further fighting.

The two nurses who shared a tent with Cathy and Norah brought news of the transfer when they came off duty. The night air was chill but the brave light from a Tilly lamp and the aroma of coffee simmering on the little oil stove made the tent invitingly cosy. Hastily the new arrivals laced up the tent flap behind them.

Cathy put down her book 'What kept you? You're late.'

'Every patient who can be moved is to be transferred tomorrow. We've been packing up their things.' Annette Taylor was a loose-limbed, big-boned girl from Coventry, awkwardly put together – with her big hands she gratefully clasped the mug of coffee poured for her by Cathy.

Small, neatly articulated Una Michelson was quite the opposite to her companion. Over the rim of her mug she solemnly regarded Norah and Cathy. 'Our poor boys would prefer to stay where they are. Wouldn't you, with dysentery?'

Una had left the Shetlands when she was in her teens to train as a nurse in Aberdeen Royal Infirmary, but her distinctive speech persisted. Each carefully enunciated phrase seemed to have been properly considered, weighed, trimmed and polished before it was allowed out. Taylor had no patience with such pernickety delivery and frequently trampled

358

all over Una's sentences before she had really finished with them.

Taylor lit up a cigarette. 'Another bloody push on the way. And then before our lads know what's hit them, they'll be back here again with Rommel at their shirt tails.' The deep draw on her cigarette was intended to lend authority to her opinion but it merely filled her lungs with smoke and she collapsed on her camp bed melodramatically beating her chest.

'That's a nasty cough,' Norah looked up from the stocking she was darning. 'You ought to see a doctor.'

'I'm not unbuttoning my shirt for any of that lot!'

'Oh, don't be soppy. They are looking at chests almost every day.'

'Not ladies' chests, they aren't and I'm shy.'

Guffaws of laughter followed this. 'Drink your coffee,' said Cathy, 'and stop talking gaff.'

Outside, in the Egyptian night, the bleat of a wandering goat, the wild call of a coyote, underlined the alien environment for these nurses from the other side of the world, but within their tent all was reassuringly British. The cigarettes they were smoking were Senior Service, the little oil stove was made in Birmingham and they were drinking precious instant coffee sent by kind friends back in Britain.

A message for Cathy from Simon, delivered by an ambulance driver, reinforced the opinion that another campaign was about to begin. 'I may not be able to get in touch for a while but don't worry. Have contacted Jacky and Eric. Both OK. Be good, both of you.'

Always at times like this, before the battle, nurses' thoughts were on those soldiers, briefed and waiting. Many nurses here in the desert had brothers, sweethearts and friends in the services, men like Simon, Eric, Jacky and Norah's Australian.

A dread shared by them all was that one day the casualty on the stretcher would be a friend or relation.

The new offensive, code-named Crusader, got off to a fine start. Simon's old position at Halfaya was recaptured and, from there, the advance gathered momentum. Casualties brought stories of success at last, of German troops in retreat. On 1 December the siege of Tobruk was relieved.

The news leapt across the miles to Britain. Success in the desert. Rommel on the run. A few days later, on Sunday, 7 December, the headlines in the newspapers eclipsed even Tobruk. Without warning, Japanese planes attacked the American fleet in Pearl Harbor and some of America's finest battleships were sunk with an appalling loss of life. Britain's 'Friend Across The Water' who had been providing war materials and food since the hostilities began now entered the conflict totally with sleeves rolled up. She declared war on Japan and Germany and began training her young men for war. Britain immediately gave support by declaring war on Japan.

'Damned unsporting, that attack on Pearl Harbor.' Home Guard Sergeant Ken Poole held the match to his pipe and sucked hard. 'Bombing sitting ducks. But, for us, things are looking up, Cyril. We've got America with us now.'

'Aye.' Cathy's father, too, was feeling remarkably cheerful. 'First Russia, now the Yanks. I could almost risk my shirt and put a bet on our winning this damn war after all.'

All their new-found optimism melted like snow in sunshine as 1942 ushered in a crop of disasters. The Japanese invaded Hong Kong and Singapore. They sank the Royal Navy's two brightest jewels, the battleships HMS *Prince of Wales* and HMS *Repulse*, with heavy loss of life.

The regulars at the King's Head reeled in stupefaction. Hong Kong, gone? Singapore? The British bastion, the unassailable, impregnable watchtower of the East, gone? Surrendered to a race of little people who, so it was previously supposed, had defective eyesight and who went to war on bicycles? Whatever next?

Japan in the south Pacific was next, threatening New Guinea and its neighbour Australia. Australia, remote from the heat of war until now, found herself at its brink and reclaimed one of her divisions from the desert war in order to protect the homeland. One of the regiments recalled was that of Norah's admirer.

Annette Taylor was leaving the sisters' mess when a dispatch rider roared up. Still astride his motorcycle, he handed her an envelope and wiped the sand from his goggles 'Letter for Miss Norah Moffat,' he said. 'Reckon it's urgent, Ma'am. Can you get it to her?'

The Australian accent put Taylor on the trail at once. 'For you, Moffat. From your gorgeous Digger.'

The note was brief and to the point. 'Emergency ... Must see you. Will call 1400 hours Tuesday. Keith.'

And today was Monday...

'The Aussies have dropped us in the dirt,' Taylor said with some heat. 'They're getting out. You tell him, Moffat.'

'They can't be expected to stay here when their own homeland is threatened. Don't be such a cow, Taylor.'

Una agreed to change duties with Norah to allow her to keep the appointment. She was waiting for him when he called at the mess and he took her to Cairo, to Groppi's, for tea. There was not much time and he had a lot to say.

'The Japs are attacking New Guinea. If they get to Port Moresby, the Australian mainland is only a short hop away – and most of our troops are on the wrong side of the world.' He was serious, unsmiling and his light blue eyes were troubled. 'My div is picked to go.' He met her concerned look with a wild intensity.

362

'It breaks me up to leave you, Norah. Now that I've found you, after Greece, after Crete, to lose you again is hard to bear.'

And she was sorry to see him go, sorry to lose someone she was fond of, but it meant more to him than that. 'There is not much time to tell you all that is in my mind. In peacetime, I would take it easy, give you a chance to get to know me for the man I am before I asked you to make an important commitment. But this is not peacetime. You and I are living in quite extraordinary times, my dear.' He took her hand in his, pale against his own, sharp veined and burnt brown. 'Listen hard while I plead my case.'

She began to fidget nervously. He could see from the anxiety in her eyes that she was unprepared for any emotional outpouring but he was determined to speak out before he boarded the troopship at Suez. His voice was level and quiet. 'From the moment I first set eyes on you in the hospital tent at Kifisia I truly loved you.'

The fidgeting stopped. She sat still as a statue, her eyes fixed on his face.

'I've known other women. I've been around, but no one has ever made me feel that I want to wrap up the world and give it to her. I'm going over the top a bit but it may be some time before we meet again. Norah, my darling, more than anything else in the world I want to make you my wife. I am asking you to become engaged. Ah!' he exclaimed when she quickly withdrew her

363

hand. 'Do not turn me down without a second thought.'

Norah was filled with sudden panic. 'I do not know what to say.'

'If you think you could love me a little, I could build on that,' he searched her face. 'Just to know that you are waiting for me would be a bulletproof vest, a suit of armour. And I will come back. I'm a lucky guy, you know.' He grinned and the lines of his face relaxed. 'The kookaburras laughed when I was born, so my ma says. And that's an infallible sign of good luck.' Serious once more, he asked, 'Do you care for me at all, Norah?' His voice lost its buoyancy, dropping into quiet control. 'Or am I just a big, brash digger?'

Her quick smile of denial lightened his heart. 'I'm very fond of you, Keith.'

'That is the first time you have called me by my name.'

'Perhaps, if I got to know you better ... I'm not sure.' Confusedly, she shook her head. 'You have taken me by surprise. You pay me a compliment, asking me to be your wife, but we hardly know each other. I'm not at all sure that I would be any good doing things an Australian wife should do.'

'You don't need to shear sheep or make damper. Only be your own sweet self. I just know my ma and the rest of my family will love you.'

He fumbled in his shirt pocket for cigarettes. The hand that held the match was unsteady. 'I'm sorry to rush you like this.'

She looked at his pleading face, at his kind, crinkled eyes and saw that he truly loved her but her own feelings were in disarray. 'I need time,' she insisted. 'Please let me think about it. I will write. I promise. When I have had time to think.'

He tried to hide his disappointment. 'I am so certain of my own feelings, I have made no allowance for any doubt on your part, but you have every right to be cautious. I must respect that.' He retreated from his impulsive persuasion. 'You have promised to write your answer – I will wait for that. Remember that wherever I am, my sweet girl, you will be with me in my thoughts.' He picked up her hand where it lay, passive, on the tablecloth and put it to his lips. 'Do not forget me when I am gone.'

'I have promised. I will write.'

He cast a long look about him, at the tables set with cakes and flowers, the laughing girls and their escorts, the smooth waiters, the slowly turning punkahs and the fiddlers sawing the air. He would never return to this place.

She saw him glance at his watch. 'When do you sail?'

'1800 hours.'

She got to her feet. 'You must go.'

They walked through the pushing crowds, and beggars and little boys pleading for baksheesh and cigarettes. He hailed a gharry. His face, she thought, looked like a man in shock. Wondering how best to say goodbye, she put out a hand which he roughly brushed aside and took her hard to his body so that she felt the beating of his heart and smelt his man's smell. It seemed to her that it was with anger that he smothered her face and neck with kisses – her hair, her closed eyes – and devoured her mouth. Fear suddenly invaded her, all pleasure gone. She pushed against his chest, scarcely able to breathe and he let her go.

'Sorry, sorry, sorry,' he handed her into the carriage behind the grinning driver. 'Take Miss to the hospital. Quick smart.' And paid him.

She turned as the gharry creaked away and saw him standing stock-still, head and shoulders above the crowd. At the corner she lifted an arm in farewell. Out of sight, she pressed a handkerchief to her lips and scrubbed away the contact. She had hated his kisses and was afraid she might be sick.

On her return to the hospital she changed quickly into working uniform and made her way to the ward where Michelson waited to be relieved. Cathy, on her way across the parking lot, paused and waited for her.

'How did it go?'

'Tell you later. No time now.'

Cathy pulled a face. Didn't like the sound of that. But later, after supper, Norah detained her. 'Don't go back to the tent yet. I don't want to discuss this in front of the other two.'

Apart from the local serving girls who were clearing the tables, the mess tent was almost

366

empty. A few nurses lingered over coffee. Talk was subdued and mostly 'shop'. Norah made for a small table in one corner and produced half a bottle of gin from her shoulder bag.

Cathy grabbed two deck chairs. 'This is serious.'

'The last of my NAAFI ration.'

'I'll get glasses.'

'And lemonade or something. I can't drink it neat no matter how suicidal I feel.'

Cathy returned from the kitchen annexe. 'You're in a fine state! Fire away. Tell all.'

Norah poured two large gins. 'He's gone. I said goodbye to him.'

'If you are sorry, then I'm sorry. He was a good type.'

'He has to defend his own country.'

'Very reasonable. Is that the end of the great romance?'

'He asked me to become engaged.'

Cathy brightened visibly. 'Norah darling! How exciting. What did you say?'

'I was taken by surprise, couldn't think what would be the right thing to say in the circs ... the war and all that. Same as you with Simon,' she said pointedly.

' "Yes" would have pleased him.'

'I know. He waxed quite poetic.'

'Lucky you. No one ever gets poetic about me. A limerick or two perhaps.

'There was a fat nurse in the army.
Whom everyone knew was quite barmy.'

'Oh shut up, Cathy,' Norah said crossly, 'this is just about the most serious moment of my life.'

'All right, old dear,' Cathy was at once contrite. 'Keep your shirt on. What's the problem? This very nice chap with the physique of a Greek god wants to marry you. You're the envy of every QA in the hospital.'

'I like him,' Norah said seriously. 'I do like him—'

'But?'

Norah topped up their glasses. 'The problem is,' she spoke very carefully, 'I cannot bear him to touch me. He kissed me, all over.'

Cathy's eyebrows rose. 'In Groppi's?'

'All over my face, I mean, silly. My hair, my eyes, my neck and ... my mouth. He ... he put his tongue inside my mouth, Cathy! I would have screamed if I could have found the breath. It was simply ghastly. I certainly cannot marry him. In fact, Cathy, it is quite obvious that I cannot marry anyone. The truth is,' Norah said miserably, 'I like men but I can't *bear* them to touch me.' Huge tears welled up and trickled over her cheeks.

'Ah, Norah love,' Cathy put her arm about her friend's shoulders and offered a fairly clean handkerchief. 'Here, blow your nose and cheer up. It's only petting after all. You could get to like it with the right person. There's no need to get worked up over it.'

'But, don't you see, I'm different. I'm different from all the girls. I'm different from you.' Her tear-filled eyes accused Cathy.

'Oh come on! Andrew must have kissed you. You didn't go hysterical over that.'

'Not like that. He never kissed me like that.'

'Huh, schoolkids' kisses. Look, Norah, right now we are all working under a fair bit of pressure. And the men we meet are under even greater pressure. How can anyone remain normal in times like these? Put it all out of your mind. You'll laugh about it in a little while.'

'I won't.'

A fleeting image of Mrs Moffat crossed Cathy's mind. 'Maybe your mum didn't cuddle you when you were little?'

Norah shook her head. 'Kissing, hugging, mother did not approve. She said it was not character building.'

Cathy thought of her own loving parents, her father's bear hugs. 'Well, that's probably something to do with it, but when the right man, etc, etc. Anyhow, you and I have hugged each other since we were bairns.'

'That's different. You're a girl.'

'Oh, come on.' Cathy got to her feet.' 'You've got this all mixed up. It'll all settle down when our lives sort themselves out.' She took Norah's arm. 'Right now, we've busted your gin ration and it's bedtime. We'll never get up in the morning and I've got a man in the iron lung.'

Into the night they went, arm in arm, a trifle unsteadily.

369

Thirty-Seven

1942

In Cathy's opinion, Norah was making a
great deal of fuss over this letter to her Australian. As she watched her friend's halting
progress with pen and paper, the thought
occurred to her that maybe there would never
be a man for Norah. *What if she's a designated
immaculate?* The unrehearsed phrase pleased
her. *Well, perhaps she is.*

Norah eventually put together a sensitively
worded rejection of Keith Russell's proposal
of marriage, but a rejection just the same.
When, on the following day, a cheery note
arrived from him, posted at the last moment
before he sailed from Port Tewfik and
crossing with her own letter, she lapsed into
despondency.

One last note to say how much I love
you.
I was never a great swot at school, but
there was a dinkum little lady who
taught us poetry. She'd been crossed in
love, I reckon, for whenever she recited

370

this poem she always had a little cry, and she was so pretty and young we boys used to bring her flowers to cheer her up. We'd pinched the flowers from our mothers' borders, of course.

Read it carefully, my darling girl, I mean it.

> *I will not let thee go*
> *I hold thee by too many bands.*
> *Thou sayest farewell and lo*
> *I have thee by the hands*
> *And wilt not let thee go*

I don't know what clever geezer wrote that, but whoever he was must have been feeling like me. Write soon, sweetheart.

'Don't worry about it,' Cathy said. 'he'll get over it. Men do.' But Cathy, so glib about others' heartaches, could not reconcile her own. Deep in her most private thoughts was a closed box with contents too painful to contemplate. Sometimes the lid was lifted a fraction as when, in the last intake of casualties, she noticed the shoulder flash of the Coldstream Guards as she cut away a young soldier's empty sleeve. Her heart contracted. Even after the passage of time the sight of that flash brought all the longing back. 'Did you ever know a certain Lieutenant Raymond Webster?' she wanted to ask but such a trivial question would have been out of place.

371

Pull yourself together, Cathy Lewis. She administered the prescribed injection of morphia, wet his dry lips, bathed his hands and face.

'Thanks, Sister,' he said.

That *he* should be grateful! Listen, she wanted to say to him, dear young man, dear sacrificial lamb, all the suffering, dispossessed people in this mad, bad world owe a debt to you. You are in no one's debt.

She removed his heavy boots and tied them to the handles of his stretcher, and wrapped his fish-cold feet in a blanket. 'The MO is on his way.'

Maybe, she considered the possibility as she laid out the equipment for a blood transfusion, maybe, after all, it was no worse to die of rotten lungs in a sanatorium than to end up on a stretcher like this young man, minus a good right arm, somewhere in Egypt, far from home.

It was obvious from the increasing number of casualties being brought to the hospital that the latest allied offensive was running into trouble. The long lines of communication which had bedevilled the German Army in its advance now hindered Operation Crusader. First Benghazi then Tobruk were retaken.

Tobruk, the name that rang victory bells not six months earlier when its long siege was lifted, was back in German hands. It was a bad time to lose the Australian divisions who had gone to fight in New Guinea. The morale of the troops was at an all time low.

'You know what MEF stands for, Sister?' a weary soldier asked. 'No. Not Middle East Forces. Men England Forgot. We fought hard for every salt pan, every dune, a year ago and now we're being pushed back over the same old ground. We're passing places where we lost mates on the way up. Now, there's just a wooden cross stuck in the sand where we left a pal – and all for nothing.'

They were sick to death of the desert. 'Benghazi for Christmas. Cairo New Year' was the bitter catchphrase. Norah laid a finger on the young man's wrist to take his pulse.

'Oh, don't let go of my hand,' he pleaded. 'You are the first woman I've seen during two years up and down that flaming desert.'

The German advance continued headlong into Egypt – Sidi Barrani, Mersa Matruh, all places fiercely fought for and now lost. Rommel stopped at last to revictual at a place called El Alamein seventy miles from Cairo.

There was panic in that city amongst the merchants. Which master to serve? Was it too soon to pull down the British and Commonwealth flags and put up the German swastika? The sight of charred paper drifting above the walls of the British Embassy fuelled rumour. The situation was desperate and called for a new hand at the helm. General Bernard Montgomery appeared on the scene.

Cathy was on night duty, trying to sleep through the hot and steamy day. Even a single loose sheet as a covering was too hot within the sweltering tent. Her thighs and back were sticky with sweat when an orderly brought a message that she had a visitor. A quick sluice with half a bucket of tepid water refreshed her before she hurried out to meet Simon.

He grabbed her in a tight hug. 'It's good to see you, Cathy. Are you OK?' He had lost weight. His skin was burned brown and his hair bleached by the sun. He wore three pips on the epaulettes of his shirt. 'Fleeting visit, old girl, I have to pick up a replacement officer in Cairo, but he can wait five minutes. I just had to see you, my pet. The next time might be a long way off.' He ran his hand over her thick, bobbed hair. 'I wanted to say, I think you and Norah and all the rest of you girls are doing a grand job.'

'What's going on, Simon? There are rumours that Rommel is about to enter the city.'

'That he will not do,' Simon said with certainty. 'We've got a smashing new Commander in Chief and Rommel is going to get his come-uppance.' He glanced at his watch. 'Got to go. Walk with me to the truck.' He put an arm about her shoulders. 'Just had to see you, make sure you're OK. Give my love to Norah,' and kissed her lightly on the cheek.

'Good luck Simon,' Cathy said seriously as he climbed into the driver's seat. 'And – congratulations, Captain.'

He started the engine and put the truck in gear. 'Promotion is easy when all your superior officers get killed.' He drove away and did not look back.

Norah was relieved when no answer to her letter arrived from Keith. Much better this way, she told herself. A clean break mends quickly, but when she heard that Japanese forces in New Guinea had pushed back the Australians almost to Port Moresby, she could imagine his anxiety for his country and the safety of his family. 'Port Moresby,' he had said, 'is only a short hop from Australia.' Her letter of rejection would do nothing to lift his spirits.

The present – and very real – threat to Cairo and the canal, however, put all other thoughts out of her head. The new Commander in Chief had said quite bluntly that there would be no retreating. His words to the troops were: 'We will fight on the ground we now hold. There will be casualties. There will be NO withdrawal.'

Strangely, these chilling words seemed to strengthen the troops rather than discourage. He had promised another thing, that he would not order an attack until he had enough armaments and men to do the job properly. And the troops could see for themselves the columns of tanks and armoured cars arriving by sea. Cathy and Norah were among the reduced nursing staff who were staying, with suitcases packed for an emergency.

'Last ditch,' Norah stated flatly. 'Like

Greece.'

'But the troops are in tremendous spirits. A few months ago they thought it was all over for us and now look at them.' Men driving past the hospital tents in gun carriers and armoured cars signalled the 'V' for victory sign, waving cheerfully to Cathy and Norah.

'They trust Monty, Simon says. Where he leads, they will follow.'

When the last ship withdrew from the canal a sombre silence fell. All remaining patients had been transferred either to Palestine or South Africa. Their beds were made up with clean linen, awaiting casualties, which would, inevitably, be heavy.

Cathy and Norah joined servicemen and women in the garrison church in Cairo for a simple service and prayers for those taking part in the forthcoming battle upon which the whole future of the Middle East depended. 'There would be no withdrawal.' Those were the words of the commanding officer.

Then doctors and nurses, FANY ambulance drivers and other medical auxiliaries who were staying, returned to their posts – the troops to battle stations to await the fateful summons.

There was a letter waiting for Norah. It was her own, the one she had sent to Keith, returned unopened. Stamped all over in smudged blue letters was the word 'DECEASED'.

At nine forty p.m. on 23 October, 1942, one thousand British guns opened their barrage in the most unholy row ever heard in the desert.

The big sunburnt Australian was dead. The man who could dance and ride wild horses, who had a wonderful mother who had wanted to show Norah his country, who had truly loved her. 'Killed in Action.' Her eyes filled with tears.

'Just think of this,' Cathy comforted her. 'He died without knowing that you turned him down.'

Thirty-Eight

For several days the battle of El Alamein waged without supremacy on either side. Casualties, as expected, were heavy. The price that was being paid for what their Commander in Chief had told them was the last chance was high. Cathy dreaded to see Simon on one of the stretchers brought to the reception tent. She knew he was in the thick of the fight. For the staff it was work and sleep, work and sleep until the battle was won and Rommel was in full retreat.

Norah, kneeling between stretchers, found herself in that most dreaded situation. She was looking down on Eric. A needle of pain pierced her temple. His face was the colour of putty. There was a field dressing bound round his head, another, soaked in blood on one leg. She dropped to her knees and loosened the neck of his shirt to feel for his carotid pulse. It was faint but regular. He opened his eyes and there was a flash of recognition.

He gave a low moan. 'Norah. Oh, Norah.'

'Just lie still, Eric, and leave everything to us.' She was rapidly opening the waxed envelope tied to his shirt button and reading the medical notes it contained. Compound fracture right femur. Multiple lacerations forearm and scalp. Morphia and anti-gas gangrene serum had been given. She tucked the report away. Through lids made heavy with morphia, Eric was watching her. 'The MO is on his way,' she reassured him with her calm. 'You will need some blood.'

The leg was in a bad mess with splintered bone showing white in the mangled muscles. Lacerations of scalp, the surgeon found, were not too deep. Those on the forearm were more serious. 'Get him ready for the theatre, Sister. I'll do him first. That leg looks pretty urgent.'

With care Norah removed his boots, slicing them down the sides with a razor blade. 'Don't worry, Eric. You'll be OK. I'll be here when you come round from the anaesthetic.'

'Norah!' his whisper was urgent. 'In my kitbag, beside my watch and wallet, there's a ring.'

'I'll hand them over to the RSM and get a

378

receipt,' she promised.

'Listen hard, Norah. In case I don't come back. The ring belonged to Jacky. He stood on a mine,' his deep, dark eyes brimmed with misery. Norah took his hand in hers. 'Jacky died in my arms, Norah. My old friend. And...' he was struggling to keep control of his emotions, 'he said, "the ring is for Evie. Tell her I love her."' Eric's eyes were riveted on Norah. 'Will you see to that ... if I get my chips?'

The surgeons managed to save the leg, although it was touch and go. The next few days were critical. Most of the shell fragments were removed from various parts of his body, 'and any that are left will work themselves out' was the surgeon's breezy prognosis.

Cathy and Norah spent all their free moments at his bedside As his condition improved, he could talk of nothing but Jacky. 'We were at primary school together. He used to bully me unmercifully because I was such a weed and then he would make up for it by giving me pear drops and letting me have a go with his pea shooter,' he smiled wryly. 'I was never allowed to have a pea shooter. Too dangerous, my parents said. That's a laugh, considering.'

Cathy was thinking of Jacky's parents. Poor Millie Whitmore.

Norah was writing reports at the ward desk when Eric's company officer arrived. She told him that Eric was making satisfactory progress and would probably be evacuated to

Britain on the first available ship.

He followed her down the ward to Eric's bed. 'I have good news for him. He has been recommended for an award.'

Norah turned to look at him in enquiry.

'Perhaps he has not told you? His mate, Private Whitmore, was sent as a runner with an urgent signal. He stood on a mine and Dotchin went in and brought him out, but there was nothing we could do for the poor chap. Dotchin then offered to take the signal himself and was almost back in safety when he stopped a big chunk of mortar shell.'

'It must have been an important message to endanger two men's lives.' The note of criticism in Norah's voice did not escape him.

This is a very attractive nurse, he thought, but none of my business. 'It was,' he assured her. 'A gun position was about to be surrounded by the enemy. We had no radio connection. Dotchin's information allowed them to get themselves and their gun out safely. I'm glad he hasn't lost the leg.'

'He's an old friend of mine,' Norah told him. 'It's odd, you know, he did not seem to have the makings of a hero.'

'This much I have learned about heroes,' the officer said humbly, 'you can never tell.'

When the boy arrived with the telegram Millie Whitmore thought she was going to faint. Some people she knew in the town had been sent these telegrams from the War Office. She kept up appearances, however, smiled at the delivery boy, who was Mrs Smart's youngest, and said, no, there was no answer. Even before she opened it she knew there was no answer. When she closed the door her legs buckled beneath her and she slithered to the floor. And that was where her husband found her, glassy eyed, clutching the unopened 'wire'.

He stopped and looked hard at her. She wasn't dead, as he had at first supposed. So what was the matter with her? He approached reluctantly for he disliked intensely dramatic situations like this and she damn well knew they upset him. 'What you doing sitting down there, woman?'

The sound of his familiar gruff voice seemed to bring her to her senses. She waved the orange envelope at him. 'Read it,' she said, and much against his will, he had to take it since it looked as though she wasn't going to read it and somebody had to do it. He sli it open and read it and stood stock-still as if hit by a thunderbolt.

'What's it say? What's it say?' Millie was cheeping like a chicken. Her voice had taken on a life of its own.

'It's our Jacky,' he said and he hadn't spoken so soft like that for years. 'He's bought it.'

The telegram fluttered down from his big, shaky hand to settle on her lap, feckless as an autumn leaf. He picked his cap off the peg and took himself off to The Lobster Pot at the head of the river, Jacky's favourite pub.

The other drinkers in the bar kept away from him that night. He looked as though he could murder the lot of them. 'Go to hell,' he growled when one of his cronies offered to buy him a drink, so they left him alone and among themselves whispered and wondered. 'It'll be his lad, Jacky. See if I'm not right.'

When Millie Whitmore had worn herself out with weeping she had a quick look in the mirror, wiped her beetroot face with a wet flannel and hurried off to see Chrissie Lewis.

Thirty-Nine

1943

The bells were ringing in Tunis. Seven months after the great battle at Alamein the victorious 8th Army met British and American troops advancing eastwards from Algiers. Rommel, forced to fight on two fronts, was beaten. The war in North Africa was won. Wooden crosses in the desert sand marking the graves of allied soldiers could, at last, be acknowledged and honoured as the price of victory.

'This round is ours,' Captain Simon Poole told his men. They had fought hard all the way from Alamein, had suffered huge losses but not as huge as the Germans'. Simon had come through unscathed – so far. There was a long way to go before the game was won and he knew the mettle of his adversary. 'The Fox has gone to ground in Italy. Take a break now but be ready for the Tally-Ho. Enjoy yourselves. The NAAFI is here. ENSA is here. George Formby, Beatrice Lillie, Noel Coward, all here to entertain you. If you haven't heard Alicia Delysia sing "Parlez moi d'amour" you're in for a thrill. You damn well deserve it. Well done, men.'

Then Simon went in search of Cathy and Norah. He had kept in touch with their hospital as it moved up, in the rear of the troops. He went at once to their location on the outskirts of Tunis. Here, in wards filled with men who would never be completely whole again – the blind, the limbless, those whose future would be dependent on another's charity – celebrations were muted.

Simon offered Cathy and Norah a spell of light relief from the day-to-day tragedy in the wards. 'I've got transport and a picnic. Can you get time off? Bring your bathers.'

Joyfully they climbed aboard Simon's jeep. Cathy held up a listening finger, a beatific smile on her face. 'No guns!'

He drove them to nearby Philipville, an undisturbed little port of whitewashed houses and sandy beaches. They swam in the Mediterranean, picnicked in the sun, conscious all the time that this was no more than a happy interlude. Preparations for the next campaign – the invasion of Italy – were already in hand.

383

This was but a moment of pleasure to be enjoyed to the full in the company of dear friends, not to be spoiled by thoughts of tomorrow.

'Any news of Andrew, Norah?'

'Correspondence cards are rationed. If he has any of his allocation left after writing to his family, I think Hilde gets them.'

'Well, I have news of Eric.' Simon refilled their glasses. 'He's back in Cairo.'

'What on earth is he doing there? He should have been sent home with that leg wound.'

'He could have gone home after Palestine, but he chose to stay in the Middle East. You know why? Love, my dears. That charming little interfering cherub. Eric is in love with his physiotherapist. The fact that he is able to walk now with very little disability is, he insists, entirely due to her devoted care in the Palestine hospital He's back on duty now but not a frontline slogger any more. A company office sergeant in Cairo, a desk job, which is where he should have been all along, with his clerical know-how. I tracked him down when I accompanied our brigade major on army business recently.' He laughed delightedly. 'He's crazy about his Rosemary. Moonie as a blackbird in May. Our dear old Eric is in love.'

The girls were astonished. 'What about Eileen?'

'Eileen has had her chips. Eric can't wait to get spliced.'

'What does the lady think about that?'

'A case of mutual adoration it would seem.'

Simon lifted his glass. 'So we'll drink to Eric and his Rosie.'

'I'm glad they saved his leg. It was touch and go.'

'The trouble is,' Andrew said to his audience of five, 'our minds have stopped growing. What is there to extend them? We have exhausted the reservoirs of experience of every single one of us. What are we left with? Cud, that's been chewed over interminably. Pap with no nourishment.'

'Oh, come off it, Doc,' Barnfather would be jolly and would put on a bright, accommodating face if he were on the way to the guillotine. 'It's not so grim as all that. We can still find something to chat about amongst the six of us.'

Winstanley stretched his long, thin legs. They had always been long, thin legs, but now they were a good deal thinner than they were at the beginning of the men's imprisonment. 'He's right, Barney. Not one of you could surprise me with an opinion. I know what you are going to say before you say it. What has any one of us done, or thought, or said during the last twelve months that is new?'

Silence fell.

'I thought I felt a poem coming on, but that was months ago. Stillbirth,' Stevens, the other airman, finished lamely 'Can't seem to get motivated here.'

Three years had passed since Dunkirk and there was little unexplored material left in anyone's head.

'Actually,' Flight Lieutenant Winstanley's normally indolent gaze alighted with a spark of interest on Andrew, 'it's the doc who's the cagey one.'

Andrew put up his guard. 'Me?'

Winstanley laughed. 'Look at him. All innocence, but who is Fraulein Müllerman, we ask ourselves? We know about my little peccadilloes. We know all about Steve's bonnie little Scots wife and Barney's mother's corns and her Eccles cakes, and Jenkins's son's adenoids. Johnnie's adolescent love life has been an education to us all but who, we wonder, is Andrew's fraulein to whom he devotes most of his correspondence?'

'We don't call her Fraulein,' said Andrew. 'She is a Jewish girl who escaped from Germany in 1938, and I love her.'

'Well, well, well. Lift a stone and see what you find.'

Andrew shrugged. 'Nothing to get excited about. She doesn't lose any sleep over me.' His eyes took on a dreamy look. 'She is the most beautiful girl in the world.'

A knock at the door and Corporal Lemington came in with an unaccustomed smile spread across his face. Terrible teeth, thought Andrew. Never noticed them before. 'Spit it out, Corporal. You look as pleased as if you had won the Irish Sweepstake.'

'Just about, sir. Just about. The desert war is

over and Rommel's beaten. His lot are either in the bag or hoofing it to Italy. The bells are ringing in Tunis, sir. All the lads are celebrating.'

The girl of Andrew's dreams was now sister in charge of the major surgical ward at Eastport General Hospital, a figure of authority in her blue uniform and white frilled cap. She moved swiftly and lightly about her ward on flat rubber-soled shoes, looking about her, registering every nuance of her surroundings: the general appearance, contented or otherwise, of each patient, his pillows, his locker and whether or not his water jug needed refilling. Nothing escaped those glittering dark eyes. She did not readily smile. Life was too earnest for that. She was utterly reliable and correct in everything she did, the admiration of junior doctors and the respected ally of consultants.

This was visiting day. The doors would be open to visitors, two for each patient, within five minutes. Today she was expecting Mr Lewis, Cathy's father. The junior probationer had been instructed to watch out for him and take him into her office as soon as he appeared. She had no idea what brought him here to see her. She hoped it was not bad news. After Jacky, one could never be entirely free from anxiety. When she returned to her room Cyril rose to his feet with a friendly smile. No bad news then.

'Hilde,' he never bothered with the title, 'my

word, it's good to see you, and looking as pretty as a picture.'

Hastily she closed the door behind her before the juniors started giggling. 'I'm very pleased to see you, Mr Lewis. What brings you here? Not bad news, I hope?'

They sat facing each other in chairs not meant for comfort. He had noted the strictly professional character of the room, with its framed certificates and reference books, shelves filled with files and stationery.

'I think you will agree with Chrissie and me that it's extremely good news. Cathy is coming home.'

Hilde was genuinely surprised and delighted. 'I haven't had a letter for some time, but I know they vork hard and now the desert war is over they need holidays.'

There was a knock at the door. A tray of tea and two digestive biscuits was put before them. 'Nothing fancy, Mr Lewis. Rationing, you know.'

'It's only Cathy who is coming home,' Cyril was not to be distracted from his news. 'She's very upset because Norah and she have been separated.'

Hilde frowned. 'I can understand. Always they are together. I was jealous of their vonderful friendship. I never had a friend like that.' A sharp brazen thrust of memory surfaced like a goldfish in the circumscribed bowl of her mind, the memory of good friend; Anna, screaming 'Jew!' at her and spitting in her face. She had to contain herself in front of Cathy's father to hide the inner cringe.

'Where is Norah, then?'

'On a hospital ship. I suppose since her father is a sailor the powers-that-be think she will be a good one too.' He had a hearty chuckle at his little joke, but kept it nice and quiet. Sick people here and he wouldn't want to get on the wrong side of this little lady.

After he had gone she continued to sit, reduced to immobility by the memories she had disturbed when she thought of Anna, memories of the last days in Berlin. 'Papa! Papa!' she had run home from school. 'They call me a Jew, Papa! I'm not a Jew?'

Up till that day she had joined the rest of the class in making life miserable for the girl who everyone knew was a Jew. After that, all her schoolmates turned on her. In fear and confusion she had fled the taunts of her one-time friends, but when she reached the tall, wooden gates that led to her father's house she saw painted there the yellow star of David. She ran, distracted, into the house, 'Papa! Papa! I'm not a Jew!'

Her father had embraced her and, for the first time in her life, she saw him cry. 'Yes, my child,' he had said. 'We are Jews and that will bring us nothing but pain and grief.'

A knock at her office door roused her. Her staff nurse put her head inside. 'Are you ready to go off duty, Sister? It's six o'clock.'

After Hilde left the ward, the staff nurse stood alone in the linen room, indecisive and disturbed. 'She was crying.' But there was no way anyone would dare to offer comfort or even inquire what was wrong. Not with Sister Müllerman.

Forty

The picnic at Philipville was to be the last occasion when these three would be together for some time to come. Simon's regiment was confined to barracks, preparatory to the invasion of Sicily. Norah and Cathy, for the first time, were given separate postings. Norah was to replace a sick sister on the hospital carrier *St Augustine*. Cathy, Una and others in the unit returned to England, to retrain for the Second Front.

The plan to liberate the German-occupied countries of Europe was no longer wishful thinking. It was already taking form in hugely ambitious schemes. Before very long they would be put into action. If Norah had been included on the draft, Cathy would have been wildly enthusiastic to be involved in this momentous venture. To leave her behind spoiled for Cathy the excitement of going home, the first time for three long and eventful years. The rest of the sisters' mess showed little sympathy. 'Lucky to have stayed together for so long.'

Cathy and Una came ashore in Liverpool on a miserable day in November 1943. After the dazzle of the desert, with its high blue skies, England's image was of a drab land cowering under the weight of leaden skies. Everything about Liverpool was grey, the dishwashy water of the harbour, even the faces of passers-by were grey and cold.

After a while Cathy was able to look beyond the bombed towns and streets of crumbling houses and discovered an astonishing strength of purpose coursing through the country like a subterranean river. The insistent anonymous demand 'SECOND FRONT NOW!', painted on railway bridges and roadside hoardings, even in tidy front windows of terraced houses, demonstrated the nation's impatience to get to grips with Germany. This country, she discovered, was not sorry for itself. Not in any way, despite the bombing and the battering and the shortages that were still being endured.

With ten days' leave, Cathy made for home. Her father beamed love upon her. 'My word, it's good to see you, Cathy pet.'

'You've lost weight,' her mother accused her and hustled up some mock-cream buns.

Cathy was taken aback by the ageing of her parents – she had not been prepared for the effect upon them of constant anxiety. There were deeply engraved lines on her father's face. Her mother seemed to have shrunk and there was a frail look about her. She had to put her legs up on a dumpty at night because her ankles swelled. The house was freezing cold. It was a plumber's winter.

Cathy steadied the stepladder while her father squeezed through the trapdoor into the loft to set a small oil lamp near the cold water cistern. 'I don't want another burst pipe, not after the last carry-on. Brought half the kitchen ceiling down in spite of my lagging.'

'I'm not surprised you had a burst,' Cathy pointed past him, 'I can see daylight through the roof tiles. It's like a refrigerator up here.'

'Well, I didn't build the house,' her father replied somewhat testily and she knew he must be very tired.

The rest of the house was only marginally warmer. Coal was strictly rationed and the price of logs exorbitant. Even paraffin for the ubiquitous Valor stove was rationed. Cathy stopped complaining of the cold.

Almost every commodity was rationed. The portions of butter, meat, cheese, tea and sugar were minimal. There was no imported fruit. If it was not grown in Britain it was not on the greengrocers' counter. Lemons and bananas were things of the past. It was no wonder, Cathy realised, that their faces looked dried up, parched. 'It's been hard for you at home.'

Despite the privations, spirits were high. The restrictions and shortages had been accepted, 'for the duration', which was in its fourth year. Now, at last, there were signs that victory was becoming a distinct possibility and the optimism was infectious. Cathy decided that, as a nation, Britain excelled at putting up with things, hardly a lofty ideal.

'The inspiration,' said her father, 'is out there with the soldiers, sailors, airmen, your pals, and,' he looked sideways at her, 'the doctors and nurses. There's no call for heroics here back home. It's our job to keep the wheels turning, to keep the tanks and guns and planes coming out of the factories ready for the day when we'll hit the Hun for six!' Cyril Lewis brandished a fist. 'It's coming, my lass. Make no mistake.'

The fever of anticipation stirred even the most phlegmatic of the bar-room generals. There were plenty of them in the King's Head ready with advice – men in reserved occupations who would not be required to fight. 'Hit him hard now. We've got him on the run.'

Everywhere, there were men in the uniforms of occupied countries, men who escaped when Hitler invaded their homeland, the Free French, Poles, Dutch, Belgians, Danes and Norwegians and the square-hatted Czechoslovakian officers, and American GIs, high-spirited, with pocketfuls of money, and nylon stockings for the girls. All of them had a score to settle and the day of retribution for the Nazi aggressors was drawing near. Confrontation was now inevitable. Britain had become a huge holding depot for troops and a warehouse for armaments of every kind.

Cathy had several visits to make before her

leave expired; to sisters, new babies and Auntie Nan, who was a big noise now in the Women's Voluntary Service. And Norah's mother.

'I never worried about her when I knew you were together,' Mrs Moffat said, 'even when you were in Greece. Some of the local lads who escaped from Greece told us that the nurses had been left behind, but I knew the pair of you would get yourselves out, no matter what. Only I wish you were together now.'

Cathy had always felt a bit scared of Mrs Moffat. Not any more. Here was an anxious mother masquerading as a stern disciplinarian. Cathy stayed longer than she had intended. There was a lot to tell – especially the story of the Australian soldier who fell in love with Norah. 'A tall, good-looking chap and he worshipped Norah, but he was killed in New Guinea.'

The fleeting spark in Edith Moffat's sharp brown eyes died away. 'Poor Norah. She's never had a real boyfriend. She never seemed interested as long as you were there.' The rare smile, Cathy noted with surprise, was Norah's. 'Inseparable, you two. There was that nice young doctor. I wondered if that would come to anything, but the poor chap is in a POW camp, wasting his life away.'

A more difficult visit was to Jacky's mother. Once Cathy said how sorry she was there seemed little else to say.

'Nice scones, Mrs Whitmore.'

'No fat.' Millie Whitmore got no further

and began to cry. Cathy moved over to sit beside her on the prickly horsehair couch and held her hand and cried a little herself, for Jacky.

Eric's parents were glad to see her, grateful that she and Norah had looked after their son when he was wounded. 'We're proud of him, of course,' his father said, 'but we hoped he would be sent home after being wounded.'

'He's in a desk job now, Simon says, so he'll be all right.'

'And he's found a lovely girl. Have you met her, Cathy?'

'Easy come, easy go, in wartime,' counselled her husband, who knew about such romances. 'Might not come to anything.' Nobody mentioned Eileen.

She visited Simon's parents. He was somewhere in Italy now. 'And a captain!' Mr Poole said proudly. 'What d'ye think of that, Cathy?'

Evie came from the country to see her. They had tea at the Haymarket Café and talked of Jacky and of Eric's courage. 'Eric didn't want to post the ring to you in case it was lost,' Cathy explained to a tearful Evie. 'He's waiting to give it to you in person.'

'Poor Jacky.' Evie poked in her handbag for a handkerchief. 'He didn't have much of a life. I'm not sure things would have worked out between us, you know.'

Hilde, genuinely pleased to see Cathy, had the latest news from Andrew. 'He has more hopes. He thinks that soon he will be free.'

She was entertaining Cathy in the common room of the nurses' home. They had the room to themselves. Deadly quiet, dustless and without warmth, it smelt of polish and aspidistras. Only the lament of a frustrated bumblebee on the wall mirror disturbed the stillness.

'A prisoner since Dunkirk,' Cathy recalled. 'Three and a half years. I'm glad he writes to you, Hilde.'

'It is hard to find things to write in reply.'

'Tell him about his friends. They are your friends too. Evie says you sometimes spend your day off with her.'

She nodded. 'Evie is my friend.' She glanced at Cathy. 'She is sad that Jacky is killed but I think she never would have married him.'

'You both went to see Alec – I'm planning to go. How is he?'

'He is wonderful, so brave about his new face, which is not so handsome as the old one. Now he has a job and writes things for the local paper. He has a very nice nurse who looks after him well and he has a house to live in near the hospital.'

'Go to the Burns Unit and ask to see Sister Fletcher,' Alec sent directions for Cathy. 'She will show you where I live. I am looking forward so much to seeing you again, Cathy, after all this time. I will bake a cake, which is something I have learned to do.'

Cathy caught the train to Basingstoke and a

bus to Park Prewitt Hospital, and made, as directed, for the Burns Unit.

Sister Fletcher regarded Cathy with friendly interest. 'You are an old friend?'

'I'm Cathy, a very old friend. I have been overseas for the last three years and I haven't seen him since he crashed.'

The sister placed a restraining hand on Cathy's arm. 'Be prepared. He won't look the same as you remember him. Since he was shot down he has had a good deal of plastic surgery.'

Cathy nodded. 'I'm a nurse. I am prepared for that.'

Esme Fletcher pointed to a row of small brick houses with gardens backing on to the hospital grounds. 'He is number three. He rented it when he was having frequent hospital appointments but he has finished with all that now. He is a reporter on the local *Basingstoke Echo*. You probably know?'

'I am not surprised.'

Cathy knew better than to expect a flawless reconstruction. From the amount of work done she could judge that the original destruction of the soft tissues of Alec's face must have been extensive. His replacement nose was blue and blobby. His natural nose had been finely drawn. Tissue for the new nose had been swung down from the forehead, leaving, darker areas on his brow. The refashioned jaw was a little underslung but functional. The smile at seeing her was Alec's own. He stretched his arms to greet her and she went right in and kissed the foreign flesh.

She followed him into a small room littered with books and magazines, and with windows overlooking the hospital. By the window, a typewriter.

'I can't quite cut the umbilical cord yet,' he said shamefacedly, indicating the large red-brick hospital. 'I am tackling the brave new world outside in stages.'

'But you've finished with surgery, sister said?' She had just noticed the claw hands.

He laughed. 'What you see is the final product. What's the verdict?'

'Different but interesting,' she stated candidly.

'No pin-up, Cathy, but I'm alive and I have this hospital to thank.' He produced the cake and somewhat awkwardly cut her a slice.

'And you can type?'

'But they won't let me fly. I'd give a lot to be in the Big Show. That's what you've been brought home for, isn't it?' He cocked a knowing eye in her direction. 'Anyhow, enough of me.' He took a seat with his back to the window. 'Tell me what you and Norah have been up to.'

He did not interrupt. She watched the fleeting shadows cross his face. 'I think a lot about our gang,' he said at last, 'and what has become of us. Andy sometimes sends a card from that hole in Poland and Simon when he's not up to his eyes in battle. I think a lot about Quentin, Colin and Jacky. I try to recall the things they said and the marvellous fun we had together.' He raised his eyes to hers, lashless with puffy lids, but still Alec's eyes. He stretched out a hand and she put hers gently over the malformed fingers, each deriving comfort from the closeness. No words were necessary. There were no words to describe the awfulness of war.

'Well, anyway, you haven't changed, Cathy.'

She gave a little self-conscious laugh. 'I'm stuck with this fizzog.'

'And I'm stuck with this nose. "Not really me, dear," ' he mimicked, 'but it's better than none at all. When you kissed my cheek you were kissing my bottom. That's where the graft came from.'

Cathy joined in his laughter and the mood of nostalgia faded.

'Would you mind having a word with Sister Fletcher on your way out? She will want to know your professional opinion.'

The sister was flitting about, waiting. 'Well?' she said. 'What did you think of him?'

'His spirit is amazing. We have you and the staff of this marvellous place to thank for that.' Cathy, greatly moved by the meeting with Alec was having difficulty in expressing herself without bursting into tears. Handsome, handsome Alec, blown away in a moment when the sky caught fire.

'Their own courage is the thing that pulls the men through.' Then she delivered her surprise. 'I suppose you knew Nancy?'

'Yes.'

'I hope,' said Esme Fletcher in a level voice,

'that you will be pleased about this. Alec and I are to be married.'

The explosion of joy that escaped Cathy was answer enough. She flung her arms about Esme and planted a kiss on each cheek. 'That's the most wonderful news! No wonder he sent me back to see you,' she exclaimed. 'He wanted you to break the news and it is the best news in the world for Alec. I'm so happy for you both.'

She ran all the way back to Alec's house to grab him in a bear hug.

'I wasn't sure if Esme wanted me to tell you. We've only just decided that neither of us can comfortably live without the other.'

'You've picked a winner. This is the most wonderful news and I just know you will be very happy.'

'What about you and Norah?'

'Oh – still on the shelf. And likely to stay so.'

At a military hospital in the south of England Cathy and Una learnt how to erect a tent, purify drinking water and efficiently disable a six-foot assailant. They attended lectures on new drugs, new methods of treating fractures, burns and head injuries.

'The only good thing to be brought about by war,' said one particular lecturer who could scarcely contain his excitement, 'is medical advance and today we are about to introduce a major discovery. Penicillin! The wonder drug! You nurses will witness a revolution in the treatment of infected wounds.

Throw away your soggy fomentations. Penicillin will cause the textbooks to be rewritten. Penicillin will save thousands of lives in any future campaign.'

It was impossible not to be carried along on the wave of his enthusiasm. This discovery would be of immense value to all servicemen and women destined to take part in the invasion of Europe.

'Norah will be mad at missing this.'

But Norah was involved in her own particular sphere of excitement.

Forty-One

1944

Hospital ships and the smaller hospital carriers, conforming to Geneva regulations, were painted white overall with a broad green band round the hull and large red crosses on the superstructure. At night they sailed fully lit. They could presume immunity while about their humanitarian business of picking up and treating casualties.

Norah's belief in human nature received a battering at the allied landings in Sicily, when she saw the Hospital Ship *Talamba* bombed and sunk while taking on casualties. HMHS *Newfoundland* received the same treatment at the Salerno landings on the mainland of Italy. Their immunity appeared to depend on the whim of the pilot at the controls of an enemy plane. She was not unprepared, therefore, when the luck of His Majesty's Hospital Carrier *St Augustine* ran out at the Anzio landings in January 1944.

The *St Augustine* was one of three carriers attending the landing. Casualties were being ferried from the shore in flat-bottomed ambulance craft and transferred to the carriers when darkness fell. All three vessels were ordered to stand off, fully lit, until daylight when they would come inshore again to complete the embarkation of the wounded. For a certain German pilot the target, although clearly identified as non-belligerent, was too tempting to resist.

Norah was settling the newly embarked casualties for the night when the bombs dropped. The ship rocked violently and exploded in a sheet of flame. Casualties, medical staff and crew were blasted into the water, Norah amongst them. The compulsory lifejacket kept her afloat as she flailed her way through the wreckage of beds, medical equipment, spars and crates. From all around came the anguished cries of helpless, drowning men. Lifeboats, launched immediately by the two remaining carriers and guided by the pinpoint red lights on bobbing lifejackets, moved over the dark, swirling water, hauling men on board. A man strapped to a stretcher was within Norah's reach. Waves repeatedly washed over him as he was tossed in the turmoil of the sinking ship. His eyes were closed. She had no way of knowing if he were alive or dead, but she grabbed the stretcher handles and, turning on to her back, kicked out furiously to pull away from the deadly maelstrom, praying that the stretcher would remain afloat. Flames were dancing among the heads in the water. Norah spat out a mouthful of oil and saw her man give a gasp. He was alive. She redoubled her efforts to reach a lifeboat.

Someone grabbed her by the shoulders. Strong arms reached down to her and attempted to lift her into a boat. 'Drop the stretcher,' they yelled. 'He's dead! Let him go, Nurse!' But she knew he was not dead and they had to pull the stretcher on board with her.

I think the navy was pretty mad with me, Cathy, but all was forgiven when my patient survived. I learned later that he had been on the operating table when the ship was bombed. Our junior surgeon had just completed a partial gastrectomy and the man was still under the anaesthetic when the MO strapped him to a stretcher and pushed him overboard as the only chance of survival for him. There was, at least, the possibility that the stretcher would float. Sadly, that MO and two of our QAs were lost. I was taken to our old hospital in Bizerta. Potts fracture and minor burns. I'm OK now and back on shore duty here with some old friends of ours but I miss you, Cat. Take good care of yourself, whatever you are up to.

Cathy was horrified. 'See what happens when they split our luck.'

German troops had met their match in Russia. After the glorious Russian defence of Stalingrad in 1943, the great mechanised German army was forced to retreat with terrible hardships. The tide turned against them in Russia, as it had done in North Africa. On Mr Mount's war map those areas which represented German occupation were shrinking.

On 4 June 1944, allied armies entered Rome. Simon's note to Cathy read, 'It wasn't built in a day. It wasn't won in a day but we're in.'

On 6 June, the Second Front was opened. Allied armies invaded Normandy. The master race was discovering that, after all, it was not invincible.

Norah was now stationed in a military hospital in Naples, a town devastated by war, poverty and disease. And Cathy was in Normandy, sharing a tent once more with Una, though in a very different environment. For sand, read mud; for desert scrub, read apple trees, but the guns were the same and the young men in the tented wards in Normandy were, like all the other young men in Greece and the desert, a sacrifice to war. One day perhaps, Cathy thought despairingly as she hurried from stretcher to stretcher in a crowded resuscitation tent, there would be no young men left.

Germany had already reached that stage. Sixteen-year-old boys were among the wounded Germans prisoners now being brought to the British hospitals for treatment. Others were too old and too infirm to be fighting in the battles then raging around them in Normandy, the battles for Tilly-sur-Seulles, St Lo and Falaise and, the hardest challenge of all, Caen.

In the first few weeks after the landings, progress was slow and the bridgehead remained tightly confined to the coastal strip. Casualties had to be moved through the hospitals and back to Britain with as much speed as possible. On some days the number of men admitted equalled the number evacuated, a challenge of logistics for RAMC warrant officers acting as wardmasters. The nurses working in battledress trousers and gumboots had no time to wonder how the balance of war lay. Care of the wounded demanded their whole attention.

When, after some weeks, the frontline moved from Normandy to Belgium, Cathy wrote enthusiastically to Norah.

'The folks of Brussels gave us a huge welcome. Chocolate to die for. Una and I are

405

sharing a room in an old people's home and we've got a flush toilet!'

A landscape of blasted poplars, dead cows in the fields and rusting tanks in the ditches was left behind in Normandy and the city of Caen was a mountain of rubble.

Italy was out of the fight, although there was still heavy fighting against the retreating Germans. The squalor and poverty of Naples appalled Norah, who was working there.

> Peter Collins, the naval officer who pulled me out of the water at Anzio, sometimes takes me out for a meal when his ship is in port, but I really do not enjoy eating in a posh restaurant with starving Italians peering through the window, begging for food. They are so poor, Cathy. And there is every disease you can think of here.

Cathy would have liked to know more about Norah's naval escort. All she learnt was that his name was Peter Collins.

1945

First Paris liberated then Brussels and now, in the early months of 1945, the crossing of the Rhine.

Andrew's father standing before his wall map made another correction in the position of the armies. 'This is more than the name of a river,' he said. His wife earnestly followed the route of his finger. 'It's the death knell of Hitler, the karate chop to the German soldier and a blood transfusion to our tired troops. I believe, my dear, that we are within the smell of victory at last.'

Cathy's hospital, working through Holland behind the troops, now reached the German town of Celle, lately captured by allied forces. The animosity of the residents resulted in no British nurses being allowed to walk outside the hospital building without an armed escort. German mothers, ill nourished and angry, who had sacrificed their meagre rations for soldier sons regarded the British women with hate. Their country, their lives, their fanatical devotion to the Führer, all was in ruins. Cathy and Una might have felt some pity for them, but for their callous reaction to a sight that would make any decent person recoil in horror.

As the two nurses walked with their escort out of the hospital gate, they were horrified by the sight of certain creatures burrowing into one of the town's rubbish bins in search of edible scraps. They looked scarcely human. Their eye sockets were deep hollows in close shaven skulls. With skin drawn tight over cheekbones and jawbones scarcely fleshed these men resembled nothing so much as a group of cadavers, dipping and diving into the binlike figures in a macabre ballet. Striped cotton uniforms like ill-fitting pyjamas could not conceal sticklike limbs supporting the gross belly of starvation.

But there was no pity in the faces of German residents who turned away, only disgust.

'Good God!' questioning, Cathy and Una turned to their escort. 'What's going on, Corporal?'

His young man's face was grim. 'Our advance troops have just uncovered a German labour camp at a place called Belsen, not far from here. These blokes probably wandered out when the gates were opened. They're still alive. Just. We're too late for thousands more. Hitler's labour force, no more than slaves, and when they were too weak they were *liquidated*.'

As the German defences were rolled back, more camps were uncovered where thousands of men, women and children, mostly Jews, had perished. Allied military hospitals took up the enormous challenge of restoring health and sanity to the victims of the Third Reich.

Cathy wrote to her father.

It's desperate. We need miracles and we are only nurses. They keep on dying even after we take them to places of safety and feed them. As well as suffering from starvation, they have every illness you can think of: heart disease, TB, kidney failure and sores on their bodies which will not heal. Poles, Lithuanians, Latvians and German Jews. Bankers, musicians, professors and common men, they own nothing. Have you ever known anyone, Dad, apart from a new born baby, who possessed absolutely nothing? Even their camp uniform was theirs only as long as they lived and then it was passed on. All that is left is the will to survive. They trust no one, not even our doctors who are so patient with them. And they do not trust us, the nurses. That is the hard bit. They think we will whisk them off to the gas chamber if they stay in bed, so even seriously ill men wander about in the woods around us.

On an impulse, Cathy wrote to Hilde. This might have been the fate of her family had they not escaped to England.

'Dear Hilde,' she began and then could not find the words to go on, All she wrote was: 'I send you my love, Cathy.'

Hilde would wonder.

The end to all the misery came when Hitler took his own worthless life in April 1945. The guns were silenced and in the poignant hiatus that followed it was as if a terrible sigh of sorrow and relief rose from all the ravaged lands of Europe.

In the King's Head, members of the Home Guard were a little stunned, not yet ready to take in the momentous news. Ken Poole and Cyril Lewis exchanged a long exultant look. A close relationship had grown up between the two men in the course of their Home Guard duty. Each respected the other for his individual qualities.

Volunteer Sergeant Ken Poole gripped the hand extended to him. 'We'll have two double whiskies, Paul,' he addressed the barman over his shoulder, 'and we'll drink to the death of an evil man.'

Volunteer Private Lewis added, 'And the end of the Third Reich, a regime fit only for the sewers of mankind.'

Families gathered round the wireless sets to hear the Prime Minister say it: 'The war in Europe is over.'

As the last notes of the National Anthem died away Tina and Gwen Mount danced a dizzy dance of joy, 'Andy's coming home.'

Quentin's father remained seated in the easy chair where he had been listening to the Prime Minister's speech. His wife had sung out with joy at the news and rushed off to put the kettle on. 'I'll make us a cup of tea, dear. Bother the rations.'

He could hear her happily busying herself with cups and saucers. A sudden weakness invaded his fortress, momentarily robbing him of self-control. He buried his clever, greying head in his hands, his fleshy white capable fingers with the broad gold ring, and he wept. He wept until he was emptied of tears and his shoulders no longer shook with grief long withheld. Tonight he wept for the son he had lost.

Forty-Two

1945

The residents of Andrew's hut were happily packing, preparing to leave for ever their tight little world of the last five years. Possessions that up till now had been jealously guarded, like Johnnie's homemade pencil sharpener and Barney's toasting fork, could be carelessly cast away. Such artefacts were superfluous in the world they were returning to.

Andrew would remain with his patients until they could be safely handed over to a British authority but the others were too impatient to await the arrival of liberating troops and took themselves off in a commandeered German truck.

Andrew stood at the wide open gate and waved goodbye to his companions of so many dreary days and nights. They would organise a reunion, try each other's favourite pubs. Meet each other's families. 'Keep in touch, old boy!' And off they went in their crumpled uniforms, holey socks and jaunty caps.

'You'd better hide that swastika on the truck,' Andrew shouted, 'or you'll find your-

411

selves back in clink.' He waited until the madly rocking truck driven by Winstanley disappeared from sight, then turned back to the hospital hut where his stalwart medical orderly was preparing twenty sick men for transit to freedom.

They were poor things, debilitated through disease and diet deficiencies. The nerves of such men were in tatters. The knowledge that they were free to go home was almost too much to bear. The jokey stoicism which had held them together in tight endurance failed them in the face of freedom and the orderly, who could have left the camp in an earlier transport had he wished, tended them without impatience, understanding their tears. But for the grace of God, he told himself, there go I.

Andrew, searching for Oberleutnant Golze, came upon him sitting in a kind of stupor at his desk. White faced and trembling, he jumped to his feet at Andrew's appearance and saluted. 'Herr Leutnant Doktor,' stammering, tripping over his words in his agitation, 'I haf alvays been freund to you, jah? Plees, Herr Doktor, you vill remember that alvays I haf tried to help you mit your work. Is happy day for you, hein? For us Chermans it is the end of our Faderland. Who knows what is to become of us.' Unashamedly he wiped his eyes.

The sight of a senior doctor in such a funk was distressing in the extreme to Andrew. 'Oberleutnant Golze, I will report that you have never ill used my patients and that you have helped within your limits. You have my word. Now,' he continued, firmly asserting his position, 'I must have soap, clean shirts and blankets and all the Red Cross articles which have been withheld.'

'At once!' Golze's heels came together with a resounding click.

At the moment of his departure, Andrew extended a hand in reconciliation. 'The fortunes of war, Oberleutnant,' and left a consolation gift of surgical dressings. There would be precious few of those available for Golze's German patients.

Stretcher-bearers, pink faced and healthy, came tumbling out of British ambulances to collect Andrew's patients. 'Let's be having you, mate.' Their voices were loud and cheery but their handling of the sick men was womanly. 'All your troubles are over now.'

Beds awaited them in a British military hospital near Bremen, a staging post before they returned to Britain. The years of captivity, of separation from their families, were nearly over. Nourishing food awaited them and a whole range of powerful new drugs. And a celebratory glass of the best French champagne from a captured German officers' mess.

To Andrew's eyes, long starved of female contact, the sisters in the Bremen hospital seemed incredibly beautiful. Such complexions! Peaches and cream. Such plump little cheeks. Pink hands like fluttering birds. He

413

imagined bosoms like melons beneath the modesty tippets and fantasised guiltily over Hilde.

He was required to rest at the Bremen hospital for several days while medical checks were carried out, all of which pronounced him fit – apart from weight loss. A seat was found for him on a Dakota then he was, unbelievably, on his way to England.

All at once everything was easy for Andrew. The deep furrow in his brow, a legacy of his imprisonment, would never leave him but otherwise the face he was shaving with a brand-new, courtesy-of-the-Red-Cross razor, radiated joyful anticipation.

After landing at Northolt airport, he was driven to King's Cross station. It had always been a busy, dirty connection. It was busier and dirtier now. There were uniforms of every description amongst the crowds struggling with kitbags and suitcases. The women looked delicious. One of them, a cute little creature in a tricorne hat, snubbed him for staring.

His warrant entitled him to a first-class seat on the Flying Scotsman to Eastport. He grabbed a window seat without any concern for other passengers' preference. All that nice polite stuff could come later. This was his day, his first day of freedom. Watching England fly past the windows he felt absurdly happy, picturing the welcome that awaited him, his father and mother, his two little sisters. His imagination, no longer shackled, lingered on the meeting with Hilde.

Hilde. Hilde. To whisper her name was an indulgence he had denied himself throughout the past years. A song he had not thought of since those far off pre-war days surfaced in his mind like a rainbow bubble.

'Blue moon, you saw me standing alone
Without a dream in my heart,
Without a love of my own.'

He felt like singing it out loud but his fellow passengers in the compartment were already looking at him in an odd way because of the fixed grin on his face. If he started to sing, they would lock him up. He hummed the rest of the song somewhere deep inside his head, in a place for special memories.

'And then there suddenly appeared before me,
The only one my arms will ever hold.
I heard somebody whisper, "Please adore me,"
And when I looked, the moon had turned to gold.'

His eyes scarcely registered the panorama slipping past the train windows; the random watering holes for cattle provided by shell craters strung like necklaces over fields and hills. Crippled buildings near the railway line, leaning on scaffolding crutches, and roped-off areas carrying the warning 'Unexploded Bomb'. But Andrew's mind was elsewhere, assembling an image of Hilde; recalling the high cheek bones in an oval face that gave her a Slavic look and the thick fringe of dark lashes against an olive skin, but the lips? The smile? That he could not bring to mind. He pictured her dark, slumberous eyes which, on occasion, had kindled with friendship. Admittedly there had been nothing more than friendship. He had never been bold enough to ask for more, but he was five years older now and five years bolder. It was time to declare himself.

His family was there to meet him as the train pulled into Eastport Central Station. Mother, father and the two girls ... could those two elegant young ladies really be Tina and Gwen? Could five years bring about such an amazing transformation, from gawky schoolgirls to mature young ladies? It was laughter and tears, kisses and hugs all the way to the station yard where the old Standard waited.

'Saved petrol especially for this occasion, my boy. We always knew you'd come home one fine day.'

'But it's been a long, long time, darling.' His mother was weepy and he had to pull her leg to make her turn off the tap.

'One of you two girls will have to sit on Andrew's knee,' said his father busily, packing away Andrew's kit and the presents he had bought on an IOU until his pay caught up

416

with him.

'Me!' both girls yelled and the alarming impression of young ladies was dispelled.

'Here, Dad,' hastily Andrew took the starting handle from his father. 'Let me do that.'

'Think I'm too old, do you?' but he gave in with good grace. 'The old boneshaker is hard to start these days ... Like me in the mornings.'

Privately Andrew was struck by the ageing of his parents, but this was not the moment for inquiries into their health. After two or three turns to get the engine going he realised he needed to do some muscle building himself.

The car rattled into life and, with his father at the wheel, they drove away from the station forecourt. His mother sat in the front waving and nodding to passersby, most of whom knew the nature of their journey. She had told everyone she had met that morning about her son's return from a POW camp, back from the war at last.

'Any news of Simon, Dad? Or any of the gang?'

'Simon's been and gone. He came home for a few days' leave at the end of the European campaign before flying out to join Mountbatten's outfit at Southeast Asia Command. Got his majority! Good lad, that. The girls are scattered. Cyril Lewis's lass was in Belgium, last I heard, and her friend Norah in Italy, but I can't keep track of them all. That pretty little girl who went to America came back some time ago and I believe she's teaching somewhere up country. She was Whitmore's girl, wasn't she? Bad show that. His mother never got over it. A bit round the bend, to tell the truth, old chap. The Dotchin boy got a medal. Did you know?'

Andrew's disappointment at missing Simon was sharp. They had been through the Dunkirk nightmare together. He recalled his last sight of Simon, seriously wounded, being lifted aboard a rescue ship under heavy fire from enemy planes. 'Major Poole now? He's done well.' Yes, he thought, while I have mouldered away in Poland. He shook off the hovering self-pity.

'His father hoped he would not be called upon for the Southeast Asia campaign,' Brian Mount continued. 'Reckons the Japs are nastier than the Krauts – and that's saying something.'

Andrew sent a note to Hilde. He would not permit this message, rehearsed and savoured over the years, to be relayed over the telephone, emasculated and sanitised by some old trout of a home sister. He was home, he wrote, anxious to see her. He would like to take her out to dinner. When was she off duty? And he was a little disappointed when her reply suggested he should come to the hospital. But he consoled himself with the thought that there would be many opportunities in the future for candlelit dinners, in the best restaurants that this battered old

418

seaport could produce. To know that he was on his way to seeing her, even in hospital, was unbelievable.

'Ward six,' she had written. 'I am sister in charge there and we can have tea in my room.'

He experienced a strange flashback as he walked once more along the white-tiled corridors of his old hospital; meeting the present day medical students, half expecting them to recognise him as they hurried past, stethoscopes swinging, in their flapping white coats and baggy flannels. Needing haircuts, all of them. Young nurses showed a passing interest in him, but he did not know them. Five years, he had to remind himself.

Hilde was delighted to see him. She broke off, instructing a junior nurse in order to greet him, hand outstretched, and there was the smile he had dreamed about during the long, dreary days in captivity, and unmistakable gladness in her dark brown eyes.

'Andrew. Liebling! How vonderful to see you safely home again. You haf lost weight but that is to be expected, jah?' He had forgotten her thick accent. It came as an unpleasant reminder of the POW camp. 'Come to my room. I am the boss here now.'

'Hilde, Hilde,' the words tumbled out, 'it's been so long.'

She opened a door marked 'SISTER'S OFFICE'. 'Come.'

There was a gaunt fellow sitting in the only comfortable chair. He rose to his feet at

419

Andrew's entrance. 'This is Doctor Weinert,' Hilde introduced him. 'Doctor Mount vas vorking here before the war,' she explained. 'He vas taken prisoner at Dunkirk and has been in a POW camp ever since.'

To Andrew's hypersensitive antennae, she seemed to make him appear both careless and somewhat lazy. His hand was taken limply by a bunch of barely fleshed phalanges.

'Then ve haf both endured captivity, Herr Doktor.' The man's voice was dry and thin as a wafer. Andrew strained to hear him,

Hilde said, 'Doctor Weinert has spent the last three years in one of Hitler's death camps. My uncle was in the same camp and did not survive. Doctor Weinert is here to recover and refresh his medical knowledge.'

The poor fellow was alarmingly thin, the lobes of his skull clearly visible on his shaven scalp. Sad eyes were set deep in a face where the cheeks had fallen away. Andrew had seen such spectres before he left Europe. Pity for him fought with anger that men could treat their fellows with such inhumanity.

Hilde pulled up a stool for him as a ward maid entered with a tray of tea. Without hesitation, Doctor Weinert reached for a biscuit. Hilde moved the plate a little nearer to him and poured tea. 'One sugar?' She smiled at Andrew. 'You see, I remember.'

Their fingers touched on the saucer. It was enough to send Andrew's spirits on a dizzy lift. The uninspiring setting and the poor chap from the concentration camp were all forgotten. 'Hilde,' he began in a rush, without a clear idea of how he meant to continue, but she broke in.

'Doctor Weinert needs care,' as if to remind him. 'He already grows much stronger since he comes. I haf put him on an easy digested diet.' Her direct, appraising glance at the man, her use of the third person singular, did not seem to embarrass him. He was staring fixedly at the one remaining biscuit. Hilde resolved his problem by handing him the plate. 'These are early days for him,' she explained to Andrew. 'He cannot yet understand that food is plentiful.'

Andrew's fire died out. She did not want to hear what he had to say. The gap between himself and these two members of a wronged and persecuted race was growing more unbridgeable by the minute. Nevertheless, he hoped that his voice reflected the compassion he felt for this unfortunate man. 'My treatment was less harsh than yours, Doctor Weinert.'

At that the stranger looked directly at him with eyes as black and impenetrable as bog water. 'Excuse me. You are not a Jew.'

He was an outsider.

And that was all there was to this first meeting, about which Andrew had built up such high hopes. There had been no opportunity to speak to Hilde in private and when he suggested an evening date, her reply had been far from encouraging.

'Telephone me next week,' she had said. 'It

depends if someone vill vatch over Sigismund for me.'

Perplexity creased Andrew's brow.

'Doctor Weinert,' she explained.

And Andrew had exploded. 'He's not a baby!'

'I think he is,' she retorted steadily.

He went away marvelling at the new self-confidence of a girl who at one time could scarcely look him in the eyes. She most assuredly *was* the boss now and he was just getting the message. Even so, for some time he did not fully realise what a non-starter he was. He had thought her concern for the Jewish doctor's welfare was no more than one would expect from a dedicated nurse. After the evening out, to which she finally consented, however, he saw that the racial bond between them was too strong for him to break.

'I hoped, Hilde, that on my return things would turn out differently between us.'

'Alvays you expected more than I vas prepared to give.' The mouth was prim and tight.

'Yes,' he admitted. His heart was leaden. 'My feelings for you are deeply sincere. I hoped that you might one day feel the same way about me. You know the English proverb? "Absence makes the heart grow fonder." I rather pinned my hopes on that.'

She shook her head. 'You are a dear friend and I vish you to be Siggy's friend, too. I vill give the rest of my life to him for all the suffering he bore for us Jews who escaped.'

422

There was nothing more for Andrew to say after that. It was he who was the Displaced Person.

Eastport was not the same without his old friends. Norah was in Italy. There was a rumour that Cathy was on her way to India and Simon was in Ceylon. He intended to visit Alec as soon as he could take delivery of the Morris Minor he had ordered from Coventry. He might have to wait some time.

Painful comprehension came with the stark reality that some of the gaps in what had been the circle of his closest friends were permanent. Never again would he listen to Quentin postulating on some elevated topic and Jacky fighting back. Even in argument, comradeship was seamless. And Colin, steady, dependable and the best bat in the Eastport cricket team. He would have liked to have delved deeper into Colin. Their days had been so full, no time to waste and now time had no value. Freedom had turned to ashes in his mouth.

He considered getting in touch with Barney or Johnnie of the old hut six association but decided against it. Later perhaps. He could hear Winstanley, 'How's the beautiful fraulein, old chap?' Much later.

'Got any plans, my boy?' It irked his father to see him aimlessly letting each day go by without any motivation of any sort on his part. 'Thinking of going back to the hospital?'

'He's changed.' Andrew's mother saw her son becoming more withdrawn with every day that passed. 'He never used to drink so much.'

'Being shut up in that POW camp for five years is bound to have affected him,' Andrew's father rose in stout defence. 'He'll pull himself together. Give him time.'

Forty-Three

The war in Europe was over but was still raging in Southeast Asia. Medical units now surplus to Europe's needs returned to Britain to re-equip. Cathy and Una found themselves on the draft for India.

Cathy was desolate. 'Norah will be coming back to England now the Italian campaign is over. If I go to India, goodness knows when we'll meet again.'

Una did not in the least mind where she was sent. She was not ready to go back to a quiet existence on Shetland and had not yet met the man she would marry, who would change the pattern of her life. That came later.

A last-minute delivery of mail arrived as the unit was about to sail from Ostend for England. There were two letters for Cathy. One in Simon's big round hand proclaimed itself at once, but the other was unfamiliar. She slit it open.

'Dear Cathy.'

She skipped to the signature and sat down heavily on the nearest tin trunk. All the strength seemed to have drained away from her legs

'You all right?' Una looked up from her own corres pondence.

'I think so.' The signature at the bottom of Cathy's letter was Raymond Webster's. 'It's from Raymond Webster.'

'Who?'

'Raymond Webster.' Cathy was hastily reading the page of neat writing.

...One and a half lungs in good working order and free of the dreaded tubercle. I've been passed fit and accepted back into my old regiment, home based as instructor. Never in my wildest dreams did I foresee this. Only one more dream remains, that I might find Cathy Lewis again, the cheeky, cheery little nurse who did more than she will ever know to get me well again. You gave me the determination, Cathy, and the miracle drugs did the rest. I don't know where you are but the War Office has promised to forward this letter so, if it has found you, then please write to me. Can we meet or are you for ever outside my reach? Worse still, are you married? That would be hard to bear.

Una was becoming concerned. 'Whatever is

the matter, Cathy? What are you crying for and who is this man?'

'I'm crying because I'm so happy,' Cathy managed to say between sobs. 'This is the man I am going to marry.'

It was some time before Cathy remembered the other letter, from Simon. He had hoped to see her in the UK before leaving for Southeast Asia.

Can you get a posting out here? The action is all in Southeast Asia now that Europe is cleaned up. Do try, my darling, my dearest girl. I love you ... Simon.

Cathy's head was in a whirl. There was no question of choice, of course, but she shrank from hurting Simon so cruelly. After much heart searching she wrote to him.

I never was the right girl for you, Simon dear. I know you will find her once I am out of the way. I will always look on you as my very best friend and I will always feel that kind of love for you.

Without delay, she applied to the War Office to be removed from the India draft because of her approaching marriage and was posted to Aldershot instead. She was jumping the gun here since marriage had yet to be mentioned between Raymond and herself. Confident that events would justify her assumption, she felt that there was no need to involve

Raymond at this stage. She had enough determination for both of them.

The rendezvous was The Corner House, Marble Arch, which was the only London restaurant Cathy was familiar with. She raced along the crowded pavements of Oxford Street, holding tight to her uniform cap. She must not be late. If he didn't find her there he might go away again, for ever.

Pink and breathless she stood at the entrance and scanned the faces at the tables. Nippies in their little aprons and frilly caps scurried by with loaded trays. The clatter of cutlery and the buzz of conversation confused her. She couldn't see him. He had changed his mind. He wasn't here. Her face reflected her disappointment.

He was standing by a table for two, a tall, upright man in the uniform of the Coldstream Guards, watching her, waiting for her to spot him. Then her feet of their own accord found the quickest way to him.

He took her by the hand and led her to a chair. 'Hallo, Cathy.'

She could find no words. Her tongue seemed to have disengaged itself. She just looked and looked while the smile spread across her face. This was no pale ethereal invalid. Hollow cheeks had filled out beneath a healthy, tanned skin. He watched with undisguised amusement as she made an inventory of his appearance. 'Will I do?'

'You have taken my breath away. You look so well.'

'Before you get your breath back I have something to say.' A serious note crept into his voice. 'I have practised my piece and you must let me say it, straight away.'

Cathy just kept smiling. To listen to his voice was enough to transport her into infinite happiness. No matter what he had to say, this moment she would treasure for ever.

'Try to stay quiet,' he begged her, 'until I reach the end or I will lose my courage and go away with things unsaid.' He hoped that she was truly listening. She was just sitting there with a faraway look in her eyes. He pushed on with what he had to say. 'Firstly, do not ask me to be patient. I have been patient for five years and not a day has passed when I have not said a prayer that you would not fall in love with some handsome soldier before I achieved a clean bill of health. At one time that seemed out of my reach but now,' he spread out his arms, 'look at me. I am cured.'

She nodded in agreement. She believed him. A slight lopsidedness of one shoulder was the only physical evidence of his long battle with tuberculosis.

'I am fit to be a husband, Cathy, and I want to know if you will have me.' Speaking more soberly, he lowered his eyelids. Cathy remembered how he used to employ this little trick when preparing himself for adverse clinical results. 'Don't speak,' he halted the words on her lips. 'Not yet. This is the difficult bit. If I am too late and you love someone else, then I must leave you straight away with many regrets for what might have been. I warned you. I cannot be patient. You must tell me now and settle this once and for always.'

The lump in her throat made speaking difficult. 'There is a man who loves me and I tried very hard to love him but it was no good.' Tears came to her eyes at the thought of Simon and how hurt he would be. 'I did not know if you were alive or dead but I could not really, truly love anyone else.'

He grasped her hands in his. 'Cathy, my wonderful girl.'

She looked at him accusingly. 'I fell for you in a big way, right at the start, when I used to come and see you in your side ward, but I got sweet damn-all in the way of encouragement from you.'

And he laughed. 'Don't be cross with me. How could I ask you to wait for someone who seemed about to make a hasty exit?'

'Well, Raymond Webster,' her eyes were brimming with happiness, 'you are not a dying man now and I have never been so happy in ... my ... life.' She ended the declaration in a small howl.

'You have a funny way of showing it, my sweet.' He reached across the table and with his handkerchief gently dabbed her eyes. 'So, if you are not married or engaged, will you marry me?'

Vigorously she nodded her head. 'I certainly will, Raymond Webster. Thank you very much.'

He took her face in his hands and kissed her

long and tenderly. 'Could you try calling me Ray, Sister Lewis?'

The waitress at their table coughed. 'Can I have your order now, sir?'

Norah would have been pleased for Cathy's sake, if someone nice like Simon was to be her husband. Simon was one of their oldest friends, one of the gang, but the news that Cathy was to marry Lieutenant Webster came as a bolt from the blue, an unheralded disaster. She had thought that Cathy had got over her great 'pash' for this ex-patient but no. Cathy had stars in her eyes. 'Taken leave of her senses' was how Norah privately described her friend's euphoric condition. She was dismayed beyond words and desperately jealous of Raymond Webster, a sick man, for taking Cathy away. Some mysterious alchemy was at work. Where she, Norah, saw scars and disease, Cathy saw pure gold.

Ever since the conclusion of the Italian campaign, Norah had looked forward to joining Cathy once more. Now, seemingly, her place in Cathy's life had been filled by someone else. She was in no hurry to confront the new situation and would have been happy to escape on the India draft with some of her colleagues, but the authorities had other ideas and sent her to England as an escort for casualties of the Italian campaign.

After handing over her charges to Woolwich hospital, she reported to the headquarters of the army nursing service to receive her award

430

of Associate Royal Red Cross for her part in saving lives when the Hospital Carrier *St Augustine* was sunk; and to be informed that her next posting was to the emergency military hospital at Shaftesbury in Dorset. Once a corrective school for naughty boys it was now, by an ironic twist of fate, considering the object of what she chose to call Cathy's 'infatuation', a centre for the treatment of pulmonary tuberculosis.

At the first opportunity after her meeting with Raymond, Cathy travelled down to Shaftesbury to see Norah and booked a night's lodging at Pump Cottage near the hospital. 'Darling Norah,' Cathy flung her arms about her old friend in an ecstatic embrace. 'Let me look at you! Tell me all. I want to know everything you have been doing, about the *St Augustine* and the man you saved, about your medal – how very, very brave you were – and this chap called Peter Collins, and our friends at Bizerta.'

'Cathy, are you really going to marry Lieutenant Webster?' Norah cut in.

Cathy nodded happily. 'And you'll have to learn to call him Ray.'

'What about Simon?'

Cathy stiffened. 'I have written to him to say how sorry I am, but I truly love Raymond. Always have done. You know that, Norah. I still can't believe it is true that I have found him again. All this time I have been thinking of him as a dying man and suddenly there he is, fit and well and we are to be married. It is like a wonderful dream. You must be bridesmaid, my pet.' She pulled a face. 'But you'll put the bride in the shade of course, glamour puss.'

'Hard luck on Simon, Cathy. He's been in love with you for years.'

'But not I with him.' Cathy's answer was tart. Her mind was made up. Briskly she changed the subject. 'Now tell me about Peter Collins. Do you like him?'

'I was glad of his company in Naples.' Norah shuddered. 'Naples was awful.' She broke off and added quietly, 'It's good to see you again, Catypus. Been a long time.' They were sitting on a bench in the grounds of the hospital. Bees buzzed on the honeysuckle. Somewhere a lawn mower joined in the music of summer. For a little while time slowed for both of them. 'Have you seen Andrew since he came home?'

Cathy looked troubled, 'Andrew is going through a bad time'

'He seemed to be in seventh heaven when he wrote to me from that holding unit in Belgium just after he was released. What went wrong?'

'Hilde.'

'What do you mean?'

'He got the cold shoulder, frozen mitt or whatever you like to call it. Oh she welcomed him home, of course, then she introduced him to her latest protégé, a Jewish doctor who has just been released from a German concentration camp. She is devoted to him and has no time for Andrew.'

'Latest protégé? Has she several of these...?'

'Displaced Persons. Europe is full of them. Hilde wants to help them all.'

'That's very noble of her. Does Andrew not fit into her plans anywhere?'

'Only as a helper in her crusade.'

'Poor Andrew. After all he's been through.'

'I took him with me to visit Evie in Slabridge. She's engaged to be married. Did you know? To a schoolmaster. I thought she might cheer Andrew up, but he was dead wood for most of the time. You, if anyone, can help, Norah. You are closer to Andrew than any of us, excepting Simon.'

'I don't see what I can do to cheer him up. Andrew is in love with Hilde. I have known that from the first day he met her, that night in the King's Head.' The finality in her tone deterred even Cathy from pressing further. 'So,' Norah continued, 'what's Evie's schoolmaster like?'

'Very schoolmaster-ish. Not much sense of humour, but a heart of gold and he adores Evie.'

'Poor Jacky. I wonder what he would have made of his life had there been no war.'

'Big noise in real estate, perhaps?'

'He might even have realised his ambition to become an engineer.'

'Remember when he got Simon's dad's car safely home after the gears went berserk halfway up Cheviot? Simon said he was a genius with engines, but he never got the

433

chance to follow that up.'

'Yet some of us, like Quentin, seemed to be born lucky. Little good it did him in the end. Anyhow, I'm glad Evie is happy. What's her chap's name?'

'Gladstone.'

'Crumbs!'

The outcome of that first meeting in Lyons Corner House was crystal clear from the start. Cathy and Raymond were head over heels in love. The wedding was fixed for Saturday, 28 July. Neither of the participants saw any point in prolonging the waiting time. They had already waited too long.

It was a uniformed wedding. Few clothing coupons were available for indulging in smart clothes. Cathy and Norah wore the grey and scarlet walking-out uniform of Queen Alexandra's Imperial Military Nursing Service Reserve, wearing their campaign medals and Norah her bravery award. Raymond and his best man presented handsomely as Guards officers.

'Goodness me,' marvelled Chrissie Lewis, screwing up her damp hankie, 'is that my little girl?'

Until recently the seaside hotel which Mr Lewis booked for the occasion had served as billets for a succession of servicemen, scarcely a festive background. The windows were curtained in serious black – or boarded up entirely. Barrack room poems still decorated the walls. Nevertheless, everywhere there was a spirit of celebration. No more air raids. No sirens to send everyone scuttling to the shelter. Under-the-counter offerings of gin and whisky swelled the legitimate liquor ration. A cadaverous gent in black wearing a white carnation squeezed syrupy wartime tunes from a battered piano for the couples dancing cheek to cheek – 'I'll Be Seeing You', 'Bluebirds Over The White Cliffs of Dover'.

The bridegroom approached Andrew with hand outstretched. 'Doctor Mount. I'm an ex-patient of yours. I have to thank you.'

Andrew gripped the extended hand enthusiastically. 'I find it hard to believe. Cathy told me. Of course I remember you, but you have made a splendid recovery. I congratulate you on that and also on getting our dear Cathy for a bride.'

'I think we need to look after the doctor for a while, don't you, Ray.' (Chrissie Lewis was already very easy with her new son-in-law.) 'He's still a bit peaky. Needs feeding up after so long in that POW camp.'

Norah came up at that moment with a cup of tea for Chrissie. Ray smiled at her a little shyly. 'Norah and I are old friends, too.'

Norah nodded, the cool smile of a nurse towards an ex-patient.

The pianist struck up the first chords of 'My Guy's Come Back', which brought Cathy hurrying to claim her husband. 'This is Our Tune,' and the new Mrs Webster was whirled away in a delirium of happiness.

Chrissie, cup of tea in hand, watching the

couples on the dance floor wanted to know who Evie Dobson was dancing with.

'He's a very decent chap,' said Andrew. 'Schoolteacher like Evie,' and he managed a laugh, 'I keep wanting to call him "Mr Gladstone".'

'Oh, he really doesn't resemble Mr Gladstone, Andrew,' ssid Chrissie firmly. 'Not at all.'

'No, that's his name,' Norah explained.

'What? Mr Gladstone?'

'Gladstone Brown.'

'What a funny name to call a baby,' then tiring of the subject she drew her attention to Eric who was dancing with his pretty wife. 'Eric is not what you'd call a good dancer, is he?'

'Not bad for a chap who was shot in the leg,' said Andrew.

'Of course,' she agreed, immediately contrite, 'trying to save poor Jacky Whitmore. But why isn't Hilde here?' She turned to Andrew.

'She has a ward full of Displaced Persons and would not leave them for the king himself.'

'She's got a heart of gold, that one,' affirmed Chrissie. 'Ah, there's Cathy dancing with her Dad. Isn't that nice?'

'And here's your son-in-law coming to claim a dance from you.'

Later, over cake and NAAFI champagne, Cathy's father confided to Norah, 'We'd always hoped she would marry Simon, you know, but Raymond seems a decent enough chap.'

Norah kept her thoughts to herself.

'Have you seen Simon's present?' Cyril Lewis was impressed. 'Cost a fortune!'

Naturally, Simon had been invited, but was unable to get leave, had not even asked for it, if the truth were known.

Momentous decisions were being taken concerning the war with Japan at the headquarters of Southeast Asia Command in Ceylon, where he was serving. Compassionate leave to attend the wedding to another man of the girl you love was out of the question. Amongst the modest presents displayed however was a superb canteen of cutlery. 'To wish you happiness together. Love from Simon.'

'How in the world did he manage to get that?'

'I shouldn't inquire too closely, Cathy dear. Probably bartered his soul in exchange.' An inspired guess from Raymond.

Before Raymond drove her away for a honeymoon in Scotland, Cathy had a special hug for Norah. 'This makes no difference to you and me,' she whispered but Norah knew that it did.

The pianist closed the lid on the upright and drained his half-pint of beer. Norah and Andrew were the only guests left. In front of them, two empty glasses and an overflowing ashtray. Conversation limped along. Norah could think of nothing else but Cathy, gone to spend the rest of her life with a man who had a history of tuberculosis.

Andrew's low spirits matched her own, scarcely those of a man lately released after five years in captivity. 'You're going to miss Cathy?'

Norah nodded. 'So will Simon. He will be desolate.'

'Let him join the Society of the Great Unloved.' The cynical tone was entirely foreign to the Andrew of old. 'He's eligible.'

A waitress hovered. Andrew got to his feet and pushed back his chair with a screech on the parquet floor. 'Come on, Norah,' he took her hand. 'Let's get gloriously tight. It helps.'

But it didn't work. A week later, Andrew answered an advertisement for a partner at a country practice in the Lake District and left Eastport. Norah's black mood accompanied her back to Shaftesbury.

The men under her care had contracted tuberculosis while serving abroad under sometimes appalling conditions – in damp caves, in ditches with no dry clothing for days on end, and scant rations. Their health had suffered accordingly and they were understandably bitter. When many of their mates were enjoying home leave, even demobilisation, their address was a sanatorium in Dorset. Their depression fuelled Norah's own low spirits. So when Peter Collins turned up she was pleased to see him.

Forty-Four

With the dropping of the atom bombs over Japan in August 1945, the war which had begun in 1939 was truly over and the men began to come home.

Not all of them were ready to return to civilian life. Some, like Simon, chose to make the regular army their career. Others, like Quentin Ford, Colin Rankin and Jacky Whitmore would never go home again. And Albert Smith, the ne'er do well son of the man who used to work in the fish shop, was another to have his name engraved on the cenotaph overlooking Eastport Bay. Albert Smith's military medal was awarded for initiative and courage on the retreat from Greece. His Victoria Cross for devotion to duty in the face of enemy fire – for putting the lives of others before his own on the Normandy beaches – was awarded posthumously. Eastport was proud of its one glorious Victoria Cross.

Millie Whitmore, with her hat askew and regardless of wind and weather, would watch the engravers adding the new names to those who fell in an earlier war. There were Smiths and Whitmores and Fords in that war, too.

'That's wor Jacky,' she would tell passers-by and point to a name that was clean and bright. *'My lad.'* And some kind soul would take her by her skinny arm and lead her home.

The destroyer on which Peter Collins served as First Officer was in a Portsmouth dock for a refit when the Japanese surrendered. His ship was to have joined the battle in the Pacific. Now her mission was changed to one of mercy, to locate and bring back released prisoners of war from Malaysia and Indonesia. With time on his hands until the refit was completed, Collins took the opportunity to look up Norah Moffat.

He had been writing to her, on and off, ever since he had picked her out of the water in Anzio Bay, a half-drowned woman covered in oil hanging on to what he had at first thought was a corpse strapped to a stretcher.

'Let him go,' he had yelled at her. 'He's dead, you bloody fool.'

But she didn't.

She had been right because, amazingly, the man had recovered despite tubes in his belly full of sea water and God knows what else. Anyhow, she would not be lifted into the lifeboat without him. She wore a Red Cross brassard on her nurse uniform. 'What good d'ye think that will do?' he'd asked her roughly. He had just watched the *Luftwaffe* sink her hospital ship. 'You must be the only people round here who still believe in God.'

The big surprise came when, bathed and dressed in a pair of his shorts and a sweater, she appeared on the deck of the destroyer. 'A bloody gorgeous mermaid without the tail,' the bosun whispered in his ear

Her long blonde hair, partly cleansed of oil, hung down her back. A belt around her slim waist held his shorts in place. Long shapely legs and feet were bare. Yes, he could only agree. All she lacked was a tail.

He saw her several times after that. Whenever his ship docked in Bizerta he took her out and, later, in Naples, but he had to admit that, apart from her gratitude for pulling her out of the water, she seemed disturbingly indifferent towards him. He had a reputation for success with birds but this one was impervious to the treatment.

When his ship was detailed to join the battle in the Pacific he had imagined that that would be the end of contact with Sister Norah Moffat, but here she was in England, in nearby Dorset. He took the day off and drove to Shaftesbury.

Parking the borrowed jeep in the hospital grounds, he walked purposefully into the main building. He was not one for asking permissions. Do it first, was his maxim. The wall plan showed him the siting of the TB wards, in open ground on the hospital perimeter occupying a series of prefabricated huts. Disregarding the signposted 'Way In', he entered her ward hut by leaping over the verandah rail.

'Hallo, you chaps.' His high spirits did not impress the quiet men in the tight white beds. He strode into the ward and there she was, stunning as ever, her starched white veil covering all but a pale gold band of hair. To his surprise, she seemed flatteringly pleased to see him. There was not even a reprimand for his irregular form of entry into the ward.

'You must take yourself off until six o'clock,' she told him quite kindly. 'I'll meet you at the main gates.'

After that, he positively pranced out of the ward past all those poor pallid buggers with their spit pots and thermometers. Peter Collins was as fit as a flea and had caught the scent of a hunt. The chase was on to win a fair damsel and he was the man to do it, another triumph for his joystick.

The Dorset countryside, having been delivered of a rich harvest, like a woman brought to bed of a healthy infant, basked peacefully in the ripe glow of a huge September moon that night.

'Harvest moon,' said Norah.

Peter looked sideways at the woman sitting so relaxed beside him in the jeep, a perfect goddess of a woman, smiling happily and appearing to enjoy their breakneck speed through the woods. Her hair, long and loose, streamed about her face like the mane of a flying horse. Her eyes danced with enjoyment. Maybe the three gins had something to do with her high spirits for she was a tiny bit

442

pickled and quite enchanting.

He pulled off the road and brought the jeep to a standstill in the shelter of a great oak where moonlight striped the shadows and magical scents rose from the cooling, mossy earth. What a night! What a corker of a night and a magical place to make love to a goddess. His hand slid over the seat to rest on her soft thigh and was at once gently encased in her own. Encouragement? Or restriction? He carefully considered the next move. Here, he suspected, was a fortress not yet taken. Gently he stroked her inner thigh and finding no opposition made a move to investigate further while he engaged her lips, but his prying fingers were swiftly caught and held, this time, remarkably firmly.

'No,' she whispered, 'out of bounds.' She was actually laughing at him. This was not in the rule book. Temporarily nonplussed he fell to the gentle fondling permitted and reviewed the situation. He was in love – again – but he wanted this gorgeous girl as he had never wanted any girl before. Any day now, his ship would sail away and he might never see her again. Some other chap would snap her up. Well, faint heart never won a fair lady and this fair lady demanded an entrance ticket. With the sketchiest of preparation, he asked Norah Moffat to marry him and, without batting an eyelid, she said yes.

Cathy was surprised and pleased. 'I hope, darling Norah, that you will be as happy as I am. That would complete my little personal heaven.'

Released from the services following the obligatory month's notice after marriage, Cathy was rejoicing in her new civilian status of housewife. Raymond had found a small flat with minimal war damage in Wimbledon, quite near his base. They travelled north in the new year for Norah's wedding, a quiet affair in the Eastport Registry Office. Cathy was consumed with curiosity to meet the man who had finally won Norah's heart.

He was tall, dark and handsome.

'Granted,' was Raymond's laconic comment, 'like a film star.'

Cathy found it hard to go further than that on such a short acquaintance. 'But he did save Norah from drowning.'

'He is no doubt very brave,' Raymond conceded.

Cathy cast a sly look at him. 'But he's not half as handsome as my husband.'

Norah's father, home for the occasion, greeted his new son-in-law enthusiastically. 'Welcome aboard, son. We're a seagoing family. You'll fit in here comfy as an old sea boot.'

The groom, in his gold-braided naval officer's uniform, ran a hand over his sleek hair. 'I'm afraid I've had little to do with the engine room, Chief.' And a tiny chill crept into the homely atmosphere.

'His father and mother don't have much to say,' said Mrs Moffat, and when Cathy said,

444

'This is a happy day for you, Mrs Moffat,' she answered, 'I just hope it's a happy day for Norah. She's not jumping for joy.'

She was putting into words what Cathy was loath to admit, even to herself. Here was no radiant bride. A smile wavered unsurely on Norah's pale face. The lilies in her hand trembled from time to time, as though a cool breeze was passing over them. Nevertheless, Cathy cheered with the rest and threw home-made paper confetti into the flower-decked jeep as Peter Collins drove away with his bride.

Later that night, in her old bedroom in her father's house, Cathy lay in bed while her husband sought space for his uniform in the wardrobe. She sighed. 'What a perfectly dismal wedding.'

'She's got cold feet.'

'Not like me.'

'Not like you. Positively brazen about the whole affair, thank the Lord.'

She giggled. 'As I remember, you didn't protest.' Idly she watched him strip. His back was towards her as he pulled off his shirt.

'Stop dissecting me,' he complained. 'I can feel you counting my ribs.'

'I carried out a survey weeks ago. You are in perfect working order.'

'Thank you. I have passed my bed test, have I? Then move over. This is a very small bed.'

'Virginal couches are small by definition.'

'Your promotion is overdue, my darling.'

Cathy switched off the bedside light and

445

sighed deep with contentment as she slid within his arms. 'No more black-outs. We can see the stars through the window.'

'The stars can see us.'

'And see how we love each other. I hope Norah has done the right thing. It has all been so sudden.'

'Look who's talking,' he whispered, and kissed the finger that wore his ring.

Norah's honeymoon perforce was brief. Her husband was recalled to his ship. 'Don't come to see me off,' he requested. 'I hate prolonged goodbyes.'

Both parties were guiltily aware of relief at the end of a disastrous honeymoon. Other sisters in the mess, seeing Norah withdrawn and silent, pitied her. 'Poor thing. Just married and now his ship has sailed.'

Her head was bent, not to hide tears but to contemplate the ring on her finger – in despair. She knew now that she had made a terrible mistake.

Forty-Five

Norah was finding army nursing extremely dull in peacetime. After the dramatic nature of treating casualties in the desert, in Greece and on board a hospital ship, housemaid's knee, tennis elbow and athlete's foot were very low-key. She was with a much younger unit now, based in Yorkshire. Very few of the sisters had seen active service abroad and she was in some way isolated because of that. Her habitual reserve dissuaded friendly overtures. The truth was that she never had made friends easily. It had not been necessary while Cathy was around. Now, she felt no desire to create a close relationship with anyone ever again.

She collected her mail from the company office, skiffling through the letters for a sight of Cathy's handwriting and was disappointed. She would be busy, she supposed, gardening, cooking, mending socks, all the things young wives are supposed to do. She picked out an envelope bearing an Australian stamp. The handwriting was not familiar.

447

Dear Sister Moffat, (obviously from someone who did not know that she had been married – and divorced!)

Shipping lines are opening up the Australia run again and my parents and I would dearly love you to visit us. You are the girl my brother Keith hoped to marry. If he had lived he would have brought you here himself. In the event of his not surviving, he asked us to act for him.

It is a lot to ask of you. Australia is a long way from England but please consider it seriously. We would be so happy to welcome you to Wirrawee, where Keith grew up. My parents will not see their son again and I will never ride again with the dearest brother any girl could have. You will be a consolation to us all. I can meet you at Sydney Harbour whenever your ship berths. Do please come. I enclose a warrant to cover all your expenses, according to Keith's last wish.

Sincerely,

Marian Reed

Norah's reaction was one of amazement. Australia! Out of the question. In any case, she had never intended to marry Keith. Nevertheless, she acknowledged that he was a good, kind and brave man.

Her mind went back to a hill in Greece. To a tent overflowing with wounded German prisoners. The earth shook and reverberated with the sound of guns. Keith Russell had grabbed Cathy and herself and ran with them to get them aboard the last truck to escape before the German troops arrived.

Other memories came sliding back as she sat in the sisters' mess with a letter from his sister in her hand, memories of starlit nights in Cairo, dining and dancing with Keith. She had been happy until the question of marriage came up.

And, sick at heart, she remembered the dreadful day when her own letter to him was returned with the word DECEASED stamped in blue ink all over the envelope, as though some bored clerk had grown tired of thumping the ink pad. Another stiff. Another stiff. Another poor God forsaken stiff. She was glad that Keith did not have the chance to read that letter for it would have broken his heart before the Japs did the job.

Since those days she had married and was now divorced. The past was over and done with. She wrote to Marian Reed explaining this. There was a silence lasting several weeks. I shall not hear from them again, she told herself, albeit with a tinge of regret. They do not want to know me now.

But they did. The invitation was repeated.

We know how upset you must have been

after Keith was killed, how easy it was to make a wrong decision. We still believe that a trip to meet us would be a happy occasion for us all. We would enjoy showing you our country.

Norah's mind was in turmoil. One part of it urged why bother? Why stir up painful memories, and under false pretences? Yet to confess that she had rejected Keith's proposal was somehow to reduce him in the eyes of his family. She had no wish to do that. Finally, for his parents' sake and, to some extent, for her own convenience, she accepted their invitation while concealing the fact that she was not and never had been the daughter-in-law they hoped for.

For her part, a spell out of the country amongst people who knew nothing of her circumstances would be welcome. After the shameful divorce (the shame was all hers since the marriage was never consummated), she would be glad to get away from the curiosity and embarrassing solicitude of friends. The loneliness which descended upon her when Cathy married would be with her wherever she went – England or Australia. No matter.

Cathy and Raymond were understandably wrapped up in each other. They had moved to a neat little house in Woodford Green with a fig tree and a rhubarb patch in the garden. Whenever Norah visited them, they made a great fuss of her, insisting upon her having the best bedroom, which was only marginally superior to the worst by reason of its splendid view of the cricket field. The worst bedroom overlooked the backyard of The Fox and Lamb. But 'two's company, three's none' went the old saw. She had to learn to take second place and that was not easy.

Viewed dispassionately, the invitation to visit Australia could be seen as a turning point in her life, an opportunity to take stock. Did she really want to stay in the army? Possibly based in Berlin with the British Army of Occupation. A lot of administrative red tape. Simon was over there somewhere. Is that what she wanted?

The opportunity to escape the dreariness of England was tempting. England was tired, her treasury empty after her Herculean war effort, her industrial machinery out of date. Widows and war wounded needed support. Where, wondered Norah were the spoils of war due the victor. 'We did win, didn't we, Dad?' Norah demanded. 'But what did we win?'

'We won freedom, my girl,' said her father, 'and that cost plenty.'

'Was it really worth it? All those young men,' she saw again the stretcher-bearers and their limp burdens, 'sacrificed.'

'Never let me hear you say such things.' The chief engineer who had been bombed and torpedoed, who had seen his engine room flooded and members of his crew roasted, all in aid of bringing food to a starving Britain,

451

was angry. 'Make no mistake about this. If we'd made terms with Hitler, as some did, there would have been no one left in the ring. By the time the Yanks came in it would have been too late, Europe and Britain would have been back in the Dark Ages and a Nazi-style labour camp would have stretched from John o' Groats to Land's End. Freedom, girl! That's what we won. That's what hundreds of young blokes died for and we have to live up to the legacy they left us.'

But Norah, lacking the burning patriotism of her father, wanted out. Australia, with its energy, blue skies and plentiful food, was a world away. Dispirited and disillusioned with her life, she resigned from the QAs, collected her gratuity and booked a passage on the SS *Himalaya* to Sydney, New South Wales, Australia. She needed a change, her mother agreed, to put the roses back in her cheeks.

Andrew took a day off from his practice at Ambleside in the Lake District to see her off when she sailed from Liverpool on 1 March, 1949.

'Come back again, Norah.' No questions. Andrew knew about the divorce. He understood.